# Areon AND Nothingness

TATE PUBLISHING
& Enterprises

*Published in the United States of America*

ISBN: 1–5988673–1-8
06.09.29

# Areon AND Nothingness

## Cole D. Lemme

TATE PUBLISHING & Enterprises

# Thanks and Dedication

I started writing at a bad period in my life. These times most likely prompt many people to begin writing, as they probably see nothing else worth doing during that time. Through that summer, I did nothing else but work on *Areon and Nothingness*, whilst my parents helped me out and let me stay at the place where I know that I will always be welcome. I would like to thank them for everything they did and do for me. The writing of this book was partly made possible because of their patience.

I also need to point out the fact that as a child, I had a very vivid imagination and fondness of things that I knew were not real, but still wished they were. Often, I would run around my backyard with a towel tied around my neck as a cape and a wooden sword that I had procured from my father's cabinet shop, vanquishing evil and keeping fantasy alive. Later in life, I lost sight of this world of fantasy that I had loved and held in such high regard as a child. I finally came back around to my old self as an older teenager. I do not know if I would have come back of my own accord or simply stayed grounded where I was, but I know that certain individuals, people that I consider close-knit friends now, helped me see that fantasy is not something that is unreal. Fantasy and adventure are two things that I see in everyday real life. They are an escape for everyone who wishes to avoid the mundane and can be found by anyone who seeks them if they only look hard enough. I want to thank my friends (they know who they are), for this book is dedicated to them for showing me the fantasy and making it possible for me to show that which we have found to those who would read this book. May Nothingness never consume these peoples' lives.

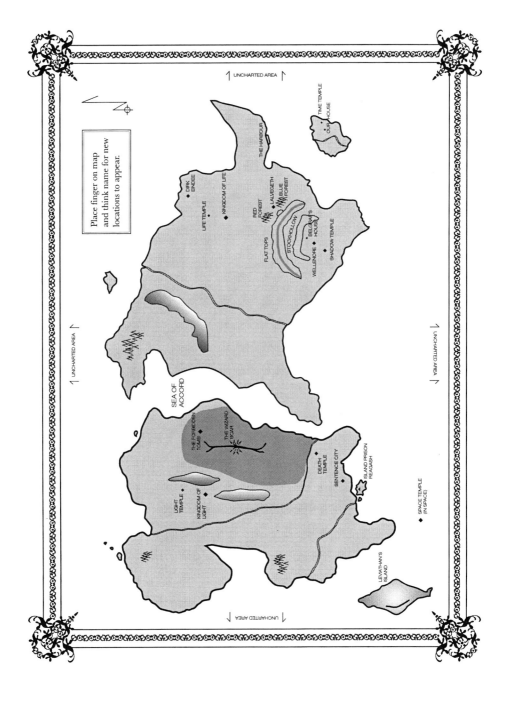

# TABLE OF CONTENTS

# PROLOGUE

## 375 Years Before the Birth of Areon

Bishop Tolok had held the position for the Kingdom of Life for thirty years. He wore a white, shabby loincloth under his tattered, brown robe, which symbolized his isolation from the rest of the world. He never cared what people thought of him or his clothes as long as he could stay in the cathedral and preach to those that still listened and pray when he was alone. His prayers were more often than not for those people of the Kingdom who still wished to stay within its walls. The philosophers of the neighboring city, Dirk Eindee, had persuaded many that God did not exist, and the false hope that they had been instilling in peoples' minds that their city would prosper while the Kingdom's would fail had been a constant nuisance and reminder of why the city only housed and sheltered half of what it could. The lack of people was also apparent in the condition of the many stone houses and other buildings; all of them had begun to decay due to lack of preventative maintenance. But the cathedral and castle still stayed in excellent condition, as they had been built to withstand the ravages of hostile invasions and time.

Bishop Tolok walked from his small sleeping room and into a larger corridor that led to the sanctuary. After he entered, he looked up at the massive pillars that stretched up one hundred spans and lined either side of the two rows of pews. He walked along the cold stone floor and gazed up at the dome shaped ceiling, wondering cynically if today would be the day all lost hope and finally abandoned the Kingdom they had worked so hard to build after the wars between men and wizards.

Tolok often wondered to himself if God was punishing them for their brash war with the wizards. The wizards did not believe in God; they thought themselves above God because of their abilities to manipulate the elements God had put into them. They called this manipulation magic.

Tolok shook his long, white hair out of the way of his eyes and looked back at the ceiling towards the heavens.

"Shall I make another pilgrimage to the Temple of Life?" he asked aloud, although the cathedral was empty. "I will go to where the very essence of life is protected if you ask it." Tolok took his hands from the long sleeves on his robes, his words reverberating off the hard walls. "I am here, Lord, send me!" and the dejected Bishop let his hands fall as no response came.

The day dragged on slowly for Bishop Tolok. He spent most of it cleaning the dirt-strewn floors and praying, as it happened to be a Sunday. As the night drew near, Tolok walked once again through the sanctuary to the opening of the cathedral. He stopped and looked at sides of the building as rain began to patter gently against the stone. He jerked his head toward the massive wooden doors as the muffled sound of voices could be heard approaching.

The unlocked doors of the cathedral swung open and smote the walls, and three warriors from the king's army approached swiftly, looking grim.

"Bishop," said the first and tallest of the armor-clad warriors. He bowed slightly, as did the other two. "The king has sent us to warn you. A dark wizard approaches."

Tolok gasped, and his hands began to tremble as they slid out from under his sleeved robe. "I-I thought the wars were over," he stammered.

"He must be one of the last remaining dark wizards left," the warrior in front spoke. "Bishop. He wears the Black Wizard cloak."

All the color in Tolok's face drained, and his mouth fell slightly open, his hands still trembling.

The guard continued, "Most of the first assault wave of our warriors died in an attempt to stop him at the front gate. We do not have the power to defeat him. The king has ordered all men back and says that you are to remain inside locked doors as well."

"Who will warn all the people?" asked Tolok.

"It is not our concern at this point," the man said coldly. "We've done all we can. Fighting him is useless. One of the survivors of our first assault says the wizard claims to have wreaked havoc near the Kingdom of Light and has traveled this far only to destroy our Kingdom as well, although our walls may stand." Instantly, the three men turned on their heels and walked briskly out of the cathedral and into the adjacent castle.

Tolok looked around quickly and then dashed outside to see what chaos had already begun. He swung to the right of his cathedral and could already see down at the beginning of the city walls houses and stables burning. Tolok forgot his orders from the king to barricade himself inside and ran toward the fires and screaming people. After running a long way, Tolok was out of breath, but had reached the nearest burning house. He looked out onto the stone street and saw him; the black cloaked wizard. He was arrogant and full of malice. The rain was light and hardly did much to put the fires out. Tolok wiped his eyes to see better. The wizard was holding a small boy as a man, who looked to be in his late thirties, rushed up to his son. Tolok watched the nefarious black-cloaked figure and cried. The dark wizard put his hand down and turned his head slowly, moving his eyes up and down Tolok, noticing the robes of a holy man.

"Which one will die tonight, Bishop?" said the wizard loudly as a wicked smile formed on his face.

Tolok looked from the man to the boy and said nothing. The wizard put his hand in front of the boy and spoke an incantation before fire magic erupted unto the boy, leaving him lifeless on the ground. Tolok put his hand to his mouth and retched while starting to cry.

"No, Lord. Please, no," he whispered. The boy's father ran at the attacker to strike, but in an instant the wizard shot out his hand and a flame leapt out so large and hot that it blew the man ten arm spans from where he stood, leaving him in flames. Tolok gritted his teeth in anger. The wizard was using elemental fire magic. He tried hard to fight back tears of despair as the wizard advanced on him and grabbed his robes, dragging him along, forcing him to watch as he killed every person and burnt every structure in sight.

"Do you not see that your God does not exist?" asked the wizard, holding Tolok around the neck. "You will learn by the time I am through with the pathetic Kingdom of Life."

Tolok tried to tug himself free by groping around at his restrainer's hands and arms, but the wizard held strong and Tolok was weak at his age. The wizard walked into an area of several houses near the market and threw him violently into a cart, leaving him dazed. In several chaotic moments, the wizard and Tolok watched as hundreds of people began running up the streets, falling at the sight of the wizard in all his malevolence. The dark wizard stretched up his hand at the crowd.

Tolok screamed, "Lord, No!"

The wizard laughed a cruel, inhuman laugh and yelled, "Your God does not exist! I am you god, and today is the day of judgment for man!"

Tolok stood up, letting the rain wash over his face. He closed his eyes and held out his hands slowly towards the heavens. "God help me! Send me your angels!"

The wizard looked at him and back to the crowd. "You will be the last to die, Bishop, so that you might understand," and as he said this, he grabbed a woman who looked age twenty or so, and killed her in the same manner he had the child, without batting an eye of compassion or regret.

Tolok cried harder at the sight of more death. "Lord, we need you!" Tolok raised his hands unto the heavens and fell to his knees. "Give me strength, King of Kings." Tolok forgot the wizard and poured his soul into his words. "Dispense justice from above unto the wicked!"

At these words, the rain stopped. The dark wizard and Tolok watched the heavens as a star began to grow brighter and brighter from the east. Soon, the bright light turned into what Tolok took to be an angel. With a white face and streaming hair, it emerged not upon the wizard, but Tolok, and kissed him slightly on the cheek and whispered, "I am watching over you, Tolok."

The angel ascended above the wizard, and before Tolok could react, another white light began to descend upon them, and the dark wizard sat stunned, yet defiant. The second light turned into another angel, yet this one was equipped with divine armor. It hovered above, and before Tolok could watch to see what it would do with its heavenly spear, another light came from behind it. After that, three more lights appeared, indistinguishable due to the immensely bright light, but all of them clearly angels of the Lord. Tolok fell to his knees. The seventh light came to them. He looked up to see the first six angels and an enormous wheel-like being with many eyes staring in every direction fly with wings of fire toward the dark wizard and knock him on the ground. Again, before Tolok or the wizard could react, another light came slowly and grandly, and the wizard could not help but show fear in his eyes as he staggered to his feet and prepared to attack this new ally of the Kingdom. The light turned into a heavenly robed figure, flying with two sets of wings, and staring at the wizard with one of its four faces, each staring in a cardinal direction. The angel's wings shone brightly and its robe seemed to be made of white light. Fire surrounded his figure and licked the open air with eager anticipation.

During this, the wizard almost seemed to be considering running, but the second angel that had come threw his divine spear, which stuck into the wizard's shoulder blade, sending him wobbling onto the hard stone floor of the street.

Tolok was forced to shield his eyes as the ninth light descended down to appear. This angel was flying on three sets of wings. It also had four faces, as its predecessor angel, but holy light and fire surround it for many spans.

The nine angels sat in a circle around the dark wizard and said nothing. The last of these that had come let his three sets of wings set him on the ground in front of the wizard, who ripped the spear out of his body and stared in terror at the four faces of judgment in front of him. The angel held out his hand from under the many wings, and from the fire surrounding him, a divine sword appeared. The angel looked at the wizard, closed his eight eyes, and struck him down with the sword made of fire.

Tolok gazed around at the nine beings of white light. Slowly, and in the same order they had come, each flew next to Tolok and spoke with angelic voices.

"I am an angel, and your guardian," said the sweet voice Tolok heard in the beginning. "I represent the choir of Angels."

"I am a messenger of the divine and represent the choir of Archangels," a voice boomed from the angel clad in armor.

And so it went on.

"I protect religion and leaders. I represent the choir of Principalities."

"I am a border guard. With a flashing sword I prevent fallen light energy from going where it should not. I represent the choir of Powers."

"I steer divine and immortal lives while overseeing the process of nature. I represent the choir of Virtues."

"Ever do I spread transcendental wisdom. I represent the choir of Dominions."

"I dispense divine justice and make up the chariot of the Lord. I represent the choir of Thrones."

"I am a glorious guardian with illuminative knowledge. I represent the choir of Cherubim."

The angel that had killed the wizard let his sword dissipate into his own flaming aura and turned to look at the shaking Tolok. His top set of wings lifted him slowly off the ground as he pushed against it; his middle set covered his arms, while his bottom set covered his feet. The four faces took a turn looking at him. "I represent the highest of the Nine Orders of Angels. I am of the choir of the Seraphim. Ask, and you shall receive, Tolok. We are at your disposal. You have earned a place in heaven. Be well until we are needed again."

The nine angels, in a magnificent spectacle, took flight, singing their praise to the Lord. Tolok heard them clearly, "Holy, Holy, Holy!" until the last trace of their light flickered in the heavens and went out.

# CHAPTER I

## Genesis

A boy, or perhaps a man at his new age of eighteen, walked down the dirty road that led to the small village known as Wellenore. The sky became dark as the day grew late and the man named Areon gazed toward the heavens. He gripped the top of the hood of his black cloak and tugged it farther down his face. His blonde hair hung in his eyes to farther conceal his identity. He knew the people of Wellenore did not particularly like him, as he was the apprentice of a wizard that he lived with north of town.

Areon walked until the fence surrounding the town came into view, and he looked up at the faithful gatekeeper known as Goffu, who opened the gate and looked at him suspiciously.

"Keep that hood wrapped about your face," he said, not unkindly.

Areon smiled back. He always held suspicions that Goffu knew his master, Belgraf the wizard.

As Areon walked into town, he scrutinized the closely built houses and looked toward the only thing making noise; the tavern called the Full Barrel. His pace quickened at the thought of being able to have some wine, which Belgraf refused to stock in his cupboards. Walking onto the porch of the tavern, he swung open the mighty oak door and looked around at the small amount of people occupying the place at this hour. He scanned the tavern that he loved so much, although he was rather unwelcome. Wood floors stained with wine ran along the whole of the square building. A large oak bar stretched across the entirety of the east wall, and the bartender stood behind it, resting on his elbows. An assortment of wood chairs and tables were strewn throughout the place and many barrels of wine and other strong drink rested behind the indifferent bartender.

Areon took a seat near the door. If a fight were to ensue, Areon knew he could win with ease, but did not like the fact of fighting those that were not proficient in lower level magic; the only magic, as far as he was concerned. He would almost refuse to call it magic, as it was simply the manipulation of elements inside one's body, but for reasons unknown to Areon, saying words of the old days brought fourth these elements such as fire, wind, water, and many more. The only way to explain it was to say "magic."

Areon raised his hand and the bartender walked over slowly.

"Bring me a bottle of the cheapest wine," Areon said quietly.

The bartender acquiesced and brought him the bottle, to which Areon threw him a silver piece that seemed to satisfy the man. Areon looked around again and saw a woman that he had missed upon walking in. She blended in perfectly with the shadows, even apart from the fact her apparel was comprised of all black.

Being proficient in magic, Areon was in tune with his aura and the elements inside him. He pulsated it quickly, as Belgraf had explained how once, out of curiosity. To his great surprise, the only one in the bar who turned sharply to look at him was this woman. Areon instantly regretted the decision to reveal the fact that he was a magic user.

The woman in black stood up and Areon looked at her slender form. She walked towards his table and sat down without an invitation. He had never seen her before, and instantly, her beauty captivated him.

"Hello," she said simply.

Areon took a drink of wine and grunted back a hello that he knew made him sound stupid. The woman had dark eyes, so dark that Areon squinted to make sure they were brown. When he decided that they were black, he leaned back and she continued.

"My name is Reiquem," she said quietly.

"Areon. I've never met another person that used magic in my life," he said even more quietly.

"Then you haven't traveled much, have you?" she returned.

They sat in silence for a little time.

"You have beautiful eyes," he blushed upon saying it, not believing he had blurted it out.

Reiquem did not appear complimented.

"It is almost with regret that I have this eye color," she said.

"Who are you?" asked Areon, leaning closer.

She smiled. "You are a lower level magic user, are you not?"

He nodded.

She leaned very close to him and stared at him with those glossy black eyes. "I am a master of shadow."

Areon started and then smiled.

"You must be joking."

She smiled and stood up to her full height, which was almost, but not quite, Areon's. "You don't know what lies close to where you live. None here do."

Areon continued to give her his incredulous smile, not really comprehending what she said or not believing it.

"I hope to see you again, Areon," and with that, she left.

Areon stayed late into the night ruminating on the matter and deciding if he should discuss things with Belgraf.

Upon taking the last drink of his wine, Areon stood and walked to the door and went out. The sky had grown a bit misty so Areon quickly walked out of the town, nodding to the gatekeeper who never seemed to sleep. He walked north for some time before Belgraf's wooden house came into view. It had a left wing which housed all the books Belgraf owned. The house was square, although the wood had warped over time leaving the building with an awkward, tilted sort of shape. Areon walked onto the porch that had an old railing and stole surreptitiously through the door, trying his best not to let it creak. He glided up the stairs and went to his bed, hoping his master heard nothing.

# CHAPTER II

## Magic and Stories

"Areon, awake!"

Areon sat up and rubbed the sleep out of his eyes noticing a small pain in his head. He looked up lazily at the wizard.

"Good morning, Belgraf," he said through a yawn.

"Areon, today do you feel up to sparring with swords?" asked Belgraf.

Areon grinned, threw off his covers, and hurried after the old wizard. He raced down the stairs and into the kitchen, sat down, and pulled on his black boots, lacing them up carefully. He went to where his cloak hanged and took out his old sword from underneath it, leaving the cumbersome cloak where it was. He walked out the door and embraced the perfect new day; the sun was shining and not a cloud was in sight. His eyes went down from the sky and to the horizon where he watched Belgraf walk out into an open area. Areon loved training with swords.

He swung his old, insignificant, but solid and trustworthy sword around a few times before stopping at fighting distance from Belgraf. Belgraf pulled his hands from inside his robes and unsheathed his sword seemingly without touching it. Areon shook his head at the wizard knowing he was using his aura to move things. Belgraf was bald, but the white hair on the sides of his head mingled with sideburns that grew down into a soft beard. He had soul-piercing green eyes and loved to use lower-level magic; fire being his favorite.

Belgraf, although old, possessed the speed of a middle-aged man and came at Areon unrepentantly. But Areon took up his sword and pushed off Belgraf's with his own. They both smiled.

For hours the exchanged blows, Areon waiting for fatigue to set in and Belgraf waiting for an amateur mistake. Neither happened. And so it went on.

Areon stopped after the long sparring session and looked up at the sun. It was near noon. He looked back down at the wizard who had stuck his sword in the ground.

"Stop this, if you are able," Belgraf muttered among other words of the days of old.

Areon looked up and the sky above him swirled into a dark cloud. He reached down and pulled up his sword in time for lightning to strike down upon the flat of the blade. Most metal would have sent electricity coursing through his body, but the sword Belgraf had given him had elemental earth magic woven into, making it impervious to all elemental attack.

Areon bent his knees to absorb the impact, but Belgraf continued making the white-hot lightning hit the blade as he coached.

"Never use too much elemental magic, my boy!" he yelled over his lightning. "The elements come from inside you. It is what you are made of, and if too much is used, you will certainly perish!"

Areon pushed his sword up slowly, his arms quivering. He then swung the sword around and down and the lightning grounded as Belgraf stopped his spell.

The two looked at each other fiercely. Areon took up his sword and ran at the wizard who simply smiled quickly, gripped his sword, and tore it from the earth, and the steel collided stinging both their hands.

"Belgraf," Areon managed to say through gritted teeth.

"What i-is it, m-my boy?"

Their swords stayed locked together, neither giving way.

"I-I met someone who says they are the m-master of shadow."

Instantly Belgraf released and Areon almost fell over.

"Reiquem?" asked Belgraf.

"How did you know?"

"We have met once or twice near … well, near here anyway," replied Belgraf.

"It's true then?" asked Areon, letting his sword fall.

"Areon, we must talk." Belgraf pushed his sword into the soft grass and looked toward the Moss Woods. "What say we go for a walk?"

Areon nodded.

The woods made a large U-shape around Belgraf's house, and the Flat-top Mountains made a U-shape around them. The two had made their way there to where willow trees comprised the whole of the Moss Woods. They were called this because everything, save the bark on the trees, was covered in moss. Areon knew the Moss Woods were where Belgraf had discovered him and undoubtedly saved him, although the two rarely brought up the subject.

Upon entering the forest Areon and Belgraf found the usual stream that ran through it and followed it until they came to their usual place that consisted of a flat, worn bed of moss and a smooth boulder on which Belgraf sat. The trees became denser after this place, so they usually stopped here.

"Areon," Belgraf said, "elemental magic is not all that exists in the world. It is called lower level because some have been able to control actual essences and therefore take large control of reality. They can manipulate shadow, light, time, space, life, and death."

"But how? I don't ..."

"I know it is difficult to understand, and only would you understand it if you were to learn from another master," Belgraf replied abruptly and then continued. "I have spoken of the ancient wars between men and wizards, Areon, do you remember?"

"Yes, some of it. Mostly it was over land, was it not?" answered Areon.

"Mostly, or should I say that was the half of it," continued Belgraf. "You must have an understanding of what the ancient wars were over before I divulge the information of why you have come across a master of shadow, which I regret." He cleared his throat. "The wars were also over religion. Wizards, generally speaking, do not believe in a perfect being, a being in which nothing greater can be imagined. Humans, on the other hand, tend to believe in God. Perhaps it has something to do with the variation in life spans. It wasn't until the nine came that I myself began to question the old beliefs of my kind."

"The nine?" inquired Areon.

Belgraf looked at him seriously. "The nine orders of Angels. Please hold your peace until I am finished. In the beginning, or shall I say before the beginning, Nothingness consumed this plane of reality, but essences started to form, or shall I say God formed essences. From his quintessence came light, shadow, time, space, life, and with it death, or so the theory of priests goes. Although I am uncertain of God, I know that these essences ran rampant throughout the universe; death and shadow consuming more than they should, and so God, or some greater being, sealed them all in stones. Great gemstones that could never be broken by mortal force, perhaps not even by immortal force, so that one would not overpower the rest and let Nothingness consume the universe and all it contained as it did before the beginning."

Areon absorbed all the information as best he could and continued to stare at Belgraf looking for answers.

"So this is a shadow and not its essence?" he asked pointing to one a tree made.

"Quite right," said Belgraf. "And if the gemstones were to ever get too close, they could be cracked. Or so the legends go. But not many can find the temples, and even if they do, it is said that Angels now guard most of them."

Belgraf arose and looked at a sliver of sunlight coming from the intricate roof of the forest. "It is time to go home."

Areon followed him out of the woods and past the clearing back to the house. By the time they arrived, night was a few hours away. Belgraf stopped on the porch and looked at the sky toward the Flattops. Areon followed his gaze and thought to himself: Someday I will stand on the Flattops, but not today, and he turned and walked inside.

"Areon," called Belgraf from his study.

The eighteen-year-old ran from his room in which he had been relaxing and went to the study housing thousands of books.

Belgraf turned from the shelves and handed him a black book with swirling silver on the front making an unknown design.

"What is this?" he asked.

"A book of the old days; not one of religion, but of the essences and a passive view on them. Read it if you must."

Areon began paging through it as he turned to go back to his room. Forgetting to make a reply, he read softly the first thing written on the old pages:

Time - time stretches eternally forward and eternally backward; nothing can withstand the ravages of time.

Space–Space is all around us and nowhere all at once; space magic can envelope a person and hold them to the wielder's will forever, or send them to the edge of the universe to suffer a cold, dark death.

Light–Light magic is a beautiful terror. When used subtly, it will light the way and cover darkness; when the full extent of its power is unleashed, it blinds good and kills evil.

Shadow–Simply put, it is the absent of light magic. An image of a person on the ground standing in the rain when lightning has struck. Shadow magic is enormous but weightless, an abyss with no depth.

Life–Life is the reasoning for all the magics being present. If consciousness were not present, the others would have no use. Life is used to restore those near death, or if a wielder of life magic has the courage, to bring back those that are in the realm of death already.

Death–Although most choose to forget, death finds everyone. While most are scared of death, it is only another beginning, a line between life and the beyond. When you embrace it, death opens your eyes to gentle light and the infinite. When your anxiety of death takes over, you may lose your mind and fear the afterlife forever.

Nothingness–Individually or all at once, it is a magic to end the others.

Areon sat in his bed with his head propped up and read until the book slid down on his chest and his eyes shut for the night.

# CHAPTER III

## The Incessancy of Areon and Learning to Fly

    Areon woke the next morning feeling refreshed, and for once without the soreness leftover from an entire day of training or the weariness of a mind that had read far too much information on the casting of magic. As he got up he took a look at the book that was sitting upon the dresser in his room. The tattered black donned a single symbol of swirling silver lines that danced on the front of it. Areon ran his hand across it as he walked out of his room.

    Areon had awakened that morning by himself. Most mornings the wizard had to wake him on account of the fact that he was always tired from the day before. When Areon walked downstairs, he did not see the wizard. Walking outside he saw that Belgraf was seated upon a hill west of the house. He began the walk across the rich green grass to give Belgraf a good morning. He approached the wizard wearily because he knew that the wizard was meditating and did not want to disturb his thoughts. As he approached and was within hearing distance of the wizard, he opened an eye.

    "Hello, my boy. How are we on this glorious day?"

    "Refreshed, and yourself?" returned Areon.

    "Deep in thought until you arrived," smirked the wizard.

    "And what of the day?" asked Areon, ready to face it.

As Areon looked down a peculiar thing caught his eye; Belgraf seemed be floating over the smooth green grass rather than sitting on it. This very peculiar sight did not surprise Areon because he had seen it before, yesterday, in fact. Thinking back, Areon had noticed that now and again the wizard seemed to float over things rather than come in contact with them, in accordance with gravity. Areon thought about it a bit and realized that the wizard was often moving things without touching them. A book that was an inch out of reach seemed to gravitate toward Belgraf in a lazy need. His sword seemed to slip up into his hand rather than being pulled out by Belgraf. Areon, of course, had learned of auras a little, but Belgraf had only taught him to pulse his a little in order for others to feel his energy.

"Belgraf, are you not touching the ground when you meditate?" asked Areon.

"Defying gravity, one of the many uses of magic. Why do you ask?" replied Belgraf.

"I've just noticed it now and again and thought I should ask. Perhaps it could be something new for me to learn," said Areon.

"I don't think I like the way this conversation is headed," grumbled Belgraf. "You notice it often, eh? When I use my aura to move things, in this case myself."

"Why do you do it when you meditate and often other times, although you do it subtly?" asked Areon inquisitively.

"I do it to train my aura. Everything living has an aura. This aura can push off things, let others sense you, and you others. Your body is pulled to other masses that loom in space. The aura of your body pushes off things. But because only living things have auras, they can push off things that do not have auras, such as the ground or planets. Most never realize they have an aura because the push is much weaker compared to the pull planets have on your physical body. I practice subtly because I must; it is rather a difficult art to learn, taming and using your aura. I have not done much with it, but I feel the need to study every matter in the world, so I practice now and again. Very difficult. Very difficult, indeed."

"One could fly with the right amount of training, couldn't they?" Areon asked almost suspiciously.

"If you must know, I have been able to before, but only in dire need."

"Teach me," was Areon's answer. The thought of flying nudged him to make the request.

"It is too difficult," Belgraf refuted.

"Teach me; never do I ask for you to teach me something in particular. Teach me."

"It is very hard to do and superfluous at this time in your life." As Belgraf said this, he stood up and started walking towards the house.

Areon, angered at being refused by the wizard, followed bitterly.

When they went inside, they ate a spot of bread and drank tea. As Areon got up from the table he grabbed a slice of cheese from the cupboard and started to walk outside, nibbling slowly and showing that he was obviously irritated. Belgraf followed him with a small smile on his face.

Areon grabbed his sword that was hanging outside on a peg and his cloak. His black cloak hung loosely around him and stayed about an inch from the ground. A good cloak will come close, but never trip you, Areon thought, reminiscing over the words of Belgraf.

They both walked into a grass-covered area toward the north of the house, the main place Areon trained and Belgraf taught.

"Now," announced Belgraf, attempting to disregard Areon's attitude and continue normal elemental magic practice, "I will throw three shots of elemental fire at you in a row. One I want you to dissipate with your sword, the next I want you to dodge, regardless of where it's thrown, and the third I want you to counter with your own elemental fire."

Belgraf took his familiar stance and began. After years of wielding a sword, Areon would be used to stopping the magic with a one-handed sword parry and the other with his free hand. Exercises such as these occurred daily; after training for so many years, monotony was common, the most probable reason Areon wanted to learn something new.

The first three went slow. Areon took a stance and saw the first of the three flames protrude from Belgraf's hand, sword cutting through the fire, and dissipating it as expected. The next went toward his feet, and he jumped just in time to hold up his hand and feel the familiar warmth come when he used fire magic. He raised his hand, thought about the element within him, and brought all of it towards the palm of his hand where it leaped out in time to meet Belgraf's flame about halfway between the two of them. After so long, the speed increased.

This exercise went on for what seemed like hours to Areon.

Sword, leap, fire.

Sword, duck, fire.

Sword, sidestep, fire.

Sword, dodge, fire.

Sword, dodge, fire.

Sword, dodge, fire.

Sword, dodge, fire. Areon could hardly stand it any longer, and the last of the flames leapt out of his palm, barely staying alight and stopping Belgraf's only before it consumed his hand.

"Good," stopped the wizard, sensing Areon's energy was almost spent. Areon dropped the sword and bent over, holding himself up by keeping his hands on his knees and his back bent. Sweat poured from his body. The cloak was soaked from the back seeping sweat through three layers of cloth.

Hours had passed, Areon realized as they stepped out of the clearing and he looked toward the sun; it had fallen to the west side of the Flattops. The sky around it looked splendid. Three stretched clouds shot out from the sides of the sun while two other billowing clouds sat in the east with caves etched in the sides of them. The sun painted the sky orange while the clouds countered with white.

Areon hardly had the time to soak up the beauty in all his exhaustion. The two decided that the training they had accomplished was sufficient for the day.

They trudged to the entrance of the house with Areon hanging onto the shoulder of his wizard. Areon walked immediately to the west wing to look up books on auras. Belgraf returned to the small green hill, albeit it was nighttime, but not unaware of what Areon was going to do.

Days went on like this one. Belgraf and Areon would train, and Areon would run to the west wing to look up books on auras and the remarkable things that one could do with a strong aura.

The books conspired against Belgraf to teach Areon the art of strengthening one's aura. Everything he read captivated him and made him want to learn, no matter the level of difficulty.

One particular day Areon ran across the last book he would read on the matter.

On Auras, the author appropriately titled the book. "When one is born, an innate aura resides in and around one. The pull of everything made of matter on everything else that is made of matter is called gravity, and the push that a living thing has against the gravity of oneself and other things made of matter is called one's Aura. Generally, the pull of the two objects made of matter is much stronger than the push of a being's aura. One can strengthen this aura and use it to do many things, not the least fascinating of which is flying."

"Amazing," remarked Areon aloud.

"And nearly impossible to learn," returned the wizard from behind him.

Areon jumped a bit. "You scared me Belgraf."

"I pray I can scare you out of learning to control your aura. One must increase their own energy level."

"Well you can't," Areon said obstinately.

"Very well," said the wizard unexpectedly. "If you wish to press the matter, we begin tomorrow."

Areon looked up with enthusiasm capering in his ocean blue eyes. "Do you mean it?"

"Yes, of course," grumbled the wizard. "But don't think for one minute that I decided to train you on this subject because of your bad moods and incessant asking as of late; it was the fact that you have learned much and need some new material before your apathy from tedious exercises overwhelms you.

"Tomorrow it is." Areon grinned as he turned and went to go to sleep.

# CHAPTER IV

## The Cloak, the Sword, and the Ground

Areon ran outside that morning to see if Belgraf was meditating. The wizard, with his way of reading minds and all, was leaning on his staff, aware that Areon had just ran outside and was waiting for him, not altogether impatiently.

"Grab your cloak," yelled Belgraf, walking away. Areon was going to anyway with the coldness still clinging to the morning breeze. Areon ran around back to the north side of the house where Belgraf hesitantly gazed up at him. The boy had not been this interested in learning something for some time now.

"To strengthen your aura you must first find it. Feel it inside you and then begin to flex it; like a muscle, except in the case with muscles you have an innate ability to use them. With an aura you would never know it was there had one not informed you," Belgraf said, starting his teachings immediately.

"So what exactly shall I do?" asked Areon with little knowledge, although he had been reading much on them. He thought back and realized that the books never really told you how to strengthen your aura, just some things you could do with it and background information.

"The books gave you little instruction on how to strengthen, eh?" said Belgraf.

"Very little," agreed Areon.

"That is because using your aura is something you almost have to figure out how do to by yourself. It is very difficult to explain."

"I'm not sure I understand," Areon said shaking his head and looking at his body.

"Imagine this analogy," tried the wizard. "Days ago, when you were watching the orange sunset, was it beautiful to you?"

"Yes, indeed."

"Why?" quizzed the wizard.

"Why was the sunset beautiful?"

"Yes, can you explain to me why the sunset was beautiful?"

"Not exactly, no not at all really," answered Areon beginning to understand.

"It was simply something you knew, correct? Something innate in you that words cannot explain or do justice?" asked Belgraf.

"Correct," answered Areon with a bit more confidence.

"Good. Now feel your aura, reach into your consciousness, and feel for it," the wizard finished.

Areon looked down, closed his eyes, and stretched out his arms, hands open and feet together. He knew not why he stood this way; it just felt appropriate. He stood and felt for minutes, staring at the darkness in front of him. He knew this would be a difficult task, not the least Belgraf had given him … or would it?

Searching his soul Areon found nothing for the longest amount of time. He waited and waited, eyes closed, refusing to give up on this, although feeling a bit nonsensical.

Finally, something happened. A light came into his being. Not a visible light, a light that he could feel, but not exactly by physical warmth either. An inexplicable light that illuminated his souland started at the bottom of his feet and the back of his body permeating to the front of his chest and the top of his head with ease and stopping a slight distance on the outside surrounding the entirety of his body, being one in the same with his anima.

"Good," interrupted the wizard, pulling Areon's mind back to everything outside his body and to his physical sensory preceptors.

Areon fell to the ground shaking; shaking from coldness.

"Why am I cold?" he asked, stuttering a bit.

"Did you feel the warmth?" asked Belgraf. "You were taken from it when I pulled you out of your peering at your soul."

"Incredible," said Areon as he stood up trying to compose himself.

"Quite," remarked the wizard more to himself while looking down. "I've never witnessed anyone find themselves that fast in all my life, which I might add has been exceedingly long."

"Now you have seen the Aura and you know how to reach it. Inexplicable, yes?" asked Belgraf. He seemed somehow distracted to Areon, perhaps amazed at his ability.

"Yes, quite," Areon agreed.

"Now all you have to do is strengthen it; rather than looking at it and feeling it, use it," stated the wizard.

So it began; the wizard told Areon to train and strengthen by pushing his entire aura into the air pocket in his cloak and make it flail out into the wind.

Areon tried this for little under an hour before he almost gave up. Belgraf scolded him and told him that it was because of Areon they were doing this, so they would do it.

After awhile, Areon would reach farther in. His mind and senses would implode on himself and would force the light that surrounded him back, and the cloak would move from time to time, although not without strenuous work. The hours passed and Areon realized what he had gotten himself into; although tired and sweating, the difference of the wind and Areon moving the cloak on his back had become altogether more apparent.

More often than not the cloak would flutter up above Areon, far above his head and

whirl around with the force of his already growing aura. The day was almost spent, but Areon persevered. Finally he took a break.

"With that learned," the wizard announced, "we will begin trying to move something heavier; your sword. Attempt to spin it on the ground, as it is far to heavy to levitate at this point."

Areon unsheathed his sword and tossed it to the ground with due disrespect. Reaching down into his being, Areon once again propelled his aura, only this time forward rather than back. The sword did not budge for hours. Areon tried until he felt spent. Finally he collapsed again as he had initially.

"You tire. Let us rest until tomorrow," Belgraf implored.

"Not yet," Areon said lightly with a hint of determined anger in his voice.

He rose and looked with an unwavering will to move the sword. Finally it spun. The hilt made a circle and Areon let the energy explode from his body. His entire day of reaching into his soul finally went the other way. He was controlling his aura entirely and reaching in only to have it gush out in a berserk burst. The veins throbbed in his head; the wizard watched with a surprise that wizards experience few times in their almost immortally long lives. Belgraf's eyes bulged and his pupils constricted trying to force out the pouring light that he could now see.

With a final burst the sword spun into the air, hung for an instant, and fell alongside Areon.

"I suppose we'll call that a day," announced Belgraf. Areon collapsed at his words.

Areon slept well that night, but even though he awoke feeling drained of energy, he arose and walked back outside to begin again.

Training resumed, only this time Belgraf told him that with the sword being moved yesterday, he thought that Areon should attempt to move something bigger; himself. The thought of this only disheartened Areon. The idea seemed ludicrous.

Hanging his head and spreading his arms out, eyes closed, he reached into his being expecting to fail. The light he felt yesterday was present, and he thought that maybe he could detect it with increased speed today despite his lack of energy. He pushed everything he felt downward, the light all moving toward his feet. It propelled downward this time, having been moved effortlessly at Areon's whim.

He pushed for sometime, oblivious to the time around him. Hours felt like minutes, and the day swept by as Belgraf watched intently. Areon could not move himself upward, a feat the wizard had hardly accomplished in his long life.

He tried into the night and the light of the stars fell on his face, his eyes still closed. Sweat ran down his cheek as he held his aura under and around his feet trying to lift himself.

Nothing.

Again he forced everything he had to the bottom of his being physically, and spiritually he was fatigued. Remembering the burst he put force yesterday, he made an attempt at it again; only tonight, he was trying to levitate himself. He flexed everything he had, muscles and aura, pushing down, trying to instantaneously lift himself if only for a minute to prove that he could do it. Prove to Belgraf that it was not a waste of the wizard's time and prove to himself that he had the energy, the will to fly.

Again nothing happened. Areon felt his aura faltering. The cloak swept up and engulfed him in all its darkness; the night hanging overhead and the carefree stars glowed in the heavens, not worrying if Areon succeeded.

He began to shiver as the light left him and started to come back to the world of physical matter. No longer within himself he fell to the ground, shaking from lack of the ever-warming light. Belgraf sat still, gazing down on him with a look of empathy in his eyes.

Areon had failed.

# CHAPTER V

## Seeing Reiquem

The hour grew late as Areon slept. He had exerted much energy and was in no mood for training that day with Belgraf. Sliding out of bed and slowly walking down the stairs, he went to see what time of day it was.

"About three hours after the noon," said Belgraf with a chuckle. He stood from his crouching position outside the house.

Areon jerked his head from the sun and eyed the wizard.

"Good morning, Belgraf. I'm sorry I wasn't awake earlier; my energy has been all but depleted."

"Its fine, I thought you might have needed a day off. Do you now know what I meant when I said auras were difficult?"

"Indeed," replied Areon.

"If it will make you feel better, you are without a doubt the fastest learner I have ever witnessed. When it comes to controlling your aura, that is," Belgraf said smiling.

"My thanks, although it doesn't help my lack of strength for when I will need it, if I ever need it," returned Areon. "And yes, I will be careful as I always am." The last comment of Belgrafs worried him a bit.

"Tedious practice, my boy. I go now to the woods, good day!"

"Good day, Belgraf." He was appreciative for the day off.

Areon walked back into the house and grabbed a jug of water, some bread, and a little cheese. He sat thoughtfully and ate. After his bread and cheese, he grabbed an apple that Belgraf and he had picked from one of the many apple trees that were scattered about their land north of Wellenore. He ate slowly and pondered the odds of Reiquem being present at the tavern in town. Come to think of it, she probably had gone a couple times since he had been absent practicing and studying so vigorously.

The day swept by on account of the fact that Areon had nothing to do and was bored most of the day. He got up from one of the chairs he had been sitting in and laid down the book that he had been reading. Grabbing the weaving wooden blinds, he shoved them up and looked out to see the point of the sun. It had already fallen behind the western side of the Flattops and the blinds had already become obsolete. He turned and grabbed the boots that lay beside the chair. After running into the kitchen and splashing some water on his face, he darted outside. Grabbing his cloak and tossing it around him, he looked at the night-bathed path that was almost indiscernible in front of him. Fortunately he knew it well and started on his way to Wellenore.

He trudged up and down a few hills and finally made his way to the gates of the town. Casting his cloak upon his head, he turned to the gate watcher and smiled.

"Good day, Areon, or shall I say night?" as he looked up at the newly visible stars.

The gatekeeper had a story, but Areon figured it went often unheard.

"How are you friend?" asked Areon politely.

"Very well, but you should have a mind to keep that hood on your cloak wrapped about your face, or it'll be trouble for me," responded Goffu.

"Always," returned Areon as the gatekeeper let him in. He smiled to himself and looked up the dirty road to the Full Barrel. As he walked in the bar a few folks drunkenly gazed up at him with half open eyes and looked away again not paying much attention to the stranger that had wandered in.

He walked passed the first table and glanced up to recognize someone he had not seen for some time … Reiquem.

She looked at him and smiled, not wanting to wave and attract attention to him so that others would look; she knew his situation as well as he did. The others in town were oblivious to the fact that Reiquem was a magic user, let alone a master. She did a very good job of not letting anyone know, regardless of how much they pressed her. Wellenore seemed a perfectly closed-minded place for two mages to have a drink together.

He smiled back and looked away, sitting at a table near the entrance. She walked over to him with two mugs in hand and sat.

"How are you?" she said with unexpected surprise in her voice. Reiquem was a rather serious person, being a master and all else she was.

Areon, a bit taken back, stammered, "Fine, and you?" he felt stupid talking like this to a woman as beautiful as Reiquem. Perhaps he was the only one that saw her beauty? Or perhaps the local drunks just did not care if they sounded stupid to her. Areon always was a shy person, but he never really had a chance to realize it due to the fact that he hardly encountered people, which was probably why he was shy in the first place.

"Very well, but I could be better, I imagine," returned Reiquem. " I haven't seen you in some time; what have you been up to?"

"Practicing with Belgraf," Areon answered rolling his eyes. He tried his hardest to act confident.

"I see, getting a little boring is it?"

"Quite," said Areon.

"Well, you'll have to start practicing with me." She laughed.

Areon noted that Reiquem seemed to be fond of him. Never had he seen her with another person, and he imagined that she often got lonely and wondered into Wellenore hoping to see Areon as much as he always hoped to see her. Perhaps her master no longer traveled with her since she was, in fact, a master of shadow. Areon had not ever thought about this and was beating himself up on the inside for not coming back more often; he had no friends either.

They talked and drank, more the former than the latter, for hours and hours on end. Areon had guessed that the time was close to midnight. The talking got easier as the wine started tasting better and better. Soon they were laughing as if they were old friends.

They decided to take a walk. The bartender eyed them as they walked out the door. He realized after a moment of brief silence that it was one of the best times he had had in his life. They strolled through the back gate where they had to jump the fence. It was against the rules of Wellenore to do so, but everyone was long asleep and dreaming of insignificant things, according to the couple that walked out on the black, dirty, cozy, winding road.

They met a stream down south of Wellenore and Areon had another realization; he had never been south of Wellenore.

"I want to thank you for this night," remarked Areon. "It is one of the best I've had in some time. Belgraf's teachings generally put me to sleep for the night and resume in the morning."

"And I you," she smiled. They had sat down next to the bank and were looking up at the stars. Areon hoped to see a shooting star grace the sky with its presence and briefly mingle with the others.

"Reiquem," said Areon, "what can you do with shadow magic? I'm not sure I grasp its importance. I didn't even believe you were a master when you first told me, but I have read much since then."

She turned to him. "Many things," she said seriously. "And I don't intend to insult your wisdom with this comment, but I'm sure you don't grasp the importance. Areon, does Belgraf ever tell you of the history of this land?"

"The ancient history?" asked Areon.

"No, the recent history, the history still being made today with the two kingdoms of the two continents of the sea we reside on."

Areon felt foolish. Along with some other realizations today, he added the fact that Belgraf never really gave him any geological information of the lands, and certainly not recent history or any news of the outside world. He figured knowing of the old days was far more important and did not interact with others enough to care about that sort of thing. "No, I guess I know very little," sighed Areon.

Reiquem looked unsurprised. "Wizards are so old that recent history matters little to them, and when they teach, they tend to teach what is known to only the oldest and wisest. For all a wizard's virtues, they have their faults. The men of the old days weren't the only ones to blame for the wars, you realize?"

Areon nodded with covered half ignorance. He was only now beginning to realize the intelligence that Reiquem possessed, and he imagined all masters had this much lore.

"Wizards realized they could not survive fighting against such numbers that men held, so they slowly compromised and dwindled away. Some stayed to watch over the men, and others, well, it is unknown what happened to the others. I suppose they are deceased and will never touch this land again," Reiquem said looking again towards the sky. "After the wars, most men stayed on the continent we live on now. The reasoning was the wizard's scar left on the other—"

"The wizard's scar?" interrupted Areon.

"Yes, a canyon on the land that was formed from one of the most powerful and last wizards ever to kill so many men, and also a constant reminder to the descendents of beings that fought of those that died. After some time, other men ventured to the other continent and formed another nation. You live in the Nation of Life."

"Why is it called that?" asked Areon, very interested.

"Obviously because the Temple of Life resides next to the Kingdom of the Land," answered Reiquem.

Areon looked back up confused. "I was under the impression most people hated magic folk."

"It is true that the people of Wellenore hate them, but not all people. For example, the intelligent people that still have scribes outlining the days of old, people such as those that live in the city of Life that surrounds the Kingdom of Life."

"And the other kingdom?" Areon asked. "I pray they didn't journey across the sea to make a Kingdom of Death?"

Reiquem laughed. "No, of course not; it is called the Kingdom of Light. The Kingdom of Light is as big as the Kingdom of Life but little inhabits the surrounding area, save the wizard's scar, which isn't even that close to it, and of course, the Temple of Light, which I'm told is inexplicably beautiful. Some say it is made entirely of white light."

"Amazing," said Areon thinking aloud.

"Amazingly late," answered Reiquem as she looked toward the river and stood up. Areon did not exactly want the night to end but was rather tired.

"When will I see you again?" asked Areon anxiously.

"Soon," she returned.

"Where do you sleep?" he questioned.

"Now that's a little bold." She shot him a quick, half joking look, almost reading his mind as of earlier.

As she said her last word she took a step towards Areon, looked him in the eyes, and softly kissed him on the cheek. Areon was so off guard he found no words, but nothing could leave him as speechless as the next thing that he witnessed. As Reiquem stepped back, she looked at the lighting of the moon, almost sizing it up; her shadow shot up over her as if it were alive, encased her body, and the next thing Areon knew he was only looking at his own shadow draping lifeless across the grass on the river bank. He sighed, and a smile spread across his face.

No one would believe that if I told them, he thought. Pondering, he remembered, Unless maybe I was in one of the great kingdoms.

He started the walk back, circling around the whole of Wellenore, not up to dealing with the gates and the hassle.

As he made his way around he found his old, well-trodden path and began up it, making his way to his own house and a comfortable bed.

Areon was rather confused that night and entirely dumbstruck by the manner in which Reiquem took her leave. As he gazed at the sky one last time before walking up the small staircase to his and Belgraf's house, he noticed in the sky amongst all the still lights in the heavens a shooting star.

# CHAPTER VI

## The Shadow Temple

As Areon and Reiquem were together they got to know quite a lot about one another. Often Areon would not spend the days practicing anymore and would run off in the morning to go and find Reiquem. More often than not, she was practicing or simply walking in the woods or thereabout.

On one particular morning Areon woke to go off to meet with her. They met the night before and planned a day together. As Areon grabbed his cloak, which was hung inside on account of the rain last night, the wizard slowly appeared in the doorway, stalling Areon. His familiar old face seemed a bit more lined, and his back seemed a bit more bent than Areon remembered. Areon was absent more than present, and the wizard found the former a bit insubordinate. He had raised him, and he felt that the time was coming when Areon would leave, although this realization did not come with regret. The wizard and the boy loved each other, but Areon needed to stretch his wings a bit and the wizard was by no means closed-minded.

"Off again, are we?" asked the wizard.

"Yes, by your leave, Belgraf."

"You have grown, my boy. I have taught you much, not the least of which is the fact that you do not need my leave to do what you wish."

"Thank you, Belgraf."

"I do hope you are keeping up with your training, though; I wouldn't want to see you go soft." Belgraf smiled.

"Me and Reiquem often spar with magic. Although she is not very fond of the sword."

"Masters rarely are," said the wizard. "They are comforted by magic and are convinced it will get them out of any plight that they may be constrained by."

"Perhaps they are correct?" asked Areon.

"Perhaps," sighed the wizard. "But perhaps not." He looked up with a little doubt in his green eyes.

Areon was well aware that wizards were ingenious, and the fact that a sword felt comfortable at his side more or less gave Areon his answer.

"You are strong lad," stated Belgraf. "A strong, intelligent mind can go far. And you may, lad, you may. I have trained many and you are quick. Practice ever your aura control; it may get you out of a bind someday, my lad."

"Somehow I doubt I will go far," said Areon with a smile, knowing that after the years of boredom and uneventful days in the world, he would be content living a simple life with Reiquem. Not that he was positive that this would ever happen, just wishful thinking.

Areon looked up again from his thoughts. "But ever will I practice magic and my aura when I feel energetic."

"I have taught you all I know, and you have absorbed much," returned the wizard. "Pass my teachings onto those you love and read the books that I have acquired over the many years and learn more; the words in them seem almost perpetual."

"I will, but for now, good day," finished Areon.

"Good day, lad. I'm off to the woods for an uninterrupted day of thought. I will see you when you return." The wizard waved and turned his back to Areon.

Areon turned and headed in the direction that Reiquem had told him to meet her. It was to the south and to the west of Wellenore, for what reason Areon remained unaware. He swerved around Wellenore and went past the stream, walking slowly and knowing that he had left a little early according to his calculation of time by looking at the position of the sun. Belgraf had taught Areon at a young age how to tell the time from looking at the world's source of light. During the winter the sun was straight overhead at noon, and in the summer it was a little to the east before noon, the rest of the time could be told by using these as a standard, although it was rather difficult to do.

Areon walked over a couple hills and down to the open area that Reiquem had told him about. They had visited it a couple times prior to this. The grass stretched down over a small slope in the land. It was extremely lush and extremely green. Willow trees were scattered throughout the surrounding area, but none were packed tightly enough for it to be called a forest. The trees did not inhabit the open area, only the green grass. It was out of seeing or hearing reach for the villagers and a perfect spot for practicing the ways of the old days.

Areon laid his back against a small hill that gently sloped. He put his arms up behind his head and relaxed for the time being. He watched the gossamer clouds slowly floating by and experienced a feeling of tranquility as he waited for the master of shadow. Time went by with the clouds and Areon fell into a light sleep.

Areon found himself waking up to a shadow cast across his eyes. According to the sun and where he saw Reiquem standing, the shadow stood in the wrong place.

"Not quite ready to go today?" asked Reiquem. Areon sat up and rubbed his eyes a little and looked toward the sun. "How long have you been here?" he asked embarrassedly.

"Not long enough to get bored looking at your peaceful face." She smiled at him. Areon thought that she had a beautiful smile, and he wished she would not conceal it as much as she liked to.

"This place is beautiful," remarked Areon while standing up. He rather regretted leaving the plush grass.

"Indeed," answered Reiquem. "Shall we begin?"

"We could," returned Areon with a little hesitancy. Practicing with Reiquem was immensely different than practicing with Belgraf. Although Areon liked the change, he would miss practicing with the wizard. Reiquem never was too hard against Areon, but it seemed as if it was impossible to counter the master or do anything that would remotely hurt her.

They both got up and looked at each other; Reiquem ready to do the usual and Areon preparing to be strained physically. Areon walked down the hill and slowly turned toward the beautiful Reiquem while she walked opposite of him and turned with a jerk. Eyeing each other in the sunlight, they fought.

For what seemed like endless hours and no time at all to Areon, they fought. Shadows constantly diffracting and slicing across the ground; she used them to move things, to move Areon where she wanted him for an attack, to disappear and to reappear where he knew not. The shadow waxed when the clouds did not cover the sun and waned when they did. Shadows need light to exist. Areon used his full strength when the sun was covered.

Reiquem stood about three spans from Areon and they both ceased movement. Eyeing each other, Areon smiled while Reiquem did not follow; her eyes had darkened, if it was possible, and she held her hands up fingers unbent and together in a cross about her chest, slicing the air with her hands going down. A shadow crept from behind her, over her, and in front of her in a long straight line that Areon approached apprehensively. He knew not what she was doing but was wary nonetheless. As he stepped on the dark ground where the shadow resided, he fell …

Areon looked around to see where he was, being no longer a part of the world he knew; he was suspended in shadow and was caught. She had lured him to the deep abyss of the shadow, and he was lost in it.

In the world of beings, Reiquem's eyes had turned to an entirely different sort of black, a black that was impenetrable. A black in the eyes that made it impossible to ever meet her gaze. Although you could not look at her, she could not look at anyone; she was lost in her spell, holding Areon to her will, bending the essence of the shadow, and holding him helpless in its grasp. She stared far off and did not blink for some time. Realizing the fight was over she blinked and Areon was spent. The shadows had taken him, and Reiquem released him.

Areon appeared on the ground where the shadow had been and where Reiquem had taken it from, returning the darkness to her slender figure behind her. It was almost as if he had been on the ground the whole time and the shadow simply blanketed him.

Areon welcomed the warm rays that the sun provided and was thankful for not being in the hands of the shadow any longer.

"I'm sorry," she said almost as if she was absent from their present time and place. "I have a need to try and reach my limits and go beyond whenever I am near the temple. You understand?"

Areon's face turned from a scowl to a look of curiosity.

"Absolutely not," he replied. "Not in the least."

"What do you mean?" asked Reiquem. "It's common knowledge, or at least simple enough to understand."

Areon paused and looked at the ground. Unbeknownst to herself, Reiquem had held her breath during the constrictive shadow attack and was now panting heavily. Areon came to an abrupt realization and scowled for being so mentally slow.

"We are near the shadow temple?" he said as more of a statement to himself rather than a question that was directed toward Reiquem. Areon pondered about how stupid he must look at the moment to Reiquem.

She laughed. "Of course we are. Were you under the impression I randomly chose where to refine the art of shadow? Why do you think we happened upon each other?" She laughed again, which was unusual for Reiquem.

Areon looked up from his fixated gaze at the ground; he was becoming a bit flustered by the whole epiphany he was having and Reiquem's fondness of his stupidity.

"I'm sorry," she said to him. "Would you like to see it then?"

This perked up Areon's spirits. "How far off are we? Is the distance in spans or miles?" Areon asked with anxiousness.

"About twice as far from Wellenore to Waholcast," she answered. "But easily close enough for me to feel the resonation of the gem."

"Another stupid question," interrupted Areon, almost perturbed by the situation. "What color is the gem of the shadow temple?"

"Black, of course," answered Reiquem.

"Are all the gems, or whatever the things are that seal essences, different color?" asked Areon intrigued.

"Well, I guess I'm not sure. I imagine the light gem is blinding, or in the least illuminated from within," answered Reiquem. "The rest I cannot be sure."

Areon was getting more worked up with every word spoken; he wanted to see a temple. At least one thing exciting should happen in his life.

"Can we go and see it?" he asked.

"Now?" cried Reiquem. "It's almost three past the noon; we would never make it. If you must see it, and I warn you to tell no one, we will begin the short journey tomorrow with the few supplies that are necessary."

"Such as what?" asked Areon.

"Food, water, and a few blankets to sleep on," she answered bluntly. "The duration of the trip will be approximately three days. Meet me here tomorrow at sunrise and we will begin."

Areon shook his head, amazed that he was going to behold the temple of one of the gems; as he looked where Reiquem had previously been standing, he realized she was gone.

Areon started his long walk home alone.

Areon passed alongside of Wellenore and back up the slow rolling hills to his little house that he was so accustomed to. He ran up the small staircase to his room and grabbed a book and immediately started reading. The familiar book had silver writings etched on the front; it was otherwise black. This particular night he read about the essence of shadow. As he read, the book slowly slanted more and more until it was level with his stomach and Areon's eyes shut, his mind lost in dreams.

When Areon awoke, he realized that he was late; he could see the light downstairs from the sun. After the realization, he grabbed his black boots, threw them on carelessly, and without a tie, grabbed his cloak and hustled downstairs.

The food situation seemed a bit more meager than usual to Areon. He grabbed some bread and a couple apples. It seemed to Areon that Belgraf had not been home much lately. The food would be sufficient for Areon, for he ate little and could easily go a day or two without sustenance. When he had finished throwing the food into sacks, he punched his hand down on the counter and ran back up stairs. Grabbing a blanket from his bed, he ran down the stairs and sprinted out of the house with his bootlaces flailing, the blanket and his hair fluttering in the wind.

Areon took the route that he had grown accustomed to as of late. He ran round Wellenore and down to the west to the open area where he and Reiquem practiced, sparred, etc. Upon arriving, he saw Reiquem standing impatiently with a bag of supplies leaning against her left leg; her arms were crossed in annoyance.

"Where have you been?" she asked.

"I'm sorry, I simply slept in. I know you've been waiting, please forgive me, Reiquem," Areon answered as he stopped and took deep breaths. He looked up tired and apologetically.

"Of course I do," was the unexpected reply. She said the words, but her face lacked a smile.

"Let us begin the walking," she said a little more kindly.

"Yes, of course," said Areon.

And so began the small, uneventful journey to the shadow temple.

After a break they began the tedious walk again.

"Reiquem, do you mind if I ask you a question?" asked Areon.

"Not at all." She glanced over at him.

"Is there a meaning behind your name?"

"As is with most names in this age, yes, mine has meaning," she returned.

"Can you elaborate on it for me then?" he asked

"You've heard of a requiem, correct?" she began. "My name is the opposite of a requiem; Reiquem. A requiem is a song for the dead that the living sing to honor them, a bit morbid, I suppose, so my parents decided that I would have a name that represented a song to honor the living; a reiquem."

"Brilliant," remarked Areon.

"My parents were always strong supporters of the Life Temple and the goodwill for all the people who are under the Life king's rule. It makes sense that they bestowed upon me the name they did," said Reiquem.

"I'm ashamed to say I do not even know who the king is," said Areon.

"The mighty Rehoboam reigns. He is a good man," Reiquem said. "I'm not surprised that you haven't heard of him. His rule does not generally exist out here although it could if he traveled here."

"And where are your parents now?" asked Areon.

Reiquem looked up at the sky and would say nothing more.

And so they trekked along in silence pondering the conversation. Areon could stand the silence no longer and was about to speak when Reiquem suddenly stopped, shielded her eyes from the direct sun, and carelessly let her bag fall to he ground.

"We should sleep here tonight," she stated. "We've already covered well over half the distance and I am weary."

"Fine with me," Areon said with some relief. He was entirely sick of walking.

"Nothing dangerous inhabits the land around us so we should be safe both sleeping simultaneously," said Reiquem. She took out a black blanket and a pillow that were both tightly packed into the bag. After placing them beside the blankets that Areon had set out for himself, they both crouched down and lay on the soft grass. Nothing much was said as Areon and Reiquem looked up at the stars that night, but before they both fell into a deep slumber, Reiquem laid her face down on Areon's chest and their hands met so that the two felt a little more comfortable and secure in the emptiness of the night.

It seemed to Areon that the minute Reiquem had closed her eyes she had fallen asleep until she woke in the morn; Areon, on the other hand, had hardly slept. He simply rested and felt snug with Reiquem lying so close to him. All in all they both felt rested and rose with vigor. The rest of the walk felt like it took no time at all. Before long, Areon forgot the monotony of the paces that they were taking because of the site that he could see in the distance: A temple.

Reiquem looked over at Areon. "We cannot enter the temple. It is forbidden. And even if it wasn't forbidden, the guardians that keep the gems would perhaps kill us before we even saw the sealer."

"The sealer?" asked Areon, a little put out that he couldn't go in. "And the guardian? I'm more than a little confused."

"Did you think any old person could walk in and take the gem for themselves?" asked Reiquem facetiously. Of course, Areon knew this was not the case, but he thought it would be a bit different.

"The temple," continued Reiquem, "is the warehouse for the gem. If a person should want to get into the temple and get the gem or whatever the things are that hold the essences are, they would have to go through two trials: the guardian and the sealer. The guardian is far worse a thing than the sealer. The sealer simply takes master knowledge to know how to get by; the guardian takes a monumental amount of strength to kill."

"What is the guardian that guards all the temples?" asked Areon.

"I only know a few and that it is different for each temple," she replied. "The shadow temple is guarded by an angel of the Nine Orders. He is of the fourth order; a Dominion ..." she stopped.

"You're joking?" Areon said in disbelief. "An angel? I never believed in that sort of thing." He shook his head

"And what are some of the others? You said you knew a few," said Areon.

"I heard a dragon guards one of the temples, and I know not the rest. I fear to imagine what guards the death temple," said Reiquem. "I've also heard that some of the other angels that have an alliance with the kingdom of life guard some of the temples. Perhaps a Seraph guards the temple of life itself, though I doubt it. Few see the indomitable Seraphim."

"How is it that people do not find these places and come to take the temples?" asked Areon. He did not wish to discuss angels at this moment. He had done a little reading up on them after Belgraf had mentioned them, but nothing more.

"It is curious how it works. Most really can't explain except for masters and some of the very wise. The temples seem to move, to not want to be found. And so they aren't," she shrugged. "Magic, I suppose."

Areon looked up at the approaching temple. "So after the Dominion, that is, at the shadow temple, what is the sealer?"

"The sealer," began Reiquem, "Is a wall, a sort of protective aura that is made of opposite the essence of whatever is inside the gem. The sealer may not be nearly as strong as the resonation of the gem, but it filters a little power so that the gems resonation of each do not spread and undo the balance that is present."

"So almost like a counterweight," replied Areon.

"Yes, sort of, I suppose, yes, that would work," answered Reiquem. "And only the masters of the magics can break these seals because the opposite of the magic that holds the seals is in fact the magic that they practice." She let out a deep breath and took in another. "For instance, if I managed to kill the Dominion, which lingers in the halls of the temple, I would then find my way to the shadow gem, which would be sealed with an aura of light. I would counter the light with my shadow magic and the gem would be mine for the taking."

"Sounds almost easy for a master," said Areon smiling.

"Although it does, it's not. I haven't the faintest idea of how to stop the sealer. Perhaps it just comes to your mind when you go into the place, but no one's been able to teach a master how to break the seal ever," said Reiquem.

"Obviously," replied Areon. "The gems have been around since the beginning of time, haven't they?"

"Correct, but I thought maybe someone would know." She sighed.

As they came over the last hill that slowly unveiled the temple, Areon took it all in as best he could. The light seemed to hold sway only so that it could show the silver brick that the building was composed of. Everything else around the area was shrouded in shadow. The trees were bent away from the surrounding land trying to find more light to live, and the grass was covered in darkness.

The structure itself looked dark, but glorious. Every silver-looking brick was laid with exact precision. No man could have constructed such a temple. Two tall pillars marked the sides of the entrance, and two slanted pillars went out from the bottom of these and met with the edge of the top of the temple. It was beautiful. The most beautiful thing Areon had witnessed, and he now realized that the trek he had made had been worth it just to peer at the temple for only a minute. He knew that the building would stand for an eternity if it had to, and it would. He lost himself in all his thoughts and knew that no one in Wellenore had ever seen anything this magnificent in all their boring lives. The walls seemed to be pulsating, as if they had veins, and magic was running through them keeping it alive for all eternity.

When Areon tore his gaze away, he realized that Reiquem was not standing beside him. She had already run down the hill to the entrance as if something was wrong. Areon followed with curiosity and wonder plaguing his mind. He did not know what exactly to do in such a glorious place, so he simply walked in, although Reiquem told him they couldn't, or shouldn't in the least. The steps were carved at an exact ninety-degree angle, and they were cold and hard to the touch. Never had they decayed and never would they. Shadow bounced off every corner of every hall. Areon didn't know where to head until finally he saw a dull light up ahead that made the shadows enormous. A faint golden-brown light bent the shadows on the wall and made them huge and terrible. Reiquem's shadow could be seen along the wall along with something lying on the ground.

"Reiquem," started Areon, "Where's the—" but he was stopped short; the unmistakable angel was lying on the ground, dead. Areon stared at its body; a slender figure with blonde hair scattered over its beautiful face. Its white robes contained a hole that a mage had torn during the deathblow. Strange lights were coming from the Dominion and suddenly bursting toward the heavens. It still clung to its flashing sword with the left hand. Areon could not tell what sort of material this majestic sword was made of, and after he looked at it, he slowly raised his head to look at Reiquem, who stood over where there should have been a sealer of light and was gazing at the altar that should have held one of the most significant things in all the universe; the shadow gem was gone.

# CHAPTER VII

## Lost Composure

The flight back to Wellenore had been almost a blur to Areon. For the day and a half after Reiquem had realized that the Gem and sealer were gone, they had been half running, half walking to Wellenore. The trip consisted of the two covering ground. They had not slept, and they had not eaten anything while they were trying to make it back. Reiquem had said nothing the entire time.

As for Areon, the situation was a bit more than perplexing. In a couple days' time he had discovered that the temple resided somewhere close to where he had lived his whole life, visited it, seen the slaughtered angel, and found the gem missing. When Reiquem had seen this, and after she had let it all soak in, she took off without even letting Areon know what she planned to do. He stopped and looked at her from behind, and she turned to face him and get an explanation for the delay.

"Why are you stopping?" she asked. "We must hasten."

"For what?" cried Areon. "We've been walking monotonously for over a day now. For what?"

"You don't understand?" she asked sternly. "The gem is missing. To the fools in Wellenore this means nothing, but if it should happen to fall into the wrong hands, or worse, should the rest of the gems be stolen and come to close to each other, the resonation of them can break one or all of them.

It will be devastating to the world and could leave no world left to be in devastation."

"I realize this, Reiquem, but what good does it do to run to Wellenore, especially if they know nothing about it?" asked Areon.

"Wellenore is the only town for a long way in every direction of the temple," she replied. "Someone there will have witnessed something."

Areon shrugged and kept trudging along behind Reiquem. Perhaps she was right. Maybe someone would know something. After all, the gem had been stolen, which Areon thought could never happen. So why would somebody from Wellenore not know about a magical situation? He corrected himself in his mind, I daresay, a universally life threatening situation.

They had reached the outskirts of the town when Areon realized that it seemed to be more of a ghost town than a bustling country town. Merchants were coming through with carts full of goods and the townsfolk were talking and laughing outside the houses comprised of wood and stone. Generally music could be heard from a walking musician out for a few bronze or silver pieces. Nothing could be heard as Reiquem jumped the fence that surrounded the place. Areon was having a hard time keeping up with the now determined Master. She looked like she wanted to end someone.

"Where is the stone?" she cried as she entered the open middle section of town. Who she was speaking to Areon knew not.

"Where is the stone?" she screamed. Areon had never seen this side of her. A man walked out of the bar and looked at her in horror. She walked over to confront him.

"What do you know?" she glared at him. He really did look pathetic in all of Reiquem's terror.

"Reiquem, you're losing your composure," tried Areon.

Reiquem tore her gaze from the man to Areon for a split second and then back again.

"If you don't tell me something I need to know this instant, you'll never see the light again, understand?" Obviously she had stopped caring if the townsfolk knew that they used magic.

The man stammered, "A wizard, hooded, came through here a spot ago; no one's been outside the houses since."

"Belgraf," she said to herself.

"Belgraf?" asked Areon, "Impossible. He knows better than any things that must and must not be done."

Regardless of what Areon had just said Reiquem was already headed north towards the little house that Areon had lived in his whole life. As she took a few more steps, a large man came out from one of the more prestigious buildings in respect to Wellenore. Areon recognized him as the head of the town. He was an old, rather fat man who some considered a blundering idiot. How he maintained his position as the head of the town was beyond Areon.

"Halt, right there," the man said putting up a quivering hand. As he did, Reiquem shot her hand from her hip up into the air making a gust of wind. A shadow materialized and followed the path of her hand; it swept over the ground and made a gash in it. Areon noted that it seemed to have solid characteristics. The shadow went out across the man's face, and he was left with a scarlet line. Blood ran down the side of his face from directly under his eye. He said no more and Areon followed closely behind as they exited the northern boundary of the small town.

# CHAPTER VIII

## The Scarlet Wizard Cloak

As the couple approached the house, they noticed Belgraf sitting on the porch with an indocile look on his face. Reiquem approached him with anger, but Areon knew better. Reiquem took large strides toward him and Areon was almost running to keep up. When they were within a span of Belgraf, Reiquem took up her hand to strike the wizard across the face; he simply raised his hand and hers stopped dead in its path. It was apparent that his magical ability was far beyond hers.

Reiquem stared at him motionless but with a look of contempt in her eyes that were locked on the wizard; the rest of her body stayed under his control.

"Master Reiquem," said Belgraf, patronizing her. "We meet at last." He was still holding his hand up with his fingers hanging almost limply in the air; magic hung heavily.

"Release me, wizard," she replied. Belgraf looked at Areon who nodded impatiently and Belgraf lowered his hand. Reiquem moved after calming herself a bit. She lowered her arm when she could.

"Shall we congregate inside and talk, or would you prefer to strike the innocent?" Belgraf asked coolly.

"Innocent?" Reiquem asked with surprise. Before she could say more, Belgraf turned his back to them, heading toward the kitchen. When they entered, he sat with a leg crossed and a look on his face that said he was now ready to answer some questions, although he knew Reiquem's assumptions were incorrect.

"I presume the sealer has been broken and the gem is gone," said Belgraf cutting into the silence.

"Of course you do," answered Reiquem, "you're the only person in a fifty league radius who was any sort of match for an angel of the fourth order."

"Thank you for the accusation, Reiquem." The wizard glanced from Areon to Reiquem with a look of annoyance.

"How else would you know it was gone?" she shot back. "The temple is miles from here."

"I'm Belgraf the Wizard, dear girl," he returned. "Not some fool. I would be offended if you had it in your mind that I would not know what happened."

Areon was thinking to himself silently. He absolutely agreed with Belgraf. The wizard had done so many inexplicably strange things that Areon thought this was rather normal. Reiquem had obviously not lived with a wizard her whole life, in contrast to himself.

"Belgraf the Meddler," she said with aggravation in her voice. She had lost the argument and felt foolish, which happens to many who disagree with a wizard. She knew the wizard disagreed with her ways and regarded her as a child with a dangerous weapon. All nonmasters who knew of the essences did.

Belgraf chuckled and looked over at Areon. "And do you think I took the stone?"

Reiquem shot Areon a look, but Areon shook his head toward the wizard. Reiquem scowled.

"Of course not, what a foolish idea you had, Reiquem," said Belgraf. Reiquem stood up and bowed toward the old wizard, knowing she had been wrong.

"I apologize," she said. "But the gem is gone and the sealer has been broken. How I'm not sure. A powerful magic user, I know I didn't do it." Her voice gave out a little and her bottom lip quivered at these words.

Belgraf raised his eyebrows and looked over at Reiquem. Areon caught on.

"Reiquem couldn't have done it," said Areon. "I've been with her the last couple of days."

The wizard looked down with a grin on his old face; it was barely visible beneath his thick beard. "I know—I know it wasn't you, master. Although you are the number one suspect, being a shadow master and therefore a perfect person to counter the sealer. The question that would need asking would be why you chose to do it."

She jerked up head up with a nasty look on her face. Before she could answer, Belgraf raised his hand.

"But I know it wasn't you," he said curtly. "Areon, follow me." The wizard got up from the table and walked up the creaky staircase. Areon looked at Reiquem and motioned for her to follow him; they both came up the stairs to see Belgraf standing in front of his room. Areon had seldom ventured into Belgraf's room. He felt no need to after he had seen it the first time. It was rather dull. A small window facing the north let a small amount of sunlight fall into the room. A bookshelf off the side of the bed housed many old and tattered books that Areon had never read. He figured he would read them if Belgraf told him, or if he ever happened to finish all the books that were in the main collection in the upper part of the house.

The rest of the room was pretty ordinary; a bed sat in the corner of the room with ancient, patched blankets residing on top. Most of the walls were bare, save a part opposite the bed where a small closet was seemingly drawn onto the wall. Areon had never really acknowledged it in his life. But the most insignificant thing in the room was what Belgraf headed toward.

As he approached the door, Areon realized that there was no handle on it, most likely the reason for it appearing drawn on the wall.

Belgraf closed his eyes and whispered something in the language of the old days that was barely audible to the two standing behind him. Belgraf made a sweeping motion with his hand that the door followed. It opened and revealed a cloak, a blood red cloak.

Belgraf grabbed at the top with care; he took it out and shook it, covering the air in dust. He coughed and walked in between Areon and Reiquem, only to walk directly back down the stairs. They followed closely in awe.

As they made their way down the old steps, they saw the wizard eyeing the cloak with what seemed like rue. It was as if he was parting with something that was alive. They stopped at the bottom of the staircase and waited for words.

Belgraf started talking very quietly; the two were forced to lean closer to hear everything he was saying. "Good-bye, my old friend, you have saved me many a time. You will be missed." He turned and looked at Areon. "Areon, my boy, I've waited long to give you this, whether it was because I dreaded parting with it, or because I thought you weren't ready, I do not know, but apparently the time has come, and you will be wise to nary take this cloak off on your travels."

Areon eyed the scarlet cloak and he walked towards it and touched it apprehensively, as if he expected it to move and turn into something. The cloak draped motionless on the table. Belgraf took a step back for his final parting with the glorious cloak. It was without a doubt the most beautiful thing that Areon had ever laid eyes on. Most of the things owned by Belgraf and Areon were from days long past that Belgraf never had disposed of, others were made by man; the cloak was obviously made by wizards.

"What is it?" murmured Areon.

"A cloak," chuckled the wizard.

Belgraf turned serious. "A wizard cloak. The last wizard cloak, as far as I know. In the old days, the wizards gathered and made seven cloaks. After magic was dripping from them from so much work, the great convention decided on the seven great wizards of the day that the cloaks would be bestowed to; I humbly say that I was one of them that received such an honor. The six others; black, blue, violet, silver, green, and white have been lost in the sea of time. If one were to come across one of these prestigious cloaks, he would be infinitely lucky and inescapably great for good or evil."

"What makes them great besides the beauty they hold?" Areon asked, still gazing at the scarlet cloak.

"Once put on," the wizard began, "they tend to become your best friend, never letting you go and trying desperately to keep you alive. They tend to grow and move to accommodate the situation. They will save you when you are in dire need, if you are not able, of course. Other than these situations that require the cloak's services, they act as an ordinary article of clothing, nothing more. Always remember that they will not fight for you, but with you."

"And you once wore this?" asked Areon with more wonder in his voice than ever.

"Once, long ago," answered the wizard. "But the fight to get it off when the wars between men and wizards ceased was so great that I dare not ever put it on again; it would hold me for eternity. I imagine the other cloaks have been buried with their masters for the fact that they were impossible to remove after the owner had passed into the afterlife."

"Amazing," Reiquem said, speaking for the first time since she had seen the cloak. "I've heard of the cloaks, but I never knew they existed. I thought it was an old fairy tale from the old days."

"Perhaps it was. Fairies exist, you know. Outside with you, lad," said Belgraf, looking from Reiquem to Areon. "On it goes. I want to see you put it on before you go to bed for the night."

"Are we staying here then?" Areon asked Reiquem. She nodded in response.

Areon went outside carrying the cloak. It shimmered in the sun and fluttered flirtatiously next to Areon. Belgraf grimaced a bit out of regret.

Instantaneously Areon grabbed the neck of the cloak and threw it around his shoulders; a magical aura surrounded him as the cloak's aura and Areon's mingled and connected. The edges of the bottom of the cloak seemed to push against the ground and push Areon only inches into the air before setting him gently down again. After this display, it became an ordinary cloak, apart from its exquisiteness. The scarlet draped his body like a solid cloud of dark blood. Areon looked glorious in it and felt that he would never want to take the cloak off in his life. It gave him security; made him feel safe from the world, the same feeling you get from a warm blanket when you are in utter darkness during the dead of the night.

After Areon got over the initial shock of the new cloak, he looked over at Belgraf.

"Belgraf, you spoke of me wearing this on my travels. I'm sorry. but what travels were you speaking of?" asked Areon.

"Ho, Ho," laughed the wizard, "Why, your travels to break the seals and collect the gems, of course," answered the wizard, as though it was an obvious answer to a silly question.

Areon's jaw dropped slowly. He looked at Reiquem, who did not look surprised in the least.

Belgraf turned and headed inside. The sun was lowering as well, and the sky had become a deep orange.

"He's joking, right?" Areon asked Reiquem. She gave him a serious look and turned to go in the house.

"I'm sleeping with you tonight," she said. "And leaving with you in the morning."

Areon stood still and watched the sun set the rest of the way. His life had gone from one extreme to the other.

# CHAPTER IX

# Not Good-bye

Areon experienced a hard time facing the fact that he was going to be leaving his lovely, secure home. He stood outside for about an hour before he realized that Reiquem would be wondering what he was doing. He shook his head vigorously and rubbed his eyes. The night had settled in, and he decided to go to bed.

When he walked up the ancient staircase, he heard Belgraf carelessly sleeping in his worn bed. Areon wondered how he was sleeping so well after giving away what seemed to be a part of him earlier on in his life. He thought a bit more and decided that it could have been a burden that was released from Belgraf's shoulders. This, of course, only made him look at the cloak nervously. What if Areon would be one that must be buried with his cloak on? He decided not to think on it any longer. It was only a cloak. He corrected himself in his mind, A wizard cloak.

When he had nimbly walked past Belgraf's room as to assure that the old man slept peacefully, he crept into his room and looked around for Reiquem. The only way Areon could tell that she was there was because she jerked her head up from his pillow to see if it was he for certain; she seemed to blend into the darkness.

"Sorry, I was outside thinking a bit," whispered Areon.

"I know, it's fine," she replied. "I wasn't asleep anyway."

His bed was rather large and could easily accommodate two people at once. Areon lifted his hand to remove the cloak he was wearing. It was not exactly stuck to his body, he just found it everything but impossible to take off. After a bit of a struggle, he decided he did not want to take it off. He could sleep in his clothes. He imagined that it was what he was going to be doing anyway for some time after the night. He stealthily lifted the covers and slid into his comfortable bed.

"We'll have to wake rather early tomorrow morning." She turned her body towards his and laid her hand on his chest and her head close.

"I know," answered Areon. "I wish we could stay a while longer."

Reiquem sat up. "I thought you were sick of this place."

"I thought I was, too, but apparently a little longer wouldn't hurt," he returned.

"Regardless," she said, "we leave tomorrow."

"You'll have to wake me when you wish to leave," said Areon.

"I will," she said sleepily. "Although Belgraf may wake us both before I get the chance."

"Perhaps," he replied and turned toward her. She had lain back down, and they both looked at each other before slowly closing their eyes and falling into a dreamless sleep.

"Wake up, face the sun, its time to rise!" chorused Belgraf. The room was hardly lit by the creeping sun.

"What time is it?" asked Areon groggily.

"Time to rise, of course," repeated Belgraf agitatedly.

Areon sank back into his soft mattress and flung the sheets over his head to block out the small amount of sunlight. Reiquem stood up and went downstairs to wash up a bit before they began to get ready. Belgraf stood over Areon with his hands on his hips and immediately after ripped the covers off Areon and prodded at him with his cane to get him up and out of bed.

"Get up, you lazy oaf," said Belgraf. "Early, yes, but you must wake."

"Shouldn't I be well rested before taking off?" asked Areon.

"You are fine," remarked Belgraf. Areon got up slowly and rubbed the sleep out of his eyes. After running down the stairs, he walked passed Reiquem, who was leaning over a tub of fresh water, washing her face. He walked outside and watched the sun for a while. After walking back toward the house, he realized Reiquem was standing outside on the porch having a cup of tea that Belgraf had given her.

"Getting along a bit better, I pray?" asked Areon.

"A bit," she replied, taking another sip. "What all do you need to take?" asked Reiquem, immediately changing the subject.

"I'm not sure," answered Areon. "I suppose food, my old bow, if I can find it, for hunting when we run out of the initial supply of food, a spare set of clothes …" he trailed off. "I don't know. I guess I'll have to run in my room and look around for awhile." Reiquem looked rather impatient.

"You should go," she replied. "We haven't got much time."

"Much time?" said Areon chuckling. "How long do you think this is all going to take? I'm not even sure why we're doing it."

"I'm sorry," she responded. "This is difficult for me. All I've had most of my life is my ability; it's as if someone has taken part of it from me. I'd like to find out what exactly is going on."

"That's enough reason for me to go, and I hope we will find some truths," returned Areon. "But obviously all in due time."

Reiquem smiled apologetically. "Thank you."

After stretching, Areon ran past her and touched her lightly on the shoulder. When he reached his room, he realized that Belgraf was already going through some things. He was bent throwing some old clothes about and looking for odds and ends that would be useful.

"The cloak and bow will be sufficient to take off with," said the wizard. "But I suppose we can send you off with a bit more than that."

After searching through his room and running down to the kitchen, Areon stepped in view of Reiquem and Belgraf with a bow strung to his back; a quiver accompanied the bow and lay flat against his back containing many skillfully made arrows that Areon, if ever, had shot and found with care; a sword at his waist, (his old sword that Belgraf had woven a bit of elemental earth magic into); a knife stuck to the other side; a bag that was tied around his neck and waist and was hidden by the cloak, filled with food; and a flexible skin for carrying water. Reiquem reluctantly carried two compact blankets and a miniature pot for cooking.

Areon looked up at the old wizard with disbelief in his eyes. "I'm not really leaving you am I, Belgraf? Where will we go?" he asked.

"Head to Wellenore," replied the old wizard. "Speak with Goffu; he knows the lands around this area better than I and will know where to steer you."

"He has never spoken of anything pertaining to his travels before, why should he begin now?" asked Areon.

"As I have said before, the wizard cloak will help you more than you know," answered the wizard mysteriously.

Areon could not help feeling a bit homesick already.

"Belgraf," he said slowly, "I will see you again, won't I?"

The wizard looked up with a smile and spoke, "Departures occur often, but rarely are they good-byes, Areon."

"Then I will see you sooner or later," returned Areon as he turned and started on his worn path toward Wellenore.

"I hope the former, my lad," said Belgraf to himself, and then he whispered. "But I fear the latter is in our future."

Belgraf watched the two until they were entirely out of his sight. Then he went back inside to do whatever it is that wizards do.

# CHAPTER X

## Goffu's Council

"What will an old gatekeeper know?" asked Reiquem.

"More than you can guess," answered Areon. "I think that especially now that I know he and Belgraf know one another and are friends. Although I'm not entirely sure he will give us any helpful advice on where to go; I've often felt that he was once a mage but had left that life behind and was trying to live a bit more peacefully, which is why I think he will 'forget' what he used to know and send us on our way."

"Well then, it's a good idea to head there, isn't it?" said Reiquem sarcastically. Areon gave her a look and smiled.

"I'll always trust what Belgraf says," he answered.

They walked a bit more in silence. It seemed to Areon that the trip was just another tedious trip to the Full Barrel, and that he would be going home after. In the back of his mind he knew this was wrong. When they finally got to the gate, they looked at the old gatekeeper who was faithfully waiting. He seemed less than happy to see the pair of mages.

"Rash decisions you made, Master Reiquem," was the first thing out of Goffu's mouth. "The townsfolk hardly leave their homes anymore; I myself am ostracized for staying out all the time and keeping watch. Some say I'm on your side. As if sides exist."

Before he could say another word, he glanced at the blood red cloak Areon was wearing. His face held an expression of disbelief.

"It can't be …" Goffu trailed off. He straightened himself up a bit and tried to remain calm.

"So that is where the last remaining cloak has gone," he said. "I should've known it was Belgraf's."

"Are you a wizard as well?" asked Reiquem.

"Ha, ha, no, no, I am just old and, according to some, wise," he responded. He returned his attention to Areon. "You know not what you possess, lad. Wear it well." He turned as if they were about to leave.

Just before Areon could speak, Goffu turned to him. "Well, let me put the pieces together; the shadow stone is gone, a cloak of infinite power has been bestowed to a new master, and the two involved in these have come to old Goffu for council. How far off am I?" he asked.

"Not far at all," returned Areon.

"Well, I guess the best thing that I can tell you to do is head toward some place that can give you better advice than I," said Goffu.

Goffu lit up a pipe that he had recently pulled from his coat. He took a long drag and blew the smoke away from Areon and Reiquem. He seemed in no hurry for them to leave.

"And?" said Reiquem.

"And you'll get nothing from me if you're going to be impatient," he snapped.

The two waited while he took another drag from his pipe and blew the smoke into a cloud above his head. He leaned on the gate and stared at the two with unblinking eyes. Reiquem noted that he deliberately took his time.

"You'll have to first head through Stock Hollow forest," Goffu finally began. "Heading in a northeast direction. Next you'll have to cross the Flattops."

"Cross the Flattops?" interrupted Areon.

"Yes, and it is not as difficult as one might expect," he returned. You will cross with ease."

"I hope so," said Areon looking towards them.

"I'm surprised you're not worried about the Moss Woods." Goffu grinned.

"Why would I be?" asked Areon absentmindedly, still looking towards the mountains.

"Because you're not going into them this time with a wizard." He smiled with the pipe hanging out of his mouth.

"We'll be fine," said Areon. "What after that?"

"The trickiest part of my advice," responded Goffu. "Get into the magic city, Lalvegeth. It is located directly behind the Flattops."

"And how does one get into the city?" asked Reiquem. "I've heard it doesn't even really exist."

"And I've never heard of It," said Areon feeling a bit foolish. His heart sped up a bit in excitement after hearing about a magic city.

"You must prove to them that you use magic," answered Goffu. "They loathe nonmagic folk."

"Well, that'll be easy," said Areon looking at Goffu. "Right?"

"Not as easy as you might think." Goffu took the pipe out of his mouth and stared at them a bit longer. "No one can see the city unless they're inside it."

"Well, that's terrific," said Areon.

"If you head in a direct northeast direction from here, you'll run into it," said Goffu smiling broadly.

"I'm sure," responded Areon sarcastically. "And should we happen to find this place, what then?"

"Obviously go to a store that sells maps," returned Goffu.

"Good-bye."

"Good-bye?" asked Areon. "That's all then?" Goffu sucked on his pipe thoughtfully and said no more for a while. When the two decided this was all they would get out of him, they turned to leave.

"Thanks," muttered Areon. Reiquem said nothing.

When they had walked a couple of spans, Goffu turned and cupped his hand toward Areon and Reiquem. "Oh, and Areon," he said. Areon turned and looked at him. "I wouldn't tell too many people what you both are up to." After saying this, Goffu turned and went back to being an old gatekeeper that kept his secrets.

They walked awhile before Reiquem turned and scrunched up her face in bewilderment.

"We didn't even tell him what we were up to," she said.

## EXCERPT FROM THE HISTORICAL
## ARCHIVES OF THE KINGDOM OF LIFE

" ... So as not to confuse the student, or inquisitive mind, we were always at peace with the Kingdom of Light prior to this atrocity. This last recent even written of earlier is one that is, in its entirely, unforgivable and will be dealt with in a manner of unforgivable ferocity. We have ever shared an alliance that seemed incorruptible, as well abidingly unbreakable, with the Kingdom of Light until relatively recent events. The time will soon come for these old alliances to end. We know of what the Kingdom of Light has done, although we will show empathy toward our friend of old. The time to strike has not yet come. Although we realize that eighteen years is a long time to wait, we need to show that we are civilized beings, capable of letting our longtime friend and ally repair their nation. A wizard scar is a thing that time cannot erode easily. Their nation will suffer, as it has since the end of the last war with wizards, not of our accord for some time without our brash invasion. We will not be negligent to the facts that are incorporated with the continents. The event that was written about eighteen years ago was, according to our most intelligent minds and according to most of the civilians, a plan of attack against us to weaken us, to stop us from having a reigning king and split our kingdom in twain. Divide us so that we would be vulnerable to attack from the Kingdom of Light and then, and only then, would they strike us down and take control of the mirrored continents that lived in such harmony. For details on the event that occurred eighteen years ago, refer to Historical Archives of the Kingdom of Life, book 52, pages 211–235 ..."

May the angels ever watch over us, keep us safe, and guide us through shadow in the afterlife.

# CHAPTER XI

# Named Not for Nothing

For the majority of the day that was left in front of them after the talk, the two walked in silence. Reiquem was apparently used to monotonous walking, but in contrast, Areon was not. They took a straight shot from Wellenore towards Waholcast forest; the Moss Woods. Areon watched as they went by his house. He wondered if Belgraf was in the house studying something. He knew not to walk to the house and say good-bye again because it would be too hard to try and leave.

As they reached the edge of the woods, they decided to take a break from the day of walking. As Reiquem sat down on the blankets she carried, Areon decided to walk around and find an apple tree to take a few ripe apples for the trip. The Moss Woods were entirely composed of gloriously large willow trees.

When he had picked some apples that looked good enough to eat, he went back over to Reiquem and sat down next to her. She looked peaceful for the first time in awhile. He sat down silently and watched her gaze up at the large moss-covered willow trees that were locked together.

"They look like they've been here forever," she spoke. "I haven't been in this forest much."

"And why is that?" asked Areon taking an apple from his pouch and taking a small bite after.

"Some say the moss changes time," she answered. "Some call it 'the living green.'"

"'The living green,'" thought Areon aloud. "I thought this place had enough names."

Reiquem looked over at him. "Well, the name Waholcast is obsolete," she replied. "None now call it that, as your wizard may have told you."

"I guess I didn't think of that," he responded. It was good for Areon to get a viewpoint from someone else besides an ancient wizard. He loved talking to Reiquem more than anything. When he stopped to think about it, Belgraf was the only person, save Reiquem, whom he had had an in depth conversation with his whole life.

Areon offered Reiquem an apple. She accepted and took a bite.

With a mouthful she asked, "Shall we sleep on the edge of the forest tonight? I'm a little less than anxious to start walking in the forest, particularly toward the end of a day."

"Understandable," replied Areon. "I think it would be a good idea to sleep out here tonight. One less worrisome night we'll have to endure."

"Areon," said Reiquem. "Have I ever told you how much I enjoy being with you?"

Areon looked up, rather embarrassed. "No, I guess not, I'm not sure you really had to," he said. "Have I ever told you?"

"You didn't have to either," said Reiquem showing the smile that Areon loved so much.

They talked for some time and the sun slowly went down. It was a perfectly windless day and a good start to a journey with Reiquem. Due to the warm summer they had no need to start a fire, and after watching the sun sink behind the Flattops, they laid one of the blankets down and used the other to cover themselves up with. The two had grown used to sleeping next to one another and fell into a carefree sleep.

When they awoke the next morning, the sun was already above the Flattop Mountains and they both felt fully rested. Areon walked to the nearest apple tree and took one off, knowing that it would be the last chance he had to grab another. He also picked one for Reiquem. After walking back over to her and it putting it in her hand, he looked up to the roof of the forest and examined the entire area.

"We slept in," said Areon, still gazing at the top of the woods.

"I know," replied Reiquem. "It's okay. I'm a little apprehensive about this journey through the forest."

"I don't know what the big deal is," answered Areon.

"Well, of course you don't. You've always been in here with Belgraf. He is very protective. He probably saved your life without you knowing it a couple times in there," said Reiquem.

"You said you've ventured through here very little," returned Areon.

"I have heard many stories," she replied.

"Well, perhaps you can tell me these tall tales while we walk," said Areon sarcastically. Reiquem scowled and looked over at him.

"Do you think some of the wise would call it the living green for nothing?" she asked.

"Yes, I suppose," answered Areon carelessly. "Look, we have you, and I've been studying magic since I was born. Nothing will happen to us in the forest. We may run into a goblin or two, but what are they to us?"

"Have you ever fought or killed a goblin?" asked Reiquem.

"No, but I'm not really worried. After all, Belgraf has slain many, and he said they would be no match for me; and that was a long time ago," said Areon rather proudly.

"Perhaps," sighed Reiquem. "But, honestly, it's not really the goblins that worry me." Areon didn't give much thought to the last comment.

After gathering up the blankets and throwing them back on her back, and after Areon had taken up all his supplies, they walked to the utmost edge of the forest.

"Well, here we are," said Areon hesitantly.

Reiquem looked at him and gave a sort of an uneasy half smile. They took the first steps through the woods and looked around. Areon had to admit that while the talk as of late had led him to believe the woods were dangerous, it was without a doubt one of the most beautiful spectacles Areon had ever seen. A zigzag path cut through the middle of the forest; they would be taking the off path to get to the destination they desired. Every tree was a willow. The farthest apart any two trees were was about two spans and no more (a span, of course, being the distance of an average human's outstretched arms from fingertip to fingertip). The trees were all gloriously tall and wide, as if they had all finished growing centuries ago and yet were nowhere near dying. Green moss covered every single one of the innumerous whip-like branches. The ground was grassy and moss-covered; even the grass on the ground had moss growing on it. All the rocks that happened to be lying by trees were covered with moss.

Areon was the first to speak. "Beautiful, isn't it?" he said.

"Don't let it deceive you, Areon," she replied darkly. "Be on your guard."

They took the first steps into the woods and soon they became tired of walking again and were less wary of the woods. Areon noticed that the moss seemed to stick to the bottom of his boots, and after some time of not looking at them, it had crawled up the sides of them and had to be brushed off, which proved a trifle more difficult than he thought it should have been.

"Annoying, this moss," Areon said.

"So I noticed," Reiquem said in response.

Beautiful as they were, the woods became rather boring to Areon. The scenery became the same thing over and over again for hours on end; simply willow trees and moss. Finally the two ran into the stream that Areon and Belgraf had been to a few times prior to this. The rock that Areon had remembered Belgraf sitting on was in the same place and still covered with moss that seemed as though it would never leave.

"I've been here before," said Areon.

"Oh really?" asked Reiquem. "Its quite lovely. I say we stop and have a rest, we've been walking nearly three hours now."

"That'd be wonderful," said Areon. He sat on the same moss-covered patch that he had sat on what seemed like ages ago now. Areon took off his boots and rubbed the inch of moss off that had accumulated on the sides and bottom of his shoe. Reiquem did the same.

After she finished, she looked at Areon, who was still busily scrapping the sides of his boots. "Looks like we still have a few hours of daylight left to travel in here," she said. "I'd like to find somewhat of a safe place to sleep."

"Yes, it'd be nice, although I don't know if it'll be possible," replied Areon.

The two stood up from the spot of which they had been so peacefully sitting. Areon went over to the stream and took a long draught of water from it. The water was clean and fulfilling. Reiquem decided that it would be a good idea to take a drink as well and not exhaust the supply of water that Areon held in his homemade skin canteen.

"Shall we begin walking again straight away?" asked Areon. He seemed as though he wasn't ready to leave the place.

"We might as well, not much else going on here," answered Reiquem a bit absentmindedly.

So the two gathered up their luggage and started walking again, heading in a northwest direction. Areon couldn't shake the thought out of his mind that he had absolutely no idea what they were looking for, but then he would just think about how far of a walk it was going to be to get across the Flattop Mountains. He had never done it before and figured it was going to be quite a walk judging from the size they were from looking at them from Belgraf's house.

Areon looked down at the moss that was already accumulating on his shoes once again.

"Looks like whoever named this place the Moss Woods didn't do it for nothing," he muttered to Reiquem.

# CHAPTER XII

## An Unpleasant Morning

When they had walked until they were starting to bump into each other due to the lack of light, Reiquem finally stopped.

"I don't think we're going to find a nice safe place to sleep, Areon," she said. "We might as well just rest up against some trees; one of us will watch while the other sleeps. We'll have to take turns like that looking for goblins and such."

"All right," grumbled Areon. He was not to keen on the idea of staying awake and keeping watch. He threw down his pack and did not even bother with his cloak.

"Which of us will sleep and which will watch first?" asked Areon.

"I'm not really tired," answered Reiquem. "I'll watch first." Areon showed a sign of relief on his face. He was not exactly at his full strength after walking all day; apparently Reiquem was used to it.

"Sleep well," was all she said before Areon positioned himself next to a giant willow tree and fell into a much needed rest.

The sun was down completely now and all the stars were in the heavens. Reiquem, however, could not see them due to the serried roof of the forest. She watched for a few hours while her eyelids slowly went farther and farther down towards being shut. Finally, without waking Areon, she fell asleep where she sat.

The two awoke sometime in the morning, unscathed and rested. Reiquem woke slowly just before Areon. She looked up at the roof of the forest and then down in horror. Moss covered the entirety of their bodies.

Reiquem was beating herself up inside her head. "How could I be so stupid?" she said. Areon looked over at her sleepily and tried to stretch, realizing that his arms were pinned underneath a bed of moss.

He looked over his green body and then over to Reiquem; the only thing on her that was not covered in moss was her head.

"You fell asleep?" yelled Areon. "What do you suggest we do now? I can't move a muscle."

"I'm thinking," she shouted back. She knew it was her fault. Areon watched her think for a while and then struggle in vain. He could barely move his body anymore, which meant the situation was worsening; when he had awakened, he could at least wiggle his body a bit.

"Any thoughts?" asked Areon. Reiquem did not reply, she only continued to struggle.

"I don't understand this," he cried. "How long have we been asleep? We walked most of the day and all we had was some moss covering our feet."

Areon looked over again at Reiquem; he noticed that the moss was now creeping up her neck and edging toward her face.

"This is going from bad to worse," pointed out Areon. "We need to find a way out of this. It's no good trying to move. It seems like every time I try it just gets harder to move and the moss grows faster."

"Okay, stop moving," said Reiquem. "We need to think."

Before Areon got much thinking done, he stopped and felt something move beneath him. Slowly the moss began to lift as Areon did. He could not fathom what was happening until he saw something familiar; scarlet.

"Your cloak!" cried Reiquem, not unduly. It had indeed begun to penetrate the moss on top of Areon and itself.

"I wouldn't believe it if I wasn't witnessing it," exclaimed Areon. The cloak was slowly breaking Areon free. It looked as though blood was seeping through the layer of moss. After about a minute of what seemed like easy work for the ancient cloak, Areon was basically free and wiping clumps of moss from his stomach. The sides of the cloak then shot up into the air, raised Areon from the ground about four spans, and then set him gently on his feet.

"Amazing," said Areon shaking what remained of the moss off himself.

He looked down at Reiquem, who seemed a bit less than thrilled Areon was free while she was not.

"Sorry," said Areon, finally running over to Reiquem and grabbing the obstinately strong moss that clung to her body. He ripped off what he could and helped Reiquem onto her feet. She shook off what was left and looked around at the piles sitting where the two had been sleeping. It must have equaled about a foot of moss that covered Areon and Reiquem.

Areon glanced over at Reiquem and turned his head away as soon as she shot him a look.

"Well, at least we're out of it." Areon shrugged. "I don't think I'm going to regret taking this cloak from Belgraf." he started picking up the supplies and brushing the moss off them. Reiquem was pretty silent until they finally had gathered the few things they had and started walking.

"That was foolish of me, I'm sorry," she said apologetically.

Areon stopped and looked at her with a small grin on his face. "Hey, c'mon, we made it out alright. How were you supposed to know?" he asked. Reiquem shrugged. Areon gave her a playful nudge on the shoulder and she gave him a little push back.

"This is an adventure, right?" said Areon. "Things happen." He was almost enjoying the fact that he was out and doing something with his life for a change. Reiquem gave him a sort of smile and looked at him with admiration in her eyes.

"I suppose you're right. I guess worse things could have happened," she replied, not knowing how right she was.

"Good, now let's forget about it and have a good day," returned Areon. He looked over at Reiquem, but she wasn't alongside him any longer. He looked back and she stood frozen where she was.

"Reiquem what are you—" asked Areon, but before he could finish, he turned to look at what had stunned Reiquem; in front of them, about thirty spans, trudged a cannibal, a thing Areon had hoped to never see in his entire life, although he expected to on his adventure. It was the biggest monster Areon had ever laid eyes on; an ogre.

Reiquem stood frozen where she was. Areon kept moving his head from the ogre to Reiquem.

"What do we do?" asked Areon nervously.

"Quiet," snapped Reiquem. "Don't move." Areon ceased movement and stared at he ogre. He had read a bit about ogres and heard a lot about them from Belgraf. Belgraf had told him that ogres had somewhere near three-fourths the intelligence an average human had, which, according to a wizard, was not much. He had read that they were cannibalistic, eating humans and other ogres alike. Areon stared for what seemed like days. The ogre was not moving very fast; apparently it had no particular place to be at this time, in fact it seemed as though he was walking in circles.

The ogre had large feet with toes that protruded out of old, worn sandal-type shoes. It had a large cloth covering its waist, which had a girth of about six feet. Its stomach was bare, and grotesque; it bulged from eating everything in site that was alive and it had a yellowish greenish color not unlike the rest of its body. On his thick fingers resided long, yellow, sharp nails that the brute obviously never trimmed. His face disgusted Areon the most: his head seemed disproportionately small compared to his body. It had a patch of unruly hair at the top and the rest of the top part was covered in brown spots. His eyes were large, yet slanted and fierce-looking; his teeth were like ivory daggers that had been sharpened for years. All in all it was enough to make Areon quite nervous, even if he had Reiquem. He would have been scared seeing the ogre even if Belgraf was with him.

It paced around some more and ran its fingers over his stomach and to his back where he scratched vigorously for some time. Areon slowly went to loosen his sword from the sheath, but Reiquem stopped him with a low hiss. He had no idea what to do so he waited. Before long, the inevitable occurred. A bird that the ogre had been eyeing swooped over toward Areon and Reiquem. The ogre watched it all the way until its ugly eyes landed on the still couple. Within seconds it began a berserk rush towards them. Human meat was rare due to the fact that Belgraf and few others journeyed this far into the woods. While running, it had managed to pull out a crudely fashioned knife or more appropriately a sword, in accordance with Reiquem and Areon's size. Areon knew not what do in the situation, but Reiquem did. As the ogre neared Areon, his cloak reeled out and grew to a size Reiquem thought impossible and wrapped itself around the side of a tree. It tugged Areon away from the path that the ogre was taking. It swung him around the tree and set him on the ground facing Reiquem and the ogre. In the meantime Reiquem had prepared herself for the attack and jumped up, grabbed a low branch, and dodged the swing of the old rusty knife that the ogre wielded.

Before the ogre could even think about making another move, Areon had drawn his sword, deciding that the cloak was not going to continually save his life. He lunged forward and stabbed the ogre in the calf. It gave out a deep cry in pain and wheeled around to glare at Areon for a split second before reaching out to grab him and strangle him.

While this went on, Reiquem had not remained idle. She had been muttering words of the old days and conjuring up shadow to fight back; it was her only defense as she was weaponless. She fell to the ground from the bow she had been hanging onto. It jerked up and knocked a few leaves down. Her eyes closed. She shot her bent left arm into the air and held the other straight and low to the ground. She launched it up straight at the ogre's eyes and it consumed them for a moment. The ogre, blinded, stopped and saw nothing. He was in utter darkness. Reiquem could not keep the incantation going forever, so she stopped and her arms fell, although she did not drop her guard. The ogre looked back at her and seemed a bit overwhelmed by the couple's resistance. He swiped a massive hand at Reiquem and she ducked. Areon seized the opportunity and stuck his sword into the ogre's back. This had little effect, as the skin was incredibly tough. It was as though he had tried to stab through two inches of solid leather. The ogre then turned and knocked the sword out of Areon's hand and with the other grabbed Reiquem by the legs. This infuriated Areon. He grabbed his strong oak bow, swung it in front of him, and knocked an arrow as quick as humanly possible. After this impressively fast display, he loosed the arrow into the ogre's neck. The arrow went in about half an inch and lazily hung in the ogre's flesh; it tore and out and seized Areon by the waist and lifted the two together. The last thing Areon heard was Reiquem muttering words, trying another incantation. The ogre then smashed Areon and Reiquem together, knocking them both unconscious.

# CHAPTER XIII

## An Ogre's House

When Areon regained consciousness, he gazed slowly around the room that he hung upside in. He could not exactly remember what happened so he let the blood rush to his head for a moment and tried to recall the earlier events. After looking around the room some more, he remembered quite clearly. An ogre had beaten them in a fight, and if Areon was not mistaken, they were about to be eaten. He was hung upside down by a rope that was very tightly tied around his angles. He must have been hanging like this for some time judging by the way his head felt. Reiquem was hanging upside down on the opposite side of the room they were in. The walls of the room looked as though they were made of strong wood. It was also cylindrically shaped. After Areon put the two together, he realized that the house of the ogre was a very large hollowed-out willow tree. For how stupid Areon had heard that ogres were, he thought the idea of living in a hallowed-out tree was rather ingenious. In fact, Areon was thinking (if he had not just been caught by an ogre) he would like to do that for a place to live for a while, just for some fun. After shaking this thought out of his head, he reached up to grab at the ropes. An ogre undoubtedly tied them. The knots were about as tight as they could be around Areon's legs. Come to think of it, as he tried to wiggle his toes, he realized the whole of his lower legs and feet were completely asleep. He let himself fall back down again and glanced around the room making sure the ogre was not present.

The tree house consisted of a doss opposite the entrance, a crude table that had bloodstains on it, and a few trinkets that looked of some value scattered throughout the room. All in all it was not the way Areon would have his hollowed tree of a house. He looked over at Reiquem, who had a nasty gash on her brow and grimaced; if he could, he would pay the ogre back the evil favor.

Areon, wasting no time and thinking about how stupid the ogre was for not tying his hands, went to grab the knife that was fastened to his side only to find it missing. He looked across the unlit room once again. On the floor was a pile of the things they had brought, including his knife.

"Hellfire consume it," cursed Areon thinking of the wretched ogre and how he was going to get his. He thought of other means of escape for sometime.

Of course, fire was the only choice Areon had, but how could he burn the ropes without burning his leg? He was not exactly looking forward to burning his legs and then falling on his back, or worse his head, but he could not wait around for the ogre to return and eat them. After thinking about it, he decided he could stretch up high enough to get beyond his legs and burn the rope from where it was tied in the ceiling. He summoned the fire within him and waited to feel the warmth as Belgraf had taught him so long ago. After directing it from all over his body to his hand, he did a half sit-up in the air and touched the rope that held up him. The flame kissed the rope and it slowly burned through as Areon's stomach muscles began to ache. The rope was old and dry and burned quickly; before Areon knew it, was he lying on the ground massaging his tailbone. When he looked up, he judged the fall to be at least two spans. If it were not for the ogre in his mind, Areon would have stopped to moan a bit more about the pain. He tried to stand up but realized how asleep his legs were again. He sat on his backside and massaged them a bit to get the feeling back into them. Finally he was able to stand again with a bit of work. Reiquem appeared to still be in an uneasy sleep. He walked over to her and put his hand gently on her face.

"Reiquem," he whispered as quietly as he could. "Reiquem," he said a bit louder. "Reiquem, please wake up." She stirred momentarily and then fell back asleep.

"Reiquem," he half whispered, half shouted. She remained motionless. Finally Areon looked over to the table; a shabby-looking shelf was above it that held a pitcher of water with a ladle. Immediately he grabbed the water and pitched a bit on her face. She slowly stirred and then her eyes shot open. She looked all around the room before finally looking at Areon.

"We're alive," she said.

"For now, but we must hurry, I expect he'll be back soon seeing as how long it took me to get free and wake you," replied Areon.

"Untie me," said Reiquem. Areon went over and grabbed a chair that sat beside the table. When he had hauled it over to Reiquem, he jumped up and started trying to undo the ropes around her legs. When this proved useless on account of how many times the ogre had wound the rope around her legs, Areon got down and grabbed his dagger that lay in the pile of all the things they brought with.

"Hold onto me while I cut," suggested Areon. Reiquem grabbed him around the shoulders and he cut furiously. Within a minute the ropes had been sliced and Reiquem fell down to the ground still clutching Areon by the shoulders. He had to bend over to accommodate her weight. When they had finished this task, they went for their supplies and weapons. Areon grabbed his sword that the ogre must have grabbed from the grass and put it around his waste, along with his knife that he slipped into his boot. He figured if he ever got into another predicament like this, it would be useful to have the weapon a bit more concealed. Next he grabbed his skin and small sack and put it behind his cloak. Areon was very glad to see that the ogre was unable to remove his marvelous cloak. Lastly, Areon grabbed his bow and slung his quiver on his back. As Areon and Reiquem headed for the door, they saw a large shadow creeping up the path.

"We can't seem to catch a break today can we?" Areon said trying not to sound nervous.

"Now we run," returned Reiquem.

They made a mad dash for the door, which proved futile; Areon had tried to avert the ogre's attention by throwing a rock out the door into the taller grass and moss, but it did not have the effect he wanted. After doing this, they ran out the door, only to see that the ogre remained aware of their situation. Areon had gone out first holding Reiquem's hand, and as soon as they had both gone completely out the makeshift door, the ogre had swung a giant clawed hand. It hit Reiquem hard. She was thrown about four spans from Areon's side. Areon's cloaked proved useful again, although he cursed it for tearing him from Reiquem.

The scarlet cloak reached out, as if it had blood red hands, about twenty spans, and wrapped itself around a tree. The other side of the cloak enveloped Areon and rushed him to where the other side had wrapped around. He was furious until he saw how this had proven useful. He had forgotten about his marvelous bow and instantaneously he knocked an arrow.

The ogre looked around to see where Areon had gone, in this time Areon had looked at Reiquem lying on the ground, not badly hurt at all, but her being on the ground was enough to send sparks with the arrow he was about to loose. When the ogre eyes finally found the scarlet red in all the forest, Areon spoke: "Reiquem sends this arrow." He let the arrow fly, sending it directly into one of the disgustingly large eyes of the ogre. It screamed an awful scream in pain and fell miserably to the ground.

Seeing that they could leave now, Reiquem stood up and ran over to Areon while he ran towards her. They embraced for a moment and Reiquem said softly, "Thank you."

Areon was having an adventure, and he was getting better at it.

# CHAPTER XIV

## The Foot of the Flattops

"Are you alright, Reiquem?" asked Areon sympathetically. They had stopped to rest after running for about half a mile from where the ogre had fallen. They stopped in a small clearing and sat in the taller grass.

"I'm fine, the oaf just knocked me over after we ran out of the tree," she replied, but Areon saw that blood was running out of the cut on her forehead. She apparently did not notice because as soon as Areon looked at it, the blood ran down her mouth and she spat a little out in surprise.

"Put pressure on it for awhile. I don't think it's very deep, besides we don't have anything to wrap it with," said Areon. After she held it for a couple minutes, the bleeding slowed significantly and Areon poured a bit of water over the cut to wash the dried blood off her face.

"It'll be fine," she said nonchalantly. Areon knew it hurt her, although she would be fine. He thought about how she acted tough and self-reliant, but Areon also thought that she needed someone in this world. He had no idea what fate befell her parents.

She got up and looked at the roof of the forest. Without another word she ran to the closest tree, hopped up to the nearest branch, and swung her body up higher and higher until Areon could see her no longer because she was lost in the leaves and branches of the willow. Areon sat down ponderously, waiting for about a half a minute and then, just as fast as she had gone up, she came back down.

Areon looked at her scrutinizing. "What was that?" he asked

"I was looking for the location of the sun," she replied.

"Oh," said Areon dismissing all the guesses that he had in his head. "What time is it then?"

"I'd say about four hours after the noon," answered Reiquem.

"Guess we were knocked out for some time then," pointed out Areon.

"Too long, let's get moving again," said Reiquem. Areon stood up reluctantly; he bent back down and sat on the heels of his feet to stretch his legs a bit. Next he leaned over with his legs straight. After he felt a bit more limber, they nodded at each other and set off again with Reiquem leading the way, seeing as she had just seen the sun and knew which way to go.

The walk was becoming a bit more than Areon could bear. Constant trees surrounded the couple, and Areon found himself longing for some open grass or perhaps a house to sit in and have some tea. The moss did not exactly help Areon's disposition towards the woods either. He found himself loathing it. Every fifty spans or so, they were forced to stop and brush the moss off their shoes and ankles. It was a constant burden. The beauty no longer helped to brighten up Areon as he walked. Reiquem, having been in the woods little, was particularly sick of the trees.

"I can't wait to get out of these woods," said Reiquem exhaustedly.

"I concur wholeheartedly," said Areon, sounding about the same. Areon was a little more than reluctant to stop after what had happened the last time they tried.

Night fell and the roof once again covered the night's stars from the couple's eyes. Areon regretted not being able to watch them over the last few beautiful nights. Finally Reiquem stopped and looked over at Areon wearily.

"Well, I guess we're going to have to try this again," she said, not sounding altogether excited about it.

"Who's going to sleep first?" asked Areon.

"I will, perhaps you'll have better luck," she said sarcastically and leaned over onto a tree.

"When should I wake you?" asked Areon quietly.

"Whenever you can't stay awake any longer," answered Reiquem sleepily. Immediately after, she fell into a much needed sleep.

Areon leaned against a tree and looked up at the roof of the forest. A gentle breeze was blowing, and he felt pretty content. His cloak seemed to blanket him. He pondered many things in the silence that followed. Often Areon wondered where he had come from. Belgraf had mentioned something about the Waholcast woods, but then dismissed the conversation. Areon chose not to pursue it any longer because he was quite content living with Belgraf and did not want to offend him. The Moss Woods were a place of mystery, and Areon knew that his discovery when he was a child was probably a mystery as well. A secret only the trees of the forest knew.

No point dwelling on it, said Areon inside his head. He looked over at Reiquem, who was fast asleep. He wished he could snuggle up and fall asleep, too, but after the antecedent events, he knew better.

After hours of waiting and thinking, he could stand it no longer and went to wake Reiquem. He was a bit reluctant due to how peaceful she looked.

"Reiquem. I can't stay awake any longer," he yawned.

She stirred a bit and then opened up her eyes and sat up.

"How long have I been asleep?" she asked groggily.

"A few hours, I would guess," answered Areon not being exactly sure. The night sky was still pitch black and Areon had no idea what time it was.

"Well, sleep well," said Reiquem. "I won't fall asleep this time, I promise."

The last thing Areon saw was Reiquem walking out a little bit from where they both stood.

Areon slept uneasily, remembering what had happened. The moss no longer grew on them; a fact that concerned him. Last time they woke up covered in the stuff and might have died were it not for Areon's magnificent cloak. Maybe the time had been changed and they had been sleeping for days. Maybe the moss did live and it did not feel comfortable trying to murder them in their sleep if one of them was awake. Maybe they were nearing the end of the forest, Areon thought wishfully, not much caring which it was and trying hard to sleep. He got up and looked at Reiquem, who seemed to be deep in thought.

"I guess I can't sleep," said Areon breaking the silence.

"You don't care if I do then, do you?" she asked.

"Not at all, I think you need it more anyway," returned Areon.

She fell asleep instantly and Areon sat down to ponder a bit more, although his body was tired.

Morning felt like it took eons to come. Areon finally saw a bit of light starting to go through the cracks in the roof of the forest. He welcomed the little bit of sunlight and brushed off a bit of moss that had accumulated on his boots and back from sitting. He walked over and shook Reiquem gently.

"Time to rise," he said, waking up Reiquem.

She got up instantly and stretched extensively. Areon looked around and decided the best course to take.

"Ready to get out of these woods?" asked Areon.

"Definitely," replied Reiquem.

"I'm not sure how much farther it is, but the Flattop Mountains are in site from my house, and it seems like we've been in here forever, so I think if we walk rather fast we can make it out of here today and to the foot of the mountains," explained Areon.

"Sounds fine to me. I'm plenty rested now and my head feels fine," she said.

So they walked. And walked. And walked some more. Areon thought his legs might not carry him any longer but was anxious to get to the top of the Flattop Mountains and see what they were really like. He had only seen them from the flat land that surrounded his house; it would be good to see them close up for once.

The rest of the journey through the Moss Woods was uneventful, and just when Areon thought that they should stop for a rest, the trees started to be not so tightly packed. The grass started to become longer and the moss lessened. Finally they burst out of the Moss Woods when the sun was setting behind the flattops. Areon and Reiquem almost sprinted for a while in the tall grass that grew on the flatland. It was a great feeling to have the wind blowing through their hair and the sun beating gently on their faces again. The mountains loomed almost ominously in front of them. The two slowed down to almost a stop after seeing the gray skies that hovered over them.

"What now?" asked Reiquem.

"Well, I'm starving," said Areon realizing they had not eaten much for quite some time.

"Yeah, I guess I haven't really been thinking about how hungry I've been with all the things going on in the Moss Woods," she replied.

So they stopped and took out the miniature pot that Reiquem had been carrying.

"Well," said Reiquem. "Now we just need something to cook."

About every twenty steps in the moss woods there had been a rabbit, but of course, Areon paid no attention to them.

"I'll walk and try and shoot a rabbit, but that might prove difficult," said Areon.

"Good luck," replied Reiquem stifling her laughter.

Areon was definitely right in thinking it would be difficult to shoot a rabbit. He walked through the tall grass for about a half an hour and lost about six rabbits and one arrow.

Before he got entirely frustrated, he saw a rabbit that was unaware he was close to it. He felt sort of bad, but he did not feel like losing another handmade arrow. He closed his eyes and muttered some words under his breath so as to not scare away the rabbit that was still chewing a piece of grass. Areon opened his eyes and stared intently at the rabbit. A single, deadly bolt of lightning struck the rabbit before it had a chance to react. Areon walked over, picked it up, and took it back to where Reiquem sat patiently. Areon skinned it with his little knife that was in his boot while Reiquem gathered up some small twigs and grass and shot a single ball of fire into them.

"I didn't know you could do lower level magic," said Areon a bit surprised.

"You can't really start out being a master," she replied. "I had to begin somewhere."

So the fire burnt nice and warm while Areon and Reiquem took turns gathering twigs from the ground around them. Areon took the pieces of meat from the rabbit and threw them in the pot to let them cook.

"Not exactly the best meal I've ever cooked, but it'll do for being out in the wild," said Areon.

"It's not that bad," lied Reiquem, who was taking a bite.

"It should be easy to get to the foot of the mountain tomorrow," said Areon.

"Yeah, we'll want to sleep at the foot, and then in one day we'll want to climb to the very top and sleep up there," returned Reiquem.

"Why's that?" asked Areon.

"Well, we can't very well sleep on the side of the mountain, can we?" said Reiquem. Areon shrugged and looked up at them. They seemed uninviting.

"I guess I'll be glad when we get to Lalvegeth," he said. "If it exists," he added.

"We'll find it," reassured Reiquem.

"Well, I'm tired, we went a long way today," said Areon.

"I suppose we can sleep simultaneously since we're out of the woods," replied Reiquem. They laid blankets down by the fire and let it burn itself out while they watched the stars. It was a beautiful night once more, and Areon was grateful for being out of the woods and able to gaze up at the sky.

Neither of the couple knew when they fell asleep, but they both woke at about the same time to the warm sun coming up. It was a particularly breezy day. Areon hoped to reach the foot of the mountain quickly so they could take another long break from walking. They both got up and gathered up what they had left strewn throughout their little campsite.

"How long do you think it'll take us to get to the Flattops?" asked Areon.

"It'll probably be a few hours past the noon by the time we get there," answered Reiquem.

They started walking in the open meadow that rolled out in front of them. It was a rather nice site in the middle of summer; the tall, plush grass gently sloping up and down as they covered more and more ground. The journey to the foot of the flattops was altogether uneventful, and they arrived prior to when Reiquem thought they would.

"We got here much sooner than I anticipated," she stated. "Do you want to begin the climb today?" Areon had been hoping to reach the town as soon as possible and hopefully rest somewhere besides the ground.

"I say we start climbing, the worst that could happen is we'll have to stay on the side of the mountain somewhere," he replied.

"Or we could just climb through the night," returned Reiquem. Areon raised his eyebrows as he looked at her. Apparently the mountain looked bigger to him than to her.

# CHAPTER XV

## An Unknown Fate

They began a slow climb on the silver gray rocks that ensued. Areon actually thought that sleeping on the side of the mountain would not be that difficult. It slanted pretty slowly, and if you walked in a meandering way, the climb wasn't difficult whatsoever. Areon could not help looking up at the top of the mountains. He could not wait to get to the top where they leveled off to start a fire and sit down.

They walk was a boring one and much harder than the walk on the flat grass that had led them to where they were. As they approached a notch in the side of the mountain that made for a good resting place, Areon noticed something out of the ordinary.

"Is that water?" he asked Reiquem. Water cascaded down a precipice that overhung where the two had stopped; it seemed to come down from the mountain and make a shield to a cave in the side of the mountain.

"It's like a glistening silver door," remarked Reiquem.

"Beautiful …" Areon trailed off as he gawked at the entrance to the cave.

"We have to go in, right?" said Areon. Reiquem shrugged as though uninterested.

"I'm going," stated Areon. He walked up to the beautifully running water that was perfectly flat against the entrance for about a span in width and three in height. He looked up at where the water was coming from and then back down at the entrance. He was about to enter when he looked back to see Reiquem standing directly behind him. He jumped.

"I didn't think you were coming," he said, trying not to sound startled.

"I can't let you have all the fun." She smiled at him and nodded toward the entrance.

Areon and Reiquem had walked through the water door coming through on the other side of it without getting wet at all.

"Remarkable," said Areon.

"There's magic in here," whispered Reiquem. It was dark in the cave, but a bit of light was visible about ten spans in. They apprehensively walked farther in.

Slowly they came up to the light. It was a magnificent site; a piece of rock protruded from the floor and slanted up into a circle, the top dipped down, and a pool of crystal clear water stood. The water looked like the cleanest Areon had ever seen; he was tempted to take a drink out of it but thought better.

"Where is the light coming from?" Reiquem whispered.

"Nowhere apparently," replied Areon.

"Supplier of the light? 'Tis I," said a dreamy, angelic, distant voice. It was the prettiest voice Areon had ever heard; that of a young woman.

"I haven't had visitors in over 3,650 rotations of the planet," the voice spoke again, lovelier than Areon could have imagined.

"Should we leave?" asked Reiquem nervously.

"If I have to die to see who that voice belongs to, I will," Areon answered. Reiquem gave him a reluctant nod.

"Your wish is to cast your gaze upon me, it is?" asked the voice in a bored sort of way.

"Yes," was Areon's flat answer.

Before Areon could think of anything else to say, the wall at the back of the cave seemed to ripple, and out came a floating object shrouded in white light. Areon could not believe that something had just emerged from the solid rock wall. The womanly figure was approximately a foot tall and very slender. Although she had a small figure, the woman, or whatever it was, looked substantially older than a child, although not old in the least. Simply put she was beautiful, however small. But it was not her size that intrigued Areon as to what she was; it was her wings that were seemingly made of light.

Areon was at a loss for words, and he could tell by looking at Reiquem that she was as well.

"How … Who …" was all Areon could manage to say.

"I have not a name, young traveler," the woman replied to his blathering. "Not for you, or for now, anyway," she said rudely.

Areon suddenly realized what she was: a fairy. It was blatantly obvious now that he gathered his wits and tried to stop staring. Fairies were immortal; not dead, but not living, at least in this world. From the ancient books Belgraf owned, they seemed to exist in both worlds at once and not at all. It was more than befuddling to Areon at the time, but the appearance of her from thin air made it a bit clearer.

"And so you shall have one question answered," said the fairy. "Just one."

"I'm not asking a question," said Reiquem, turning her head from the fairy at once.

"One of you will ask before you leave," was the fairy's reply. "It is my curse, for which I am thankful."

Areon could think of about a million questions he would like to ask.

"You might not know the answer," said Areon, making sure to not ask any questions and blow his one chance.

"'Tis a risk you will take," said the fairy gazing at the cave, as if she had never been there. "Never have I heard an unanswerable question."

Reiquem seemed as though she wanted no part of this forceful attitude the fairy was having and turned to leave.

"The door," exclaimed Reiquem. Areon took his eyes from the fairy and looked at it; the water had turned to solid ice making the doorway impenetrable.

Areon thought hard for a long time. It seemed that the fairy and the two could not leave until a question was asked. This being the case, Areon was going to make it a good question.

He sat down and thought while the fairy gazed round the room, Reiquem felt the ice and decided that there was no way to get out of the cave until Areon asked his question.

Areon was thinking to himself. Most people that came here were probably fools, he thought, if no one's ever stumped her before. Asking if they would be rich or what happens when one dies. He thought and thought and thought and thought, and thought some more.

The fairy did not move from where she was perched in the air. Areon sat cross-legged on the hard ground, biting his fingernails, and Reiquem stood glaring from the entrance at the fairy.

For a reason of which Areon couldn't explain, he blurted out, breaking the silence, "Am I to save or end the universe?"

Reiquem looked down at the ground and then turned toward Areon. The fairy stopped any movement she had been doing indefinitely.

"Ask that again," said the fairy very quietly,    "Am I to save or end the universe?" repeated Areon awkwardly and slower than the first time. The fairy squinted her eyes in disbelief. She stared at Areon for about ten minutes unblinking. Areon and Reiquem could not figure what was going on, but they knew one thing; the water over the entrance remained frozen.

"One thing is all that I can tell you about your imploration," said the fairy. Areon nodded in response.

"While all, but very, very few men throughout eternity are fated to neither save, nor end the universe, you, Areon, are fated to do one of them without question," she said.

Areon stood up. "What?" he exclaimed. "Which one?"

"One was allowed, and one was asked," were the last things the fairy said before she disappeared back into the rocks.

After the disappearance, the ice began to melt at the doorway and eventually water flowed once again. Areon and Reiquem walked out of it and sat down on the rocks. Night was approaching.

"Areon," asked Reiquem, "how come you asked that question?"

"What do you mean?" replied Areon absentmindedly.

"You realize you asked if it were possible that you end the universe?" she said.

Areon stopped looking out from the mountainside and looked over at Reiquem.

"I didn't even realize it," he said. "I can't explain why I asked that question at all. It just sort of poured out of my mouth."

"It wouldn't have bothered me," Reiquem said quietly, "But the fairy said that she didn't know which one you were fated to do."

"I know," said Areon, looking back down the mountain and ending the conversation.

## EXCERPT FROM THE HISTORICAL ARCHIVES OF THE KINGDOM OF LIFE

" ... Rarely spoken of and denied existence by our students who are more mathematic, fairies have been sighted in mountains and in forests. Upon encountering a fairy you are forced to ask a question, to which it must answer to the best of its knowledge, which is everything but infinite. Fairies are cursed to reside in the same realm as humans, although they are neither living nor dead, they're flesh never decaying while never becoming immortal. They are angels, cast out of heaven, never to return, although their crime not worthy of the depths of hell ..."

May the angels ever watch over us, keep us safe, and guide us through shadow in the afterlife.

# CHAPTER XVI

## The Fate that was Lived Out: The First Part of the Last Chapter

Kings surrounded Areon; scepters were laid before his feet. He did not know if he deserved this or not, nor did he care. The angels sat at the front of the capacious room in the kingdom that Areon sat in. The angels flew, the things of unsurpassed beauty that all, save the wicked, loved to look at and be in the presence of. They had a way of making anyone around them feel happy and warm inside, as if a light were in you, keeping you safe. They were called the Nine Orders of Angels. But Areon felt not this happiness or warmth.

Friends he had met along the way, Myriad and Infinitia, sitting together and laughing at their witty senses of humor; Scine brushing the locks of hair out of his eyes; Eanty, the wise old man, could not stop staring at the angels. And even the one that people called the Rapturer sat with a half smile on his face; it was a bit crooked and demonic, but Areon knew he was not evil. They all looked happy, benign. But Areon felt none of these feelings of goodness.

More wine was brought from the back of the room, a place Areon was not used to. He longed for Belgraf's house, his wood porch, and a day in the woods. He tried to clear his mind but could not. Lords and ladies were approaching him jovially and bowing low. He knew they would have never cared for him in the least had he not …

"Areon, my lad," said Myriad. "You could do with—" but he was cut short as Areon slowly lifted his head from his hands and gave him a cold look; one that says, "You do not understand." After this, Myriad looked away and no longer laughed with his wife. Eanty was still gazing at the angels, as if longing to float up and join them. It seemed funny, a man so serious, so obsessed with something; but then again the angels were not exactly ordinary or earthly. The Rapturer seemed to be the only one knowing what was occurring. He slid his chair back slowly and looked at all the fools who were dancing and laughing and talking in the room. Then he looked out the doors and across the bridge that provided a way across the moat and into the city. The Rapturer saw all the people that were longing to join the celebration, all the people, all the world outside. He looked at the angels; the light that was streaming in from the high windows. He looked at the shadows, some cast on the ground, and all the life that filled the world. He, for the first time Areon had ever seen him, pushed the brim of his round, large hat farther back so that one could see his eyes more clearly. He watched time go by and tried to gaze up into space through the large doors, the space over the city that held things that many knew not. The Rapturer looked around at all the reasons the essences were present. He saw the people, the life.

After his drawn out survey, the Rapturer slowly stood up, looked down to the end of his nose where his magical glasses now sat, which saw a week into the past and a week or so into the future. He turned to Areon, his crooked half smile flickered across his face, not for a reason of some jest, but for friendship toward Areon. It disappeared instantly afterward as he turned, knowing that he would never look at Areon again. Areon had not a clue if the Rapturer knew what was going to be, but he saw him do all this, and lastly, he saw him take off his hat and bow slightly. Areon watched with the rest of his friends as the Rapturer walked down the middle of the hall and out the doors into the never to be again sunlight.

Areon stood up slowly. The rest had no idea. No one had any idea. Nobody knew how Areon felt. Nobody knew what was always going on inside his head. Now especially that the time had come; Areon wanted nothing, not wind or sunshine, darkness or old age. Not the feeling of walking along or traveling farther than one should ever have to. Areon wanted not the feeling of laughter; he had no more laughter in him. Areon ran his hand along the table once more, as to feel the feeling that matter possessed. He watched things around him as the Rapturer had done. He almost smiled; the fairy had undoubtedly been right, although Areon thought it would be the other she had said. The dance and celebration seemed to have quit as Areon walked to the middle of the large room. It was over for him. It was the only way. He would have these feelings in this life and the next. The afterlife held no comfort. He realized this after something he had done that he did not want to think about again. These thoughts that would be ever present in his mind for eternity were it not for one thing: Nothingness. He outstretched his arms and looked towards the heavens; he raised his outstretched arms, almost as if asking for forgiveness for what he was doing. The angels jerked their bodies toward him in fear; they felt the ominous uneasiness of life ending. They flew toward him with beating wings faster than a normal human eye could catch, but it was a feeling had to late for the life bringers. Even the Seraphim, with their four ever watchful faces, were not fast enough. The last tear in Areon's body ran down the side of his face before he was consumed by nothingness. Next came the angels that had so desperately tried to stop him. Nobody could explain what they saw, but it mattered not, for they were consumed only seconds after the things that they saw, or didn't see; they saw nothing. No more did life exist, nor death, the afterlife with it, nor light and shadow. Time ceased, and the essence of nothing consumed the universe and every dimension and form of life that it contained.

# CHAPTER XVII

## The Freedom of the Flattops

Areon woke up the next morning on the side of the flattops still thinking about what the fairy had said. It was easier to climb now that nagging thought constantly occupied his mind. Reiquem said little, and Areon wondered if she was in some way angry with him. The two trudged up the side of the low mountains ready to get to the tops any minute so they could have a breather and walk on some flatland for a change.

The flat did not come any time soon; they walked up on rocks for hours. The gray rocks were rather large, and Areon found himself leaping across them from time to time for a little entertainment. Reiquem glanced at him with a smile on her face every so often.

Areon stopped once and looked back down the mountain.

"It's really not as big as it looks," he said. He looked back south toward Belgraf and his house. The mountain ran down for a long ways, and Areon saw where he had run into the fairy, then he saw the flat grassy area before he looked at the moss woods and then down to the town of Wellenore and Belgraf's house. They had traveled so far that it was impossible to make out the house, or even the town, but Areon looked longingly anyhow.

"Thank heavens for that," answered Reiquem. She turned and started walking back up the rocks.

"Don't you want to stop and take in the beauty of it all?" asked Areon.

"You've not seen anything yet," replied Reiquem, stopping again. "If you think this is beauty, wait until we travel farther toward the end of the earth."

"Not to mention you'd like to get to the top," muttered Areon.

Areon turned back up the mountain and looked at the clouds that hung lazily over the flattest part of the mountain range.

Trees started to litter the path that they walked on. More than once they were forced to take a winding path to get around a clump of trees or bushes. Areon welcomed these growths on the side of the mountain because of the change they gave from the flat dusty rocks.

Finally, without farther walking, something happened. Reiquem was in the lead and Areon was following mindlessly. She stopped and ducked behind one of the larger rocks.

"What is it?" asked Areon louder than Reiquem would have liked.

"I'm not sure," replied Reiquem, showing Areon how low she wanted them to talk.

Areon gazed farther up the mountain and saw a path of bushes shaking vigorously. Next, a tail shot up from one side of the bush.

"Should we just go around it?" asked Areon. Reiquem replied with a look of stupidity towards Areon.

So they waited a bit longer until the thing finally emerged from the bushes and glanced around. It was about one span tall and three long, while resting on four legs. Its tail looked like it had a razor sharp sword embedded in it.

"A Grendel," said Areon quietly and with a little apprehension.

"A what?" asked Reiquem.

"A Grendel, you know, the scaly beast with a tail like a knife? They kill by flipping up backwards and slicing with the inside of their tail."

"Great, sounds like we can't move for some time," answered Reiquem. And so they waited, watching the Grendel flip back a few times and roam around the area looking for smaller beasts.

"How did you know about Grendels?" asked Reiquem out of boredom.

"I read it, of course," answered Areon. "Mountains Fiends, I believe the book was called. Quite short, but interesting and pertinent, if you want to climb a large mountain."

"Anything we could do?" asked Reiquem impatiently.

"Not really," answered Areon. "It said the only weakness it has was bad eyesight."

"Perfect," replied Reiquem. She stood up and glanced at the sun; it was covered by some of the gray clouds in the sky that hovered above the mountain. She waited while standing up. Areon wished he could grab her and tell her to crouch down as to not be seen, but he waited patiently.

She stood for a while longer, waiting for the planet's slow spin and the sun to come into focus a bit better. Finally a crack in the clouds sent rays of sunshine down on the side of the mountain, but as this happened, the Grendel caught site of Reiquem standing patiently. It began running furiously at her, and still she sat. but Reiquem stood still. The Grendel cocked its tail up a bit, but Areon noticed that Reiquem still sat; before he knew what had happened he was blind. The mountain the trees, Reiquem, the Grendel; all were gone. He looked around and saw his hand vaguely. He realized what had happened; Reiquem had shrouded the three of them in a thick shadow. Before he had a chance to even look up at Reiquem, she had grabbed him by the cloak and jerked him up, almost sending him down on his face. As they ran they could hear the Grendel snorting impetuously and kicking up small rocks, trying to see anything. Once in awhile they heard it flip backwards and cut a few larger rocks in half. The two did not stop running for at least another twenty minutes.

Finally when Areon had slowed to a worthless jog, Reiquem bent over and put her hands on her knees and panted heavily. Areon sat down to see where they were. They had covered a lot of ground and he looked up; the top of the mountain was approximately ten spans away from where they rested. The only problem was that a precipice stopped them from getting up top. Areon did not want to stop now that he was so close.

"C'mon, lets get this over with," he panted as he walked over to Reiquem and helped her up. They walked over to a spot where the precipice went straight up instead of looming over them. Inch by inch they made their way up to the top of the mountains they had been climbing on for so long. Areon reached his hand over the top and climbed up; before he took in the beauty, he grabbed Reiquem's hand and hoisted her up as well.

The two sat and looked in awe at the countryside that lay north of the Flattop Mountains. Stretched out before them was a gray mass of rock that meandered to the other side of the mountain that angled down to their destination. Next came the land; it was all beautiful. Areon noted in disbelief that he saw several places that looked like forest colored in unnatural color; one looked blue and another looked violet, while yet another looked reddish, a more scarlet red not unlike his cloak. These forests were captivating, and Areon did not tear his gaze off them for the longest time. Next, the sky came rising like a dome. It had a dark look, and the moon was like a ghost in the air, while the sun slowly sank into a horizon that Areon had never seen before. A lone star materialized in the sky as Areon took in the beauty and the unbelievable forests. He walked out onto the flat gray land and forgot all his worries. He forgot the journey for the time being, the dangerous part of the journey. He remembered how all the people of the town had ostracized him and how Belgraf had always been there to help him out of situations beyond his control. Now Areon had none of these shallow minds or guardians. He was with Reiquem, who would help him, but need help as well. He felt entirely free of all the world. As if before, the world were his master and now he was the master and his world a mere friend that supplied him with what he needed; and he would get it himself. He looked up at the sky as a chilly wind blew in his face and welcomed him to the other side of the mountain. Areon put his hands in the air toward the numerous stars and felt pure freedom.

Reiquem strode over and took his hand in hers. He was used to Reiquem, and he felt no awkwardness at all. He took her hand back and smiled down at her. They both felt wonderful together, and finally Reiquem broke the silence.

"Areon, this is beautiful," she said.

"I know, its almost overwhelming," he replied, not looking at her anymore but at the sky and the beautiful forests that lay out on the flat, grassy land.

"But one thing does bother me," she said.

"What's that?" he said almost sounding worried.

"I don't see Lalvegeth," she said as Areon gave her questioning look. "The magic city," she tried. Areon's spirits sank a bit.

"I don't either," he said

They decided to set up camp in the middle of the gray plain; it seemed the best idea. They could hear monsters or other things coming up to attack them and hopefully wake in time. Areon and Reiquem were both rather tired and did not feel like staying awake while the other slept. The two arranged the blankets in a comfortable fashion against some rocks and sat down together. Areon had his arm around Reiquem and they both watched the sunset go slowly down. The clouds had lifted from the top of the mountains. Areon took it all in and looked down at Reiquem.

"I'm very glad I've gotten to share this moment with you," he said.

Reiquem looked up at Areon, smiled, and snuggled up closer to him. He knew the feeling was mutual and fell into sleep.

# CHAPTER XVIII

## A Shorter Way Down the Mountain

The next few days consisted of Areon and Reiquem staying on the top of the large mountain flat and gazing wonderingly at the lands before them. They knew they should have gotten a move on but found it difficult to leave the beautiful place that gave them such a view.

Finally, on one particular morning, something spurred them to start the hike down the other side of the mountain: a heavy downfall of rain. The rain came as not a surprise to Areon because of all the nice weather they had enjoyed thus far on the journey. Although he did not much feel for rain, he was not altogether flustered because it was coming down with no wind and it was rather warm in the beautiful summertime. Areon wrapped his bow in one of the blankets and unstrung it and placed it on his back while turning north toward their destination. Reiquem had been watching in the rain, sensing that Areon wanted to get going.

"I suppose its time we leave the top and start down the other side," stated Areon ruefully.

"Yes, I know we've lingered here too long," replied Reiquem. She looked up at the rain and let a couple drops fall in her mouth. Areon watched her and smiled when she saw that he had caught her doing it.

"Let's go," she laughed.

"Wait!" said Areon with enthusiasm. "I've just had a crazy thought."

"What's that?" asked Reiquem, raising her eyebrows. Areon did not reply; he only looked down toward the other side of the mountain. They had made their way toward the other side and were almost at the precipice that hung over the slant that lead to unknown lands and, he hoped, Lal-vegeth, the magic city. Areon looked around for something that he thought would be useful. He glanced around some more and leaned over the edge to look down the entirety of the slant. Next, Reiquem watched as he went to a spot that was letting water pour over the side and was etching a path in the mountain.

"What if we built a sort of sled type thing to glissade down this side and save us a bit of time?"

"I think you're crazy," Reiquem responded. But Areon just stared at her with a sort of half grin on his face. He was thinking about how much fun this was going to be; Reiquem was thinking about how dumb of an idea it was.

"We would be down in no time," tried Areon. "If we can find a spot where the water runs for a long ways, I can do ice magic in front of it while we slide down."

"You could hold an ice spell that long?" asked Reiquem skeptically.

"Well, I could at least hold it for some time and we would have that part of the trip out of the way," answered Areon.

"When was the last time you've done ice magic?" asked Reiquem, sort of changing the subject. "All I've ever seen you do is fire."

"Well, Belgraf sort of favored fire magic," returned Areon. "But I've definitely done ice before. And a lot more of the elemental magic," he added.

"Sounds like a pain," said Reiquem.

"Yes, it probably will be," he said. "But if all goes well, we'll be down the mountain days before we originally were going to be, and in a city for once, hopefully in a bed."

The sound of a bed must've been what it took for Reiquem to say, "Okay. Let's try it."

So they set to work, gathering up flatter pieces of wood and tearing off the bark to tie the wood together. Areon was tying the last piece when Reiquem brought over another and set it down.

"That should do it," he said looking at his shabby toboggan.

"Now ..." Areon looked around. "We just need to find a spot where the water has run off and goes down in some what of straight—"

"I already did," cut in Reiquem. "And I pushed out some of the dirt so we can set the, well, the whatever that is that you made down and rest on it, so we should just be able to rock on it for it to send us over." She stopped and looked at her spot a little apprehensively. Areon turned and looked at her dug out V in the side of the flat part of the mountain.

"Good," said Areon. "Now I just need a little bit of time to think about this ice magic."

"Take all you need," said Reiquem. "We should let it rain as long as possible."

"Yes, good thinking," returned Areon.

Areon delved into his memory. Fire had been coming so easy to him lately and for quite some time on account of the fact that that was all Belgraf really used. He had told Areon how to do other elemental attacks and Areon, out of curiosity, had practiced them, but he was much younger when he had done it.

Just concentrate. he thought to himself. Reiquem waited patiently and watched the rain for signs of ceasing.

The key to elemental magic, Areon quoted Belgraf in his mind, is to understand that all matter is composed of all the elementals, while some contain much more of a certain element and others less. For example, fire contains a very miniscule amount of ice and ice fire. Wind contains very little water and water wind. He continued, almost hearing Belgraf speak the words. So naturally we live on this plane of reality with all the other elements and we possess them in us. We need to understand that fires can be put out and ice can be melted. The reason for this is the fact that they hold some of what extinguishes them in them. Fire, when held against ice, will interact with the fire that is so insignificant in ice and therefore melt it. This is the same for all the elements, while I use this example because it is the simplest. Therefore, if we can summon these small amounts within us, we can build them and harness them for however long a time, given the mages abilities. You need to concentrate your mind on the element you wish to harness and bring it forth so you can use it for your desire. I use fire magic often because humans contain a lot of fire within them to keep them warm, but be wary, Areon, these life sources within can be depleted. When they are, you will die. They must rebuild after you use your magic. Now, the final ingredient to a magic spell is the words of the old days when magic was discovered; granted it is possible to do magic without the words, but it takes a very skilled mage indeed. The name of the certain element must be used. For first-degree magic, numerous words for fire, for example, exist and you need only mutter them. But for second degree there are only three words for three different levels of fire. And for the last and strongest degree of fire magic there is but one word. Now begin with these words.

Areon stopped and looked up at Reiquem who was staring at him thoughtfully.

"Have a magic lesson, did we?" she said.

"Precisely," answered Areon, paying no attention to her facetiousness. "Let me have some practice before we try this."

"Better hurry," she answered. "The rain's letting up. I think it would be a good time to take off. The waters flowing pretty good in that spot I found."

"Alright." Areon turned and looked at a rock near them. He closed his eyes and put his head back, cracking his neck. He thought down and reached the element of ice within him. Instantly he felt the coldness as one feels the warmth with fire magic; Areon preferred the warmth, although he always regretted the burning sensation when he pushed it out his hand. He thought for a while, and then finally a freezing feeling so cold it almost seemed to be burning went through his hand and the rock beside them turned to solid ice.

"Impressive," remarked Reiquem. Areon crouched low and spun around, smiting the rock with his foot, making it break into thousands of tiny shards that looked like glass.

"Let's go," said Areon with more enthusiasm than Reiquem wanted.

She shrugged and grabbed the makeshift sled for the trip down the other side of the mountain.

Areon drug it over himself, seeing as how apprehensive Reiquem seemed. He took her hand and they both sat down, Areon in front, ready to fly off the side of the mountain. He had apparently been a bit too excited because one time he looked back and the sled fell off the side, making Reiquem and Areon land in the water and a bunch of mud to the side. They both looked at how dirty they were and, to Areon's surprise, Reiquem was smiling, getting ready to give it another go.

"Okay," she said. "Do the ice magic, and remember, we're going to be going fast, so once we start, don't stop," she said and then added hastily, "Unless we're going to hit a tree or something."

Before Reiquem could say another word, Areon lunged his body forward, making them both sit up a couple more inches in the sled; Reiquem had to grab Areon around the waist to stop herself from falling off the back of the sled. Not realizing what had happened, Reiquem opened her eyes in fright. She saw that Areon was staring forward with a fixed gaze at the path in front of them. He had done the ice magic, and it was rocketing out of his hand in a straight stream that slowly enlarged as it neared the ground. The reasoning Areon had taken off without so much as a word was because he had started his elemental ice magic and did not want to waste his energy waiting. Reiquem clutched Areon tighter around the waist and looked forward.

Areon concentrated like mad on trying to steer and turn the water in front of him into ice. It was a difficult task to say the least. He had taken off and felt Reiquem almost fall off the back, but she had managed to stay on. The trees were rushing past them at an incredible speed. They were flying down the mountain; Areon's plan working tenfold better than he thought it would. Reiquem had chosen an ideal spot and they were staying well on course. The layer of ice in front of them was not thick, but sufficient enough to keep the sled sliding at an incredible rate.

But after awhile the sled starting swaying from side to side, and Areon was having difficulty keeping it on course and on the water that he was so desperately trying to turn to ice. He felt sweat pouring off his face as all the coldness in his body left him to aid the ice magic that ensued. Next, he felt Reiquem face to face with him, grabbing the front of the sled and trying to jerk it on course. It worked, and they continued to ride down the mountain. Areon thought that it might be working so well because of the width of the small river that was running down the mountain, and he was covering this all with magic, instantly turning it to ice. It was rather brilliant, and Areon found himself, although tear-streaked because of the rushing wind, enjoying himself immensely.

It was rather chaotic for the next couple of minutes between Areon trying to continue his elemental spell and Reiquem trying to jerk the sled on course, the wind whipping in their face, and the tears blurring their vision. They both knew that the ride had to end, something they had not thought about before they set off on this crazy venture. Areon noted that fewer and fewer trees were rushing by them and the ground was leveling out slowly. He also realized he was growing more tired as the energy left his body along with the ice. It was nearly impossible to keep the spell going, and finally and abruptly he let his hand fall and they were suddenly skidding across mud and gravel. They whipped around and traveled sideways for some time before the sled caught and left the two sprawled out on the ground with all their things strewn throughout the side of the mountain. Areon got up to make sure Reiquem was all right. She was moving around, looking for Areon, so he knew she was fine. Finally she looked at him and he at her. The two had mud streaked across their faces and all their clothes were wet. Areon's once blonde hair was now a muddy brown color, and Reiquem's had clumped spots that appeared to be mud. It was all Areon could do to keep from laughing at the sight that was before him, and finally, when he could take it no longer, he burst out and looked at Reiquem, who was laughing with him. They started gathering up their things and Areon stretched his spelling arm. It felt hot and totally useless. His body felt weak, and he knew he could not have kept the attack going for much longer. The reason they had gotten so far was because they had gone so fast.

"Well, that was interesting," was the unexpected remark from Areon.

"And look where we are," said Reiquem.

Areon looked around and noticed that they were on the edge of a beautifully colored forest that was somehow crimson. He looked back up the looming mountains and noticed the ice path that they had made on the side of them.

"Excellent," said Areon. "We're at the bottom." He collapsed from fatigue.

# CHAPTER XIX

## Lalvegeth

The strangely colored forest began almost directly at the north foot of the Flattop Mountains. Areon took out his skin and filled it with water that trickled off a smooth rock. It was a rather dazzling site. Most of the forest was covered in a cherry red. The leaves on the trees were painted with red, the grass was a reddish color, and all the flowers seemed a shade of red. Reiquem and Areon simply stared at it for a few moments before Areon turned to say, "Well, shall we enter?"

"I suppose we should," answered Reiquem. "Nothing else to do at the time," she said it rather sarcastically. After looking around a bit and waiting as Areon gazed up into the trees, they walked through the first part of the forest.

It was a bewildering site to say the least. Each tree seemed to be strategically positioned in a way so that they were lined up in perfect rows. Areon and Reiquem had no trouble walking through them. They both took their time as the gentlest breeze swept up red leaves that had fallen and made them dance in front of the couple. The red forest was glorious, and Areon felt anxious to see the blue forest, his favorite color. He thought to himself that they should perhaps go through all the colored forests he had seen; regardless of if it was out of their way or not. They did not have to step over bushes or the red grass. It was all as if someone had been managing the forest, keeping it perfectly groomed for visitors. The trees ran so straight that they did not have to veer off their northeast course. Another odd thing that Areon recognized was the way the trees were spaced; they all had almost a perfect two spans between them. It was magical.

The red forest was uneventful, and Areon had found himself wishing he knew the proper name for the forest rather than having himself and Reiquem call it the "red forest." It seemed to him that as soon as they had stepped into the forest, they stepped out of it. It was significantly smaller than the Moss Woods, which Areon regretted.

When they stepped out, they looked around for a sight of this city that they knew so little of. Nothing at all was in front of them, save more the roofs of some forests that were way off in the distance and some that started to get lost where the land met the sky.

Areon had guessed it to be two hours after the noon and looked over at Reiquem, who had said little, as he had, during the short trip through the glorious red woods.

"Now what do you suppose?" asked Areon seriously.

"I'm … I'm not sure," she said finally. She held up her hand and looked at the horizon, as if it would give her an answer.

"Well, shall we just keep heading in a northeast direction?" he asked. "I can't see much of what we've traveled over, save a bit of the flattops."

"Yes, sure." Reiquem shrugged.

They walked farther over streams and light hills that were of no trouble to get over. The two both thought that the easy traveling was nice. After awhile, they stopped and ate a little food.

"This'll be the last of our food then," said Areon regretfully taking another bite.

"I hope we find this place soon," she replied.

So they kept walking as they sun slowly thought more and more of going down and finally—Wham!

"What was that?" shouted Areon as he held his nose where a bit of blood had started to fall into his upheld hand. Reiquem stopped to stare and would not have believed what Areon said if she had not see the slight nosebleed.

He had run head first into nothing at all, nothing visible anyway. Reiquem went forward disregarding Areon's cursing as he held his head back to stop the bleeding. She held up her hand and felt something solid but not visible.

"I don't believe it," she whispered. "I could see them making the city disappear for brief moments, but not invisible," she spoke to herself.

"I'm fine," Areon said a bit annoyed. "What is it?" he asked.

"I would've thought it obvious that it's Lalvegeth," she replied nonchalantly.

"And how do we find the door?" Areon had stopped holding his nose and began to be amazed. He was looking up now as though he could see something if he looked up towards its highest part. To his amazement, he was correct.

"Magic to enter," said an indifferent voice. A person had appeared about ten spans above them, the lower half of his body invisible and the other looking as though it was floating in the air.

"What?" Areon and Reiquem said simultaneously.

The man had not looked at them the whole time they had been standing there. He turned his head down and looked.

"Do either of you practice magic?" said the man again, only louder. Apparently he was some watch guard.

"As a matter of fact, we do," said Reiquem defensively.

"Oh, well, good," said the security guard sarcastically while making a funny sort of face. "You'll need to show us that you practice magic before I can let you enter," he said turning serious again. "Unless, of course, you're a nonmagic folk here for the tournament."

"Don't show them you're a master," said Areon very quietly to Reiquem, disregarding the guard for the time.

"Alright, you do it then," she said comprehensively.

"Can you disappear?" asked the man excitedly, trying to guess what they were about to do.

"Disappear?" said Areon to Reiquem. "Is he serious?"

"Come on then," said the guard.

"I can disappear," returned Reiquem quietly to Areon.

"What?" he said scowling "How? Why didn't you tell me?"

"Let us see it then," said the guard anxiously. "Some things from the old days, eh?"

"I can't disappear," Areon yelled to the guard. "Half a minute," he said impatiently. The guard looked a bit offended and put his nose in the air and waited without a word.

Areon stretched out his arm and muttered some words under his breath, next he felt deep down for his aura, his immaterial self. In the next few seconds Areon had made his sword rise out from its sheath and float in front of him without touching it, his cloaking flailing randomly in the air. After it sat for a minute, he sent fire magic sailing toward the hilt of the sword, which spun it around perfectly and made it stick into the ground a span away from Areon, who was now barely sweating.

"Show off," said Reiquem.

"Impressive," said the guard. "Pretty good with you're aura there, traveler. Let 'em in!"

Instantly a wall appeared in front of the guard covering the lower part of his body. Next, purplish bricks starting coming into view, and Areon and Reiquem beheld the marvelous magic city of Lalvegeth.

It began with a large gate that was shimmering with magic. The bricks that went off the sides from the gate were purple and precisely laid. Lalvegeth, from the outside, was a simple square in the middle of the land. It had little notches in the top where the security guards stood, but other than that it seemed fairly normal apart from its color.

"Come in, come in!" yelled the security guard. The gate behind opened slowly and Areon and Reiquem walked into the city where they beheld something of magnificence, something that had taken years upon years to complete and to flourish.

Lalvegeth was a town not of war. It was a town where all folk of magic could gather peacefully and in secret if they wanted to. The city was a lot bigger than Areon had originally thought. It had a cobblestone street that ran all the way through the center of the vast city. On either side of the street were buildings, shops, and houses. For the first part of the walk into Lalvegeth they saw a lot of taverns and shops; the houses were put more towards the back, but a few shops and inns were strewn throughout the more residential areas. Everything was buzzing in Lalvegeth. The streets were moving with people. Most were wearing cloaks, some covering their faces and others with the hoods down. Things were flying around from who knew who was controlling them. Traders were lingering around stores, trying to sell in bulk on highly stacked carts. Businessmen were trying to sell anything and everything. Areon and Reiquem walked slowly and wondered where to go or what do to.

A little boy was running away from some friends who were playfully chasing him; he had dirt on his cheeks and was smiling broadly before he ran directly into Areon.

"Sorry," the boy said sincerely.

"Hey, boy," said Areon casting a look at Reiquem. "I'll show you a bit of fire magic if you lead us to an inn with good accommodations."

The boy squinted his eyes. Areon guessed him to be around seven or eight. He had on old clothes, but by the look of them, his mother must have tried her hardest to keep them clean.

"Name's Rop," said the boy holding up his hand so that his palm faced upward. In the next second a small blue flame burst up from the center of it and stood dancing for a few seconds before it went out of the boy's own accord.

"I live here," he said before dashing away again with his friends. Areon chuckled to himself and kept walking. Reiquem gave him a little nudge and they both laughed for a while walking deeper into the city.

"Wish I lived here as a child," remarked Areon wonderingly. "Might've had some friends."

"Well, what now do you suppose?" asked Reiquem, changing the subject abruptly.

"I'd like to see a shop of some sort," answered Areon, not really looking back at Reiquem. He was still gazing at the city.

"How about here?" asked Reiquem, pointing. The shop was sitting to the right of them and it was sunk back and sandwiched between two taller buildings. It was called …

"The Humpback Adventurer's Shack?" said Areon skeptically.

"It looks fun," said Reiquem, pulling on Areon's arms so that he was forced to go inside after Reiquem, who had already pulled open the faded wooden door.

A musty smell filled Areon's nose as he walked into the store. He looked around to find no one attending the counter.

"Where's the owner?" asked Reiquem. Areon did not answer; all the things that were scattered throughout the shop bedazzled him.

On one part of a wall was an array of different colored cloaks. Below these sat an assortment of walking boots, some armored on the toes and some not. On the next wall there were shelves lined with glass bottles full of different colored liquids. A particular green one bubbled as Areon ran his eyes across it. Some had nothing on them at all, and others had labels that were unreadable at a distance. At the very bottom were several little bottles that had nothing in them at all. To the right of these liquids were a few nets of various sizes, one as small as the palm of a child's hand. Many outfits were folded neatly in a corner. The next thing that caught Areon's eye was the basketful of walking sticks. Some were twisted and looked rather old, while others straight and looking very sturdy. He would like to have a walking stick, he thought to himself. A few leather bound telescopes were set off the counter, and in the counter lay various trinkets and superstitious items used for warding off evil. As Areon finished looking around, he noticed that an old humpback man had made his way out from behind the counter. A raggedy blanket was over a small walkway that led to a backroom.

"'Elp you, traveler?" he said in a gruff voice. He had slicked down hair that was almost amusing in a way that looked as though he tried too hard. He had on a green tunic and kilt that was a brownish color. Some teeth were missing as he smiled at the couple who had graced his store.

"We're sort of just looking around," said Areon politely.

"'Oo need a walkin' stick, eh?" said the old hunchback.

"How'd you know?" said Areon, a bit surprised. He was scrutinizing the man from head to toe.

"Been workin' 'ere longer than 'oo can 'magine, son," said the hunchback. "Know me a traveler when I see one, and 'oo need a walkin' stick."

"Unfortunately I've got no money," replied Areon ruefully.

"No money?" returned the hunchback. "Well, you won't get far in Lalvegeth wit no money."

"Even an inn?" piped in Reiquem.

"'Ell, you might find someone 'oo'll give you a room up in the attic," replied the storeowner. "Try me friend Karnt. It'll just be the inn that says the word 'Inn' on a rusty, old sign at the end of the city. North side."

"And who shall we say sent us?" asked Areon.

"Ahh, just say the ol' hunchback sent ya,' eh? Wouldn't want him to give you the best room in the house now, would ya'?" the hunchback smiled an almost toothless smile before waddling back into the backroom from whence he came.

Reiquem scowled. "Well, very nice wasn't he," she said dramatically.

"At least we've got a place to stay," replied Areon. "Let's get going farther uptown."

They went out of the shop and turned northward and hurried toward the edge of town. It took them a better part of ten minutes to get towards the end where they saw a run down old inn that had an aptly hung sign. Areon regretted not being able to stop at more of the stores that they saw.

"Here it is," said Areon. "It just says 'Inn' on a rusty old sign." They walked through the door together and found a bored-looking man sitting at the front desk that was in between two sets of wooden staircases that undoubtedly led to the upper rooms.

"We seek accommodations," announced Areon. "The hunchback from 'The Humpback Adventurer's Shack' sent us."

"Did he?" said the man pompously. "Well, lucky for you he's a good friend of mine and I owe him a favor. Did he give you his name?"

"No, he did not," said Reiquem crossing her arms.

"Must not have bought much then, did you?" said the man with a grin.

"We've got no money," replied Areon.

"Well, you can stay up in the attic tonight, but only for a night. You'll get a meager breakfast in the morning," said Karnt.

"Beggars cannot be choosers," stated Reiquem aloud.

"No, they cannot, but I do have a way for you to get a bit of money," returned Karnt. "It'll be the hard way, but you might want to buy something in Lalvegeth, especially since you've never been here before now."

"And how do you know that?" asked Reiquem

"I know, as does everyone who's lived her a long time, when a visitor comes," returned Karnt.

"And how do we get some money?" asked Areon, trying to keep the conversation on track.

The innkeeper took down a piece of paper that was nailed to a post beside him and handed it to Areon.

### FIST FIGHTING TOURNAMENT
To be held outside of Lalvegeth on the northern side,
tomorrow at noon.
There will be a strict no magic rule
**100 pieces of gold to the winner.**
Open to the people and visitors of Lalvegeth.

"Fist fighting?" asked Areon. "I know how to fistfight. Belgraf taught me a little when I was younger just for the fun of it. And for defense," he said looking at Reiquem hopefully. She raised her eyebrows.

"Why would Lalvegeth want to hold a fist fighting tournament?" asked Reiquem.

"Two reasons mainly," said the innkeeper. "The permanent residents of Lalvegeth hardly ever get to see a fight that doesn't involve magic, so when this comes along it's quite popular, and another is the fact that Lalvegeth is always overflowing with visitors that want to win some money. So the city folk get to see the fight while not having to participate at the same time."

"Ingenious," said Reiquem facetiously. "No magic, whoever heard of such a thing?"

"I have," said Areon still looking at the flier. "In Wellenore, when I would travel there as a younger lad, the kids would pick fights with me and Belgraf forbade me to use any sort of magic. So I dealt with it."

"Well, good," said Karnt unsympathetically. "You can be there at noon. If you're not up by then, I'll wake you." He walked up the stairs briskly and turned when he realized that they were not following him.

"Well, up here, you two," he said

"Are we staying in the attic?" asked Reiquem hesitantly.

"Nah, you can stay in beds since you've decided to be in the fist fighting tournament," replied Karnt.

"Well, one good thing will come out of you getting beat up," said Reiquem turning and following Karnt.

"You forgot the money," Areon called after her confidently.

# CHAPTER XX

## The Small Tournament

Karnt had just left the two to go to sleep when Reiquem turned and sat down on the bed looking at Areon.

"I'm so glad we're indoors for a little while," she said exhaustedly. The room was pretty nice considering where they had slept as of late. It was a wooden building. Two rooms sat above the room where they had entered; they both had four beds in them each. The beds had nice soft mattresses and a fluffy white pillow on them. It was entirely better than sleeping on the ground. Toward the back of each room sat a basin with fresh water for washing and a mirror. Reiquem got up and walked over to it and splashed some water on her face.

"I could use a bath though," she said.

"How like a woman, to want a bath when we're out in the wilderness," returned Areon.

"Wilderness?" said Reiquem. "We're in a city, and now that I think about I, I hope you win that money because I want to visit a bathhouse. They've got to have them in Lalvegeth."

"I'm sure they do, and I'll try my hardest to win," replied Areon. He turned and went over to where Reiquem had been standing and splashed some water on his face as well; after, he rubbed some water on his dirt-caked arms.

"Well, I'm going to go to sleep and enjoy this soft bed as long as I possibly can," announced Reiquem. "Good night, Areon."

"Good night, Reiquem, sleep well," he replied. Areon did not go to sleep directly after he had said it. He laid on his bed and put his arms behind his head and stared up at the ceiling while listening to the quiet, slow breathing of Reiquem, who slept soundly. He refused to admit it to Reiquem, but he was a bit nervous about the fist fighting tournament that was to ensue in the morning. He wondered how big his opponents might be, and how he was going to refrain from using magic, and what about his cloak . . .

⋙⊙⋘

"Wake up!" shouted Reiquem. She and Karnt had been standing over him; he had fallen asleep while thinking.

"What time is it?" he asked groggily.

"About an hour before the noon," said Karnt pompously. "And you, lad, should have been up with breakfast in your stomach, stretching out."

"Stretching out?" said Areon laughing. "How about the breakfast?"

"Yes, well, follow me," replied Karnt turning around and heading back down the creaky wooden steps.

"Hey, just thought you oughta know that only four people are participating in the fistfights today," said Reiquem.

"Four?" said Areon sounding a bit less nervous. "Is that all?"

"Yes, I was up eating already with Karnt, and he said that two fight each other and the winners of those fights fight. Pretty simple."

"Indeed, does second place get any money?" asked Areon.

"No," said Karnt shortly. "So win. And I'll be expecting a little something if you do." He had come back up from downstairs. "Now get down here and eat."

Areon got up slowly and went over to the sink where he splashed a little water on his face to wash the sleep out of his eyes and walked down the stairs with Reiquem following him closely.

Karnt led them to a room in the back that had a large wooden table with a plate on one side that was obviously for Areon. Karnt gestured to him to sit and he did.

"Eat up," said Karnt. "It's still as warm as ever."

"Thank you," said Areon sincerely. He ate two pieces of toast and two scrambled eggs with a glassful of milk. The people from the city were different. Nice, but different.

"Very fulfilling," said Areon pushing the plate away and standing up. Karnt took the plate and rushed it to a room in the back.

"Now, we must get to the grounds outside," said Karnt. He grabbed Areon by the arm and hurried him through the front door with Reiquem directly behind them.

"Why are you so eager to help us?" asked Reiquem suspiciously.

"As I mentioned before, I expect a bit of the winnings for my services, and perhaps you can stay again for a nice discount," returned Karnt after locking up the door to his inn.

Areon glanced over at him and then back at Reiquem, which was difficult because Karnt was holding his arm tightly and hurrying him along the cobblestone path towards the north entrance of the city. Areon was still trying to catch glimpses of things that were strewn throughout the city, not least of which were the people who had obviously lived there for some time. Everything looked so very interesting.

"And here we are." Karnt had led them outside the gate, which was open to an area in which a huge bench with ten rows of seats sat along with a booth with three chairs in it and in front of all this a big circle dirt patch outlined with a glittering white chalky substance. Areon easily distinguished the fans from the judges and the fighters from all of these.

The fans were all sitting in the seats or walking around them talking carelessly. The three judges were standing outside their booth talking seriously, and the fighters were to the north of the dirt patch. One was very tall, taller than Areon, and skinny; he wore no shirt. Another was about Areon's size, but his head was shaved and he looked extremely affronted. He had scars up and down his back and a few on his face. Areon thought that if he could choose, he would not fight him at all. The last fighter was shorter than Areon and not all that much more muscular. He was smiling and talking jovially to people that passed by.

"Alright. I think we'll start here soon then," said a loud, heavily accented voice. "Fighters, to the center of the ring, and face the crowd." Areon looked over at the crowd; it had swelled from the seats being half full to all of them being full, and many more people of Lalvegeth were standing around the dirt circle. There were even more pouring out of the northern gate. It was getting bigger than Areon would have liked, and his stomach did a quick somersault.

The man that had spoken was one of the judges, or referees. Areon could not decide, but it was obvious that he was doing the talking for the other two. After the four fighters stepped in and faced the crowd, which was difficult to do considering how many were around now, the man spoke again.

"The fights will either go for ten minutes, until one of the fighters gives up or is unconscious, or until one of them is knocked outside of the circle," said the announcer. "If, by chance, a fight happens to go for ten minutes, the judges will decide who won the fight."

"Do the fights not usually go for ten minutes?" Areon asked the smaller, happier fighter next to him. The smaller guy just shrugged and gave him a nervous of smile.

"Most people are knocked unconscious," said a gruff voice that belonged to the man who was about Areon's size and had many scars. He lifted his head up and cracked his neck while still giving Areon a cruel stare. Areon raised his eyebrows and turned his head away nonchalantly; what the man said made him rather nervous.

"The fighters that have appeared today do not reside in Lalvegeth. All residents who wish to make bets may do so now on the boy with the red cloak." Areon knew the announcer was talking about him, but not very many people moved or made any transactions. "And now place your bets on the skinnier man." He saw a couple more people turn and make a few exchanges with bits of paper and gold and silver coins. "Now on the other man with no cloak." No one moved, as they had not with Areon. "And now place your bets on our last year's traveling champion." Areon guessed they were talking about the gruff looking man with scars on his back. Everyone seemed to want to place a bet on him.

"Now that that's taken care of, we can begin," shouted the announcer. "The boy in the red cloak will fight the man his size not wearing a shirt." Areon felt entirely relieved at the thought of having to fight the one who seemed happy and not intent on knocking him unconscious. His spirits had dropped, and now he was more concerned about staying alive rather than winning all the money. He knew with magic, or so he thought, that none of the people in the dirt circle would be any sort of match for him, but it was strictly forbidden during a fistfight for the entertainment of the people of Lalvegeth.

"The other two fighters will step out of the ring and watch," stated the announcer. "You two," he said pointing to Areon and the apparently nervous man beside him, "will start whenever you both are ready."

Areon turned to face the man that he would be fighting. He had not been in a fistfight in some time and was curious as to how it would go. The man, who was a little smaller than him, turned and gave him an uneasy smile. Everyone had left the ring and was standing out of earshot. The little man turned to him and said: "We're not going to take this entirely seriously, are we?"

Areon stomach settled a little bit. He was fighting someone who did not even seem out to win.

"Nah," whispered Areon. "I'm not taking this too serious." The little man gave an appreciative smile and backed away, putting his hands up and nodding at Areon. Areon put his hands up in a ready to fight stance.

They walked around in a circle around each other for a half a minute and then started throwing out a few jabs that did not connect. Areon, not wanting to look like they were staging the fight, gave the man a sharp shot in the nose that put a more serious look on his face.

"C'mon, Areon," shouted Karnt from the side. Everyone was cheering on one or the other to try and get into the fights a bit more. He threw a few more punches at the littler man. After they did not connect, Areon felt a fist smash into the side of his head. He shut his eyes and then shot the man a look before throwing a big right and connecting in the same spot that the man had just hit him. Areon kept looking over his shoulder to make sure that he did not get close to the white line that would disqualify him.

The little man made a rush at Areon and sent him back a few paces, closer to the line than Areon would have liked. He was so busy worrying about falling outside of it that he took a few shots to the stomach and bent over in pain. The man had a smile on his face as Areon looked up and over at the crowd, who was not cheering for him. He decided to get more serious. He ran over to the man and ducked out of the way of a punch and landed his fist directly in the little man's ribs; it was a clean shot and the man fell over. Areon then fell to a knee and hit him hard in the face under the eye. Areon remembered telling him that he would go easy, so he backed off to let the man up. The man did not get up. Apparently Areon had taken his last punch a little to far. The man was bleeding from under the eye, and he looked over warily at Areon. He was holding his hand under the cut that Areon had inflicted and a pool of scarlet was forming in his hand. The man clearly saw that Areon was letting him do a lot better than he normally would have. Areon was physically strong, and he was hiding it from the crowd.

"Well, I think that'll do," said the little man. He got up and stepped outside the circle while a judge from one of the three seats had come over to hold up Areon's hand.

The man that Areon had been fighting went over to a small group consisting of a woman and a few other men who were patting him on the back and telling him good job; they all looked rather rich.

"The next fight will take place immediately," shouted the announcer. The man with scars who was about Areon's size stepped in slowly while the skinnier man bounced in and threw a few punches into the air. He looked more than ready, regardless of the look of the scarred fighter.

"Start when you're ready," said the announcer. The fight began differently than Areon's and his opponent's had. The two stared at each other for some time and then walked up closer to each other without putting any hands up in ready to fight stance. The skinny man suddenly threw out a long arm that connected solidly with the scarred man's ribs and a better part of the crowd grimaced. It looked like a painful blow, yet the scarred man stood without putting up his guard. The skinny man wasted no time, and he simply threw a few more long-armed punches out that connected with the scarred man's solid stomach. Yet the scarred man did not move. Areon could tell he had been in his fair share of fights. Finally, the skinny man threw a big hook punch that landed perfectly on the side of his opponent's face and sent him to the ground. Before Areon even had a chance to predict what was going to happen next, the man with scars stood up swiftly, faced the skinny man, and headbutted him directly in the nose, sending a shower of blood over the dirt circle. The skinny man lay motionless on the ground while the crowd fell silent.

"Cease!" yelled the announcer. "He is finished." Two men came and carried off the skinny fighter to people who would tend him until he woke up with what would probably be the worst headache of his life and a broken nose.

Areon glared at the man with scars. It was a mean thing to do, playing with his opponent like that. They waited a few more minutes for people to carry off the unconscious man and for things to calm a bit.

The announcer looked at the man with scars and asked, "Are you ready to begin, Brek?" Areon guessed the man that had just won was named Brek and that the announcer knew this from last year.

"'Course I am." stated Brek. He did not remove his glare from Areon's.

"Then you two may begin," stated the announcer. A cheer rose up from the crowd and the two circled around each other, not putting up hands. Areon refused to make the same mistake that the skinny man made; he had to approach this fight cautiously. Areon warily approached the man as he intended, and surprisingly the scarred fighter threw out a fist that almost connected with Areon's face. The next few minutes were a blur; after the big hook from his opponent, Areon started throwing a storm of punches. He and Brek were going toe to toe and the fighting was not pretty. Areon was feeling his face getting beaten severely, and once he backed out of it, which was a mistake, to take a blow to the side of his head that sent a burst of light through his vision. Brek stopped and looked to see what effect this had. Areon rushed at him and tackled him to the ground. He was throwing punches with his left and right that smashed into the nose of Brek, which bled profusely. Finally, after seeing the blood, Brek threw Areon over himself and did a reverse somersault that landed on Areon's stomach and knocked the wind out of him. The two both stood up and looked at each other; they were both apparently very tired. Areon absentmindedly conjured up a fire attack and was sending it toward the palm of his hand when he remembered the rules. The fire subsided back into him. Brek walked over to Areon, and just before Areon was about to throw another enervated punch, Brek threw his forehead at Areon's face, which landed directly where it had on the skinny fighter and sent Areon on his back. This did not have the effect on Areon that it had on the skinny fighter; instead of knocking him out, it only enraged him. He got up and started walking swiftly toward Brek, who was standing unconcernedly, when the announcer walked in and pushed Areon away from trying to beat up Brek some more.

"This fight is over!" yelled the announcer in Areon's face.

"What are you talking about?" screamed Areon back. He knew ten minutes was not up yet. "I'm still standing!"

Before Areon could argue any longer, he looked at what the announcer was pointing at: he had landed outside the white line when Brek had headbutted him to the ground. He could do nothing save smile regretfully and walk over to shake his worthy opponent's hand.

# CHAPTER XXI

# The Bathhouse

"Well, it was a good fight anyhow," remarked Karnt as they made their way back into the city. "The last one, that is. You looked like a caitiff during your first match." Most of the people had already left when Areon and Reiquem had decided to go back into town and try to figure what to do next.

"I think that's a little overboard," Areon returned to Karnt.

"Are you okay, Areon?" asked Reiquem. She sounded rather worried.

"I'm fine," Areon smiled at her. He was donning a fresh bruise under his eye and had blood under his nose from a nosebleed that had stopped a few minutes after the fight. Reiquem did not smile back. He also had a nice bruise on his upper stomach, but he was not going to mention the thing that hurt him most to Reiquem.

"Hey, kid." Areon turned to see who owned the voice.

"Hold up there a minute," said the little man who had been the first to fight against Areon.

"Oh, yes," said Areon turning. "Good fight."

"Yes, yes that's all very well," returned the little man. He was standing with his group of friends, who all looked rich. Areon also noted that the man was wearing new clothes that said he was a lot more than well off. "I wanted to thank you for taking it easy on me during our fight." He had dropped his voice to a whisper that could not be heard by his yuppie friends. "I entered this fighting tournament to impress some of my friends. And I realized that you could've been much harder on me that you were."

"I don't understand," said Areon.

"Well, we were talking one night, and one of them thought none of us rich folk could enter the tournament. Most of them are stuck up," replied the little man. "I entered just to prove them wrong, but you took it easy on me and it made me look good, at least for a while. For that I would like to thank you. You're a nice person."

"How do you know I took it easy on you?" asked Areon politely.

"I saw you fight Brek," said the man.

"Well, you're welcome," said Areon and he turned to leave and made it a couple steps before the little man grabbed him by the arm and said, "No. I really want to thank you," and the little man dropped a small sack in Areon's hand and turned around and went back to his group of friends before Areon could refuse.

"What was that all about?" asked Reiquem suspiciously.

"I'm not really sure," answered Areon. He took out the little leather sack and poured the contents out into his hand. It was a bag half full of silver and half full of gold coins.

"Well, I guess you won anyhow!" exclaimed Karnt taking two gold coins and stuffing them in his pocket.

"Hey, what the …" tried Reiquem.

"It's fine," said Areon. "He did let us stay in the beds."

"I'll let you stay for free tonight," said Karnt. "Good-bye 'til then. Don't spend it all in one place," he said as he walked away from them.

"And how'd you get that?" asked Reiquem.

"The little man gave it to me," said Areon. "I took it easy on him during our fight, and apparently he appreciated it."

"Apparently?" said Reiquem. "There must be thirty gold pieces and thirty silver pieces."

"I know. Should be enough to find us a map," stated Areon.

"And a lot more besides," said Reiquem, who had started walking back up the dirt path that led to the gates of Lalvegeth.

When they got back to the inn, the beds were made and a fresh basin was set out beside the mirror.

"I guess things will be more accommodating now that Karnt knows we have money," said Areon.

"Good, and by the way, speaking of accommodating, we should really try and find a bathhouse," said Reiquem. "I'm filthy."

"Yeah, I guess I wouldn't mind getting clean," replied Areon.

"Well, let's go look around the city a bit more and come back and have a rest," said Reiquem. "Tomorrow we'll look for a bathhouse and a map."

"Sounds like a plan," said Areon, who'd just cleaned his face up in the basin, which was now housing bloody water. "Lets go."

They walked out of the inn and into the streets. The city was buzzing just as it had been when they walked into the city for the first time. Areon had his hand on the sack of money that was in his pocket.

"Let's head to the Humpback Adventurer's Shack," said Areon. "There was a few things there I wanted to get." They made their way, which did not take long and wandered into the store. It held its initial musty smell. The humpback sat on a bench behind the counter.

"Goodday," said the storeowner.

"Hello," replied Areon.

"Got a bit ruffed up in the last fight eh?" the humpback smiled.

"A bit," said Areon uninterested in the conversation. He was looking at the small nets. Next he turned his attention to the walking sticks.

"I think I'll buy a walking stick, but I don't know which one," Areon said to the storeowner but after looked at Reiquem with a questioning look. He then took out a rather plain stick.

"Made of willow," said the humpback. "Strong, plain but dependable."

"Alright you think Reiquem?" asked Areon.

"I would say strong and not to flashy would be good for our travels," she replied.

Areon left the store with a small net, an empty jar, a jar full of substance that helped heal wounds, a substance that helped bring back ones wits, and a plain, but new walking stick.

The rest of the day was rather uneventful, Areon and Reiquem ventured around town looking at all the prestigious pillars and statues that were about the city but soon after they became tired from the day and went back to the inn.

"Hello," said Karnt as they entered. "Have a good day?" he asked more politely than usual.

"Yes, it was nice," replied Areon. "Shall we?" he turned to Reiquem and headed up the stairs where they both got into bed and went immediately to sleep.

Areon awoke before Reiquem and sat and watched her sleep for about a minute before she stirred and looked over at him with half open eyes.

"Good morning," she said groggily.

"Morning," replied Areon glad that she was awake. "Shall we take off right away, I think we woke up rather early so we can get some things done today."

"Like the bathhouse?" asked Reiquem eagerly.

"Yeah, sure we can look for that first," replied Areon wondering why she was this set on taking a bath.

They set off down the stairs and out the inn with renewed vigor. It was a glorious day and the sun was shining brightly on the two of them as they walked heartily up the street. They went until they found a man sitting in a booth type structure with his elbows on the counter and his hands holding up his head. He looked extremely bored.

"Does Lalvegeth have a bathhouse?" asked Reiquem to the bored looking man.

"Does Lalvegeth have a bathhouse?!?!" replied the man sitting up and looking shocked yet excited. "Does Lalvegeth have a bathhouse? The best one in all the land my dear. Follow this cobblestone down to that sign that has a knife crossing a shield, it's the armor/weapon store, take a right and head straight and you won't be able to miss it."

So they went down to the armor/weapon store and took a right. The man could not have been more right about them not being able to miss the bathhouse. After they walked toward it a ways through what seemed like an alley they emerged into a structure that equaled amazing. They stood before four large white stone pillars that held up the stone roof that slanted from the middle. Through the pillars you could see an open area where people paid and the women were led to the right and the men to the left, beyond this nothing else remained visible. The floors were pink and made of some material that Areon could not place. It was gorgeous to say the least and Reiquem pulled him to get in. They walked through the pillars and up a small flight of stairs that led through the pillars and up to a woman sitting behind a stone desk that went from one side of the room to the other which led to the men and women sides of the bathhouse.

"Good day," said Reiquem hastily "We wish to have a bath."

"Of course dear," said the old lady that was behind the counter. "A gold piece each is all it costs, and you may stay as long as you like."

Areon gave her the money and looked at Reiquem.

"Well now what?" he said. "How long should we take?"

"Take as long as you want," replied Reiquem. "Let's just meet back at the inn." She gave him a quick kiss and hugged him. "I'm glad you're alright from the fight."

Before Areon could reply she was already walking to the area where the women stripped down and walked in. Areon walked over to his side and remembered his cloak.

"Come off me," he commanded to the cloak as if it were alive. He grabbed the neck and gently tried to take it off but it constricted around his neck.

"You will come off." he gave it a sharp tug over his head and it scraped the sides of his face but it came off nonetheless. He hung it up and looked over to the women's side. Reiquem was the only girl standing there. Her shirt was off but she was not facing the direction of the men's side. Areon could not help but look at her beautiful figure. Next she took her pants off and Areon turned away blushing as she ran toward the bath with her long black hair streaming behind her.

He took the rest of his clothes off and walked in through the steamy entryway that led to the enormously large pool of hot water. Nobody was in the place at the time, which Areon guessed was the case on the women's side and he was grateful because he felt odd, being nude in so wide a space. He walked in slowly and took a look around. The square room was lined with smaller pillars similar to the outside pillars holding up the roof. These pillars held up the upper part of the bathhouse that led to store rooms. In the center was a large bath that was steaming and large puffs of soap were sitting on the top of the water. Bubbles were floating around everywhere inside the room. Half of the stone floor was pink and the other half white. It looked spotlessly clean and Areon walked over to the bath where he, not overly graceful, got in. He simply sat and gazed up at the stone ceiling that was covered in paintings that looked as though highly skilled artists had painted them. He sat for some time without doing any scrubbing but finally he thought it would be a good idea. He looked around for a sponge or scrub of some sort and found that none were sitting around the large room. But as he looked one way and back again a bucket with a scrubber a sponge and a few bottles of oil had materialized next to him. He gave a jump and then settled back into the water taking out the sponge and started to get clean.

When Areon returned to his clothes he found that they had been washed and folded neatly, all his clothes save his cloak. It looked as though it had been in a fight and Areon guessed what had happened. He dressed quickly and walked out of the bathhouse.

"We couldn't get your cloak clean ..." yelled the old lady, but Areon pretended not to hear and continued walking back to the inn at a brisk pace. He did not exactly feel like explaining his cloak to her. He suddenly stopped and looked up toward the sky, it seemed to him that the sun was going down already. But how could that be? He wondered to himself.

"I didn't think I was in there that long," he said aloud to himself, shrugged and hurried back to the inn figuring that Reiquem was already there.

# CHAPTER XXII

## Time and Love

Areon returned to the inn to find Reiquem sitting on the side of her bed with a look of concern.

"Hey sorry I took so long," said Areon. "I didn't even think I was in there an hour and the day suddenly disappeared."

Reiquem stood up and walked over to him. "I only got here a half an hour ago," she replied airily. She was standing face to face with him and she slowly took the neck of Areon's cloak up and gently lifted it over his head, for some reason it did not struggle at all. Reiquem did not have her flighty attitude as she had earlier. Areon looked into her black eyes and lost himself for the moment.

"Reiquem …" Areon said quietly but his words were lost as she leaned over, embraced, and kissed him fervently. Areon returned the kiss acquiescently.

They made their way over to the bed before Reiquem said:

"I've known you a long time Areon. I've wanted to do this for some time but I was scared you didn't feel the same." Areon thought she smelled wonderful and her hair was very clean and bounced as she moved.

"Reiquem," Areon said in disbelief. "I feel entirely the same."

"Please don't ever leave me," she whispered.

She lifted the blanket over their bodies.

So it will ever be, with souls such as Areon and Reiquem when they encounter each other: with time will come love.

# CHAPTER XXIII

## The Magical Map

Areon awoke the next morning with the smell of the oils from the bathhouse in his nose. He had not used any, but apparently Reiquem had. She slept peacefully and Areon slipped out of bed without waking her. He went over to the mirror and looked at himself for a long time before stepping out of the room and going down to see if Karnt had made any breakfast.

"Lovely day," said Karnt as Areon walked into the breakfast area in the back part of the building.

"It is a lovely day," said Areon distantly and slowly. Karnt raised one eyebrow at him and put a plate of breakfast in front of him. It consisted of a few muffins and some bacon strips along with a glass of milk.

"Will you be staying another night?" asked Karnt hopefully.

"No I think we need to continue through," replied Areon taking a bit of a muffin and washing it down with some milk. He reached in his pocket after and handed Karnt three pieces of his silver.

"Thank you for letting us stay and giving us breakfast," said Areon.

"You're welcome sir," returned Karnt who took the money graciously and stowed it away in his pocket.

Reiquem came down a bit later and sat down beside Areon and looked at him with a smile.

"Do you know where we could get a map of the continent?" Areon asked Karnt.

"Lalvegeth does have almost anything you could want, I suppose you could find one, but I'm not exactly sure where," he replied. "I'd say just start roaming around town, you'll probably see a place on your way out."

Areon pushed his chair away and looked at Reiquem.

"Well I think we should get going," he said. "We've hung around here a while to long."

"Well thank you for gracing my inn," Karnt said, as he bowed not too low to the ground. He walked back farther into the room from whence the breakfast came.

"Shall we?" asked Areon.

"Lets go," replied Reiquem and they walked out of Karnt's inn with rested muscles and full stomachs.

"Where do you think we'll find a place that sells maps?" Reiquem asked.

Areon shrugged and looked around at the city for what would be the last time. They went through a few alleys and up some more cobblestone paths that led to ...

"The official Lalvegeth bookstore," said Areon reading a wooden sign on what appeared to be a very old, but still prestigious building. "Should have some maps in here shouldn't it?"

"I'm sure of it," returned Reiquem. "Its huge." They both walked in.

The building was narrow but long in a way where you could see both the long walls which were covered in books and ladders, but you could not see the back of the store. It seemed to distend forever back into a sea of books.

"Hellooo," said a voice of a very cheery old man. "What brings you here? Looking for something to read in your spare time?" he squinted one eye at them before continuing. "No, no you are here in need of something by the look of the two of you." Reiquem and Areon both looked at each other, raising their eyebrows.

"We need a map," stated Areon.

"Of the entire continent," chimed in Reiquem.

"Entire continent," said the old man distantly. "Well it shouldn't be a problem to find something like that. Would you like a map with both continents of the middle part of the ocean of the middle part of our planet?"

"Yeah I suppose that might come in handy someday," Areon said slowly while looking at Reiquem doubtfully.

The old man looked up at the ceiling while putting his index finger and thumb on his chin. "This will be a bit difficult," he said while squinting and thinking a bit longer.

"And why is that?" asked Areon.

"You don't live in Lalvegeth that's apparent enough," replied the old bookkeeper. "Maps are eccentricities around here, the ones we have are ones that have been made from explorers from all over the earth. Some are reliable and some aren't."

"Can you elaborate on that a bit for us?" asked Reiquem.

"Well you see at the bottom of most maps reside the key, and a note that goes something along these lines: 'Place finger on area and think of the name for new locations on your map.' When they do this a picture appears in accordance with the key of the map and it's permanent. But problems often sprout from this," said the old man.

"Such as …" Areon asked.

"Well some explorers, or map makers as some call them, are not as proficient as we would like them to be." he answered.

"So some maps are screwed up and will lead us off." Reiquem said loudly.

"Some," replied the bookkeeper. "The less you pay for a map the more of a chance you take of it not being infallible."

"Well we need a map that will get us there no matter what the price," said Areon.

"And the amount of information?" asked the bookkeeper.

"As much as possible," replied Areon. Before the bookkeeper could speak again Areon said; "And the price is of no matter."

"You're looking at somewhere around 10 gold pieces, perhaps some silver." The old bookkeeper said.

"Fine," said Areon shortly. The old man walked back and disappeared into his abysmal hallway of books, and then returned with something that looked about ten inches tall and three inches across, folded and completely flat.

"Here it is." the old man replied. "According to what you wanted it's the best map I own. It'll be 10 pieces of gold and two pieces of silver. It is completely worth it in my opinion and the map makers of Lalvegeth have put a spell on it that makes it terribly difficult to tear or get stained. It also contains the legendary locations of the temples, but I doubt you will ever find those. Perhaps it was a joke from the mapmaker, but I can assure you most other places on it are accurate. Oh and if you ever wish to return it for money the places you yourself have put on that particular map must be approved by an official geological map maker that ..." before he could finish Areon cut in while shoving the money in his hand.

"I doubt we'll ever make it back here after what we're about to attempt," he said. Reiquem looked down at the floor.

The old man scrutinized them with one eye half squinted, his index finger and thumb back on his chin. "And you won't," he said. "Not with that attitude anyhow." he turned on his heel and went back into the sea of books.

Areon and Reiquem walked out of the store and down the cobblestone path out the south side of Lalvegeth from whence they came and sat down to examine their map.

"Lalvegeth certainly is the magic city." was the first thing Reiquem said after examining the map and watching Areon do the same. "They have the temples on here."

"Not Lalvegeth though." Areon responded. "Whoever made the map."

"Curious." Reiquem said distantly.

"What's that?" asked Areon.

"Well as I've said before, the temples are near impossible to find," she said. "It's almost as if they have to want to be found."

"So you're saying ..."

"I'm not saying anything as of now." Reiquem said cutting off Areon. "But I see a harbor on the map and I see where the next closest temple is supposed to be." she continued. "I find it hard to believe they could map the temples though. Whoever has owned this map probably tried to get to them but it was in vain."

"There's a house relatively close to it," said Areon only half paying attention to Reiquem. "That can't be just a coincidence can it?" he looked up at here from his squatting position.

"Who knows." she answered. "But it's on an island and we'll test the maps validity first by heading here." she pointed at a spot straight east of them that simply said:

"The harbor?" asked Areon. "So we'll have to sail there?" he asked meekly.

"Apparently," replied Reiquem. "Anyway it is one of the lesser dangers in the worlds when you're attacking temple guardians."

"Let's do it then," said Areon standing up. "Destination: The temple of time."

# CHAPTER XXIV

## Areon the Sailor

"Hey, I've an idea." Areon said breaking the silence of his and Reiquem's walk. "We should head south a bit and go to that forest that looks as though it's blue."

And so they did. Walking only slightly southward while still going on an easterly bound course they walked into the blue forest that was identical to the red one they had encountered directly before they walked into Lalvegeth.

The rows were entirely perfect. They had a certain amount of space in between each tree so that a clearing was left on either side of a tree that one could walk through without hassle. The grass was also blue along with all the flowers. As Areon entered he closed his eyes and tilted his head up before opening them to see all the small, blue leaves floating about and the grass swaying gently in the little breeze that the forest allowed in. It was better than the red forest. It was a color that was impossible but still present in all of what was supposed to be green. They walked through slowly trying to take in as much of it as they could but these strangely colored forests that surrounded Lalvegeth were very small and soon they emerged out the east side of the forest. After a bit more walking and a bit more wondering of why and more mind boggling, why these forests existed Lalvegeth, the blue and last forest disappeared out of Areon and Reiquem's site as they continued to make their way toward the harbor town.

The next few days were as uneventful as they could possibly be. Areon and Reiquem had slept a few nights over the long journey to the harbor but they were still walking at a very fast pace and were sleeping very little out of boredom. The land was beautiful although the beauty was taken away once in awhile by the fact that they had to climb over large hills with jagged rocks. A few times they stopped at small rivers and filled Areon's water skin with water and drank but they did not have to cross any big rivers. For food Areon would hunt rabbits, or when they got tired of that they would eat a little of the food that Areon had bought at Lalvegeth.

"You wouldn't believe the dream I had." Reiquem stated as they were gathering everything up after one night of sleep.

They walked for a time in silence before Areon cut in. "Soooo? What happened?"

"It was incredible." answered Reiquem. "I was flying through clouds and past Rainbows that littered the sky. It was excellent. Ever have I wished to fly."

"Maybe someday it'll come true," replied Areon.

She only half smiled at this.

When they had walked for a whole day Areon watched the horizon start to break into blue. They quickened there pace to see if it was finally true; they'd gotten to the east sea, and the harbor was approaching them exactly as their map had told them it would.

When they arrived at the harbor town Areon looked around to see what the place consisted of. A few large vessels were tied up lazily on the east side of the inlet of land while other smaller ships had greater numbers. The place where the land and the small town began was rather difficult to distinguish. The whole area blended together forming a place of nature to a place of inhabitants and then a way out into the sea. Many sailors roamed the area, looking at large ships, or looking for taverns to drink in before they had to set sail with their crew for fishing excursions. Areon and Reiquem immediately blended in with the multifarious crowd. Part of the little town had a cobblestone walkway, but beyond that, the rest of it stretched out into the sea. Many large planks and docks stretched far out to provide docking places for people to live on boats if they felt tired of traveling. The town also had many more inns and taverns than it had houses. All in all, the place seemed to be for staying short amounts of time rather than for living. They made their way to the south end of the harbor town where they found a store that rented out and sold small boats.

Areon knocked on the door, which simply swung open. A man that was sitting on a chair about fell off it in precipitance to see who had come in. He had been sleeping and drooling on the counter, which made Areon, chuckle under his breath, then cut it off before asking ...

"We require a catamaran if you've got one, I'm afraid we haven't much money for anything else," he said.

The man seemed middle-aged and fat and one could tell that he spent the majority of his time sitting and waiting for apparently rare customers. "Oi?" he said. "And for what?, Might I ask." he added with a gruff voice. He coughed a little bit while Areon simply raised one eyebrow at him.

Reiquem spoke brashly. "We are going southeast to the temple ..."

"A temple you wouldn't have heard of." Areon cut her off. "We're on an insignificant pilgrimage." The man squinted his eyes at them. "Well to you anyhow." Areon added. "Nonetheless we require means to get there."

"Here's how I work it," said the man in his gruff voice. He coughed a bit more and spun his chair 'round to face them better. "For one of the smaller boats you require, with two sails it'll be 20 pieces of gold. When you return me my ship I give you back 5 pieces and keep the rest for you using it."

Areon took out his satchel of money and poured it on the table counting out the right amount, it mostly consisted of silver because the gold was running quite low. "There you are," he said.

The man eyed the money. "Alright," he said. "Follow me, unless you'd like to stay longer."

"Nahh, it's early in the day we might as well set sail if the sea is right and the sails sturdy." Areon replied.

"Oh the sail's will hold," replied the fat man getting up, with what looked like a bit of effort. "Me and my father hand made the smaller boats and stand by their quality."

They walked out of the old wooden shack that was near the sea and walked onto the docks to a set of small boats. The fat man led the way bumping into people while Areon and Reiquem tried to keep up.

"Which would ya like?" asked the fat man waving his hand toward the boats. Some were bigger than others, but they did not look as sturdy.

"We're going to need a larger one." Reiquem whispered to Areon.

"Right, the biggest one for the amount of money I gave you," replied

Areon. The fat man walked on the creaking dock and untied it and handed the dusty rope to Areon.

"Can't we pay you to come with us? I'm not sure how to sail." Areon asked.

"Hahahah. Good one mate." was all the fat man said before walking away with the money jangling in his pocket. "Sail with us …" Areon heard him mutter sarcastically as he disappeared into the crowd and made his way back to his pathetic shop.

"Well I hope this island comes into site soon, because we haven't much food left." Reiquem got on their boat. The hull was pretty ordinary and sunk down so that it had sides so as one would not fall over into the water. The sails were white and stained with many various things that Areon could not figure out, but they looked reliable and strong. The boat was made well and looked like it had not rotted anywhere. He boarded with Reiquem and looked out into the sea.

Areon stretched out his hand and the air around him whirled into a vortex that spun toward the center of his hand. He held it out west and suddenly they were blown out into the ocean. Reiquem had barely finished putting up the sails when he did this and was almost knocked over, but had gotten a hold of one of the masts. She shot Areon a threatening look as they made their way past the conglomeration of docks, boats, strings, and sails into the vast sea that lay ahead of them.

"I guess it's not that hard." Areon said over the noise the rushing wind was making. Reiquem turned her head toward the southeast while laughing, and hers and Areon's long hair flew back as they made their way toward the horizon and the temple of time. Many people in the harbor town watched in awe as the couple sailed out of site from the force of the wind magic Areon had created.

# CHAPTER XXV

## Our House

Areon did not stop his wind magic for quite some time. The breeze in their hair and the feeling of being on something different than solid ground for a change was quite exhilarating. He absolutely loved the open sea. He had never been as far as the sea and did not know if he would ever care to but now that he was out there it was the time of his life. Their little boat held up quite nicely. The water remained quite calm apart for some very small waves and there was no wind, save what Areon was producing to keep them going at a speed that would have been superlative to all other boats and all other sailors in the world who could not do elemental magic. Reiquem took Areon's things off his waist and put them all down on the logs that were lashed together. She threw the old jars and the potion he had obtained alongside them and all her sleeping things. Areon left the walking stick down too. He sort of regretted buying it he thought to himself as Reiquem laid it down. After, she could not stop looking at their map.

"What's so interesting about that old thing anyhow?" asked Areon a bit annoyed.

"Well I was just going over some of the information on it, making sure it was correct and all, according to where I've been, when I stumbled across this." she pointed down at the island they were heading for. Areon had stopped using his wind to propel the boat and was now just letting it drift along lazily at whatever speed it desired. He was tired now and felt that he would not be doing magic any time soon without Reiquem's help. The compass that was located directly in front of and below the wheel told Areon that they were headed in the southeast direction they needed to be to get to the island of the temple of time, according to the map.

"What is it?" Areon asked as he walked across the deck to where Reiquem stood.

"Well down on the island where we're headed I didn't much pay attention to it because all that was on there was the temple of time, supposedly. Until I looked a bit closer after examining it all twice, and I noticed a tiny brown spot on it that simply says 'our house,'" replied Reiquem.

"Well that's odd now," said Areon putting his hand to his chin and rubbing it lightly. "I don't think I like the sound of that."

"No, that's great," replied Reiquem.

"And why is that?" asked Areon.

"Well, don't you think it's odd that on one island, resides the temple of time and a house?" Reiquem said, "According to the map." she added.

"I guess that is rather odd." Areon returned. He was thinking harder than ever. "You know what it has to be."

"Of course I do," replied Reiquem. "The time master must live there by himself. I've heard of him to. They call him Myriad. What his real name is we'll know soon enough."

"We're going there first?" asked Areon apprehensively.

"Well of course, have you forgotten about the sealers?" replied Reiquem. "We'll need him in fact."

"Should we be wary of him?" asked Areon watching the sea go by faster than he would have liked.

"Of course not." answered Reiquem brushing off the comment and continuing to stare at the map. "If it is in fact him."

"And why is that?" asked Areon trying to keep her attention.

"The only requisite for being a master is benevolence." she answered. Areon looked at her with raised eyebrows.

"They have to be good at heart, opposite of evil, all that." Reiquem tried. Areon just shook his head thoughtfully. "No master will take you as an apprentice if you are not."

"What??" she asked him vehemently, after seeing him shake his head.

"Well it's curious isn't it?" replied Areon. "I mean can you imagine the master of death a person good at heart?"

Reiquem shook her head in aggravation. "Death is a part of life." was all she would say.

"Right then, so we make our way to the Myriads house." Areon said, sensing tension and changing the subject.

"Yes, we must." answered Reiquem thoughtfully. "We'll tell him what's happened and I'm sure he'll go with us. Well, no actually I'm not sure."

"He has to," said Areon. "What'll we do without him?"

"We'll do it ourselves, I guess," replied Reiquem. "Now, we need to get there faster." she started grabbing some old rope and tying it around her waist.

"What're you doing?" asked Areon. She began tying it around his waist as well.

"We can both do strong wind magic, but I daresay we'll need to be tied to the boat to keep from pushing ourselves off of it," she said.

"I can't do that much, you'll have to do most of it," replied Areon. "I feel tired, and I don't want to risk anything."

"You can never be to careful with elemental magic," returned Reiquem seriously.

Areon helped her tie the old rope around his waist and then they tied a few tight knots to the main mast.

"Here we go …" said Reiquem.

"WAIT!" cried Areon. He quickly ran up to check which way the compass was pointing to make sure they blow themselves off course. He then used the ore to correct the catamarans direction and got ready to go once again. "Should be alright for a while I guess but we probably shouldn't go for too long without checking."

Reiquem thought for a minute. "Well the island is big enough so that we should hit it, but we'll check after some time unless it gets dark too soon."

They looked at each other and then held out their hands simultaneously. At once, two vortexes appeared which stood so close to each other that they combined almost immediately and began pushing the boat along at an incredible rate. Areon thought it a good idea that they had tied themselves up.

They were moving the boat until Areon finally lost track of time and decided to stop for a minute to check where they were. He had hardly done any of the work as far as moving the boat. Just when he was done untying himself they heard the noise of sand scraping against their boat and Areon was hurled forward by the sudden stop.

He did a flip from the center of the catamaran and landed on the soft, wet sand on his backside.

"Are you okay!?" yelled Reiquem who was still untying herself from the mast.

"Fine, I just landed on the sand," replied Areon. Reiquem ran over and looked over the edge of the boat down at him. She swung her body over the edge and landed next to him still holding the rope.

"Guess we got going pretty fast." remarked Areon who began to stand up.

"I'll tie the boat up," replied Reiquem searching for a tree. She found a solid looking one some way in and tied a strong knot that would hold for the duration of their visit to the island.

"That had to be some sort of record from the harbor to here," said Areon rubbing what he had landed on. He stretched out slowly and looked around. The island looked beautiful. It was not a tropical island by any means; probably because it was so close to the continent. Trees shrouded most of the land and the sand was a wet light brown color which stretched all the way to the turning of the land where it was impossible to see any farther. It looked like many grass paths were etched into the forests, but no wildlife seemed to be present at the moment.

"So you have come at last," said an unfamiliar voice.

"Who was that?" asked Reiquem.

"For now you may call me Myriad," said the voice.

A man walked along the shore making footprints in the sand and getting closer to Areon and Reiquem by each step. He had his hands behind his back. The man looked around middle-aged, perhaps slightly older and had on a deep purple robe with a pointed mage hat that had stars on it. The stars seemed to real to be on his hat. His nose was rather large and he looked quite content.

"Myriad," said Reiquem bowing a little. "I know of you, master of time."

"Ahh, master Reiquem." Myriad bowed a little, but none to low. "A young master, very young," he said as though she was too young to be so. "I expected to see you, but not this young man, who is he?"

"This is Areon." she replied.

"Areon," replied Myriad. "A name of the Old Days if I'm not very much mistaken. None now use it."

"Well I do," said Areon.

"You need to ask me many things and I you, but first we will go to my house and have some food as I'm sure you want and you can meet my ..."

"How did you know when we were going to be here?" asked Reiquem.

"When was easy, where was not. I knew you would seek me out some-day," replied the old man. Now come with me."

"But we don't have time ..."

"Time?" said Myriad turning around, his hands still behind his back. "There is always time ..." he said grinning and turning to continue walking. "And I hope there will always be time," he said chuckling to himself.

Areon thought him a bit eccentric.

They must've walked for about an hour before anyone spoke.

"Are we going to your house?" asked Reiquem out of the blue.

"Questions, questions." muttered the man they were calling Myriad. "Whoever asks the most questions will, without a doubt, be the wisest." he muttered to himself.

Reiquem was about to say something else when he cut her off. . "Yes, young master, we are going to my house," he said.

They walked until the sun started to set; Areon thought his legs would give out any minute. Myriad stopped and looked back at them with squinted eyes and then he lifted one eyebrow.

"Do we wish to get there tonight or would you like to sleep under the stars?" he asked.

"There is no way we can get to your house by tonight, according to our map," replied Areon.

"I did say earlier that their was always time, but I did forget to mention that for some that don't know how to use it, their may not always be time to do what you wish when you want," returned Myriad.

"What?" asked Areon very perturbed.

"Now once again," said Myriad seemingly irritated. "Do we wish to sleep on the ground or under a nice roof."

"I suppose a roo. ." before Reiquem could get her words out Myriad had begun saying words that were inaudible to both Reiquem and Areon. He made arbitrary gestures with his hands and then suddenly he made a movement with them outward that sent something toward all of them and made a circle around them. It was something that was there and yet it was not, something you knew was there but could not feel or see.

"Haste," said Myriad.

The world looked different to Areon. He was looking around at things that seemed to be moving entirely too slow. A bug on the ground looked like he was traveling an inch per hour. He stepped over to examine the bug and felt as though time had rushed him over there at a rate immeasurable. The day was going by too slow now. Areon could see the clouds moving the slowest they had ever moved. He could have beaten them in a running race.

"Throw this rock into the air," said Myriad breaking Areon's gaze upon the cloud. He handed Areon a rock. "And then go and catch it. Make sure to throw it as far away from you as possible."

"It can't be done," said Areon looking over at Reiquem who was in awe of the slow moving world. She watched a drop of rain fall off a leaf that was three spans from her and Areon saw her walk over and catch it. She had walked the distance and stretched out her hand in the time it took for a drop of water to roll off a leaf.

"Just do it lad." tried Myriad who had a curious smile on his face as though he was enjoying the bewilderment of the two of them.

Areon gripped the rock and gave it a nice throw, according to Areon's application of force the rock should have gone about three spans high and about ten spans away from him, but it did not. After he watched his arm fly by his face at the speed of sound Areon watched the rock linger only a span from him in the air. It was not moving the speed it was supposed to be moving. Areon looked at Myriad in amazement.

"Go and catch your rock." commanded Myriad. Areon did not even have to run to catch a rock he had just hurled away from himself. He started walking past the rock that was still climbing into the air. He walked to a place where he thought the rock should approximately land. And there he stood while the rock made its way over to him where he finally caught it with ease. Reiquem was in complete awe of the whole situation.

"You're amazing," said Reiquem.

"And we are all very late." answered Myriad. "Let's be off then, a brisk walk should do it. Areon and Reiquem would have very much liked to stay and fiddle around with the haste magic that they were in, but Myriad started walking away and as they had no other way of finding his house they followed.

Walking equaled nothing. The sun did not even seem to move as they walked for a half of an hour. Then an hour went by and another and still the sun did not seem to move. If they encountered an animal of some sort that tried to run from them it looked like it was in slow motion. They would catch up to it and have to walk around it. If Myriad pushed aside a branch that was in his way Areon and Reiquem would have time to watch the movement of the branch bending back to where it originally sat before they ducked easily out of its way.

Finally when the sun did seem to move a little bit the trio stepped out into a clearing and saw a small house that had many flowers and trees surrounding it. It was made of stone and had a chimney that billowed out smoke.

"Ahh good, here we are." announced Myriad. As soon as he said this the haste magic that had shrouded only those three seemed to disappear and time returned to normal.

Reiquem stopped, looked at the house and then at the map. "I don't understand …" she trailed off. "Why is your house on the map? And why does it say our house?"

"Map? Hmm, let me have a looksee eh?" he walked over to Reiquem and grabbed the map out of her hand and looked at it for some time chuckling now and again.

After he had done this he simply handed it back to Reiquem and looked away from her.

"And …" tried Reiquem.

"Hmm?" replied Myriad giving her a confused look.

"Well does the map maker live in this house, or did he, or what?" she asked exasperatedly.

"Live here?" replied Myriad. "Oh yes, yes yes, we do live here; this is our house."

"What?" asked Areon joining the confused conversation.

"This is our house," said Myriad throwing his arms toward it. "We live her and we made that map along with many others."

"We?" asked Areon.

"Me and my wife … Elm, er, Infinitia, as she likes to be called."

"What's with all this secrecy?" asked Reiquem who could not believe a master was treating her like a child.

"Well you see you haven't exactly proven to me that you are a master and I have proven it to you so therefore you have a right to trust me but I have no right to trust you, not to mention, on your little quest, you brought this young man who seems unfriendly enough," replied Myriad with a wide closed mouth smile on his face.

"You make maps?" asked Areon not paying any attention to the last comment.

"Of course," replied Myriad. "I'm old, not much else to do. Besides with the dragon king and …" he stopped and looked at the house. "Yes, well we have much to do, to show, to talk about, and I would like some tea so in we go for now. Welcome to our house."

# CHAPTER XXVI

# The Married Masters

Soon after, they all walked into the house. It had a wooden door with a golden knocker on it that resembled a half moon. As they walked into the house Myriad took off his shoes and set them aside, Areon and Reiquem did the same in order to be polite. A smell of hot food filled their nostrils as they walked along following Myriad. It was really a beautiful little house. While the outside was made of brick the inside walls were lined with wood which meant that somebody had built this house to last quite some time. Instead of a normal house where most rooms are square, every room in this house was different shaped. One room was octagon shaped, one pentagon, on looked circular, and another looked like a triangular shaped room. Areon walked by a spiral staircase that piqued his curiosity. It lead to a high upper level.

"Where does that lead to?" he asked. Reiquem gave him sort of an awkward look before Myriad turned around to see what he was talking about.

"Ahhh, to the observatory," replied Myriad. "Infinitia is a star gazer."

They walked into what appeared to be the kitchen and a woman who looked slightly older than Myriad, turned around from her cooking to see who had entered.

"Hello," she said simply.

"Good day," said Reiquem. "Hello ma'am," replied Areon at the same time.

She was fair looking and a tad skinnier than Myriad. She wore a robe that matched Myriads color only it had wings coming out the back. Her hair was brown and she had it done up for the time being in the kitchen.

"Well dears," she said. "You must be famished. You've come a long way." Reiquem and Areon looked at each other in silent agreement.

"We are actually," said Reiquem. Now that someone had mentioned it they had not eaten for quite some time and they did not eat a good meal since they left Lalvegeth.

"Well you're very welcome," said Infinitia. "What're your names?"

"I'm Areon." Infinitia cocked her head sideways and squinted a little bit.

"I'm Reiquem." Infinitia looked over at her husband inquiringly.

"Reiquem?" she said. "Very interesting. We have much to talk about but and I'm very sorry to ask this but you must prove to us you're a master. And if you're a master you will think that it's obvious that you should prove it. Especially now."

Reiquem nodded in approval. Everyone just stared at her. She did not seem to be doing anything out of the ordinary. After they looked at her a couple more seconds Myriad realized that all the shadow in the room had been bent to Reiquem's will. All of them leaned in towards her and hers ran all the way across the room and up the wall almost taking on solid characteristics.

"The master of shadow bending them all to her will." proclaimed Myriad.

"Excellent," said Infinitia. "I believe Myriad has proven himself to you, will that be sufficient for now?"

"Of course." Areon and Reiquem said simultaneously.

They sat down and ate the meal that Infinitia had been preparing. It consisted of chicken, and fresh vegetables that the two grew outside. Also strawberries and other fruits from the island were put on the table and Areon and Reiquem ate heartily, hardly stopping for a break to talk. They had fresh water and Infinitia smiled every time they asked for seconds. When they had finished eating Areon felt the fullest he had ever felt in his entire life.

"Now Reiquem," said Myriad. "You're name is symbolic of the song for the living which I'm sure you're aware of."

"I am." she replied.

"Are you also aware that not many in the world possess that name, or are parents given the right to name their children such names?" he asked politely.

"I was not aware of that," returned Reiquem. "I don't remember much of my childhood. I left my home when I learned my parents had been killed."

The married masters looked at each other slowly.

"What is your last name dear?" asked Infinitia slowly.

"Iferias," replied Reiquem. "Did you know them?"

"We knew them well." responded Myriad as he took his wife's hand.

"When did you leave your home?" asked Infinitia.

"How is this relevant?" asked Reiquem a bit flustered. "Do you not know why we have come?"

Myriad and Infinitia just looked at each other for a moment. Then Myriad stated. "I thought that you wished to learn of your parents death. That is why I was confused as to why you brought this young man, but I assumed he was for companionship on your travels."

"The sealer of the shadow has been broken, and the stone holding its essence is gone." cried Areon.

Infinitia whipped her head to look at Areon. "You will not say such things unless they are incontrovertibly true." she snapped.

"But it is the truth." Reiquem said standing up for Areon.

"All joking aside," said Myriad. "Is this the absolute truth?"

"Yes," said Areon and Reiquem together.

"This is terrible news at best," said Myriad. "We have much on our hands now. Responsibility lies in us, being masters."

"I will go with to the end if I may." bowed Areon. "I am not a master, but I am skilled in lower level magic and it sounds as though help is imperative."

"Of course lad," said Myriad. "Very brave of you indeed."

"Now for our real names as I feel I can trust you both, especially you Reiquem as we knew your parents well." announced Infinitia. "While we have feminine and masculine nicknames of an eternal nature, my real name is Elmyra Daridyn."

"While mine is Labert Daridyn." stated the man they earlier called Myriad.

"Labert and Elmyra Daridyn," said Reiquem memorizing their names.

# CHAPTER XXVII

## To the Observatory

When the dishes had been cleared and everything that Areon and Reiquem had seen and endured had been explained, everyone was on their way out of the kitchen Areon was taken aside by Elmyra.

"Areon I heard you showed some interest in the observatory." she stated.

"Well the staircase looked rather alluring," replied Areon honestly.

"Would you like to see what's up there?" she asked excitedly.

Areon looked at Reiquem.

"Go on," said Reiquem.

"Yes, me and Reiquem have some things to discuss as well." added Labert

"To the observatory then." Elmyra said as she took Areon's arm and Labert and Reiquem went around one of the many turns in the oddly shaped inner-house.

So up the winding staircase they went until they popped their heads up through a hexagon shaped floor that was the base of the observatory.

"Here we are," said Elmyra. They climbed the rest of the way up and walked around the railing that stopped one from falling down the staircase. Areon then looked up.

The ceiling above was hexagon shaped as the floor, but instead of being flat and made of wood it was made of something transparent and it slanted upwards revealing the heavens and all the stars in it. At the point where the glass should have met at the very peak sat a round object made of silver and other alloys. It was about a span in diameter and as it came closer to the floor of the room, within reaching distance, it got smaller until it was the size of ones eye. The thing was supported by various bars of metal that made it possible for it to swing at all angles making it possible to look straight up or directly at the horizon. Along one of the walls sat maps that had thousands of pins sticking out of them. Instead of maps of the earth though, these were maps of the heavens, the stars being cities. Along another wall was a desk and above it sat shelves of books on numerous subjects.

"I venerate the stars," said Elmyra as she gazed through the glass. She seemed to be saying it more to herself than to her guest. Areon nodded while still staring up. He did not realized what time it was and the stars all shone brightly.

"Well would you like to have a look?" she asked after a minute of beaming at the sky.

"A look?" asked Areon never having seen a telescope, at least one of this size.

"Yes just pull the lower piece down or push up to adjust it to your height." she replied.

Areon did so and looked into it. He jumped back and hurt his eyebrow a little as he hit the telescope. Elmyra laughed silently and acted as though it had not happened. Areon looked over at her in amazement and then back into the eyepiece. It had expanded the dots in the sky to a magnificent size. To Areon's surprise the gigantic head of the telescope swiveled smoothly as he walked slowly around the room taking in all the night he could. Often he would glance at he maps and see if he was looking at the same thing in the sky that was pinned down on the map. He did this for some time before Elmyra interrupted him.

"Amazing isn't it?" she said. "The planet we're on seems so big, yet it's only another one of those tiny specks that you're looking at."

Areon sat and took in her words. She pointed out many constellations and planets that looked like they were ordinary stars, yet colored red or yellow or blue. Just from the few moments he listened to the lady, he figured she and her husband were rather brilliant. At least they both seemed highly intelligent to Areon. He finally put the piece down and looked up at all of the stars as one again. Elmyra turned to him before they went down.

"The knowledge of how one could not want to be a master of the heavens eludes me," she said.

"You are in fact a master of space magic then?" asked Areon.

"Indeed." she answered.

"And how does this knowledge escape you?" asked Areon keeping the conversation.

"Imagine myself being able to control space, even if it was just around me in a diameter of a few spans," she said. "What if one could control all of that?" she said pointing up towards the glass. "It would be something to work for and if it could be accomplished it would be something for people to be in awe of."

"The ones that are aware of masters of magic are in awe of them." responded Areon.

"This, I think, would be in a greater way," she said.

Areon said no more; he would have to agree, at least from her perspective. He supposed it would be different if he were talking to Labert or Reiquem.

"What is the drawback to using master magic?" asked Areon. The question had been bothering him for sometime.

"You see none when you watch master Reiquem?" smiled Elmyra.

"None." he answered.

"While physical strain is present, the consequences are more dire than you can imagine," replied Elmyra sadly. "When we use our magic we use a part of the essence. When you see master Reiquem use shadow, she depletes some of it from the universe. We must use our powers scarcely, and if peace ruled the world, not at all. You see Areon, when a master uses their magic it transfers from the universe into their being."

Areon gave her a look showing that he did not understand.

"In Reiquem's case, when she uses shadow magic the shadow becomes part of her physical being and the aura of her body and soul. Reiquem has used shadow magic so often that it has seeped through her self and into her outward appearance: her eyes. They reflect the amount of shadow master magic done. Some masters have gone to the point of containing too much of their essence," said Elmyra.

"What is too much?" asked Areon a little worried.

"When the resonation of that person's essence is something along the lines of one of the gemstones themselves."

Areon was beginning to understand.

He smiled at her as she gestured for him to go back down the stairs seeing as how they had finished. The thought of master magic disturbed him.

When they made it back to the main level Reiquem and Labert were in the kitchen again, laughing over tea they sat drinking. They seemed to be getting along marvelously and Areon was quite fond of Elmyra.

"Well, I suppose we're all ready for bed," said Elmyra after a bit more laughter.

"Yes, yes I suppose so," replied Labert after getting up.

"I'll show you to your rooms." stated Elmyra. "In the morning we have much to do and more to discuss."

She led them up to another normal shaped staircase and led to a room that had one large bed in it covered with many quilts.

"Come wake us if you need anything we're only a room away," said Elmyra.

"Thank you for your hospitality and for showing me the observatory," said Areon as she left the room.

Areon and Reiquem snuggled up in bed and had a much deserved, and needed, comfortable sleep.

# CHAPTER XXVIII

## Sashethalest Irohalaproteidranasheth

When they awoke the next morning, the smell of fresh fruits and smoked meats filled the entire house. Areon and Reiquem walked down the steps slowly; they were still tired but had slept plenty. When they finally made their way to the kitchen they were greeted with a hearty ...

"Good morning," said Myriad. "Are we ready to break the fast of the night?"

"I am." responded Areon. "Please."

"Yes, please." Reiquem responded.

Elmyra, being the exquisite chef she was, had prepared eggs from the chickens outside along with all the fresh fruits they'd had the night before. When everyone was through eating Areon looked at them seriously.

"What are we to do next?" he asked.

"Well, I thought that would come up," replied Labert.

"We must make the journey to the temple of time first." Elmyra put in.

"But why?" asked Areon.

"To defeat the guardian, break the sealer and pilfer the gemstone!" exclaimed Labert.

"Myriad, I mean Labert," said Elmyra. "Sorry dear, but you're being silly about something serious, although he is right," she said looking back at Areon and Reiquem.

"It won't take us long my dear Infinitia, er Elmyra," said Labert mockingly. "I will put us in haste and we shall be there in no time."

"You'd think the shadow gemstone missing was good news the way you're acting." muttered Elmyra. And in a way, to Labert, it was good news; he was dreadfully bored as of late, although he would never say such a thing about the atrocity.

"We've sat around far too long my dear," said Labert looking at Elmyra. "We need some adventure in our lives again. What's it been 150 years?" Elmyra leaned over quickly and slapped Labert.

Reiquem and Areon looked at each other with wide eyes.

"Dears," said Elmyra changing the subject. "This will be a serious quest and many dangers will be involved. Myri-Labert and I will be fine taking it on alone."

"I'll not let them sit back and miss the most monumental adventure one could have in a lifetime." yelled Labert.

"But why!" cried Areon. Everyone stopped to look at him.

"What do you mean?" asked Reiquem.

"Why don't we just find the shadow gem and replace it?" said Areon a bit flustered. "It would be much more simple than finding the rest of the gems."

"You've never read the Historical Archives have you," said Labert slowly, his voice fading away.

"Never, so someone please explain." requested Areon.

After all had been said that needed it they began the long day of packing supplies and getting ready to leave the house, for Myriad it had been, apparently a long time. Many things were lain about and none of them had been put in bags, Areon was curious as to why.

"How're we taking all this?" he asked pointing to everything lying about.

"In this," said Elmyra holding up a small satchel that had laces around the top. It was about the size of Areon's water holder, no bigger than a hood on a cloak.

"You're serious?" asked Areon. There must have been a room full of things waiting to be taken.

Elmyra looked into her bag, muttered words inaudible, next she wove spells into the air, into space, and consumed the entire room and bent the space to her will, she turned everything impossibly minuscule, Areon felt himself shrink and all the walls shrank as he started to panic. The objects were then lifted and began filing into the bag, which, Areon failed noticed, had not shrunk like everything else, it was consuming most of their space which everything else needed little as they were all so small. The various items large and small were disappearing in the abysmal depth of the now large satchel. It was utterly amazing and when all was done being put into the sack, everything returned to normal without Areon even realizing what had happened.

"All packed up," said Elmyra swinging the now small again sack over her shoulder and walking out to get ready to leave.

After three days of sleeping at the Daridyn household, everyone formed a consensus that they should all leave, seeking the temple of time, the temple of space, and then seek other masters to help them finish the quest. The map was returned to the mapmakers and they took control of it, knowing better where the temples were and so fourth.

Elmyra took up her satchel, which now contained everything they would ever need, including all the things Areon and Reiquem had been carrying. The only thing Areon insisted on carrying was his magnificent bow slung on his back with the flat leather quiver under his cloak, and his ruddy old sword.

The masters he was with did not carry weapons at all.

"So our journey begins," said Labert as they all stepped out into the sunshine on the glorious day that was to ensue. They had gotten all ready and had a day of practice before leaving the marvelous little house that Areon had grown quite fond of. Him and Elmyra had spent a lot of time in the observatory while Labert and Reiquem spent time talking and planning.

"Haste," said Labert in a sneaky voice that caught everyone unaware. The group had no more than looked over at him when they were all moving impossibly fast again as Areon and Reiquem had done the many days earlier to now. They began walking and again the sun hardly moved as they went. Areon wondered if they could do this the whole trip and make it go by faster. His hopes were dropped a bit when he looked at Labert sweating heavily, his hands clenched at his sides and his knuckles white.

They continued on like this for some time. The land was quite beautiful. Most of the forests led to clearings with large jagged rocks sprouting up from the trees and hanging over beautiful rivers. Waterfalls and such were common, and with the spray of the rivers over the rocks, came rainbows.

"Look there!" shouted Areon. Everyone stopped on the rock they were on to look across the stream.

"What was it?" asked Elmyra worriedly.

"I saw a man, or a boy perhaps." answered Areon. "He was smaller than a normal man."

"I might know whom that one is," said Labert as he kept walking.

Before anyone had time to respond to this the person Areon had seen, sprang out from behind the forest wall, on the other side of the river, he was opposite the side Areon had seen him on, which Areon thought impossible for he had not been seen nor was he wet.

"Goodday Myriad," said a man approximately a span and a half tall; he might have gone up to Reiquem's height if lucky. He had dirty blonde hair that one could tell would have been brown were it not for constant exposure to sunlight that made his hair a bit blonde. He had pointed ears at the tips that were in direct contrast to human beings. His hair was a bit long, not as long as Areon's, and started to curl around the bottoms. He wore a green tunic and brown shoes.

"I thought that might be you lurking about all these river made rainbows, Sasheth," returned Labert.

"Oo're you're friends?" he asked.

"Reiquem, the master and Areon her companion," said Labert gesturing toward them. Then he added. "Sasheth is a leprechaun, a false gold chaser if you will."

"Sashethalest Irohalaproteidranasheth," said the leprechaun rocking back and forth on his feet. "You can call me Sasheth though if you're friends with Myriad here."

Reiquem and Areon were rather speechless.

"And by the by Myriad," said the leprechaun. "The gold is real." He walked over to the edge of the rock they were on and held his hand under a spray of water where gold appeared in his palm, when he removed his hand the gold disappeared.

"Only as materialistic as the rainbows you chase," replied Labert.

"Speaking of rainbows," said Sasheth. He was looking behind all of them where a rainbow had appeared and they all looked at the most beautiful rainbow they'd ever seen, the violet the most prominent color for the first time Areon could remember. When they looked back Sasheth had vanished.

"Someone had a dream about rainbows relatively recently?" asked Labert. "Its usually the only time he shows up."

Reiquem looked at Areon with wide eyes before they both saw that Elmyra and Labert were getting too far ahead of them and had to run and catch up.

# CHAPTER XXIX

## The Cherub of the Kingdom of Life

If one were to say that traveling with Elmyra and Labert would be like traveling with anyone else, they would be entirely mistaken. Time flowed mysteriously and the land seemed to be never ending while not taking up any of their time at all while they passed over it.

They only had to spend one night out in the wild but it was rather lovely sleeping on the edge of small forests while at the same time on the edge of rivers that flowed into jagged rock that occasionally lined them.

While everyone was lying down next to the fire that Labert had made while Areon gathered wood, Areon got up and decided to go and explore a bit. He walked out of the clearing the forest and up a small path that had silver rocks on either side. The rocks led to a square type of mountain that hung over the river. He decided to climb it, which proved more difficult than he initially thought. It took him around 20 minutes before he got to the top of the small rock structure, but when he did he realized that it was worth the time. He sat on the edge with his legs dangling, he could not see the riverbank, only the water, the sky looked as beautiful as it could, the moon shrouded by wisps of gray cloud. He leaned back and put his hands behind his head.

"Areon!"

Areon awoke on top of the same rock when the sun was coming up; he had not even realized that he fell asleep.

"Hellfire," he cursed. The others had probably been looking for him for some time.

"Areon." he realized it was Elmyra calling for him.

"I'm up here!" cried Areon with a cupped hand around his mouth. He got up and looked back to see Elmyra on the edge of the woods calling out his name.

She looked up at him and finally found where he sat. "What are you doing?!" she asked impatiently.

"Sorry." he laughed. "I fell asleep up here last night."

"We were worried something from the forest got you during the night," she said seriously.

"Sorry about that." he replied as he started to climb down which was much easier than going up.

When he arrived back at the campsite everything was picked up and ready to go. He put on his own things and apologized to everyone for holding them up.

"Quite all right lad." responded Labert. "Been up on that rock myself I have. Very lovely. Shall we?" And at once they all immediately began following the old master of time magic into the forest.

If peculiar was one of the many words to describe the temple of shadow then Areon knew no words that would describe the temple of time properly. They had been walking a few hours when into a clearing they went and a wall popped up in front of them. A wall made of forest and stone. It was the same type of square blocks that the shadow temple was made out of but they seemed infinitely older. The magic still coursed through them, just as strong, though not as vibrant, slower to Areon. Above what he knew was the temple of time, rested a clock. The clock itself looked ordinary, save the numerals of the old days. It was about a half a span in diameter although it looked smaller being above the doorway. But one thing stood out on this clock that Areon had never seen on any clock in the world. It had, instead of one set of hands, two sets. He had to watch for a moment to realize that one set of hands was spinning back time at an incredible rate, while the other was spinning time forward at the same rate.

"Here we are at last," said Labert. "Be wary of the guardian. It senses us, and will be the only thing we need worry about until we compromise or defeat it," he said at almost a whisper.

"Will it be a Dominion guarding this temple as well?" asked Areon in the same voice Labert had used.

Labert looked at him quickly. "No," he said with all seriousness. "It is much worse than the Dominion, the time temple, in a way, has been around longer than any other of the temples."

"That's not possible." refuted Reiquem.

"In its own way." whispered Labert patiently. "Time is one of the most difficult things to understand my dear."

"What will we face?" asked Areon, his whisper barely audible as his fear rose.

"Myriad of myriads," said something low and ominous from within the temple. "You have strayed too close before this, I will allow you to leave, but do so swiftly."

"We will not leave," said Labert becoming the master he was, straightening his back, making his face stern and speaking swiftly but carefully. "We seek the gemstone, although it is not in your nature to let us take it while you live, which poses a conflict."

"Indeed," said the low voice. "If you seek the gemstone you seek death. God alone can take the gems."

"We're not evil," said Areon.

"We don't have the time, but you must understand that we need the stone and do not wish to battle," said Labert. "Something evil precedes us on this journey, and it is imperative that we obtain a stone before it steals them all to manipulate them all for its evil purpose."

Before Areon could ask for the second time what the guardian was, it stepped out into view. The shape of a man, although it had four faces one, facing each cardinal direction. Everyone, save Labert, shielded his or her eyes upon his emergence from the temple. It was as though most of him was made of white light. When Areon finally adjusted to the thing's illumination, he realized that it also had two sets of wings. One set him in the air while the other revealed his faces.

"What is it?" asked Areon amazed.

"I am of the Cherubim," replied the being of light. "The second highest in the order of the nine. Your ender." As he did this, he seemed to flex his aura, and fire licked at all of the company in an act of malice.

Areon spat out three words of the old days after the display of the Cherub.

"Kireth! Nasai! Saeth!" he shouted as three huge balls of fire shot from his hand, leaving a gap in it that showed cauterized sides of his skin. He had done fire magic of the second degree. The balls of fire leapt out at the Cherub with purpose. As Areon sank to his knees, he saw his own fire magic hit the force field of fire magic surrounding the Cherub. They only absorbed into his being and it laughed cruelly at Areon's attack. His magic had consumed a substantial amount of his energy, and he felt like he could hardly stand.

"It begins," said the Cherub lowly. He raced out and hit Reiquem and Elmyra, knocking them five spans away with burnt clothing where he landed the blow. Areon could not even see him moving; he would seemingly disappear to attack one, then instantly after appear to hit them again. Areon knew he had made a mistake with his second-degree fire magic when the Cherub appeared in front of him. He stopped for an instant and spun his head around revealing all four faces that he possessed. Such a wrathful look was in them that Areon turned away. The being materialized a sword from his light enshrouded figure, which looked as though made of fire. Due to lack of energy, Areon did nothing. He wished he had not done second degree magic. It felt as though part of his soul was missing now.

Areon looked at Labert, who had his eyes closed.

"It's too fast for all of us," cried Areon, desperate and scared at seeing the faces of wrath as the being was about to strike with his flaming sword. Just then hope sprang into Areon's heart as Myriad seemed to finish his incantation. Instantly, slowing time master magic leapt from Labert to the Cherub. The sword was coming much slower now, and Areon was swift enough to duck out of its way even in all his fright.

The Cherub did not need to turn its head to look at Myriad. A face was looking directly at him already. But before it could do anything, Myriad had finished another incantation.

"Haste!" he cried, and the time master magic went to his three comrades. Labert had made the fight fair by using the essence of time to slow the Cherub and put his friends in haste.

The Cherub, outraged, swung again at Areon only to miss; Areon saw it slowly coming at him. He was moving faster now. Areon drew his sword and swung heavily at a wing. The Cherub leapt up and began flying with all four wings beating rapidly as he loomed overhead all of them. Areon began to draw his bow out of his scarlet cloak. He got it out and stealthily slid an arrow out of his flat, concealed quiver. He knew he could do no more magic, but his bow would help, he hoped. Then the Cherub saw him. It flung the sword of fire at him only to be surprised as Areon's cloak whipped up and formed a shield above him, instantly changing to an unbelievable size. The sword smote the cloak, but it held and the sword turned to nothing. The cloak began to decrease its size again as the Cherub watched. But as the cloak subsided, Areon held his bow with an arrow knocked. As the Cherub came into view, Areon loosed. The Cherub, surprised, used a wing as a shield as Areon had used his cloak. But the arrow wounded the wing and the Cherub was forced to come down. As he landed lightly, he ripped the arrow from his godlike feathers. Before he could do anymore, Elmyra was standing behind him, using the haste magic to its max. She wove her hands into the air, making the arrow disappear out of his hands, disappearing from space, and in the next second, it materialized in another wing, as though someone had shot another arrow through it. The Cherub grimaced with all four of its faces and turned slowly to face her. She had done the spell two more times by then, making the arrow disappear from the wing it was in and reappear in another. He was now incapable of flying and severely confused. The four of them was overwhelming him.

Next, Reiquem decided to take part. The material shadow that Areon had grown accustomed to formed behind her, and she sent it over her body into his flames; he was no longer bright; only on fire, but consumed by darkness. The fire barely had the will to live anymore under the thick shadows. Reiquem held her attack while she felt the flame suffocating. The four heads of the Cherub now faced his four enemies directly. Myriad was holding his haste spell on all of his allies while conceiving another spell for his enemy.

"Stop!" yelled Myriad. And so the Cherub did, albeit it was not of his own accord. He could not move or act in any sort of way; even his fire that still lived was a frozen flame.

Although the spell was highly effective, it was very hard to hold by the look on Labert's pained face. Sweat poured down his twisted features. He held his arms outstretched, but his knees were bent.

"Finish it!" he cried. "It will kill us!"

Reiquem gave all she had, and her shadow finally peaked and sent a solid black blade through the west cardinal face and out the east.

Elmyra closed her eyes, saddened, and made the arrow disappear and reappear in the north cardinal face.

By this time, Areon, who sat at the south cardinal face, had knocked another arrow and loosed it toward his enemy. The arrow flew true and the angel fell dead.

The four walked in towards their enemy, haste falling and shadow dissipating into the sunshine. Elmyra made the arrow disappear for good, but Areon left his in the south mark.

"He was asked to serve the Kingdom of Life by guarding this temple," said Labert ruefully. "The Kingdom of Life shares an alliance with the Nine Orders of Angels. They strive to protect the gems and keep the universe balanced. I fear we will encounter more of them."

"Can we survive all of the temple guardians of the order or otherwise?" asked Reiquem wearily.

"Although we are out to do good, the kingdom will not be on our side once this is heard of," said Labert, not answering Reiquem's question. "Now that we're doing it, I'm not sure we went about this the correct way, but I suppose we had no other choice." He looked at Reiquem. "I'm not worried about surviving anymore, master Reiquem," he said as tears welled up in his sage eyes. "Angels do not deserve to die …"

## EXCERPT FROM THE HISTORICAL ARCHIVES OF THE KINGDOM OF LIFE

" … The Nine Orders came only hither when we asked for them to come. Light, Life, Darkness, Space, and Time, even Death. Some worship these as essences, but God created them and God created the angels. We have the upper hand as they are with us. God has sent them. The nine orders of angels, called the choirs by some, as each order sings majestically, eternally.

The Ninth Order–Angels; beautiful beings. They guard the short life we have in this universe and seek to heal. Never sleeping and ever watching the human they were assigned to by God.

The Eighth Order–Archangels; warriors, illuminators, the divine messengers that carry envoys where they are needed.

The Seventh Order–Principalities; they watch over our nations, ever trying to keep in check our order and peace between the nation of light, which is necessary for the survival of the inner continents.

The Sixth Order–Powers; the threshold defense. They guard the layers of the afterlife with swords made of pure lightning. They also prevent fallen light energy to enter our world.

The Fifth Order–Virtues; they control star movement and bestow upon us miracles that are unfathomable. They are the shining ones.

The Fourth Order—Dominions; they have wisdom of the afterlife. They hold flashing swords. They constantly overshadow the other angels, making sure they do their duties that God has assigned.

The Third Order—Thrones; wheel-like beings with many eyes. They translate the law and make up God's chariot.

The Second Order—Cherubim; they have knowledge beyond reconcile. With a disposition that loves riddles. They are second only to the first order and have four faces and two sets of wings.

The First Order—Seraphim; the highest of the nine orders. They have four faces and three sets of wings. They are closest to God and must fly with their middle set of wings, cover their feet with their lower set of wings, and shield their eyes with the upper set of wings to be in the presence of God. Most find the Seraphim hard to look upon, as they seem to be made of fire …"

May the angels ever watch over us, keep us safe, and guide us through shadow in the afterlife.

# CHAPTER XXX

## The Temple of Time

It was nighttime now so the group decided to make a campfire outside the temple before going in.

Areon looked at Labert.

"Look, Labert, it's not our fault. We have to get the gemstones before, well, before whoever got the shadow gem," he said.

"I know," said Labert.

"I know, I know," said Labert sounding a bit better. "I think for the good of the universe, we must do what we are doing. If something gets the gems before us and lines them up in the proper order so that the resonation of all of the gems break free one of them, an unbalancing of the universe will occur. God will judge who did the good and who did the evil."

"Right," nodded Reiquem.

"Right," said Elmyra and Areon together, although Areon did not believe the whole God business.

"Let's all get some rest before tomorrow when we must enter the temple and then continue," suggested Elmyra.

So they went to sleep for the time being.

Areon and Reiquem slept well, but Labert and Elmyra stayed up late into the night, thinking and whispering.

At about sunrise Areon awoke from a night of iniquitous dreams. Labert was putting out the fire with a small bucket, and Reiquem sat eating a small breakfast. He stretched and started to get his things ready. As he was doing so, he walked the distance to the body of the angel of the Cherubim that was far from the campsite. When he returned, he looked over at the group.

"What's happening?" asked Areon, not taking his eyes of the place where the angel lay.

Everyone stopped what he or she was doing and walked over to look at what Areon was looking at. The angel seemed to be decaying but not in any grotesque or indignant way. It was as if it had turned to light and small dots of light were floating around lazily before rocketing skyward and disappearing.

"Angels are made of the light of God. His light will return where God will remake their consciousness." Labert smiled.

"Fascinating," said Reiquem.

"If you believe in that sort of thing," said Areon skeptically.

"It's right in front of your eyes, lad," said Labert. "No time for philosophical arguments. We must enter the temple now. Leave your things out here; they will be of no use."

Areon put down his things and waited for the others to lead the way.

When they walked into the temple, Areon realized that a staircase led the way at a steep angle, an almost dangerous one. They went in slowly, and Areon, in the back, made a small fire in the palm of his hand that lit the way a bit. They did not really need it, which was a good thing because Areon's hand still hurt from his antecedent attack on the Cherub. He let the fire die away as they went farther down.

When they got towards the bottom, one could see a lot more than, say, from somewhere at the middle of the enormous staircase. They walked into a large room with pillars standing out from the walls and surrounding the source of light.

They very essence of time stood at the back of the room, and Areon realized that the sealer of space was what illuminated the room. The gemstone was in their grasp. Areon almost had a greedy feeling inside him, a feeling to go and grab the stone.

An aura surrounded the gemstone, Areon could see. It was an aura of nothing really and yet, something infinite. Space magic was sealing the gem that bound the essence of time. It looked dark but not pitch black and had tiny specks throughout all of the darkness. The specks looked like moving glitter on a black surface shrouding the gemstone.

"Space must be countered with time," said Myriad. As he said it, he put his hands up over the darkness that looked like a brightly lit sky during the dead of night. He let magic pour out his hands; magic that he had been taught to master—time magic.

The space tried to stop him from doing so. It fought back, the lights turning to rods as though one were flying through space at the speed of sound, then the speed of light, and then beyond. The lights rushed fourth at Myriad, the master of time as he continually made them disappear with time. Time was eroding space before their eyes. Space was hurling itself forward as Myriad was killing it with time magic. He broke a sweat and began to breath heavily. Then, taking control, he pressed his hands down into the shroud of darkness, the sweat disappearing from his face due to the dark cold of outer space, and yelled out in an effort most have never known. The space began to turn to nothingness. The stars turned back to small specks, rather than traveling beams, and then began to twinkle and then to fade. The darkness turned to the light of the room, and in front of them sat the gem that held the essence of time.

Myriad stepped forward as he beamed at the gem. It was a grayish golden color inside a translucent orb that had a silver base to keep it from rolling. The base had small protrusions of the silver that crawled up the sides of the orb, wrapping around it as it keeping it safe. It is merely the size of an orange or apple, thought Areon. He had expected it to be much bigger.

Elmyra lifted it into the air and handed it to Labert. He took out a secretly kept satchel and placed it inside. When this happened, it looked as though nothing occupied the bag.

Labert noticed Areon's confusion.

"One of Elmyra's spacious bags. Should be able to fit all the gemstones in here." He smiled.

The room had darkened, and Areon felt they were no longer welcome. One by one they began crawling back up the steep staircase that led to the sunshine.

# CHAPTER XXXI

## The Forbidden Excavation

"Hmph," snorted the trespasser of the Mirrored Continent of Light as he read the words of the old days that were carved into the stone above him. Translated nowadays they went along the lines of: "Whosoever passes under this stone will be forever cursed by the Kingdom of Light. Whosoever excavates to any depth will be beheaded without trial. If one finds what one is seeking, in defiance of our land, they will be pursued by the angel of death. Azrael will find you sooner or later, and we will pray for the former."

The snort sounded in defiance. It was nighttime and none came to this place at night. Even the garrison did not stay at night. They were afraid to come back within a league of the place before sunrise. The sign was supposed to be enough to keep others out; most did not like the thought of being beheaded, but they abhorred ever seeing Azrael full of malice and vengeful wrath. All witnessed Azrael, but only a second before they died. Some said you could see him before you died but would never know, for he conceals his wings at all times, save when he brings a soul to heaven, or hell, for that matter. Azrael was not to be trifled with, but soon, soon the thing would get what it sought and it would be more powerful than Azrael himself.

Few in the universe would travel into the place after seeing the name.

But the thing moved on. The thought of being free moved him, gave him courage and strength.

———————◆-◆-◆———————

The land was barren all around, every cardinal direction for leagues covered in the driest of sand, but the spot where the stone carvings was built was plush, full of life and foliage. No one was quite sure why the trees and plants did so well here, but they cared little. All they knew was that it was unnatural in a place like this and they stayed away for fear of the unnatural, or perhaps for fear of what they knew lay buried.

The thing ripped at the branches and tore through the thick weeds and small trees until he came to two trees that hung. One hung to the west and another to the east, making an X in the air. The thing looked at the map, the map a wicked man had given him. Out of fear or desire for more wickedness, the thing did not care. The X marked the spot on his magical map. It laid a bent finger on the map and thought the words: The Black Wizard Cloak, and thus it appeared on the map, as it should. The being knew that the dark wizard that donned the Black Wizard Cloak hundreds of years ago had been defeated by the Seraphim on the Kingdom of Life's land, but the Kingdom had brought the body back to show that the wars were undoubtedly over.

The being dug for hours and hours not needing a shovel or a device of any sort for digging. Its fingers were bloody as it stopped for a moment to look at them. It forgot blood would come, but it had. Still it dug. Suddenly the ground he was standing on was below sea level, where it had once been spans and spans above. Still the thing dug with inhuman strength and determination.

Finally the ground became solid, and when digging began to fail, fingernails were broken. It stopped to look at its accomplishment thus far.

The tomb lay enshrouded by a thick barrier of light magic.

"He he ha ha." The thing laughed a cruel chuckle. Light. It only made the thing laugh now, when once, it banished.

It fell over the tomb and let shadow drip. The shadows were consuming every inch of light, killing it. It saw shadows from trees, from bushes, fall lifeless and swim across the ground to help kill the barrier of light.

Nothing could stop it now. Only Nothing could stop it now. After the barrier had been broken, he beat relentlessly at the rotting wood. It took little time to penetrate the coffin that was over three-hundred-years-old.

The body inside was merely a skeleton with a shiny black cloak that still hung around its neck. While the body turned to dust at a touch, the cloak looked as though someone had just made it.

It grabbed the cloak now and forced it over its head. This would have to do for now. He would manipulate this, as he did many other things. And people. He would manipulate the black wizard cloak to put an end to the kingdom of the thing it hated most: the light.

⇒▸•◂⇐

## EXCERPT FROM THE HISTORICAL ARCHIVES OF THE KINGDOM OF LIGHT

" … Kingdom of Light, once in days of old, referred to hereafter as the 'old days,' men and wizards were at war with one another, refer to Historical Archives of the Kingdom of Light, book twenty-one, pages 547–995 for farther details. During this time one particular wizard, whose name will not be printed in the Archives of the Kingdom of Light, left something that will be forever etched in our land and our minds after the wars were relinquished. A wizard with that kind of omnipotent power endowed upon him by nature or of some perfect power will undoubtedly never be forgotten in our time or our children's children's children's time, as it has been remembered throughout the ages thus far. He arrayed the Black Wizard cloak, which was the most significant nuisance, nay the bete noire of all men who fought the wizards so desperately for our land. A malevolent cloak it was, never letting us kill the wizard and killing men who tried. May the true black cloak stay buried with his wizard for all eternity.

The Wizard Scar; a canyon now that stretches for some thirty leagues from the beginning to the end. The scar is ever haunting our past while reminding us of our future. We were triumphant against the wizards, by victory of our own accord of theirs we will never say in hopes that wizards never turn against us again. But peace is ours at last, and we are reminded of that from the Wizard Scar. The magic that the wizard should never have used, a magic that killed the conjurer, the magic that caused many to perish during the battle that created the Wizard Scar, warriors, mages, and wizards alike. Deep in the earth and black it will stay for all eternity after the Seraph ended the last battle of the Kingdom of Life. May peace linger forever, and may men never have to endure something of that power ever again …"

May Light ever show us the way and give us illumination in the afterlife.

# CHAPTER XXXII

## Goin' Fishing

Not one of the party said much during the walk back. They had gathered up their things in silence and begun to walk. Labert had not used haste magic to speed up the journey. He was probably depleted of energy. And then, of course, there was what Elmyra had said about masters using magic, a scary thought to Areon.

Once or twice they stopped by the river that led to the Temple of Time. Labert had looked out of the water for some unknown reason to Areon. No one, yet, had said much. Reiquem and Areon held hands along the trip, and now and then they would stop and she would sit with her head on his shoulder, pondering as he was. Finally they figured out why Labert was looking at the water.

"Aha!" he exclaimed. Areon noted he was back to his old, eccentric self.

"I feel like fish tonight," said Labert after a bit more examination. They had been walking all day without food or rest.

Labert had his hand over his eyes to shield out sun, although the sun was not out. He was looking rather excited.

"Get the poles, dear," he said. Elmyra reached into her small bag and pulled out poles that were impossibly large for the bag.

Two were all they had, but Areon did not know how to fish. Belgraf and he had lived mostly on bread and meat. The meat was from Areon's bow hunting, which explained his unnaturally good aim and stealth with the longbow. Belgraf made the bread, and during some seasons they would grow vegetables, but not most. The apples were always a good source of food as well; they grew perennially throughout the years Areon had lived there. On some occasions Belgraf would send Areon into Wellenore to find good cheese. Belgraf loved cheese and a little wine.

Only then did Areon realize he was homesick.

"Reiquem, Areon, would you like to have a go?" asked Labert.

"I've never fished," replied Areon.

"And I never will," said Reiquem obstinately as she sat down on a rock and began to think more in depth.

"Well, then, Areon, nothing ventured, nothing gained," said Labert handing him a pole.

"What?" asked Areon. But Labert was already tossing in his line. The river was flowing slowly and the water was so clear, one could see the trout swimming against the current.

Labert had dug up a couple worms and Areon put one on his hook.

It did not take long before all four of them were sitting around a camp-fire—compliments of Reiquem because Areon's cauterized holes were still healing—eating trout. Even Reiquem, who would not participate in the diversion from their excursion.

"Very good, dear," said Elmyra trying to lighten the mood.

"Yes, and thank Areon, I believe he caught one more than I," said Labert humbly.

Areon chuckled with a mouthful of fish. It really was very good.

After they all ate their fill, Areon got up and got his pan, which he took to the river and filled with the cold water. When he returned, he sat down against a tree and dipped his hands in slowly while relaxing his head against the tree.

"Dangerous lower level magic you did, my boy," said Labert, not wanting to leave Areon's sacrifice unnoticed. "From the look of your hands, a third degree fire magic spell would have been the end of your life source, which you know, of course, would've meant the end of you."

"Yes, I am well aware," said Areon. He felt like a child.

"An attack that shows you were scared and are brave," said Elmyra.

"I suppose, yes, that would be correct," replied Areon, wishing they had not brought it up.

"Speaking of unusual magic," said Areon changing the subject. "Can either of you two disappear?" asked Areon nodding toward Labert and Elmyra, who were now against a tree cuddling up together.

They looked at each other.

"No," they said in unison.

"Why do you ask?" asked Labert.

"Reiquem can," returned Areon, looking at her.

She looked annoyed.

"Now that's dangerous magic," said Elmyra. "I pray you haven't done it more than once."

Reiquem shook her head. "Only the time my master showed me where the Realm of Disappearance resides."

"We lied for your sake, Areon," said Elmyra. "We can both disappear."

"I don't understand," said Areon shaking his head at Reiquem and the other masters.

"You see, lad," said Labert. "When one learns to disappear, they don't really disappear; to disappear would be to become Nothingness. Instead one goes to the Realm of Disappearance."

"And that is …" asked Areon.

"Obviously the realm where everything goes when it 'disappears," he replied.

"Parallel dimensions," said Elmyra. "Except the Realm of Disappearance contains nothing except things that have gone from this dimension to that one."

"And how does one learn to get there?" asked Areon intrigued.

"By going with someone that knows how to get there," said Labert. "No one knows any other way, so if everyone stopped going and stopped showing the way, then the Realm of Disappearance would never be gone to again, which would be for the better."

"And why is that?" asked Areon.

"Well, put simply," replied Labert, "the Realm of Disappearance eats up time unlike this realm. To go there for a second would mean you left this dimension for days, sometimes months. To go and stay there for a day, you would come back and all the life you knew would be gone and new life would've already replaced it. A scary place, lad, but some do find it necessary to go to now and again."

"Interesting," said Areon almost wishing he could go there for a second or so.

"Let us hope we do not need to go there on our journey," said Elmyra.

The group sat in silence for a few more minutes before Reiquem spoke up.

"I've been doing a lot of thinking on our quiet trip back," she said.

"Yes," said Labert.

"In order for the gemstones to be a threat ..." she started.

"I was hoping those wouldn't get brought up for some time," groaned Areon.

"In order for them to be a threat, they must all be together; a certain closeness is need for a threat," she continued. "We really only needed to be swift in collecting one gem; now the rest will be safe no matter who has them because they will always be looking for all of them or none, so obviously they want all if they obtained one."

"Very good, master Reiquem," Labert responded. "Haste was needed but now it is not, although we will not abandon swiftness in our mission, we do not need to hurry as we did."

"Unless, of course, whatever it is that killed the Dominion comes looking for us and the gemstone we took," said Areon.

"We will stay at the house until we have a group consensus that we should go to the Temple of Space; nothing will find us," said Elmyra. "Now let us sleep."

And so they did.

# CHAPTER XXXIII

## The Dragon King

When the party emerged through the final group of bushes and trees that blocked the way to the Daridyn's house, Elmyra picked up the pace and rushed inside before any of them could say anything. Areon realized she was going to hide the sacred gem, perhaps do some magic on it to keep it in place.

Areon went around back to the well and retrieved some water with an old bucket. Reiquem and Labert went inside.

When Areon came back in, he poured half the cold water into a basin and left the rest for drinking. When he was about to go look for Reiquem, Elmyra almost ran into him.

"There," she said exhaling heavily. "The gem is safe for now. And while one is safe, as Reiquem pointed out, they are all safe. Now let us relax and gather our thoughts."

Areon followed her into the main room of the house, which had a bunch of furs sprawled out across one side of the floor and on the wall to provide for a comfortable sitting or lying position. A few other chairs were set out with furs on them as well. In the corner was a fireplace and chimney. All in all it was the coziest-looking room. Labert and Elmyra sat down on the chairs and Labert sighed heavily. The fire was already going; someone must have done the magic before he got there. He did not feel like doing any. The cauterized holes in his hands were now the size of silver pieces. He almost felt like getting ready to start sparring with elemental magic again, but not today.

"Oh, before I forget," said Elmyra standing up and reaching under her garments. "A panacea." She handed Areon a small bottle full of a white liquid. "It should heal your hands."

"Oh, thank you," replied Areon taking the bottle and drinking it all in one gulp. It tasted horrible but had a tinge of mint to it. "Ahck," he said sticking out his now white tongue. He could not help it.

"I know," said Labert. "Tastes horrible. My wife has made me drink it a time or two."

"Where do you get panacea?" asked Reiquem. As she said it, she noticed the holes in Areon's hand close up. "Surely you can't make it?"

"No, a family of alchemists lives on the island," returned Elmyra. "They sell to us and Lalvegeth, along with other major cities and small time, trustworthy mages."

Areon then sank into the furs and fell into a deep slumber.

———————➤●◄———————

When Areon woke up, Reiquem was lying beside him with her hand on his chest. He put his hand on hers and squeezed lightly enough so that she would not wake.

He got up slowly and did not move around much and then walked out of the room into the kitchen. Elmyra and Labert were absent. He walked out the front door and around to the back where they were sitting on a porch that sat out a long way from the house, watching the sun come up.

Areon had slept a long time even though it was only morning. He walked up and sat on a chair beside the two masters. They said nothing as they watched the orange sun rise into the white clouds.

———————➤●◄———————

A month passed before Areon would have guessed two weeks had gone by. The four had spent the days fishing (Labert taught Reiquem how), and stargazing. Areon and Elmyra's friendship had grown quite strong. She sensed that the boy was very good at heart and very strong. His aura, coupled with his abundance of life source, said these two things on their own. But while Areon and Elmyra had grown to be friends as Labert and Reiquem had, Areon and Reiquem's love grew for each other. They spent much of the nights walking out into the forest hand in hand, laughing and talking over their journey. It was all in one of the best times in Areon's life. He felt that although the unspoken love between he and Reiquem was mutual, he should voice it before they left to their next destination, which Areon chose to forget about for the time being.

"A month has gone and we must depart," said Labert. Reiquem and Areon had been sitting in the kitchen having a small bite to eat; hot bread fresh from Elmyra's kitchen.

"He is right." Areon had not noticed Elmyra standing behind Labert.

"And where exactly do we go?" asked Areon, less than thrilled at the prospect of leaving.

"Areon, do you remember when we discussed my wife and I making maps?" asked Labert.

"Yes, of course," replied Areon.

"I suppose you haven't seen enough of the world or lived long enough to know of how one might map so accurately in such little time," remarked Labert.

"I suppose not," returned Areon a bit annoyed.

"Neither have I," said Reiquem, habitually taking his hand.

"Have you ever heard of the Dragon King?" asked Labert.

"Leviathan?" asked Areon laughing. "It is a myth, a fabrication of some explorer, nothing more."

"He is real," Elmyra snapped looking angry. "We can summon him, Areon," said Elmyra seriously while not looking at him.

"According to the Archives of the Kingdom of Life, summoners are extinct," stated Reiquem.

"Elmyra is the last of their kind," said Labert sadly.

Areon and Reiquem were at a loss for words.

"Can you guess why I am a summoner, Areon, Reiquem?" asked Elmyra sounding equally sad.

"We need Leviathan to get to the temple of space," hinted Labert.

"The Temple of Space is in the heavens," said Areon wisely.

It took everyone about a week to be entirely prepared for the trip. They were going to head west and sail across the sea via Areon's boat.

When all was said and done, everyone felt pretty confident about leaving the homestead of Labert and Elmyra. No one brought much with him or her. Areon left his bottles and nets and walking stick at the house, but decided it best to take his bow and sword. Some other insignificant things were taken, and Areon assumed Elmyra held the satchel that housed the magnificent gemstone of time. The party walked to the north side of the island where Reiquem and Areon had initially landed. The boat was still in tiptop shape. Apparently not too many people visited the island.

Areon undid the rope that Reiquem had tied to a sturdy tree. He sat and looked at the sand where the boat sat and recalled when he had done a flip out of the boat upon running into the island unaware. The sand had washed up around the small catamaran, making it difficult for the party to set sail.

He chuckled to himself.

---

"Set us for a westerly course. It will not take long," shouted Labert. They were all in now, and the wind was blowing hard, making waves and drowning out their voices.

"How far must we travel?" Areon shouted back.

"We go into the uncharted lands to the south for some time before running into Leviathan's island, which is mapped," shouted Labert.

"The uncharted lands?" said Areon, a bit startled. "Are you sure you know where we're going?"

"Of course he knows," joined Reiquem. "He made the map." She laughed as she whipped her head so that her hair was blown out of her face. Areon watched her for a while in silence. She really was beautiful. Areon shook his head and looked into the wind as well.

"Are we ready to get there, or do we wish to enjoy the sea air all day and night and another day and night?" asked Elmyra.

"Let us begin," replied Labert. He began tying a rope around his waist, leaving much extra. Elmyra took the extra and tied it to her waist. Areon and Reiquem did the same. When they were all linked together, they took the sturdy rope and tied it to the main mast.

The four of them gazed into the west. They were around the island heading southwest into the uncharted lands to head into the sea that led back to the charted areas and Leviathan's island.

All four raised their hands at once. A monstrous vortex of swirling air appeared as the combined efforts made immense amounts of wind magic form behind the boat. It took little effort by each individual, but the combined effort meant that they would be traveling at four times the speed that Areon and Reiquem had made the boat go.

Almost dangerous in a boat this size, thought Areon.

When this had gone on for some time Areon started to feel the life source within him deplete a little bit. It was not dangerous, but he was startled to feel the symptoms of fatigue.

"Keep it up, lad!" shouted Labert, giving an extra push of his aura to show he was trying hard as well. The boat went fast, very fast. Areon could not believe how far out into the uncharted sea they were. Areon kept trying hard. Finally, one by one, the group started getting too tired to continue. Reiquem and Elmyra quit first and untied themselves before sitting down to make sure not to get blown overboard.

Surprisingly, Labert quit next. Areon was the last mage to keep the wind magic going.

"Very good, lad," remarked Labert. "The wind had calmed down a bit now and they could all talk at a normal volume. You've almost got us there."

But it turned out Labert had been joking. The group sailed on for the entire day without seeing an island, and when night fell, they all were forced to sleep on the cold boat.

The next morning the group got up and ate a silent breakfast comprised of dried meat and bread from Elmyra's kitchen. When all was eaten, they regained more strength and continued to use the vortex of wind magic to keep them headed in a westerly direction and towards the island of Leviathan. They could travel at a much faster rate opposed to the walking they had done. Areon knew they had traveled back west far enough to be the distance west of his and Belgraf's house that they had been the distance east. And so it went for two more days until they were all finally getting tired of sailing.

On the fourth morning Areon turned his head and dropped his hand. He could see a relatively small island approaching.

Leviathan's island.

Areon had no idea what to expect to all come out of this. What do dragons eat? he thought to himself. Where do they hide? The latter question was answered as he looked farther into the island. A single small mountain stood with smoke curling up from the top.

"His bed," Elmyra murmured.

After all of them got out of the boat, they walked up the sandy beach into a barricade of palm trees. Immediately after followed the foot of the small mountain and what was apparently Leviathan's resting place. Smoke still came out in breaths.

The entire company moved surreptitiously through the foliage. As they walked farther on to where they could actually touch the side of the mountains, trees became sparser and rocks more abundant. Now the ground was rocky and hard to travel over. They had to walk over these rocks up farther and farther to get to the very side of the mountain. It smelled of campfire, the walls golden brown as though they had been slow-cooked for centuries.

"Stay here," said Elmyra shortly. They had apparently come to some sort of entrance. Areon did not notice due to the fact that he was trying to stay balanced while walking over the sharp rocks.

Elmyra disappeared into a large fissure in the mountain.

After some time of waiting, Areon finally sat down on one of the flattest rocks he could find and said nothing. Before long, Labert and Reiquem did the same. When Areon tired of sitting, he got up to inspect the mountain a bit. He walked out from the base of it and looked toward the top. It had a giant hole as far as Areon could tell. As if someone had built a mountain and then taken a knife and chopped off the top …

Areon could hear muffled shouting inside the mountain. He ran over to the fissure where Labert and Reiquem were also eavesdropping. Before long, Elmyra emerged. She breathed out with her lower lip curled up to blow her unmanaged hair out of her face.

"He's being stubborn as always," stated Elmyra.

"I'll go in with you the second time," offered Labert.

"I have to go in and see this," cried Areon.

Everyone looked at him.

"Please," he added.

"Very well, we'll all go and see if that does not arouse his curiosity enough to help us," said Elmyra. "Be very careful of what you say to him. Do not, under any circumstances, insult his intelligence. Do not let him think that you think that you're smarter than him. No sarcasm. He hates to be patronized. He hates condescension. Act humble. Show respect."

"Perhaps we should not say anything?" said Areon.

"That may be a good idea," replied Labert "But answer him if he asks you a question."

Into the fissure the four went. It took a longer amount of time for Elmyra to get to the center of the cave because Areon and Reiquem were walking so slowly, so apprehensively.

They had to travel down a smoothly cut walkway that was about the perfect height for a little less than fifteen spans due to the winding of the tunnel. Areon noticed that the walls were charred.

When they emerged into light, Areon saw and believed. An entirely azure dragon sat curled up in a ball facing the wall opposite of the one they had come out of. He was as big as Belgraf's house. Areon could not tell from his position now, but he guessed his wingspan to be four times as big as Belgraf's house. His scales shimmered in the weak sunlight as the dragon drew in deep breaths every seven to ten seconds. Areon sat amazed and watched for quite some time. Finally the silence broke.

"Who is this you've brought with you?" said a low, menacing voice. It sounded human, save the volume.

"Our company," said Elmyra. "Reiquem and Areon."

The dragon turned a giant head to face them. He looked extremely flexible. Leviathan only opened one eye as he turned his head and shut it again immediately, as if he did not want them to know he looked.

"And you know Labert," added Elmyra.

"Unfortunately," replied the dragon.

"I ask you again to help us, Leviathan," said Elmyra firmly. "We need to get to the Temple of Space. You're the only who can reach it."

"Am I?" said Leviathan sarcastically. "I doubt that is the case." He whipped his body around and launched his head forward, getting within a span of Elmyra's face. "Find other means, human!" he yelled. Everyone in the party fell over on their backsides from the forceful voice.

Elmyra got up. Areon and Reiquem stayed on the ground. Labert finally arose and dusted himself off.

"We need you're help, Leviathan," pleaded Elmyra. "The world is in danger. The universe."

"Good," replied Leviathan, settling back down. "We could use a little chaos."

"You don't understa—" Elmyra stopped and shut her eyes.

"I don't understand?" smirked the dragon. "Yes, how could I understand the ways of humans? After all, you have such profound intelligence." He stared at Elmyra. "I don't think you understand that God will destroy me completely someday, whether it be tomorrow or a thousand years from now, so it matters little to me what happens to this universe."

Areon noted his dangerous way of sarcasm.

"Leave this place, or I shall dine on your flesh," said Leviathan seriously. "Are you not scared, boy?"

"Me?" asked Areon.

"You will learn to fear me in time," stated the Dragon King as he reeled up one large five-fingered dragon hand with long sharp claws.

"Enough!" yelled Elmyra. "I summon you, Leviathan! Fulfill your sworn duty to me now!" The dragon's hand stopped in air. It seemed as though he could not move. Elmyra had used her summoning abilities, and now Leviathan had no choice but to obey her command. The dragon let down his hand and burst forth from the musty smelling cave. The four ran out of the fissure as fast as they could, following Elmyra. Leviathan's long body streaked through the air and dived into the sea for a moment before emerging and shooting upward. He then opened his wings to reveal their immense size and roared a mighty roar toward the party, showing that he was forced to play a part he did not wish to. His long body and large claws reminded Areon of a monstrous lizard with shiny blue scales and enormous wings.

"Light bones and large wings," said Labert to himself. "We can travel anywhere with Leviathan."

# CHAPTER XXXIV

# The Throne of Space

When Leviathan had been calmed down and had landed, Areon noticed that he did not talk to them much after, which was fine with him. The group walked all the way back to the sandy part of the island so that Leviathan had enough room to get down and lay flat so they could all get on his extremely rough, scaly back. Areon stopped before getting on.

"He cannot let us fall now, Areon." Elmyra held out her hand. He climbed up. He realized how much he now trusted Elmyra and Labert. He'd always trusted Reiquem.

The top of Leviathan's back was easily large enough for the four of them to sit; Areon just wondered what would keep them from falling off when the dragon took off.

"How do we stay on?" asked Areon nervously.

"Leviathan will fly in circles until we reach the temple," replied Labert. "It will be a slow ascent but necessary due to the fact we have no saddle."

"I will not let you fall," said Leviathan, picking up his complaining. "We're off." He launched into the sky from simply pushing off the sand with his hands and feet. His large wings started beating against the still air. The noise they made was incredible. Areon tried to grab onto something but found it rather difficult to claw onto smooth scales.

After sometime of panic, Areon realized that he would be okay. The flat of his back was rather large and with him flying in a slowing ascending spiral, it would be difficult to fall off.

"What is the purpose of this trip, oh myriad of myriads?" asked Leviathan mockingly.

"Someone has managed to steal the shadow gem," replied Labert, ignoring the comment. "We must find the rest and move them to safety."

"Why did you not simply find the one who liberated the shadow gem?" enquired Leviathan.

"We decided to be a step ahead at all costs, rather than a step behind, if possible," returned Labert.

"Impeccable thinking," stated Leviathan. "I do wish humans' cerebral cortexes would enlarge."

"Our what?" said Areon and Labert at the same time.

"Don't try to understand everything he says," answered Elmyra.

"Of course, don't," returned Leviathan as the wind carried his voice away. "You might learn something."

Areon found his backside starting to become raw along with his hands. The scales were the hardest, roughest things he had ever felt before. The monotonous beating of Leviathan's wings caused them to come up ever so slightly each push down, and it was starting to hurt.

Despite the aggravation on his skin, Areon could not believe his surroundings. The wind was becoming stronger as Leviathan flew higher and higher into the clouds.

Areon couldn't believe he was flying on a dragon. The dragon. Probably the last dragon left. Areon dare not ask. He never believed in such things. Magic was one thing. The sun was setting about now, and before Areon knew it or realized it, Leviathan had soared above the clouds. It was like a white barrier underneath them. Wisps of clouds played around Areon's face now and again, but for the most part they remained in the veil that surrounded the earth. It was beautiful. Areon almost forgot they were headed to the Temple of Space until he saw it.

A giant wheel covered in eyes; human eyes, unblinking human eyes.

Areon jumped up and almost fell off the dragon. He did not even realize Leviathan had stopped flying in circles. He was staying in one place with his wings beating to keep them above the layer of cloud cover.

Areon stood up and looked around. He could see it now, the Temple of Space. Far off into the distance toward the horizon, yet still suspended in space. It wasn't moving, and Areon had no idea what made it hang in the air the way it did.

Silence greeted these thoughts.

Areon returned his gaze to the many-eyed wheel that sat suspended about thirty spans from Leviathan. Fire licked the open air around it. It was as though the wheel used fire as wings; fire to suspend it self in midair. Sullen flames that knew these five were after the gemstone that contained the very essence of space.

"Leviathan, you will fight with us," commanded Elmyra. "Do not let one of us fall."

"As you command," said Leviathan; he had not torn his gaze from the wheel, the guardian.

Areon looked down at the dragon. Leviathan had never acquiesced to a request so easily since Areon had met him. He distrusted the dragon, and he looked at him with incredulous eyes.

"We haven't had a chance to voice our thoughts or our circumstance—" Labert started to say, but before he could get the words out, the wheel lunged at them with marvelous speed. From its distance, the aim was impeccable. The innumerable eyes took credit for that.

Leviathan whipped higher into the air, pressing the party flat against his back. The whole party, save one, Reiquem, who was now falling.

The combination of the upward thrust and Reiquem's position on more the side of the back sent her falling down into the clouds and to her inevitable death.

"No!" cried Areon. He looked down at the clouds and saw Reiquem's arms and legs spread out, a look of terror on her face. She was going to die, Areon knew, as she disappeared out of sight through the layer of clouds.

"Leviathan, go and get her!" screamed Areon.

"I did not let her fall," yelled Leviathan. "As I was commanded to do. I will not serve you."

Elmyra was toward the back of the dragon. She had not realized what was happening. Labert was staggering across trying to get to her as she fought off the deadly wheel of fire and eyes. Neither of them saw Reiquem fall.

There is no time for this, thought Areon. He leaped off the end of the dragon's back to what would be his own death, as well as Reiquem's.

Areon kept his legs and arms pointed straight as he raced down, gravity pulling him fast. Tears streaked across his face though his eyes were closed. He would be traveling faster than Reiquem. He remembered Belgraf and all he had been taught. Instead of thoughts of his death and Reiquem's, he thought of life. He reached into his own life source and beyond. He reached out to his aura. He reached out for what might be the last time. He forgot the wind in his hair, the sinking sun at his back. He even forgot the reason he jumped. He felt deep within himself and pulled outward, pushing everything that composed his being, his immaterial being. Areon felt for Reiquem's aura. He felt it as he reached out for her and felt her falling underneath him. He felt it as he grabbed her in midair, halfway between the Temple of Space and the planet. Then he unleashed all that he had been digging down for. He unleashed his aura, the warmth; he unleashed it all down and propelled the two of them upward, back toward the fight. His love had saved them. His love for her had unleashed new depths within him.

Now, he only felt hate.

As suddenly as he had stopped in midair, he began to climb back up. He raced through the sky, through the clouds that shrouded the earth, his cloak flapping relentlessly in the air. He held Reiquem in his arms, and she held him tightly around the neck. Only then did she realize that she had no idea what Areon was doing. He should have set the two of them down and left the fight up to Labert and Elmyra. They had been through enough.

But the love that he had felt had all but turned to anger and hate. He felt vengeful. Reiquem began to get scared when Areon kept gaining speed as Leviathan and the Throne came into view. It was impossible to tell if the throne was facing the mighty azure dragon or Areon. Its eyes watched east, north, west, and south. The wheel did not move when it saw Areon's look of hate. Areon did not stop when he saw the wheel's ominous eyes. Areon pushed all he had, all his energy toward the Throne.

Labert and Elmyra watched as a something scarlet hurled up toward the Throne they had been so desperately fighting. They both gasped as they realized what Areon was doing. Leviathan flapped his wings indifferently. They had both taken Reiquem for dead and figured Areon attempted suicide to die with his love.

"Thank goodness," stated Elmyra.

"Incredible," said Labert.

They had been wrong, at least at first. They realized Areon was now flying, and he had saved Reiquem. But only to kill her? It made no sense.

Areon continued his suicidal course toward the Throne that protected the essence of space. Areon continued even as Reiquem began to yell for him to stop. She was helpless. She could neither fly, nor stop Areon from crashing into the wheel at full, flying speed. Areon still continued his course as Labert and Elmyra yelled from atop Leviathan for him to stop. Areon continued his course as he saw the flames enlarge to engulf all around. Areon continued his course after his magnificent cloak formed a solid sword of scarlet above him and Reiquem and cut the Throne in twain.

# CHAPTER XXXV

## The Temple of Space

Elmyra, Labert, and Areon were now all safely inside the temple of space. The suspended temple held their weight without wavering in the slightest, albeit nothing seemed to support it.

No one had said anything about what Areon had accomplished. He had not even said anything about it. He only felt rage at the thought of Reiquem being thrown off Leviathan's back to die from gravity. Reiquem had decided to stay on the back of the dragon as he stood perched on the edge of the front of the Temple of Space. Areon followed as Elmyra and Labert led the way in.

The Temple of Space was not unlike the Shadow Temple. The Temple of Time had led them underground, while the Temple of Shadow and Space had an even floor with many pillars inside. Elmyra knew what she had to do apparently. She walked right up to the sealer without hesitation.

Areon remembered Reiquem talking about the sealers. According to her, no one knew how to break them, but apparently these masters did. He wondered if all the masters knew how to break the sealers, save Reiquem. She was relatively young, especially for a master.

"It really is amazing in here," remarked Areon.

"Quite," replied Labert.

"Quiet," commanded Elmyra. They had walked to the back of the great temple and were now able to behold the sealer of time in all its magnificence.

Areon could not quite explain what the sealer looked like. It was just erosion, a mass of erosion. Time hung over the gemstone of space. Elmyra reached her hand over it. As she had replaced the arrow in space, she was now replacing the time sealer with space. It was as though the time sealer was hungry for space. It was hungry for something to destroy and Elmyra was supplying that. In the end the time sealers own lust for space was its end as the time was destroyed and the gemstone remained for the taking.

It was a beautiful thing. Areon gazed at it in wonder. It had the same silver base as the gemstone of time, except this silver swirled underneath it to form many rings under a ball. Inside the ball sat many tiny glimmering lights that looked like the sky on a clear night.

"Beautiful," marveled Areon.

"We should go," returned Elmyra. "The dragon king grows impatient." She took out her satchel from her garments and stowed the gemstone inside.

"I have a question," said Reiquem. "Why did we not leave the rest of the gems alone after we obtained one?" They all now sat on the back of Leviathan.

"It is complicated," replied Labert. Areon looked over at him. "The world wasn't as populated when the stones were placed in temples. Not near as populated. These temples and the guardians were all it needed. Now the world grows and humans multiply. With this enlarging number comes a greater chance of some being evil."

"And that means?" asked Areon.

Labert looked at him seriously. "It means the gemstones need to be found and put in a safer place, a place where no one will ever be able to obtain them again. It should have been done two centuries ago, but apparently God left the task to us."

Areon turned his head from the conversation, letting the wind blow his hair back. He looked toward the place where he had destroyed the Throne. Even as Leviathan made the descent Areon could still see the floating lights coming off the Throne, as if light were decaying. It was being sent back to heaven to gain a new consciousness, and that was a good thing.

# CHAPTER XXXVI

## Unexpected News

Areon watched the sun go down from atop Leviathan as the dragon landed on his sacred island. He had been kind enough to give them a ride back. Areon hoped he would be kind enough to give them a ride to the island where the Daridyns lived. After his antecedent attitude, Areon did not figure it would happen.

It was dark now. As soon as Leviathan let them off, he took off again to rest in his mountain. The mountain, which had been smoking when they arrived on the island, was now still. Areon watched as Labert went to gather wood. Areon gathered some small, dry brush and did a small amount of elemental fire magic to start a fire. Elmyra and Reiquem sat and watched. After a small amount of silence, they both stood up and walked to where Areon sat.

"We need some time," said Reiquem as Areon stood up.

"What's wrong?" asked Areon.

"Nothing," replied Reiquem as she gave Areon a quick kiss and a thoughtful look. She and Elmyra walked toward the beach.

"What are they being so secret about?" Areon asked Labert as the master walked back with an armful of wood that would last the night.

"Elmyra told me earlier that she may not be going with us to our next destination," replied Labert, dropping the wood next to their sitting area.

He grabbed a few of the larger branches and threw them in the fire that Areon had started.

"Why?" asked Areon "What is our next destination?"

"I don't know, to the island of Reagash," replied Labert without looking at Areon.

"What is there?" asked Areon. He looked down the beach to see where Reiquem and Elmyra had gone; he could not see them, but he took in the beautiful night air and all his surroundings. Palm trees lined most of the beach in front of the mountain.

"Long ago," said Labert, sitting down while exhaling heavily. "We learned the master of death magic was imprisoned in Reagash prison. While we knew the information, we did nothing to save him. We had no reason to. Elmyra and I didn't know this man, this master of death. We have been around a long time, Areon, but while we were still young, as you and Reiquem are, the master of death looked approximately our age now …"

"So you've met him?" asked Areon, intrigued by this new information.

"Seen him," corrected Labert. "Anyhow, we ran into him again years upon years later, and he still looked the same age. He still had the same sinister eyes. We are now older, yet, and I imagine that he has still not aged. Some say he is an evil man. They say he kills at will. They say he uses his power to stop the life of most sentient beings he comes upon. Some even say he takes the life of those he does not even come upon."

"And we're going to do what when he get to this Reagash prison?" asked Areon fearfully.

"If he's there, we are to break him out, unnoticed," returned Labert staring into the now large fire.

Areon thought about this conversation for some time before replying, "I was under the impression one could not be evil to be a master."

"And under the right impression, you were," stated Labert.

"Then how can the master of death magic be evil?" asked Areon, sure he'd won the argument.

"He's not," said Labert shaking his head. "Some only say he is evil, while the sad truth of the matter is that death is not evil, not for the master of death."

"But murder is evil," argued Areon.

"I never said it wasn't, but being the master of death is not evil," said Labert.

"It's sort of a circular argument," stated Areon, giving up.

Labert clapped his hand on Areon's knee for comfort. "Death is only another beginning, Areon, whether you believe it or not."

Areon shook his head in disbelief.

"I do not believe in God."

"Why not, Areon?" asked Labert. "He believes in you."

After Areon and Labert sat for some time in silence, warming themselves by the fire, Reiquem and Elmyra showed back up to the makeshift camp.

"Reiquem," Areon stood up and went over to her immediately.

"Areon, we must have a talk," said Reiquem seriously.

Elmyra went and sat down by Labert, who seemed uninterested in the whole deal.

Areon and Reiquem were now walking down the sandy beach, their feet leaving tracks in the wet sand, only to disappear as the waves came onto land.

"You can fly now, Areon," said Reiquem breaking the silence. "It was really quite amazing what you did. I was getting worried up there, you know."

"I knew what would happen, Reiquem," he responded.

She smiled.

"Areon," she said as a tear ran down her face. "We've had quite an adventure so far, haven't we?"

"Of course," replied Areon. "I would not have wanted to go with anybody else."

They were now stopped on the beach; the only sound that could be heard was the gentle coming and going of the waves.

"What's wrong?" asked Areon with concern.

"I can't travel with you any longer," she said. Areon stared at her.

"I don't understand ..."

"Areon, Elmyra and I must go back to the house." Reiquem was still trying to smile although the tears were coming. "You and Labert must go and move the gemstones to a safer place."

"Tell me why," said Areon softly.

"Areon, when I fell, you saved two lives, although you didn't realize it," replied Reiquem. "Areon that night, in Lalvegeth, our love was unspoken. I love you, Areon," voiced Reiquem.

"And I love you, Reiquem," returned Areon without a moments hesitation.

"And," sighed Reiquem, "because of that love, I am now with your child."

Areon took Reiquem into his arms and they held each other as the time slowly slipped away under the pale moonlight.

# CHAPTER XXXVII

# The Island Prison

Areon and Reiquem did not sleep much that night, nor did Elmyra and Labert. When the former couple came back from their walk, the married masters were still awake. It had been a somber rest of the night.

Areon was now gathering his supplies; he still had his faithful bow, although his quiver was not as heavy as when he had left. As for the rest of the things that Labert and Areon would need, Elmyra was pulling out of her unbelievably spacious traveling case. She handed them a tightly rolled set of blankets and tiny pillows, a pan for cooking, which Areon tied to his quiver on his back, and some panacea.

"Leviathan will give you two a ride to Reagash," stated Elmyra after all had been packed. "After that, he will take us back to the house where we will wait for news."

"How will you get news?" asked Areon.

Elmyra turned toward Labert. "Send Scine once you have news; until then we will wait at the house. It would be ridiculous to come and try to find you."

"There is no telling where we'll be at that time," replied Labert. "If we have nothing important to tell you, we will send Scine as soon as we reach the Kingdom of Life."

"We're going back to the Kingdom of Life?" asked Areon with wide eyes.

"Yes," said Labert flatly.

"But it's so far. How we will accomplish such a feat. It will take months if we travel from the Kingdom of Light on foot."

"You will have to explain to them our situation and why we took the gemstone of life," explained Elmyra. "Or there will be dire consequences," she added, ignoring Areon.

"I only hope they give us a chance to explain," said Labert. "And that we get there prior to your calculations, Areon."

Leviathan was forced to carry the boat in his mighty claws from underneath as they company flew northeast to the island of Reagash, which was directly off the mirrored Continent of Light. Areon had been inspecting the map as they took the journey toward the island. He had not realized all the land they had gone over. He was now a very long way from his home according to his map. All the sailing they had done really took them far away.

Areon watched Leviathan fly over the open waters back toward the Continent of Light. Areon had never been off the life continent in his entire life. In fact (he thought back and chuckled), he had not even known the continent he had lived on his whole life was called the Continent of Life, let alone that it mirrored the Continent of Light which was the destination after they attempted to break the Rapturer out of Reagash prison.

"What exactly is this place like?" yelled Areon over the loud flapping wings and streaming wind.

"Not much to it, really," Labert yelled back. "A small island about the size of Leviathan's with a dungeon in the middle. The cell doors never open. It is a circular dungeon with cells lining the walls; after that, it spirals down and leads to many underground cells for those with long lives. Guards roam the area all day and night; they take shift breaks when a boat comes from the larger continent to pick them up. The guards are also criminals but with less severe charges If they do their duty and guard the prison for their term, they won't have to live in one of the cells. They only have to feed the prisoners."

"Sounds horrible," replied Areon.

"Not a place you'd want to live," said Labert. "The beauty of it is its simplicity. All it consists of are brick walls against the earth and a small hole for food to be fed through."

"It seems to me that a master, especially one such as the Rapturer, should be able to free himself from this place," stated Areon.

"I am sure they have special accommodations for our friend," said Labert smiling. He seemed to be enjoying himself immensely.

They flew like that for hours, talking now and again, but never stopping. Areon was beginning to grow tired of sitting on the hard scales.

Areon stood up and braced himself against the wind.

"How far away are we?" he yelled.

"Not far," said Elmyra. She was toward the front of Leviathan's neck beside his head, peering ahead into the distance.

Areon was now getting altogether tired of sitting on the rough scales of the dragon's back. He walked carefully toward Elmyra and watched with her for some time. Before long, the horizon, no longer water, turned to land.

Areon could see it now; the island prison. Night was falling fast, and he wasn't really looking forward to going into that place. Who knew what kind of people were there? He guessed the worst of the light continent were sent.

Waves crashed onto the island steadily. Areon noticed that it did not have a nice beach area, only jagged rocks running around the whole of the island. He was thankful Leviathan would be dropping them off over the rocks. Leviathan flew steady and lowered without the company even realizing it; before long Areon and Labert were climbing off his back. The dragon took the small boat he had been carrying (much to his annoyance) and set it down in the water. Labert followed him and tied it to some larger rocks and ran back up to the group who waited.

"We'll see you when we get word," said Elmyra. "Do not forget to send somebody as soon as possible."

"It could be months," stated Labert plainly.

"No, I can't wait months." Areon looked at Reiquem.

"How pathetic," snarled Leviathan. "Let the boy return to the house where he'll be safe."

Areon knew better than to reply.

"I need your help on this, Areon," Labert said somberly.

"Months? But do you know what this means?" asked Areon. Reiquem stood silent.

"I'll be alright," she said, covering up her tears. "But come back as soon as possible."

Areon grabbed Reiquem and they hugged for what would be the last time in quite a while.

"Be careful," said Reiquem to Areon.

"I love you," he replied.

"And I you," she said.

"And good-bye for now, my love," said Elmyra, giving Labert a quick peck on the cheek. He smiled.

Areon sat in a blur of emotions watching Reiquem, Elmyra, and Leviathan fly away toward the house of the Daridyns. Out of all the exhausting sparring sessions he had had with Belgraf, this was by far the hardest thing he had ever done.

Dusk was gone. Night was present, and Areon could hardly see his own hands in front of him. Labert and he had sat for a while, mapping out their plan. Areon had not really paid attention.

"Areon, are you ready to do this tonight?" asked Labert. "It will be best to attempt the breakout at night. The guards won't be as plentiful. Most of them will probably be asleep."

"Why would the guards try and stop us if they're criminals?" asked Areon

Labert looked from the prison, which was approximately one hundred spans away, to Areon. "If they do not do their job, they will be found and made to spend the rest of their lives in a cold, dark cell, rather than being freed early. Trust me, Areon, they do their job, and they do it well."

Areon looked toward the prison. The moon hardly provided enough light. "We won't even be able to tell where to enter."

"We'll feel our way around," replied Labert. "And once we're free, we'll race to the ship and head toward the continent, which isn't much of a sail."

Areon didn't reply. He was still thinking of everything else going on in his life. Reiquem filled most of his mind.

They were now running toward a small dark tower that was darker than the night itself.

"We're here," said Labert, stopping Areon with his hand. Areon was breathing heavily.

"Haste!" whispered Labert, and the time magic consumed both of them. Areon could not tell his speed had increased due to the nighttime darkness.

"Follow me," whispered Labert, and they grasped hands and raced around the outside of the old, dark tower. It was made of old bricks that had numerous fissures along the outside but seemed sturdy. They raced around at an incredible speed until Areon was stopped by Labert's hand once again.

"The entrance," said Labert. "This is it. The guards will try to kill us if they see us."

"What should we do?" asked Areon. He was almost ready to dare one of the guards to try and harm either of them now.

"Don't be seen," answered Labert.

Labert led the way in. Down a brick walkway sat an old, rusted cage door. It was only crosses of metal that hung loosely on its hinges. Areon looked in as Labert opened it slowly. It creaked loudly, and Areon winced, hoping it would not wake the guard who Areon saw sleeping in the middle of a circular room. They both walked in and kept low to the ground. The guard sat in the middle of the large, circular room still sleeping peacefully. He probably thought no one in their right mind would ever come to this place, especially on this dark a night. Areon looked at the cells. There were not even doors to the cells. It was simply bricks for walls, save one slot that was left out to feed the food through.

It was after Areon saw that some of the bricks looked much newer than others, that he realized the prisoners were bricked up inside their cells to stay for the rest of their miserable lives.

"How terrible," remarked Areon a bit too loudly. Labert whipped his head toward the guard. Areon did the same and noticed his eyes beginning to open. Areon remembered that they were in haste, and they both ran quickly to the spot of the room where the guard was not facing. He woke up and looked around, but he was moving in slow motion and Areon and Labert easily had enough time to sprint around to the other side of the room and back before the guard realized that he was hearing things.

Labert looked at Areon and smiled while shaking his head. "This way," he said much quieter than Areon.

Labert walked to a part of the circular room that had a tunnel leading to a walkway that spiraled downwards. From this spiral, many other walkways branched off and went farther into the side of the underground. The entire place must have taken years upon years to construct. Areon and Labert continued to walk downward.

Finally they came to the end of the spiral. Areon guessed they were now two hundred spans down, but the walk did not take that long due to Labert's magic.

"May death come to whosoever opens this door," read Labert. He was reading an inscription above the last doorway in the spiral, the doorway at the very bottom.

"And so it may," returned Labert. He then looked at the bars of the door, formed invisible symbols in the air with movements of his hands, and slowly, time magic began to flow from him. It was as if Areon was watching one thousand years of erosion go over the bars in second's time. Before long, they turned to pure rust, then dust, and the door fell open. Areon let fire come to his hands and shed light inside the doorway.

Inside was something that Areon would have difficulty explaining his entire life.

"Dear God," stammered Areon.

"We are here to liberate you," stated Labert.

Areon watched a man, if you would call something with wings a man, lift his head slowly and stare down his rescuers. The Rapturer was a very tall, slender, yet slightly muscular man, with wings four times the length of his body. His wings were not tucked behind his back. They were spread out across a wall with large metal spikes pinning them to the bricks. His hands were above his head, shackled. The chains ran from his hands to the ceiling. Blood dripped from every metal stake that pierced the wings of the Rapturer.

"Then liberate me," rasped a voice.

# CHAPTER XXXVIII

# Hospitality

"I now resided in hell. Not hell as a metaphor, but actual hell. When I had established this, I needed to find a way out. It didn't matter how I ended up there, not anymore anyway. It didn't matter who put me there, if it was of God's will or not, I didn't care anymore. I simply needed to get out."

Areon sat entranced listening to the Rapturer's voice. Breaking him out had been quite the endeavor. He thought back as the Rapturer continued talking to Labert. Areon had had to use all the elemental ice magic in him. He had made the stakes holding the Rapturer so cold that they soon shattered; the only idea Areon could think of to free him. Labert had used his time magic on the shackles. The trio had then run off the island carrying the Rapturer as best they could, his wings a constant large menace.

Not only were the wings a menace, but prisoners were awake. Most of them shouted obscenities and curses. Some tried to persuade Areon and Labert to rescue them, but to no avail. Others grabbed at Areon's cloak and arms. One man held on so obstinately that Areon was forced to burn him severely with the touch of his palm and the fire within him.

Once they had made it up to the top, the guard was awake, summoning other guards that had gone unnoticed. But the Rapturer was now ready to be free, and he killed the man instantly. Areon remembered him saying something like: "He was an evil man, and his time to go had come. Now for my things."

Next, they had to rush to the place where the prisoners were forced to leave everything they came in with. Areon had to carry a monstrous cloak, thick and black, a pair of glasses with an opaque blackness to them, a round, brimmed black hat, and a large, dusty, black book with a writing utensil attached to the side.

The land that they ran across was rocky, and twice they had all three fallen over trying to carry the injured master. Finally, when they had made it to the boat, a small stream of arrows had been loosed at them compliments of the rest of the guards that had been awaken. Labert had quickly untied the boat and Areon did elemental wind magic to get them going. But after their effort, an arrow still stuck out of the right wing of the Rapturer.

Areon shook his head. They were on the Continent of Light now. The Rapturer's healing rate was incredibly fast. Not like a human at all. He looked into the fire they had all made. The Rapturer must have been done talking with Labert, for all was silent. He was wrapped in his large cloak, his wings no longer visible, although he looked rather odd trying to conceal such a thing. His hat and glasses sat perfectly on his slim face.

"Morning will be coming soon," announced Labert breaking the silence. "We will leave then and head east toward the temple." He looked at the Rapturer, who looked in no state to be traveling.

"What about his injuries?" asked Areon nodding toward the Rapturer.

"We'll travel slowly," replied Labert.

"It makes no difference," rasped the Rapturer. "I'll be healed by morning."

Areon turned and looked toward the island they had come from. It was no longer visible; the hills now concealed it.

"We will be safe to sleep?" asked Areon. "I mean, the guards, will they come looking for us?"

"I will keep watch," announced the Rapturer. "I hadn't planned on sleeping."

Areon nodded slowly and turned on his side. He took the bow and quiver off his back, put his old sword down beside him, and laid on his small black pillow that was now propped against a tree.

Areon awoke and blinked lazily. He rubbed the sleep out of his eyes and looked around. Labert lay sleeping, and the Rapturer stood some spans away peering into the distance, toward the northeast, where Areon knew the death temple stood.

"Do you know why everyone calls this continent the Continent of Light?" asked the Rapturer quietly and unexpectedly.

"No," admitted Areon. He stood up and walked closer to the man whom he feared so much.

"Have you ever been to a land where death resides?" the Rapturer asked.

Areon stayed quiet.

"Have you ever been to a wasteland? Or a place where ogres run free? Or have you been to a place where hope no longer lingers in the hearts of most?" asked the Rapturer.

"No," replied Areon quietly.

"You can say you have now," replied the master of death. "You will see it all."

They both stayed silent until the Rapturer spoke again.

"What optimism the people of this continent must have to name it the Mirrored Continent of Light, and keep it named that." He looked at Areon over the top of his glasses, his dark eyes piercing into Areon's being. "Light symbolizing hope."

Labert stirred now. The cluster of trees around them had provided a good shelter for the night. Areon grabbed a tree limb and looked out into a small grassland.

"What will we be traveling over?" he asked.

Labert blinked several times and turned his head toward Areon. "You've never been to the Mirrored Continent of Light?"

"Never," replied Areon.

"I suppose I could see that," he returned. "Some parts, as a matter of fact, most parts, are not to most people's liking. Until we reach the Death Temple, we will see mostly small communities of farmers who join their cropland to make food. But after ..." he trailed off.

"Yes?" asked Areon.

"The Wizard Scar," said the Rapturer in his usual raspy voice. "It's rumored that a dark wizard is buried somewhere near it."

"Yes," Labert began again. "Barren wasteland as far as the eye can see, the Wizard Scar in the middle of it all. And then farther up the mountains of Alklolock."

The Rapturer sat down and took out his immense black book. He took up the crude writing utensil and vigorously scratched out something.

"Straight north of us?" asked Areon.

"Not exactly," said the Rapturer. He smiled wickedly and went back to his book in which he was now writing.

Labert looked at him warily. "No, not exactly. We must first cross the River of Light, an amazing spectacle. Ever does it shimmer, even while bordering the wasteland from the Wizard Scar. It's as though it is a barrier of light against the spreading of hatred."

"This, of course, you remember, lad, is if we defeat the guardian of the Death Temple," smirked the Rapturer. His glasses covered his eyes, although they did not really need to on account of his hat. He smiled demonically. Areon noted his psychotic way of staring at people and turned from his gaze.

"Right, hmm, well, yes," continued Labert. "Across the river, through the wasteland, and across the famous bridge of the Alklolock mountains and we will be in the Light Kingdom's domain."

"And this fellow Scine?" asked Areon.

"Directly in the mountains," replied Labert. "And now we must pack up our things and be off. Rapturer, will you lead us?"

The Rapturer scratched off something else and chuckled coldly. "Of course."

Areon secured his old sword in its worn leather scabbard. He made sure his bow and quiver were secure. Next, he rolled up the blanket and pillow Elmyra had given him and tied it to his belt. Thinking of Elmyra made him think of Reiquem. He would have wept were it not for his company. The Rapturer tucked his book under his enormous cloak and pulled his hat farther down. Labert put away the panacea under his robe and tied his blanket and rolled up pillow to his waist.

The group took off following the Rapturer out of the cluster of trees that led into the lush green, gently sloping hills. They walked through many small forests and over small farmlands. Occasionally they were forced to walk directly through a cornfield or vegetable garden. Areon could not help but see all the food and wish he had some. The only thing that they had eaten were the fruits that they had come across, mainly berries that looked okay to eat, and one of the nights they had captured a pair of rabbits and skinned them with Areon's small knife that he kept in his boot now. But for a week they ate little and walked much.

On the seventh day, after walking by the third house with a large garden in the front, Areon stopped.

"We need food," he stated. The group had been walking the entire day, and Areon realized how hungry he was after he had stopped thinking about Reiquem.

"He's right," agreed Labert. "I can't remember the last time we've actually stopped to have something."

"So stop," said the Rapturer.

"We will see if the next farmhouse will take us in," said Labert. "I do not feel up to catching our dinner again."

As Areon walked over a dirt road that had trees to either side, he looked at Labert. He noticed that he had become rather skinny compared to what he was when they had met. Areon then took up his shirt and looked at his stomach. He could see his ribs, although he had been rather lean his whole life. All in all, the trio looked emaciated. Areon thought about the whole trip; he had been hungry the entire time, save when they stayed at Labert and Elmyra's house.

Areon looked at the trees on each side of the path for hours until they emerged into a flatland that turned into dirt, and finally a small field in front of a wooden house that had a small wisp of smoke coming from the stone chimney. In front of the house sat a garden with carrots, onions, cabbages, and the like. Areon's mouth started to water at the sight.

They walked up across the lawn and to the cozy home. Before they had a chance to knock, a middle-aged woman came out with a suspicious look on her face.

"What do you want?" she called out before they were too close. The company halted and Labert spoke for them.

"We only need food, ma'am, we beg of you."

She gave him a scrutinizing look and said nothing.

"We haven't eaten for days, ma'am," added Areon.

Her look softened a bit. "I'm sorry," she said. "But it seems as though you can't trust anyone these days. If we don't help each other, we're all going to die off. Come in, come in."

"Thank you very much," said Areon and Labert simultaneously.

"I will wait outside," announced the Rapturer.

"If you wish," replied the woman. Areon noted that she seemed almost glad.

The three walked inside a very humble house. A small table sat in the middle and a fire sat crackling in the corner. A large cauldron bubbled as they walked by and took seats at the table. A small entrance led to a different and only other room. The woman brought them glasses of water, which Areon downed in one gulp. She refilled it with a smile on her face.

Before long, a large man walked in. He took up most of the small doorway. He had a large beard and carried an axe.

"Oi, gentlemen," he rumbled. "Who're these lads?" he asked his wife.

"Travelers," she replied. "I was going to wait until supper to ask them any questions, they are skinny and weary."

"I can see that," he replied and took a seat beside them. Areon put down his head to show some sort of respect. The man looked well fed and muscular.

"I am Labert, and this is Areon, my traveling companion," exclaimed Labert. "And outside is … is a man we picked up along the way that looked as though he needed help."

"The homely lookin' fellow I saw outside?" roared the big man.

"Yes, that is him," replied Labert.

"Thought I was gonna have to take me axe to his head," said the man. "Can never be to careful. You lads should be more careful the company that ye choose. Anyhow, me name's Driscol, and I'll be happy to answer any questions you like, you seem like good folks."

"And so we are," answered Areon.

"Good," said the woman. "I am Blair." She set down bowls for each of them and used a large ladle to dish up the hot cabbage stew that she had been preparing. "Eat up."

Areon had never tasted anything so good in his entire life. He ate until every last drop of soup was gone and his stomach had a slight bulge to it.

"Now then," rumbled the large man called Driscol. "What are you doing out traveling through the farm communities, eh? You're getting pretty close to the wasteland."

"That is our road," replied Labert still eating slowly. "We are traveling to the Alklolock Mountains to visit a friend."

"That's quite some distance, lads," replied Driscol. "At least a week's worth of steady walkin,' maybe more. I hope you're ready for utter boredom and many ogres while traveling through the wasteland."

Areon and Labert sat silently. After dinner was over, they made their way into the living room, which housed a small fireplace. Areon watched as Driscol pulled out a grayish rock and another type of rock and strike them together until a spark made the small kindle go up in flames, and finally logs were placed on the top. He raised his eyebrows and looked at Labert. Labert chuckled at the fact that Areon had never seen a fire started by any other means than one's own elemental magic; it was how he and Belgraf had started fires their whole lives.

"Amazing," he said.

"What's that?" asked Driscol.

Areon blinked and shook his head away from the fireplace. "Oh, oh nothing," he responded.

"Well, this will probably be the last safe haven you'll come across, I expect," said Driscol as he laid back into a large pillowed chair. "None travel farther than this, unless, of course, they have business with the Kingdom." He eyed them suspiciously while reaching down and taking out a small cob pipe. He stuck a long stick in the fire and pulled it out to light the tobacco that was in the old pipe. After, he looked away from them and took a long drag from it and exhaled slowly. He thought for a little while before talking again. "You are welcome to stay here tonight."

"We are in debt to you," said Labert.

"Have you come across many farm communities?" asked Driscol.

"Many," replied Labert.

"It is the only way we on this continent survive," he said sorrowfully. "We live life to sustain it. Unless, of course, you live in the kingdom."

"How many live there?" inquired Areon.

"Thousands upon thousands," responded Driscol. "The fortified walls surround every house. It is quite safe to live in the kingdom, which is why many have given up the privacy of the country to live the way they do. It's dreadfully packed inside the city walls."

A moment of silence followed this statement before Areon spoke up.

"Why are their so many ogres in the wasteland?"

Driscol laughed heartily. "Because that is where ogres can survive. They breed and live off each other. Cannibals. Nasty business. It is barren because they have eaten and destroyed everything else that once lived their, not that the Wizard Scar didn't take care of much of it." He shrugged at Areon. "It's just where a group decided to go. Maybe they could feel the evil and they enjoyed it. Who knows? Of course, this is only what I've heard. I never travel north of this house, hardly any do. Strange things lie to the north."

Areon looked around the room. It was cozy. The nice brick fireplace had windows opposite of it with painted shutters. The large chair for Driscol, and in the other room a nice table for dinner.

"Well, lads," boomed the large man. "You've probably been through much, being travelers and all, what's say we break out a barrel of wine, eh? Me and Blair haven't had company in ages."

"Oh no, I couldn't," replied Labert. But Areon came in right away not wanting to refuse the offer.

"Of course, I would be very glad to accept." He had not had a wine since the night he and Reiquem had spent together south of Wellenore. He winced and reminded himself not to think of Reiquem being so far away at the moment.

"Good!" exclaimed Driscol. "Let's have it then." He walked over the creaky old floor and down to the cellar, which Areon had failed to notice. When he emerged again, he carried a large Barrel with a small tap at the bottom. He let it slam down on the kitchen table and got out two large mugs, which he took to the bottom of the barrel and filled to the brim. After which, he handed one to Areon.

"Here's to life bein' no good!" exclaimed the man. Areon laughed and held up his mug to Driscol's, and they both drained their glass.

Areon woke up the next morning with a pounding head. He was lying in the cellar on a soft bed made up many quilts, one of which, someone had draped over him. Driscol came loudly down the stairs.

"Aye, couldn't quite keep up with ol' Driscol, eh, lad?" roared the bearded man.

"I guess not," responded Areon, rubbing his head. He thought about the night before and remembered Driscol drinking much more than he.

"Where is Labert?" he asked.

"Me wife is helping him pack food upstairs," Driscol replied. "For your journey, you'll need it."

Areon had now gotten up. He walked to where he had laid his sword and sleeping things.

"I'm not really looking forward to going on another excursion into the unknown," complained Areon. "Walking for a week without food. It was a nice break stopping here, I thank you."

"Well, we'll get you another good meal before you go, and you're welcome," replied Driscol and he walked up the stairs. Areon followed.

Areon ran up the stairs and outside to the water bin that sat on the west side of the house and dunked his head under. After, Labert came up to him and told him to be ready to leave soon.

"Where is the Rapturer?" inquired Areon.

"Sitting in the forest with his book," replied Labert pointing. "Over there."

Areon looked to see a small forest off the flat grass land to the west of the house. To the east lay the garden, and over a hill, Driscol's cornfield. He refused to look north.

It remained early in the morning, and soon Driscol and Blair emerged from the house.

"Are we ready to break the fast for the morning?" boomed Driscol.

"I certainly am," answered Areon. His stomach felt a little upset.

In the group went and sat down to bacon and sausage along with bread and honey. Blair poured Areon two glasses of water and a glass of milk before his thirst was quenched. Areon ate heartily, knowing this might be the last good meal he would get in a long while.

"Your friend is a strange fellow," declared Blair. "Doesn't he eat?"

"I do not know or care to ask," replied Labert evasively.

"Well, at any rate, if he is scared to eat with us, you'll have your pack of food for you and him," said Driscol.

"We will forever be in your debt, Driscol," said Labert and clapped him on the shoulder. "You and your wife are good people. I wish more like you still lived in the world."

"You are kind," returned Driscol in a softer voice than usual.

———————⟫•◦•⟪———————

Areon now followed Labert, and Labert followed the Rapturer. He turned one last time and waved to the couple that had walked a few spans north of their country home to see them off.

"Two nights until the Death Temple will be in our view," stated the Rapturer. "Be prepared for the worst you can imagine."

Areon let himself fall behind with Labert. "Does he even know why we're doing this?" asked Areon.

"I started to tell him the first night when we freed him, but he cut me short and told me he already knew," replied Labert. "Very mysterious indeed."

"Indeed," whispered Areon more than perturbed.

# CHAPTER XXXIX

## The Realm of Disappearance

As it neared nightfall on the day the three had left Driscol's house, the Rapturer held out a hand to stop the group.

"We rest here tonight," he whispered. Areon looked up ahead to witness what had stopped him; all he could see was a small hill that led to a drop off.

"Well, it is near dusk," responded Areon.

"But why here?" asked Labert, slumping down on a fallen tree trunk.

"The Temple of Death draws nigh," replied the Rapturer sitting down cross-legged in one fluent motion. "It lies just across that overhang of land to the north, as does the guardian who does not fit inside the temple."

"What is it?" asked Areon nervously.

"You are a brave lad, Areon, to face such dangers with us always; but tomorrow you will stay here when the Rapturer and I go to the temple."

"I will fight with you!" cried Areon standing back up. "I would feel disgraced if I were left behind."

"Then you will die," the Rapturer said nonchalantly.

"Think of your child, Areon," said Labert placing a reassuring arm on his shoulder. "You are young still. I don't want anything happening to you. You have things to look forward to in life." Areon knew Elmyra had told him the story.

"You cannot treat me like this," Areon said boldly and stood facing Labert as a man. He refused to say another word the rest of the night.

When dawn broke, Areon awoke to find that he was alone. He looked toward the north and steadied his thoughts. He could actually hear the battle waging. Areon would not sit idle while his friends faced death. Finally, being able to take it no longer, he ripped off his blanket and stood, secured his old sword, made sure he had his well-made bow along with the quiver, and left his sleeping utensils.

By the time he neared the edge of the land he was in an all out sprint. He had not the time to slow his momentum, and before he knew it, the overhang of land was before him. He fell down into a ravine. The next sight made Areon regret his decision.

He looked up to the see the Rapturer torn to pieces. His wings ripped off and all of his limbs were only connected by trails of blood.

"Oh no …" said Areon. His stomach was empty, but he still heaved.

"Areon, look out!" yelled Labert, but before Areon even had time to tear his eyes off the dead master of death, a hard, jagged, scaly tail smote him in the stomach and sent him flying over fifteen spans away.

When Areon looked at what had hit him, he gasped out of utter fear, for before him sat on all fours an enormous red dragon with seven heads. The three heads to the either side of the middle one had a horn on each, and the middle head produced four horns to equal a total of ten.

It belched forth a thick wall of fire at Labert just after he had yelled out, and now Areon could only see the remains of the Rapturer.

Areon tried to spring into action only to find that his stomach hurt unlike any hurt he had ever felt before. He fell to his knees in pain.

He quickly glanced at his shirt. It was torn along with his stomach, which was bleeding profusely. He also would not doubt if some ribs were broken.

We're all going to die, Areon said to himself inside his head. He fell to one knee and looked for Labert. The dragon now reeled his middle head back toward Areon. The rest of his heads looked for Labert, who must have been in haste. Areon thought that he might have tried to make a run for it seeing as how Areon would be dead in a matter of seconds.

"Foolish of you to come, human," roared the only speaking head the dragon possessed. It growled mightily and went to devour Areon in a single gulp.

Areon grasped his sword with what remaining strength he had and thrust it into the upper mouth of the large dragon. It hissed and whipped its body around violently. Areon had only infuriated it. His sword was gone, his side bleeding. Areon fell and could only see the head of the Rapturer torn from the body. It spoke.

"You must go to the Realm of Disappearance now," commanded the severed head.

Areon thought he was hallucinating. He shook his head and looked at the seven-headed dragon, which shook violently trying to dislodge the sword from the roof of his mouth.

"Do as I say!" yelled the head in the raspy voice Areon had grown accustomed to.

"What is going on?" Areon said as Labert whipped around the back of the dragon in haste.

The blood of the Rapturer that had left trails leading from arm to leg to head to torso now moved slowly with purpose. His wings began to be pulled back together by the blood left on his back. His arms and legs moved like fluid to find their way back to the bleeding torso.

Labert grabbed Areon under the arms and hoisted him up. Areon cocked his head back with effort.

"If we go for a second, you will be waiting a month!" yelled Labert to the severed head of the Rapturer.

"If you don't go, you'll die," it said. "The red dragon will soon cast Flare." Slowly, the entire form that lay on the ground lifted itself up to comprise a barricade of body parts, sinew, wings, and blood. The dragon snapped his head through it all leaving large amounts of crimson on his heads and necks. He lunged forward with all his mouths, hoping to come back with a mouthful of the two that were left alive, only to find that they had disappeared.

As blood gushed out of Areon's wound, he gripped Labert's hand on his shoulder and looked at his surroundings while cringing in pain. A white floor stretched as far as could be seen. White surrounded everything while nothing occupied the room. There were no walls. The white floor stretched infinitely underneath them. All of a sudden a new pair of people appeared fifty spans away. As soon as they appeared, they vanished. Next to Labert a man appeared with sweat on his face. He glanced at the two on the floor and then vanished again. Two seconds came and went. A group of travelers materialized some distance away. Three seconds had passed.

Areon knew how to enter the Realm of Disappearance.

—————⟫•⟪—————

When the two materialized back into the plane of reality in which

Areon had lived his whole life until now, three and a half months had gone by. Areon cried out in pain as they reappeared. The pain in his side was excruciating. While on his knees, Areon gazed around at his new settings; blood no longer covered the ground. The red dragon, apparently, ceased to exist, although Areon did not see a lifeless body of the dragon. The Rapturer had built a camp under the overhang of the cliff. He looked as he always did; his body back together and normal. He had brought all of their things from the night they had stayed before the fight with the red dragon. Labert walked over to where the Rapturer knelt praying and set a hand on his shoulder.

"We have returned," stated Labert.

The Rapturer opened his eyes and spoke, "I have stayed awake while you were gone."

"And the gemstone?" Labert looked toward the horizon and the Temple of Death.

"Acquired," replied the Rapturer. Areon looked over at the temple. It looked old and weathered.

The Rapturer reached into his cloak and pulled out the gemstone to hand it to Labert, who pulled out the satchel that he had secretly obtained from Elmyra on the day she and Reiquem had departed. The gemstone of Death looked hideous compared to the other two gemstones Areon witnessed earlier on. The size seemed approximately the same, but the silver base was gnarled. It had sharp spikes coming out from underneath, like a nest of silver thorns. The inside blackness moved violently, as if living pitch were inside trying to get out.

Labert placed the third gemstone into the satchel with the other two that had been obtained on the long journey.

The three decided to stay the night in the same place that the Rapturer had stayed while they had been in the Realm of Disappearance. Areon nary looked over at the Temple of Death. He was almost glad he had not entered to see the sealer. He presumed a sealer of life covered the gemstone of death. Death countered the life. Areon was glad he had not entered. Glad he had not seen what the Rapturer did.

The Rapturer had made a small pile of wood under the overhang of the cliff, which Areon took some of and used to make a fire. He had a hard time doing the magic with his injured side. The wound drained his energy.

"Labert?" said Areon as he squatted down by the fire. "It is imperative that I bandage this wound of mine."

"Of course, of course," replied Labert with concern in his voice. "I just can't think of what to use for it."

Areon lifted his bloodstained shirt to find that the bleeding had stopped, and the wound was not as bad as he originally thought, although it still hurt him immensely. He doubted if any ribs were broken.

"Well, give me your knife, Areon," Labert said finally. He took it and cut off part of his purple robe and wrapped it around Areon's entire torso. "I guess that will suffice."

The three sat around the fire discussing what the Rapturer had been doing for the last three months until Areon finally asked, "How did you defeat the red dragon?"

The Rapturer closed his eyes and would say no more. He turned on his side to sleep but before bed he announced, "I will not speak of the events that took place while you two were gone, and I will be eagerly anticipating our departure tomorrow at dawn."

Areon let sleep take him.

"Your side must be tiring you," were the words Areon awoke to. He looked around and blinked a few times. It was far past dawn. Blood now seeped through the robe, although it did not look crimson.

"An infection has set in." It was the Rapturer's voice. Areon felt fatigued. The Rapturer took the purple cloth off Areon and undid his bloodstained white shirt. The wound looked disgusting. Puss and crusted blood covered the whole of the wound.

"This will be painful to say the least," remarked the Rapturer. Before Areon had a chance to say anything, the master of death pushed Areon gently against the ground with his hand on his chest and pinched the wound. Areon yelled out in pain, but the Rapturer's hold did not lessen. He pinched the wound together so that puss started oozing out slowly.

Areon clenched his teeth and looked down. Nothing was coming out, save puss and a greenish colored substance. He gripped the Rapturer's hand but to no avail. When Areon did this, the Rapturer squeezed harder on the wound until more puss and green liquid spilled out. Blood started to come again, and only when it came out completely did the Rapturer stop pinching. He let go of Areon and pushed the dark purple cloth against it once more before tying it tightly around his torso again.

"It was necessary," stated the Rapturer before getting up and walking over to pack up his things.

Areon waited while Labert packed up their things. Although Areon was weak, they were headed for the Kingdom of Light.

# CHAPTER XL

## Wasteland Ogres

Walking proved to be difficult for Areon due to his injury, which still bled now and again. The trio was twice forced to stop at the side of the large river they now followed to wash Areon's side. It was the mirrored River of Light.

On the second morning after the red dragon's defeat, Areon's side itched, which definitely signaled that the wound was now healing. The Rapturer and Labert always let Areon eat a little extra of what Driscol had given them for provisions, which consisted of many strips of tightly packed dried meat, two large loafs of bread wrapped in thin cloths, and the cheese, which they were currently finishing. It was a cold morning but not too cold. Areon's cloak kept him warm.

"We approach the wasteland by nightfall," stated the Rapture in a flat, raspy voice. "Which is not what I had intended. We will have to cross the river at night."

"It will be easy to avoid the Ogres," added Labert, noticing Areon's worried look toward the north. "The land is wide open, and we can run in haste in order to avoid them."

"Ahh, yes, I wondered when you would be contributing to our journey," the Rapturer voiced with what seemed like disdain to Areon.

Slowly, but sure enough, the land began to die. Grass began to grow sparser, and trees grew farther and farther apart. The land seemed to whither slightly as they headed in a northwest direction toward the Alklolock Mountains by which Scine, the apparent master of light, resided. At night the sky reflected the rust orange ground that sat on the north side of the river, with streaks across the white. The group walked on until the greenness that resembled life was behind them, and the river was the only thing that stopped the continuing spread of the dead landscape that occupied the north.

On the south side of the mighty river, the land was green, plush, and alive; on the north all had turned to orange dust and decay. A tall row of yellow grass seemed to be the only barricade to the drop-off, which led to the mucky side of the River of Light.

The Rapturer set down his mighty book. "We will take turns watching. I think no ogre will cross the River of Light, but we will be on the safe side of things. Unless you prefer to be elsewhere?" he looked at Areon.

"I will take the first watch," volunteered Labert. He took a seat on an overhang of land on some dry yellow grass. The Rapturer walked off some distance to the east and sat down as well. Areon, being tired from walking all day, grabbed his small pillow and blanket and went to sleep immediately.

"Areon, my lad." Areon jumped up and unsheathed the knife in his boot immediately while looking around. It was Labert.

"I simply need a rest, lad, would you take the watch for awhile?" he asked, taken aback.

"Oh, oh, of course," replied Areon yawning loudly and stretching his arms into the sky. It looked like dawn was a few hours away, but Areon could not be for sure. The Rapturer was not in sight.

Areon went over to the pack and the place where Labert had been sitting, and got out some dried meat, which he ate aggressively, and then he sat.

After a half an hour or so, Areon decided to look over his things. He grabbed his things from where Labert slept and brought them over to where he was sitting watch. He sheathed his small, razor-sharp knife in his boot and unsheathed his old sword. It shimmered in the moonlight. He was glad the Rapturer had kept it for him. He sheathed it again and set it beside him, not feeling like putting it back on his side under his scarlet cloak. He looked at his magnificent bow. Although his bow and sword were old and relatively normal, they served him well, and he was thankful he owned them and had brought them with him. He looked at his leather quiver, which had been hardened with oils, and saw that the arrow supply had diminished since he had left. Occasionally arrows had fallen out from various unknowns while he had been on this adventure.

God.

Areon thought it strange that people believed in such things. He only thought philosophical thoughts when he was alone; alone at the Full Barrel drinking and alone now. Belgraf taught on theology now and again, but he never gave Areon his beliefs. Areon just took in the information as facts and never established what he thought would happen when he died. He was too remote, too jaded. He knew of the churches and of angels, and perhaps he knew of heaven, yet Areon had no beliefs. He knew that people had established churches and bishops preached, but he had never prayed, even after seeing the angels. He thought of the only thing he knew he wanted to ask God.

Dear God, I whole-heartedly miss Reiquem … please protect her and our child from anything that …

"This is stupid," he said aggravated at feeling so foolish. Soon after, a twig broke and the Rapturer came walking up from the east.

"A nice night to pray; no one here to cloud your thoughts. Just you and God on a night like this," the Rapturer said with interest, while trying to appear uninterested.

"How did you know?" asked Areon aggravated.

"I know more than you might think," the Rapturer stated as he looked up at the moon and kept walking by.

Areon followed the man with his eyes until they caught something else in the distance; ogres were running at them from across the river.

"Rapturer!" yelled Areon waking Labert. The Rapturer jerked his head to see the herd of ogres falling over each other to try and get the fresh meat that they could smell from leagues away.

Areon looked at his supply of arrows; six left, six good ones at that. Six he did not feel like losing.

Labert was already gathering up the sleeping supplies and tying them securely around his waist. Areon pulled the quiver over his head, slipped his sword under his belt and tightened it, and gripped his bow tightly by the black handle that contrasted the light golden brown of the flexibly strong wood. He bent the bow behind his leg and restrung it due to the fact that he had unstrung it to sleep. He was ready for a war with the ogres.

"Labert, give me some panacea for my wound. I would like to be completely healed if we are to get away from this attack," requested Areon loudly. The ogres already knew they were there.

"I lost it all during the fight with the red dragon. You'll have to make due. Isn't it almost healed?" asked Labert.

"I fear it will break open again, but it doesn't matter now."

"Can we not fly from them?" Labert asked, turning his head toward the Rapturer.

"There is no way I can carry even one of you for very long. Thirty spans at most," returned the Rapturer. "Let alone both of you."

"I can fly myself," declared Areon defiantly.

"I'll believe that when I see it, for we need to cross the river quickly. I will carry Labert and either see you on the other side or return to get you. The ogres approach swiftly now. Something has stirred them by the Wizard Scar," said the Rapturer.

Areon smiled, knowing that the Rapturer did not believe him. Labert swung the pack of food over his back while the Rapturer uncloaked himself to reveal his mighty wings, which had healed long ago. Labert, knowing they were out of options, swung his arms around the Rapturer's chest and clung tightly. The Rapturer was at the very least a foot and half taller than Labert, which made the master of death look almost nonhuman, if not godly. The picture of the two masters taking off the ground left Areon's vision, and he shut his eyes and felt for his inner warmth, his aura, and found it with greater ease than the last time. It was as if now the aura had tasted its true strength and hungered for more. It bubbled up and erupted forth from Areon as he took flight for the second time in his life. He was not in a mad state of trying to save his and Reiquem's life this time around, so he took some time in the air to get used to his new ability. It was truly amazing. The Rapturer and Labert sat on the north side of the river waiting for Areon, who followed swiftly while looking odd flying after the Rapturer, who had wings, while Areon had none. He landed beside the two and smiled arrogantly.

"He would be impressed. A mortal flying," said the Rapturer.

"Who is that?" asked Areon, beginning to shake slightly.

"The one you prayed to earlier," returned the Rapturer.

An ogre bellowed out one of the most ominous noises Areon had ever heard in his life. One ogre, larger than the rest, led the pack by twenty spans at least. The leading ogre stayed approximately forty spans from the trio and was closing the gap fast.

As if in slow motion, the Rapturer and Labert began sprinting toward the northwest. As the Rapturer closed his wings around himself under his arms, he took up his mighty cloak and swung it around the enormous wings as it flailed while he ran. His giant book smote him in the right wing from inside one of the secret pockets. Areon, being the last of the company to depart toward the Alklolock Mountains, reached back for an arrow and knocked the chosen one silently. He aimed true, and the arrow sang a song of death for the murderous ogre that led the pack.

# CHAPTER XLI

## The Flight to Scine's Mountain Home

Areon quickly turned and began running at his top speed in order to catch up with the fleeing masters. He ran with his mighty bow still clutched in his arms; the ogres were gaining on them, the bodily odor of them now all to real in Areon's nostrils. A cloud of dust was billowing up steadily behind them. When Areon caught up to the Rapturer and Labert, Labert started muttering incantations under his heavy breathing. From the pack a larger ogre had come fourth, running with all his might, drool oozing out his mouth. Areon felt a stitch in his side form as he tried to run as hard as possible to escape the hungry ogre. In the last seconds before Labert's spell, the ogre had almost over taken Areon. Finally the time magic flew from Labert and the three were now running in haste. The ogre swiped with his giant, disgusting, long fingernailed hand, as Areon turned his head to see that it slowed to an unnatural speed. Areon quickly put distance between himself and the ogre, who could no longer keep up. The Rapturer turned and started running backwards to look at the ogres. The ones in the very back looked as though they were running at a very slow pace and soon turned lackadaisical and stopped following altogether. While this was good news, the bad news was that the much larger ones in front, such as the one Areon had killed with his long bow, were still coming. They refused to give up; the prospect of raw meat, not their own flesh, was very alluring, and the haste was barely enough to give the three speed to get away.

They ran at a sprint until they could not take it any longer. They had put much distance between themselves and the bloodthirsty ogres, but they continued to jog. Areon watched as his foot would go down; the dust would take several seconds before it would start to rise. It was fascinating running while they were in haste.

The barren wasteland was a horrible sight to behold. It smelled of rusted metal combined with decaying flesh. The land all around them was brownish orange, charred from the direct sunlight. In the wasteland no trees survived, no plants grew.

The group ran until none of them could stand it any longer. They ran until the only thing they could see in every direction was the wasteland. Areon wondered if they would lose their way not being able to see anything at all, save the dust.

"We … have lost them for now, but they will soon pick up our scent again," said Labert struggling to find his breath.

Areon threw down his bow while dropping to his knees and gasped for breath. The run had taken a lot out of him. In contrast, the Rapturer looked as though he had barely used any of his energy. Labert looked as tired as Areon.

"Even if they pick up our scent, I do not know if I will be able to make it," exclaimed Areon while panting heavily. He sprawled out on the ground facing the sky. Areon sat and simply sucked in air until the stars begin to glow, while the sun barely stayed above the horizon. Areon shut his eyes and all his thoughts turned to sleep.

"Areon, arise!" screamed the Rapturer. Areon jerked his head up and around. It was light again, and he could hear the familiar stamping of many large feet.

"The ogres have found us again?" asked Areon groggily, jumping to his feet while searching for his bow. The rest of his supplies stayed tied to his body.

"Come, we must make haste." Areon realized that he and Labert would have been dead in a matter of minutes were it not for the Rapturer, for Labert lay sprawled out in the dust as Areon had been, snoring loudly and sleeping deeply.

"Labert!" screamed Areon. "Awake!"

"I have vigorously tried to wake him; he pushed the limits of his power. You yourself were a chore to wake," said the Rapturer, clearly intent on helping the two in need. Areon looked at him and tried to understand how a man, who wished to help life so much, could take it just as easily.

"Can't you kill them all?" asked Areon mockingly. He hated the way the Rapturer seemed to be on both sides of mortal life.

"No, I cannot." The Rapturer looked toward the ground.

"Why not?" asked Areon, growing impatient at the growing noise of the ogres screaming behind them.

"It is not time for them to die," the master replied.

"Was it the red dragon's time?" Areon grew bolder.

The Rapturer finally could take no more insubordination. "I never said I killed the red dragon. You simply asked how I defeated it, and when I replied that I would not discuss the matter farther, you assumed something terrible, something most fool mortals like yourself do all too often. I haven't the time to discuss philosophical views that someone like you holds, but it will suffice to say that we need to find some way to get to the Alklolock Mountains before it is your time."

Areon scowled and looked back towards the southeast where the howling came from. A cloud of dust now billowed up. Ogres had the best sense of smell out of any creature on earth.

"How far are we from the mountains?" asked Areon quickly.

"Three quarters of the way through the wasteland. We covered much ground while in haste, but Labert is paying for it," replied the Rapturer. "But I don't know how far they will follow us out of here. Probably until we can get up into the mountains."

"We have to carry him." Before the Rapturer could respond, Areon had grabbed Labert, untied his food supply, which did not house much food anyway, and stuffed the remaining meat and bread in his mouth for extra energy before discarding the bag that Driscol and Blair had given them. He put his head under Labert's arm and looked pleadingly at the Rapturer.

"I don't know if we can make it, but we have to try."

The Rapturer nodded resignedly and took his place under Labert's other arm. Labert stayed passed out, unaware of the current danger.

Slowly, the three started moving again. Labert's feet dragged on the ground. It was slow going at first, but the Rapturer and Areon began to get better at carrying, although they heard the ogres getting louder.

For an hour they carried Labert, and for an hour Areon's hope slipped away. The ogres were within fifty spans of them and nothing could be done to lose them without leaving Labert behind, which Areon refused to do.

For a few more minutes they traveled and the mountains did not seem to get any closer, although they were visible towards the west and the north. Labert still showed no signs of waking.

Areon, panting loudly, stopped and dropped the right side of Labert. "We have to fight, or we will die."

"We will die if we stop," the Rapturer declared indifferently.

Areon, refusing to believe this, took up his mighty bow and knocked one of his three last arrows. The ogres were clearly visible and clearly hungry. Areon loosed an arrow, which hit the leader of the pack in the shoulder and only hindered him. His hand flashed behind his head, and in the next second another arrow was knocked and loosed. This one imbedded itself in an ogre's shin, causing it to fall and trip three others. Areon could do nothing. The Ogre's skin was too tough, and it was too difficult to hit them in the head from the distance he was from them. He unstrung his bow and thrust it into the back of cloak. He reached down into his elemental self, searching back into his memory for the word that would invoke fire magic of the third degree. He felt strong enough to use it but figured that even if it came close to killing him, he would die if he did not try it.

"Even now they come," whispered the Rapturer.

Areon ignored him as beads started to form on his forehead, and his knuckles began to turn white on his clenched fist.

Directly before Areon was about to unleash hellfire, he noticed a white light glinting behind him. It surrounded his face and went beyond. The ogres were now shielding their eyes as they ran.

"Areon, look!" exclaimed the Rapturer.

Areon flung around quickly to see what had slowed the pack of cannibals. A white light illuminated the side of the Alklolock Mountains.

"Areon, fly with me!" yelled the Rapturer as the ogres tried to continue even though the light seemed to be burning their flesh.

Areon whipped around and grabbed Labert by the arm; the Rapturer flung off his cloak and let it float to the ground, giving it one last look. His mighty wings spread, and he and Areon burst fourth into flight as Areon found his aura and flexed it against the ground, ascending at a speed he had never before thought possible.

"Fly towards the light!" yelled the Rapturer over the ogres' futile cries.

As soon as they took flight, the lead ogre jumped and caught Areon by the cloak, threatening to tug them down into imminent doom.

"No!" yelled Areon as the Rapturer flapped as hard as he could, barely holding the three up by the left side. Areon was not only not helping hold up Labert, but holding onto him hoping the Rapturer could hold them both up. They slowly fell, but as they did the light grew stronger, almost material, and the ogre let go with one hand to shield his eyes. Areon took the moment of weakness to hold out his outstretched fingers.

"Die."

The ogre fell from the sky; the puke green flesh on his face and hand still flaming as Areon regained his strength and made the rest of the flight with ease onto the perch of the mountainside.

# CHAPTER XLII

## Scine's Plan

"Welcome to my home," said an unfamiliar voice. Areon dropped Labert to shield his eyes. He let a slit of vision through a crack in his and and behold pure white light. The light subsided to a normal color, then to a ball of light, to an illuminated figure of a man, to a normal man.

"I am Scine, the master of light." The man bowed.

Areon nodded while still breathing hard. While the fire magic and the flight had taken a lot out of him, he realized that he was growing in strength and felt as though he could still do more before going overboard. The Rapturer stood up and folded up his wings around himself under his arms.

"You may call me the Rapturer, master of death magic. These are my comrades, Labert, master of time, and Areon, the mortal flyer. I require a cloak, if you have one of the appropriate size," replied the Rapturer.

"How very interesting," returned Scine as he rushed back down some stone steps and appeared again with a large white overcoat. "It is the best I can do."

"My thanks," said the Rapturer.

"Follow me," said the man. Areon did so instantly.

He led them down a small flight of stone stairs to a large room. After they went through two more cavernous rooms and two more stone staircases, they found a ledge that wrapped around the inside of yet another room.

Areon looked around in awe. A fireplace in the corner, a few chairs, and a lustrous table set with empty plates. Along the other wall sat a counter and some food stocks.

"You must be hungry, and he looks as though he needs a bed," Scine said   The three lifted Labert up the staircase and into the room that was Scine's sleeping area and also led to the porch to the other side of the mountain. When this had been done, the Rapturer sat down and pulled out his black book. Areon squinted at him and wondered how he had retained it after the scuffle they had been in prior to this. Areon took a seat next to him at the table as Scine boiled some water and threw in deer meat chunks along with salt and herbs. He offered them tomatoes that had been growing on a plant near the perch where sunlight spilt in. Areon took one gratefully and ate it like an apple, although he was not particularly fond of them. The Rapturer respectfully refused and began to look through his book, writing and scratching off things to the annoyance of Areon.

Areon almost fell into a sleep, but as his head was tipping Scine put down a plate of meat and vegetables before him. He came back with a large loaf of bread and some butter along with a plate of sliced cheese.

"Now, I know the master of time, Myriad, or Labert, as his closer friends call him, but we have only just met a few times. I will need a full account of your trip and why you chosen to come through the wasteland," said Scine after he had finished serving his extravagant meal.

Areon ate, and through many mouthfuls he told the story of what had happened from the occurrence near his old home at the Temple of Shadow to their last run-in with the ogres in the wasteland.

"How long has this trip taken?" asked Scine, taken aback.

"It has taken Areon three months longer than it seems to him," cut in the Rapturer. "He occupied the Realm of Disappearance."

"So approximately … six months," replied Areon sadly. His child would be born before he could make it back to Elmyra's house with Labert.

"You did the right thing, taking on the guardians. They have grown weak as men have grown stronger in the ways of magic. If whatever stole the gemstone of shadow had discovered you were leaving and went ahead before Labert found out, it could have been disastrous. You would not have had the time to come warn everyone. While you were traveling to the Kingdom of Life, this evil could have gotten to the rest of the temples before you," thought Scine aloud, understanding their deeds.

"So, the last stop will be to the Kingdom of Life, to give them the gemstones so the king can find a better place for them," Areon said, voicing his thoughts aloud.

"Precisely, the Kingdom of Light has not the necessary means to hide such things, not in their current stage," returned Scine. "Their technology is advanced, and they have many people, but other needed things are not here."

"Such as?" asked Areon.

Scine turned his head toward Areon and smiled. "Such as the choirs alliance."

Areon thought for a moment. "But angels already guard most of the temples."

"Yes, but they guard them from far away. If the king's warriors help, and new temples are made along with the angels, then the gems could possibly be safe for all eternity."

"So many live in the kingdom because most of the continent is desolate and dangerous, correct?" he continued.

"Exactly," Scine answered flatly.

"How many live in the kingdom?" asked Areon.

"Within the walls? I'd say twenty thousand, at the least, but I am not really sure these days."

Amazing, thought Areon. He wondered how many resided in the Kingdom of Life.

"Why do the angels only ally with the Continent of Life?" questioned Areon.

"The angels were asked by the famous Bishop Tolok," replied Scine. "Or so the story goes."

"Why does the Continent of Light not ask for help?" asked Areon, full of questions.

"Perhaps they are obstinate, ignorant, who knows?"

"I know," said the Rapturer quietly without looking up. "But I do not wish to disclose that information to you." He added as they all turned to him, "I will say that if you ask, you shall receive."

"Well, back to the task at hand, I believe I have proven my worth to you," said Scine.

"Yes, and we thank you very much for all your help. I am sure I speak for everyone when I say you will be welcome on our trip," interrupted Areon.

"Yes, and I say we head to the Temple of Light as soon as possible. It is not far from here. We will wait for our friend, Labert, rest up for awhile, cross the bridge of the Alklolock Mountains, and head north to the Temple of Light," finished Scine.

"That's an impeccable plan, but what shall we do after?" asked the Rapturer deprecatingly.

"What do you mean?" Scine questioned back picking up his disapproval.

"Well, I, for one, do not wish to walk clear across the continent on foot, for we cannot go back around on a ship and then cross the Sea of Accord, which would be equally impossible for we do not have a ship at that location. No one lives on the coast of the Continent of Light to lend us one. It will take us months upon months and perhaps more to get to the Kingdom of Life," stated the Rapturer.

Scine looked at the table and squinted his eyes, a barely visible grin forming on his face. "That's not entirely true," he said.

---

## EXCERPT FROM THE SCIENTIFIC ARCHIVES OF THE KINGDOM OF LIGHT

" ... many years ago, our excavations produced ancient materials discovered deep beneath the earth, which we have extracted in order to burn and thus fuel the device created. We will not employ the vessel until farther research has been completed. If one wishes to access the blueprints to our most unique project, they must set up an appointment with the king ... "

May light ever show us the way and give us illumination in the afterlife.

# CHAPTER XLIII

## The Iferias Shadows

"Elmyra, will you come help me?" yelled Reiquem from behind the house. She sat and waited for Elmyra to come lift the water out of the well that lay far behind her house. Approximately six months had gone by since Reiquem last saw Areon. She missed him dearly. In this time she had grown older and wiser. She had a grown-up way about her now. She looked down at her stomach, which now had a large distention. She could feel her baby kicking ever so gently now and again. Tears came to her eyes as she thought of Areon, and how he would not be present for the birth of his child. She hoped he was safe.

"Yes, dear?" said Elmyra running back and grabbing the heavy pale of water. She unhooked it off the chain and took Reiquem with her other arm.

"I'm sorry, I just couldn't carry it. I feel weak lately," Reiquem said seriously.

"That's normal," replied Elmyra.

When they entered the house, Reiquem sat down heavily on a chair in the kitchen. She wore a large shirt of Elmyra's that concealed her growing belly and tugged at it aggravated. Elmyra poured the water into a pot so it could boil for soup. She brought Reiquem a glass of water and sat down by her.

"Elmyra," Reiquem said. "Tell me of my parents. When I first came to this house, you and Labert thought I had come to learn of them but other matters were at hand. I have grown close to you, and I am ready to hear how they died."

Elmyra paused for some time. "I have waited patiently until you were ready to hear this. Are you sure dear?" she asked. "I cannot tell you what happened exactly, but I can tell you what they were, although my lack of knowledge may infuriate you."

"I've thought a lot about it over the last months, and I am ready to know what you can tell me. These long years by myself and now I am with Areon. I feel I have people to give me strength now. I have decided. Please elaborate," replied Reiquem resolutely.

"Your parents did not live on this island, as you may have originally thought being as we knew them. They lived on the Continent of Life, where you are originally from. To be more specific, they lived within the walls of the enormous Kingdom of Life, which is where you were born," started Elmyra.

"I vaguely remember leaving the kingdom," Reiquem said.

"You, in a way, took after your parents. They roamed all across the land. They had adventures. They traveled throughout the kingdom's domain, nay through the whole of the Continent of Life, and if they could acquire a ship, they would cross the Sea of Accord and travel into the wasteland to the Kingdom of Light. They worked for the Kingdom of Life as shadows. It's ironic that you are the master of shadow magic." Elmyra stopped with a distant look on her face.

"What do you mean 'shadows'?" asked Reiquem becoming intrigued while sadness welled up inside her.

"Shadows is a name the Kingdom of Life uses for their most secretive, most trusted allies. Your parents were unsung heroes. They did the greatest work for the kingdom while never being recognized for it. Thus the name shadows. They worked in stealth. No one knew of them, save the king. The king trusted your parents with his life, and sometimes they saved it. He would send them on the utmost important errands. The king called them the Iferias Shadows. The final task the king bestowed on them proved fatal." Elmyra stopped again.

"Do you know what it is they did?" inquired Reiquem.

"The last message I received concerning them stated that they died in the Moss Woods like so many before them. I suppose it is fitting that they died in a place that takes so many lives," finished Elmyra.

"What were they like?" asked Reiquem, holding back tears of sorrow.

"Parents whose dedication to their job was second only to the dedication to their daughter," said Elmyra. "They were good people and loved you very much. If they would have known something was going to rend them from you in the Moss Woods, they never would have gone."

Reiquem, overtaken with grief from losing her parents and being away from Areon, began crying uncontrollably. Elmyra put her arm around her for comfort.

"There, there, dear ..."

# CHAPTER XLIV

## Alklolock Mountains

Labert had awakened, and the days slipped by slowly as he recovered some of his strength. Scine's plan to leave straight away did not go quite as he planned. Labert had exhausted himself and needed the extra days. Areon spent the days roaming parts of the mountain. Scine lived on a perch that allowed pathways to either side for easy travel. Occasionally Areon saw a grendel, but it had not the eyesight to see him before he began walking back towards Scine's house. As he walked and ventured farther and farther, he practiced his elemental magic, and occasionally, he flew. It gradually became easier for him.

Areon walked in the side of the mountain from one of these particular excursions. Labert sat at the table eating some food for the first time since the company had arrived. He looked older than he had when Areon met him. The Rapturer had been gone for some time; where he was Areon did not know. Scine played his guitar quietly while resting in one of his many comfortable chairs; his long white hair hanging in his face, and Areon noted a hint of flamboyancy in him.

"Good day, lad!" yelled Labert, back to his usual eccentric self. His antecedent casting of time magic truly took a toll on his old body. "I guess the old man Myriad is older than he once was."

"You should take it easy, old man," joked Areon. He was glad that Labert seemed okay. "I'm glad you'll make it."

Areon sat down in a chair and rested. He looked toward the perch and to the outside world. A light rain sprinkled down, which turned into a heavy rainfall.

"Ahh, I do so love the rain. It seems to wash away the troubles of this land for the duration," remarked Scine.

Areon closed his eyes and fell asleep while listening to the pattering of rain on the side of the large mountain.

Areon lost track of the days as Labert recovered and went over plans with the Rapturer. Often he and Scine practiced magic or went hunting. After over a week went by, Areon and Scine went down towards the foot of the mountains and killed a doe for more food. Scine had been running low trying to feed his guests. Areon figured that approximately three weeks went by before he grew restless and actually felt like continuing on their long journey, although he had no idea how they planned on getting to the Kingdom of Life now that they had traveled so far.

Areon sat in the house while Labert and Scine chatted lightheartedly. He rose from his sitting position and walked over to the table.

"When will we leave?" he demanded.

"Are you in a hurry to face such dangers ahead?" asked Labert.

"Yes, as a matter of fact, I am," Areon shot back almost yelling. "I want to get back and see Reiquem as soon as possible."

Labert hung his head. "He's right," he said and looked up at Scine. "We've lingered here far too long."

"I have sat idle far too long. I will join you on this journey," stated Scine. "We leave at dawn, destination: the bridge of the Alklolocks and beyond towards the Temple of Light."

"Thank you," said Areon.

Labert woke up Areon with a vigorous shake. Areon blinked several times to clear his eyes and rose. He felt as ready as Scine seemed. The group ate a big breakfast consisting of cheese, bread, and deer meat. Areon had gained a little weight while staying at Scine's house and for that he was grateful.

Areon stood up in the large main room and looked at his company; the Rapturer stood with his book in hand and Scine's cloak wrapped tightly about him; Labert, with his torn purple cloak, gathered up the sleeping supplies and wrapped them to his belt; and Scine sat cross-legged, filling a bag with hunks of meat and wrapped bread. Areon fastened his sword to his belt and made sure his small knife was snug in his boot. He hung his bow over his back, although it was now obsolete without arrows. The group left through the back door that someone had chiseled out of the stone. The company walked in silence down a long, narrow tunnel. Areon ran his hand along the solid rock and wondered who had built the place. The path led to the west side of the Alklolock Mountains where finally the group emerged into the weak sunlight.

"We all can walk along this path until we get to the bridge of the Alklolocks, then we walk across the smaller of the two Alklolock Mountains. We will be able to see the Kingdom of Light from the west of the mountain range and to the south of the kingdom the temple. With our strength combined, the guardian will be no match. We approach the Kingdom of Light from the south," explained Scine.

Areon could barely see the bridge, which was suspended less than a league away.

It took the group the better part of two hours to reach the bridge due to the jagged, unstable rocks that lay underfoot. When they did finally reach it, Areon wished they had not. It consisted of old, narrow planks of wood, strung together by rope. The rope stretched up to waist level where thicker ropes ran along either side for handrails. The party stopped to survey the surrounding area. The bridge looked securely fastened to fat stakes stuck deep in the ground, but everyone still looked a little apprehensive about crossing, so Scine took the initiative. Before long, the whole party was walking along the creaking, swaying bridge; it held strong, and before Areon could look down twice at the ground so far below them, they were all across and walking up along the rocks over the western range of the Alklolocks.

The bridge was so high up on the range that it took only a matter of minutes of climbing before everyone could see over the mountains and down into a gigantic valley. In the western most part of the valley, Areon could see a city. The houses looked the size of ants from where the party stood. Areon could see thousands of people walking about, although it looked as though they were not moving much. The castle seemed to be the only thing easy to make out from the distance. It was enormous. Farmland sat to the south of the land, which looked as if it were very fertile. When Areon looked farther south, he could see a dip in the land, which was where he guessed the temple resided.

"If we make our way down the mountain heading straight west, we should travel directly over the dip and down into to where the temple is.

But I must warn you that the kingdom doesn't allow any to travel down there ever. We must camp at the foot of the Alklolocks and wait until nightfall to make our way, which we will do in stealth so that the guards will not see us," Scine said.

"We are south enough so that we will not be seen if we head straight west," stated Labert.

"Yes, but sometimes scouts are sent out to make sure all is well; though they are wary and do not wander to far south," replied Scine.

After the group formed the consensus, they all began to make the long trek down toward the foot of the mountains. It was a slow journey of which Areon seemed grateful due to the fact he had hoped not to have to sit and wait much at the bottom of the mountain. When night neared, the group neared the bottom, and Areon saw flickers of light form on the watchtowers that loomed above the city walls from all four corners. Some time later he noticed smaller moving lights that the guards carried as they walked the battlements of the castle.

Everyone sat down on some sort of rock or near a bush and said little. Areon took a seat by Scine. Scine seemed like a very nice person, granted he was a little flamboyant. He was close to Areon's age and dressed in some sort of holy robe. They chatted idly until the moon was high in the sky and after still. Scine seemed awfully lighthearted, and Areon found himself rather fond of the master of light magic. He seemed more like Areon than the rest of the more serious group, which had fallen asleep. Areon watched the great city as he leaned against a larger tree while putting his hands behind his head and looking up at the large moon; the last thing he saw before shutting his eyes.

Everyone slept in the next morning. Every person who woke up woke the next person. Areon was the last person, and Scine was the one to wake him by yawning heavily beside him.

"It's a quarter of a day's walk to the temple. Hope not to meet anyone but expect to," Scine said, being the first to talk. They took off in silence.

Areon watched the city and castle go by, and they walked farther west. When the sun had risen in accordance with noon, the group decided to take a break and eat some food. Scine and Areon got some water from a small spring and boiled the deer meat. The meal paralleled a meager one, but it was sufficient to keep them on their feet. Finally the group found themselves going down the small dip, and Areon was face to face with the next temple.

# CHAPTER XLV

## The Powers' Understanding and the Temple of Light

The Temple of Light stole Areon's breath. It was a building composed of pure light—foreboding light sending out a message that all should leave the area unless they wanted to be blinded. Areon looked back to make sure they were out of the site of the great kingdom. They were and Areon prepared to fight. The four headed down farther and were now directly in front of the shining temple. It shone so bright that Areon could not tell what it was made of. Perhaps it was pure light. Out of the entry some light seemed to detach itself from the rest of the building, and before them stood a Power.

"The sixth order banishes you from this place. Leave now and no harm shall befall you," a voice echoed out.

"We cannot leave," yelled Scine. "The gemstones are no longer safe from the evil in this world. We have all come to claim it."

"Then all of you shall die," replied the echoing voice, and in front of their very eyes the light turned into an angel. He faced them with a cold, handsome smile on his face and then raised his left hand where a sword made of lightning materialized. A horribly large, white-hot sword crackled with blue sparks. Scine acted quickly forming a barrier of light around himself while stepping in front of the group. The power struck and sent sparks flying from both sword and barrier. The light rippled around Scine and he smiled.

"Your sword will not avail you, Power of the sixth order," he said impudently.

"We could use Reiquem's help now," remarked Labert.

The group stood ready to fight for some time. The angel watched with curiosity.

"Why do you not attack?" it asked without malevolence.

"We do not wish to fight, only to obtain the gemstone," Labert exclaimed quickly.

"What will be the consummation of your quest?" asked the angel.

"A safer place for the gems, nothing more," said Areon, sensing more death could be avoided.

"The Cherub was not given time to understand your intentions; he must have been attacked first, and the Throne would never have listened, as the rest will not. But I have wisdom paralleling the Cherubim, and I sense your benevolence and know when mortals lie. Go now, bringers of better days. I will not stop those who would not attack me." The Power melted back into the light, and a gap in the Temple of Light formed, making it possible to enter.

"Excellent," said Labert.

Scine still had a mischievous smile on his face. "Let us enter." He led the way in.

The temple was undoubtedly gorgeous. Light perpetually reflected off every wall, although Areon could not tell where it originated. All four decided that they would go in the temple and see what it was like. Around several corners and up a small set of stairs, a black blob blocked what Areon knew to be the gemstone of light. Scine approached first and looked back at everyone with the same smile. He did not put his hands up as the other masters had done. He simply let the light resonate off himself. Areon remembered seeing him do the same thing when they entered his mountain home. Soon Areon was shielding his eyes. Scine flexed his aura, and the light grew brighter as his hands fell to his sides, palms open. Areon finally lost sight of Scine and only beheld light. Blinding light once again. Areon now had his eyes shut with his hands covering them. It almost became truly unbearable to stand in the presence of the master. Slowly, the red in Areon's eyes subsided and the warmth coming from Scine resided. When Labert, Areon, and the Rapturer opened their eyes, the block of darkness was gone and a shining orb remained.

Scine grabbed it expeditiously and handed it to Labert.

"Now we make for the Kingdom of Light," Scine said.

# CHAPTER XLVI

## The City

Not much time had gone by. The daylight still remained, although it would soon be gone. The group wandered out of the temple stealthily, making sure no person had left the village in order to see what the four were up to. None were seen, so they made their way over the hill and far away from the temple without heading too far east, so as not to seem suspicious. By the time they reached their destination the sun had turned from bright yellow to orange and it was slowly sinking toward the horizon.

"We'll camp here. We will be safe from danger because of the Kingdom of Light; nothing evil comes near this place," Scine said.

Areon slumped down in the grass, lay back, and looked up at the stars; he thought of Reiquem. He thought about how they would get to spend the rest of their lives together after this journey was over. He wondered where they would go and thought about all the things they would do. Even if he never got to meet another woman in the world, he knew she was the one for him; as he knew she thought he was for her. Those thoughts made him happy because he forgot about the present separation and only thought of the future.

Before Areon fell asleep, he tried to mentally prepare himself for the next day. While he had gotten to know Scine as the others did during the stay at his mountain home, he had explained the plan to everyone of how they would transport all four of them to the Continent of Life in a timely manner. He said it could be done within days, a statement Areon did not believe. The Rapturer mentioned that it would take months to walk back, cross the Sea of Accord, and get into the great city of the Kingdom of Life if they were all forced to walk. Areon thought it might even take longer, considering how far the party had sailed with elemental wind magic. While the Rapturer disagreed that the whole group could get there in days, he also mentioned that he could do it in the time Scine allotted were he to travel alone. Areon knew he meant fly, a feat that only the Rapturer could do. But he doubted the Rapturer would leave without them; the company offered great protection. During the debate that went on at the mountain home, Scine finally revealed how he planned to leave the continent; not by land, but by air, and not with wings. He planned to steal some sort of airship that the kingdom's finest engineers had been working on for years. Areon did not know if this was such a good idea, but it seemed the only feasible way to get the gemstones to safety as soon as possible. Scine had not gone into much detail, but Areon knew that large cloth balls were strapped to a large wooden ark. The round balls of cloth had holes in the top and bottom. A special substance was burned at the bottom to supply hot air that lifted the ark off the ground. The engineers wanted a ship that could fly without magic use. Areon knew the four would need to use wind and fire magic to get the airship going, especially since they would not have the help of any scientists, and it was unlikely the wind would come from the west to help push the large blown up ... well, whatever they were. The idea sounded mad to Areon, but if it worked, they would cross the Sea of Accord within two days and be into the great city of the other continent within three days. An accomplishment worth noting, he thought, and fell asleep.

Scine woke everyone when three hours had passed since sunrise. Areon left his money at the Daridyn's place, but Scine said his gold would pay for the group to stay at an inn where they would spend the week while Scine and Labert figured out how to get at the airship. Scine's bold reckless-ness and Labert's wise surreptitiousness would go together quite perfectly. Areon planned to spend the week mingling with people. Socialization he had missed out on his entire life would be welcome.

The group walked slowly over the grassy land. The castle sort of sat in a wide-open area at the bottom of an enormous valley. In front of it ran a river, which happened to be the city's source of water. Several acres of farm-land and large farmhouses sat to the west of the kingdom's domain. Areon decided that the location was suited for attacks. The guards could clearly see something coming from any way, provided they were close enough to be over the valleys very short, slow sloping walls, which was quite a distance.

When they arrived at the river, an old man, who looked bored, waited patiently for them to get to the ferry. He smiled and said, "Where do you all come from?"

Labert answered smoothly, "My friends and I traveled far from an island on the west side in order to visit a relative of mine. I dare not travel alone over that distance."

"Good thinking. I would try and point you in the direction of your relative, but odds are I wouldn't know them. Too many live here nowadays, and the city grows larger every year."

"We will do fine, I'm sure." Labert bowed a bit, and they all four hopped on the wooden ferry that was tied to a large wooden post. The Rapturer grinned nastily at the old man, who could not meet his gaze. Areon felt bad for him and smiled as he got on. The ferry made Areon sway a bit as the old man kicked it away from the river. A young man on the other side grabbed the rope as Scine threw it to him. The young man tied it up quickly and everyone, save the Rapturer, thanked him and waved to the old man on the other side.

As they approached the mighty city, Labert said, "Do not so much as mention the gemstones. That's the last thing we need brought up."

Everyone nodded.

Upon reaching the gates to the city Areon found himself last to enter. It was truly magnificent. The entrance was open since it was daylight, and it lead to a cobblestone walkway with multiple stores, shops, inns, and taverns to either side. Eventually this walkway led to the castle, but Areon could only see the upper level while standing at the beginning of the city. Behind all of the buildings, houses were packed tightly together, thousands of houses. Areon saw a stable nearby as they walked farther down looking for a run of the mill inn. Many people filled the streets. Several times Areon bumped into someone, but they seemed to hardly notice and went about on their way. He also saw several shrines and wells, butcheries, everything one could ever need. It was no wonder that the city grew every year. Areon felt very safe inside the city walls, like everything he would ever need was inside.

"Ahh, here we are, the Lost Travelers Inn. Cozy place; very lively folk. It's a tavern with an inn on the second floor. Should suit us well," said Scine.

"I'll be ready when we leave," said the Rapturer and disappeared into the crowd.

"Very cold soul," remarked Scine, and they all three walked in.

Being later in the day only a few men sat around. They looked up with bloodshot eyes and then back to their drinks. The room was much larger than any inn or tavern Areon had ever been to. The bar sat in the middle, and the bartender was leaning over it looking at the three that had just entered.

"We need a room for under a week." Scine threw the bartender some gold coins and he smiled and said, "This way, gentlemen."

That night Labert and Scine left the inn. Areon left their room to go down and see who would come to the tavern. He ordered a beer and sat down at a small table toward the back of the room. The tavern was, apparently, home to many regulars. It seemed that as the night went on more and more people came in that knew each other. As more time passed a group of three men got up and went to the most occupied part of the tavern. They raised their drinks and sang a song for the crowd:

> Try as you might
> you'll never find a plight,
> as dreary as ours.
> As we sit and drink away the hours.
> Oh, it's sad and true as the sea so blue
> that we never find a thing to do.
> But with ale and wine, and beer so fine,
> we can laugh away the time.
> So pick up your mug and
> chug a lug a lug.
> Don't say no ...
> 'Cuz it's a secret to
> everybody new
> that like a handless yarn raveler,
> no one from this inn is a lost traveler!

Areon raised his mug and cheered with everyone else who happened to be cheering and laughing. It really was a good time for everyone there, even Areon, who did not know anyone. The group of three men hugged and laughed merrily while everyone settled back in (or kept on laughing and shouting), and Areon stayed late into the night talking with various people from the Light Kingdom.

When Areon awoke the next morning, Labert and Scine had come and gone again, and the Rapturer showed no sign of himself. He went over to the basin and drank some of the clean water that the innkeeper had apparently poured. After refreshing himself, he walked down the staircase and through the large tavern out into the city to explore.

More than once Areon found himself close to the truly magnificent castle. A small moat surrounded the entirety of the structure with soldiers stationed beside small ferries. A large drawbridge, which at the current time was down, made a public walkway for any who had business at the castle. It looked like it was made of solid oak and had straps of black metal running across the large planks. After the winding moat, the drawbridge attached itself to a large wall with large battlements for guards to keep watch. A large stone staircase preceded the final doors to the castle, at which a guard stood to either side. The walls reached up toward the sky for half a league. Several silver stone walkways linked the main castle area to other parts of the enormous palace. Several wings also protruded out the side of the castle. The great walls housed a cathedral inside them that had large pillars in front of the stained doors. Areon could not see beyond all this but decided that more probably lingered behind all these buildings rooms, ferries, and so on.

Areon wanted to figure out how people traveled across this city so fast. Two large walkways occupied the city and crossed each other forming an X through the entire city. In the middle, where the two roads met, four large posts with enormous wheels on top stood. Ropes crossed through in a pattern that was easily identifiable to Areon. He realized that at one end of the city a carriage sat with a rope tied to it, and that rope led to the middle of the city, around the great wheels, and to a horse where it was tied on securely. If someone on the outskirts of town wanted to get to the middle, they simple got in the carriage and a man would blow a large horn, thus making the man riding on the horse in the middle ride to the a different outskirt, and the person would fly forward to the middle of the city. The horse would make its way back as fast as it wanted. Areon noted that it was a truly ingenious plan if most could not ride horses, which seemed to be the case.

The days began to take longer for Areon, who was bored. Although the city owned much to offer and show, Areon saw most of it on his visits. He wanted to know what Scine and Labert had come up with while on their stealth mission. He knew not at all where the Rapturer might be waiting for them in all his mystery.

Also by this time he realized the city was much larger than twenty thousand people. It had to be closer to fifty thousand. That many people and Areon had not even managed to make a friend. He did not much care, for the last day neared and Labert would make ready the mission for tomorrow. They would all steal the magnificent airship, and Areon would have to leave the place that he was growing accustomed to.

When Labert and Scine walked in the room in the inn where Areon currently sat, they greeted him without as much as a hello. Both seemed agitated, and they sat down, breathing heavily.

"What happened?" asked Areon.

"A very long story indeed," returned Labert hastily. He noticed that Scine had a very peculiar grin on his face, as though he loved seeing Labert in such a flustered mood.

"We were trying to get word on the whereabouts and blueprints of the airship," offered Scine, so Areon turned to hear him speak. "We figured out where they house this beast, compliments of some drunk guard. See, Labert paid this young temptress a few of my gold pieces so that she might entice a guard to come with us drinking. Of course it worked, seeing as how she was beautiful and all. Labert filled her in on the matter as far as that she needed to get him drunk and make him think he would bring her home, all the while staying and talking with us. She didn't ask any more questions after we flashed her the gold. Then we got the information long after his shift was over, mind you."

Then Labert stepped in. "We forgot the blueprints for the time being, as we still had time. We waited until the next morning to get into the place."

"Which was where?" interrupted Areon. They heard a woman walking down the hall outside the room, and everyone, including the confused Areon, sat still and made sure not to breathe. The walking sounds and her faint singing subsided, and the story continued.

"In one of the underground parts of the castle, which we've not yet been to," finished Labert.

"But, we tried to get there and survey the area and all, but we figured some would still be in there at night, and if they were, we would need you with us, and, of course, the Rapturer, if we can ever find him."

"Of course, the first and foremost reason we didn't go in deals with the guards that caught us lurking around the castle," added Labert.

"How did you get in and out?" asked Areon, but he immediately knew the answer after asking.

"Haste, of course, my boy!" cried Labert, but he quickly stopped his excitement and looked toward the door.

"Haste, indeed, and we'll need it tomorrow, for we are going back and leaving with the airship with or without the Rapturer," finished Scine. He plopped down on the bed and slept.

"Indeed, my boy. Are you ready to get back to the other continent?" asked Labert.

"I am," Areon said sincerely.

"Good. When we get there, we shall send Scine out with news to Elmyra and Reiquem. He can travel on light without us and will reach them before we ever could," continued Labert. "Now rest, for tomorrow we embark and fly to the Continent of Life."

# CHAPTER XLVII

## A Questionable Exploit

Areon slept little that night because of his anxiousness at the thought of trying to steal something from the Kingdom of Light. If they were caught, the consequences would be harsh. He could not shake the thought of everything they might do. Perhaps the royal guard would hang them immediately. Thieves were not treated as kindly on this continent as he heard they were on the other. He looked over at Labert as he stirred. The old master of time looked up, blinked several times, and threw the covers off.

"Ahh, Areon, you're awake," he stated.

"I can't sleep," whispered Areon.

"It doesn't matter anymore, we must depart."

Scine woke up to their quiet voices. He did not say anything, but he looked out the window and saw that the sun was not up yet, although signs of its presences on the horizon were apparent.

"We must leave soon," he whispered finally. "We should make haste while the sun is not yet risen."

Areon and Labert acquiesced and put on their things. Areon slept in his clothes these days due to his fabulous cloak. He had not even tried to take it off for some time. He took up his sword and strapped it on. He placed his bow across his back along with the quiver that now contained arrows. He bought them while Scine and Labert were out on their mission to find the airship. He looked over at the two masters, who did not wield weapons, and all three nodded in unison. The time to depart had come at last. Areon could feel himself becoming excited by the fact that every step made in his endeavor was a step closer to him being with Reiquem. Scine opened the door surreptitiously, and they made their way down the creaky steps of the inn and out into the streets of the Kingdom of Light. Very few were out on the streets at this early of an hour, and it was easy to make their way toward the castle without anyone being the wiser of what the three were about to do. Approximately halfway to the glorious castle, Areon felt a gust of wind come across the back of his head. As all of them turned the Rapturer stood behind them wrapping a new cloak about his massive wings. The brim of his hat covered his face until he looked up, and Areon saw the mysterious glasses he always wore.

"It is time then?" the Rapturer asked in his coarse voice.

"Indeed," replied Labert sincerely. The group then continued in silence, feeling naked as they walked along the bare streets like criminals.

"This way," motioned Labert as they all crossed swiftly over the large drawbridge that led across the moat and into the labyrinth-like castle. Immediately after they entered the castle walls, Labert stopped them with his hand and looked around to the left. No guards were present at the early hour except up on the battlements. The castle doors were shut tightly, and Areon wondered how they were going to get in. Labert led them farther to the left where they walked down a flight of stairs and into darkness. Areon held out his hands in front of him as he tried to make his way in the darkness that ensued. Torches started appearing on the walls and the steps stopped. They were all down in the underground levels of the castle. Labert grabbed a torch off the wall and walked around the twisting tunnels that were the under the castle. No guards needed guard the area, for it had not led to anything except for more stone hallways. But then, around one of the turns, a guard sat on a wooden stool, staring straight ahead at a large mahogany doorway. Areon was the last of the company walking, and he had not seen the man sitting. Labert stopped, and he stopped Scine, The Rapturer stopped well behind them. Areon was looking apprehensively behind the group for followers. He walked right by the Rapturer and into Labert, who could not quite stop Areon from running into the guard. . The guard had been drinking wine, and he looked up lazily at the man that had run into him. Areon and the man looked at each other dumbfounded for a second, and the stupefied look in his eyes quickly turned to one of dread.

The guard arose to seize Areon, but Areon was too quick. He grabbed the empty wine bottle, ducked out of the way of the guard's gauntleted hand, and smote him on the head in one fluent motion. The guard yelled and fell to the ground unconscious next to the door he had been guarding.

"And now we must hurry," stated the Rapturer irritated.

Labert grabbed the door that the party needed to get into. They walked into a small corridor. To the immediate right they went up to another large door, which was locked from the inside.

The group contemplated what to do for a minute.

"I hear guards coming from down the corridor," hissed Scine. "This is the room, correct, Labert?"

"It is, but I do not know if the airship is ready to fly. If we break this door down, many guards will come without a doubt," replied the old time master.

"From the sounds of the guards, we'll be caught anyway," said Areon louder than the other two. The Rapturer gave a despondent look toward the voices coming their way.

Areon spread his fingers at the door. "Nasai!" he shouted, and second degree fire magic leapt out at the door. A large hole with a fiery outline was now the path that led to the airship.

Labert shook his head, Scine grinned, and the Rapturer looked back at the loudening noises coming from the advancing guards. Everyone walked through with bent backs led by the master of time.

Areon thought it strange that he hardly felt drained of energy at all. Perhaps he was getting used to all the magic, and he would be ready for third degree fire magic. Belgraf had only given him the old days' incantation, yet never let him attempt.

The group burst in through the hole in the door to find an enormous room and, of course, the enormous airship with its clothed balls suspended in the air by giant breakaway ropes; it was ready for takeoff.

"And, uh, wh-who might you be?" said a voice

The entire group whirled around to find a very old looking man with thick spectacles on that made his eyes abnormally large. He was balding with white hair, not unlike Belgraf's.

Labert bowed ever so slightly. "We are on a mission and plan to take the airship by force, if necessary."

"And who, pray tell, is going to fly this contraption?" said the old man.

Scine spoke up. "I have heard of the workings of this airship and believe I might be able with a little help from my friends."

"Where are you going?" said the old man curiously. Areon glanced around to see if any of the guards had made it his far yet.

"The Continent of Life, and our intentions are noble," replied Labert.

The old man looked at them shrewdly. "I will not lie. I have known how to fly this for half a year, and the king refuses to grant me permission to fly it. I will accompany you if you swear none will get hurt as we try and escape."

Labert nodded quickly and went to climb the slanted ladder that led to the ark of an airship.

"And," continued the old man slowly. Labert pursed his lips. "If we happen to get caught, you will all hold to the story that I was kidnapped and had no part of this, for that is what you're doing." The old man winked at them.

"We promise," said Scine, and Areon nodded. The Rapturer climbed aboard after Labert. The old man grabbed some supplies and boarded with Areon and Scine.

Areon turned to the old man, who seemed to be inspecting the ties that led to the breakaway ropes. "What is your name?"

"Gremwold the Inventor. Pleasure to meet you, thief," replied Gremwold.

"We're not—" but Areon was cut short by the man's upraised hand as he continued to prepare for take off. Everyone crowded around Gremwold as Labert watched the door warily.

"Aren't you a bit nervous about simply leaving everything behind and coming with people you've never met?" asked Areon.

Gremwold stopped and stared at him with huge eyes through his massive spectacles. "Well, no, not really. The king keeps me locked up in here day and night trying to stimulate me to muster up ideas for his kingdom's glory. I will be glad to be out and about for a change. I trust since I have decided to help you that you will return me someday?"

"Perhaps," replied the Rapturer coldly.

Gremwold looked at him for a moment and then continued.

"Now, I wonder ... We could start a fire using my tinderbox and keep the fires lit with the black substance we have uncovered ..." he trailed off. "Then we must hope the wind is coming from the west in order to get us where we need to be ..." he started talking quieter now. "I can't quite remember where the wind was coming from today."

"None of that is necessary," said the Rapturer voicing what Areon was about to say. "All of us are sufficient in elemental magic."

"Are you, then?" said a rather surprised inventor. "Good, that will save us a load of trouble. Now if I'm not mistaken we must leave this instant, as the guards will be checking this room shortly for news of the disturbance caused by your friend's fire on the doo—" Gremwold seemed to finally understand. "Ahh, yes, the fire magic. Ho ho! Good, good. Well, all that's left is for us, that is to say you, to do is shoot small burst of fire from the bottom into the holes that are provided on the cloth balls."

Areon immediately began letting the fire magic surge forward from his palms and up into one of the balls that, to his surprise, started to expand slowly so that the cloth was stretched. Labert began doing more fire into the second cloth ball in short bursts, and soon the ark and cloth was struggling against the ropes that held the entire contraption down. Gremwold quickly ran to certain ropes that ran from the bottom of the ark and to the top of the stretched out ball type things. He tugged on one of the knots, and the ark tilted up, forcing the entire party to stagger on the deck of the large wooden ark. Gremwold quickly ran to the other side and pulled the binding loose and the ark started heading toward the ceiling, but a sudden realization hit him as he did this.

"I've forgotten to open up the roof!" he yelled frantically. In moments the ark would hit the ceiling and the advancing guards would catch them.

"How do you open it?" yelled Areon.

Gremwold pointed to the sides of the large room. "Those weights are held up by large pillars. You must knock them out in order for the weights to drop and rend the ceiling in two."

Areon jumped quickly from the ark and everyone ran to the sides to see, save the Rapturer, who took off his cloak and hat and jumped to the other side where the weight sat.

"They're stealing the airship!" someone screamed. Areon landed lightly on the ground and the Rapturer behind him. They looked at each other momentarily, and Areon, running low on strength, mustered up all the energy left and forced out a word.

"Kireth." The pillar was hit by weak second degree magic, but it had been enough. The Rapturer, with inhuman speed and strength, leapt up ten feet and kicked the pillar on its side and the ceiling split in two being forced open by the weights that were no longer held up.

"Stop them immediately," yelled a castle guard. Two ran forward at

Areon, who was closest and fainting, but the Rapturer grabbed Areon by the stomach before he fell and looked at the guards menacingly.

"It is not your time, but I will kill you to save it from being his."

None of the guards moved as they gawked at his wings.

"You are of the Nine," one managed to say.

"No," returned the Rapturer shortly. "Never." He raised his mighty wings and pushed them down with such great force that the three castle guards were knocked over. He and Areon were back in the ship as it slowly climbed higher into the sky.

Immediately when the Rapturer and Areon were safe inside, Labert and Scine began shooting bursts into the cloth again and eventually the castle became very small.

"That is enough short bursts for now," stated Gremwold, who looked very pleased at the prospect of being out of the castle for some time.

Scine ran to the back of the large ark and held his hand in the air where a vortex appeared. He muttered softly to himself, and the company started flying east at an incredible speed.

# CHAPTER XLVIII

## Crossing the Sea of Accord

When Areon awoke, he remembered everything that had transpired. He regretted, once again, his weakness at using second degree magic, as he hoped to be proficient in third degree one day. Areon wondered how he was in an enclosed room on some sort of bed but then realized that the ark was so large it probably had a few rooms under its large deck.

Areon was tired so he laid back on the pillow and thought more of magic. Rarely did he speak words of the old days aloud when he used first degree magic, but second degree only had three words that could summon it, and all three varied in strength and size. For the third and final degree of magic there was only one word that would bring forth such a burst from within one, and Areon had never even dared mutter it, although Belgraf had hesitatingly showed him on one special occasion. Even the master wizard was drained of energy as he had finished.

Areon brushed the thoughts of Belgraf from his mind, remembering the feeling of homesickness. His thoughts turned to Reiquem, which did not help to boost his morale. He longed to see her more than anything. Sometime soon their child would be born, and Areon hoped more than anything for him to be with Reiquem when it happened, but he thought that it might not be. He also wished to see the gemstones to safety, and if it meant keeping Reiquem out of danger, then he could wait awhile longer before seeing her again.

Areon stopped thinking as the sound of footsteps became louder. Labert entered the room smiling warmly seeing that Areon was now awake.

"Glad to see you awake." Labert had a tray of food that must have come from the ship's supply. "Here, eat. You must regain your strength."

"Thanks," replied Areon wearily.

"You won't be thanking me when you're better." Labert smiled slyly. "We need someone to do elemental wind in order to keep us headed in a westerly direction."

"How long have I been asleep?" asked Areon.

"No longer than a day, but I'm afraid we all grow weak, and Gremwold doesn't do magic of any sort."

Areon nodded. "What is our plan after we cross the Sea of Accord?"

"The master of life lives near the temple and farther to the East lies the Kingdom of Life," returned Labert as Areon tore into a loaf of bread.

"Who is that?" Areon asked through a mouthful.

"I'm afraid none of us have met him actually. Our shady friend the Rapturer has only been able to tell us that his name is Eanty, and he lives near the Kingdom of Life serving as one of their Shadows."

"Shadows?" asked Areon, as he ceased to eat for the moment.

"You've never heard of Shadows?" asked Labert incredulously.

Areon shook his head. "I am uneducated in the ways of the kingdoms."

"Has Reiquem told you how her parents died?" asked Labert quietly.

"She would not discuss them with me when we first met, and I never bothered to bring the matter up again until she was ready to tell me about it," Areon said quickly.

"I will tell you what they were only because I am positive that Elmyra has told her. You see, Areon, when you and Reiquem arrived, I was expecting her to come," began Labert.

Areon squinted his eyes and kept eating the bread and water.

"I assumed she wished to know how her parents died." Labert continued looking down at the floor. "Elmyra and I used to live and be in closer contact with the Kingdom of Life. This was long before yours and Reiquem's time. I knew her parents well, and I knew they had a daughter when they died. From what I understood, Reiquem ran away at a very young age when she heard her parents had been murdered in the Moss Woods. This is the reason she is so independent. To this day I know not who her master was, as she was an apprentice master of shadow, but as I grew older I decided to leave the continent and live out my days mapmaking with Leviathan, living on our island, as Elmyra could summon him. When I saw Reiquem, I instantly recognized those abysmal black eyes marking a master of shadow." Labert looked at Areon for the first time. I hoped to tell her that her parents were Shadows for the kingdom, but as the news of what had happened took precedence at the time, I did not press the matter and only waited for her to ask. I am certain that Elmyra has explained Reiquem's mother's and father's occupation and where they died."

"What are Shadows?" asked Areon.

"Spies for the Kingdom. People sent on the utmost important missions that pertain to stealth and quiet," answered Labert.

"What killed them?"

"We're not sure, but judging by where they died, it could've been anything." Labert shrugged and shook his head.

They both sat in silence for several minutes.

"Well, now I will be there for her," announced Areon resolutely.

"You're a good man, Areon, and I am glad someone faithful with take the place of her loving parents, although she did not have long to know them."

They both sat again for some time before Areon spoke again. "So what is our plan then?"

"According to the Rapturer, Eanty's house is two weeks' walk into the continent, but with our airship it should take us less than two days to get there from here."

"From here?" said Areon with skepticism apparent in his voice.

"Its speed is incredible with our wind magic, and the hot air inside the cloth balls does not need to be replenished that often. This device is incredible. With the proper people on board, we travel even faster than with our catamaran and the proper mages," said Labert.

"But our speed was incredible with the boat, surely this can't be faster?" said Areon.

"It is, but barely, and now," he said standing up, "we need your help when you're ready, so I will be on board. Our plan of action is to cross the Sea of Accord and find Eanty's house, which is near the Temple of Life and the kingdom."

"What then?" asked Areon.

Labert stopped halfway up the stairs. "And then we see what he has to say, what he knows, and so on and so forth. We see if we can acquire the gemstone of life, and if we do, we take it to the kingdom. Hopefully they will believe that the shadow gem has gone missing and see the need to take more precaution in the future."

"You're using the gemstones as bait," replied Areon shrewdly.

Labert grinned. "Whatever evil stole the gemstone will undoubtedly want the rest, whether it be for ransom or for destruction, and will come to the kingdom looking for them. Then we will get the gemstone from whoever did it and put them in proper places where they can never be touched again."

"What happens if whoever stole the shadow gem gets too close to the other gems?" asked Areon.

He could tell Labert was growing weary of his questions. "At least some sort of alignment is necessary in order for the one to break free. We think. I will let you read about it in one of the books I have at home someday, but I assure it will not happen. If it does, may God and the angels be with us." He ran back up the steps.

Areon kicked his feet over the side of the bed and decided that he should probably go and help the others. He put his hands in his face and tried to brush Reiquem from his mind for the time being. He thought about how he would get to see her in the future when the gems had been delivered to the Kingdom of Life. They could all deal with it then; it would no longer be his problem. They would be in good hands, and if Labert wanted to stay, he could, but Areon would get back to Reiquem no matter the cost at that point.

He got up and went onto the deck. There sat Gremwold by the deck railing staring out at the sky. The Rapturer was doing wind magic that shot out toward the west. He looked tired. Scine walked over to him. He looked equally tired.

"Gremwold has it timed pretty well when to keep the hollow balls full of hot air, but you can tell if it needs it because we start dropping." Scine put his hand on Areon's shoulder. "But for now I need rest. You have to take the next shift. Don't use second level whatever you do. It's too hot, and you'll waste all the energy we're going to need." He walked back underneath to where Areon had been sleeping.

Areon looked over at Labert, who relieved the Rapturer. After he came to Areon and grinned nastily at him with sweat on his face, sat down against a railing by himself, and started writing in his book again with his crude utensil. Labert began a lazy elemental wind magic that continued to push the ark along at an incredible rate. Areon glanced over the edge, and to his great surprise, the land was rushing by them from so far below. The party had covered so much sea on the little boat they had, but it was not as fast as they were covering ground now.

He turned to Gremwold. "Incredible."

"It would not be possible to go this fast were you all not sufficient mages," replied Gremwold. "The wind would just carry you along at whatever speed it felt like."

"How long until we get to the continent?" asked Areon.

"Not long. Another day and night perhaps, if my calculations are correct, and if you can all continue on like this."

"It will be easier with plenty of food," returned Areon.

"There are large food supplies under the deck."

"Good."

And so it went for the rest of the day; Areon did the fire magic when Gremwold thought it time, and Labert shot out large vortexes of wind that pushed the ark at an incredible rate. Finally Areon walked over to Labert, who had taken a break when they were high enough in the air to do so.

"How will we know where to go?" yelled Areon over the rushing wind.

"The kingdoms are in direct alignment with each other. We set our course for an easterly direction so that we would not stray north or south. When we cross the Sea of Accord, we should see a beacon the kingdom has put up so that they might see invasions from the sea. Eanty lives in the woods directly to the east of the beacon, so we should be able to find him rather easily," Labert yelled back.

"Is the beacon that big?"

"It is three times the size of a normal watchtower. We will almost have trouble clearing it." The master of time smiled as he let another whoosh of wind protrude from his hands. Labert was taken to his knees.

"Labert, are you okay?" asked Areon worriedly.

He did not respond, but he looked drained of energy. Areon picked him up and put Labert's arm around his neck and carried him down below where Scine sat, eating on one of the stools.

"He overdid himself again," remarked Scine. Areon placed him on the bed opposite of where Scine sat.

"With the wind and fire within me, I shall take his place." Areon said looking over at Scine. He walked over to him and grabbed a piece of meat he had been roasting with fire and shoved it in his mouth before walking back up onto the deck where Gremwold sat indifferently. The Rapturer stared over the edge into the distance, his wings concealed once again.

Areon continued to shoot large gusts of wind out of his hands and to feed the hot air that was necessary. Gremwold only kept track of the direction and told Areon where to go. Into the night Areon worked tirelessly, and the Rapturer began to help him. Before Areon knew it, the sky had turned from azure to orange to indigo, and his energy had been depleted. He slumped down on the deck and put his head against the railing as the ark continued to float in an easterly direction. Areon looked at the staircase that led below deck and just before his eyes shut, he saw Labert and Scine come to relieve him.

Areon again awoke in the bed below deck, but this time it was not to Labert's calm voice, but to Scine shouting something inaudible. Areon whipped off the sheets and ran above deck.

"The beacon! We're going to run into it!" shouted Scine again above the rushing wind. This time everyone was wide awake and looked worried. Areon ran to the front and peered over the railing to see the massive watchtower. It was already halfway into the day, but a large fire was still lit at the top. He looked back and saw they had crossed the sea already, but they were undoubtedly going to crash into the large beacon if something was not done soon.

"We have to freeze the hot air balls," yelled Areon, "and stop before we hit it."

"We'll crash in the landing. It will fall too fast!" yelled Gremwold.

"Get some rope!" yelled Scine. "Everyone tie themselves in somewhere at the back of the ark; make sure to tie yourself at several different points on your body. Do it quickly!"

"Why don't we fly?" said the Rapturer fiercely to Areon, grabbing his arm.

"I will share their fate!" yelled Areon back, and he jerked his hand back out of the Rapturer's grip.

Labert had already tied Gremwold in securely to a post in the back, and Scine was running up the steps with more lengths of secure rope. He helped tie in Labert.

"Who will stop the hot air?" asked Scine frantically.

"Only one of you will die," the Rapturer said to Areon, who was the only one in earshot. "I will do it," he yelled to everyone on deck.

Areon stared at him but began to tie himself to the back of the deck with Scine. "You lie." He glared at him, and Labert, Gremwold, and Scine looked at him for an answer, although Areon did not have time to give them one.

Everyone took hold of each and braced himself for the impact. Gremwold had shut his eyes long ago, but Areon looked up bravely. He saw the Rapturer take off his cloak and take flight, pushing against the planet with his massive wings. The beacon was closing in on them fast now. The Rapturer shot shards of ice that ripped through the balloon, and soon the only thing left of the cloth was the frozen strips that barely hung onto the ark. He saw the Rapturer fly away toward the forest after the beacon. Areon saw the ship take a sudden nosedive and knew the ground would come fast. He shut his eyes for impact.

The ground came much faster than anyone expected. They had stopped doing the fire magic that supplied hot air and were fairly close to the ground now. The bottom of the front of the ark hit first, producing a scratching noise that could be heard for a league in all directions. Areon heard the front shatter into a thousand splinters of large wood that shot off in all directions. He felt a surge of pain from his stomach and chest where he was tied and yelled out in pain. The initial impact hurt the most, but everyone managed to stay tied in. After what seemed like a half an hour, the group managed to look around; the whole front of the ark was demolished, but fortunately for them it had not broken to the point of where they all sat. Areon looked to Labert and to Scine. Scine was grinning and shaking at the same time, but Labert was untying himself while looking at the still figure of the old man known as Gremwold. Areon undid himself with a short burst of fire and grabbed his knife out and cut Scine and the old man loose, but Gremwold remained motionless. Areon slipped his knife back in his boot.

The master of time put his hand on Gremwold's chest, but he felt no heartbeat.

"He died," whispered Labert. "But it was not from the impact. It was just too much for his old heart."

Areon clenched his fists in rage. "We asked him to come along."

"It's our fault," Scine said slowly.

"No," said Areon. "It isn't." He jumped out of the ark onto the land of the Kingdom of Life.

# EXCERPT FROM THE HISTORICAL ARCHIVES OF THE KINGDOM OF LIFE

" ... but if one is accessing these records, they have undoubtedly been given permission by the king himself. A reminder must be set in place now, at this given time, before one is to read the following information, which should never be spoken of again, although it is unlikely there are those strong enough in the world to capture the gemstones containing the essences of the universe. The singular problem with the essences and the reasoning Nothingness has a chance of being present is due to the fact that the essences were constantly expanding exponentially on themselves, causing unbalance throughout the universe, making Nothingness possible due to the destruction caused by too much of one essence. But the perfect being, the one who alone has control over the Nine Orders of Angels, sealed the gemstones so that a balance would occur for eternity and Nothingness would be expunged from this reality for all eternity. But the gemstones alone were not enough to keep the essences inside. If one knew of the proper alignment, a certain essence could be set free and would expand on itself, causing a certain unbalance and the undoubted extinction of everything that is in this universe. The gemstone wishing to be cracked and the essence wishing to be set free must be surrounded by the rest of the five gemstones. They must also be within a certain distance of the middle one in order to let the resonation of the surrounding gemstones to penetrate the middle one properly and release it with the power of the others ..."

May the angels ever watch over us, keep us safe, and guide us through shadow in the afterlife.

# CHAPTER XLIX

## The Dark Forest

Grim and fury glowed inside Areon like hot coals waiting to burst into flame. He ran from where the others were still getting out of the ark and into the forest that started immediately after the beacon. After pushing his way through a couple of bushes and tree branches, he found the Rapturer leaning casually against a tree. Labert stayed and carried Gremwold's body out of what was left of the ark. Scine ran after Areon and caught sight of him in the forest yelling at the master of death.

"You!" screamed Areon. "You killed him!" He glanced back and saw Scine but did not look twice.

"I did not kill him," replied the Rapturer coolly. "It was his time."

"You lying murderer." Areon took up his hand to strike the Rapturer, but as soon as he tried, the master of death grabbed his hand in the air, pulled Areon close, and threw him aside like a rag doll. Scine ran to where Areon fell and helped him up.

"Come on," muttered Scine. "This won't help."

Areon jerked away and glared at the Rapturer before spitting at his feet and walking away.

The rest of the day was spent burying Gremwold's remains. Areon took one of the shattered pieces of wood and stuck it in the ground over his grave, which Scine was now covering with large stones. When they were all finished, everyone bowed their heads in silence and said nothing.

"We must enter the dark forest to find the master of life," announced the Rapturer. He jerked his head toward where he and Areon had been earlier. Everyone gathered up their supplies and the little food that was left on the ark and followed the Rapturer closely.

The Dark Forest was aptly named. When the sun began to set, all of the trees blended together due to the blackness. It was difficult to see the way for some time until Scine held up his hand; a ball of light made the company visible once more.

After trekking along for two hours, the group emerged into a large clearing with ash-colored ground. The Rapturer held out his hand to signal that this was the place, although they knew they were uninvited guests. The clearing led to a stump in the ground and an old house. Above the house were many ropes and a few ladders that led high into the trees and out into the forest. Smoke came slowly from the stone chimney and the group remained silent.

"Don't dream of moving," said a voice. Areon instantly recognized it as a young woman's. They all started to turn, but when Areon felt something sharp poke him in the back, he knew better, and apparently so did the rest of the group. He glanced at the Rapturer, who smiled, and Areon knew that he was only going along with this person. They were all pushed to the front of the door and the young woman screamed, "Master! The master of death!"

Nothing happened as Labert turned his head a little to look at the woman.

"Hey! I said don't move," she said.

"Ma'am, we mean you no harm whatsoever," tried Labert. "Our friend here knows Eanty ..."

"And my master knows him." She gave the Rapturer a sharp look. "They hate each other, so I don't trust anyone with him."

A sound came from the house of spilling pots and pans, and the door flung open to reveal a very disgruntled looking man. He was taller than Areon with a large beard and curly brown hair tied with a bandana. He had stern eyes. He was rather muscular but looked old.

"What is all this then?" he asked, but before anyone could answer, he caught sight of the master of death, and they locked eyes in a fierce glare that neither seemed to want to break.

"What are you doing around here?" he asked. "Who are these that you have brought with you?"

"They are masters such as you and me, save the one in red," returned the Rapturer.

"Masters?" the man said surprised, finally taking his eyes off the Rapturer and looking at the rest of the group. "I've never seen anything like it. If you're telling the truth," he added suspiciously.

Scine held up his flat hand and a beam of light shot through the forest roof. Labert then put himself in haste, and as Areon had never seen Labert in haste without being in it himself, he could not see the time master as he whipped around, grabbed the weapon from the female behind them, and thrust it towards the neck of the old man.

"Now, if we intended to kill you, I would." Labert dropped the weapon, a double-bladed sword with a handle coming out of the middle, and handed it handle first to the supposed master of life.

"I am Eanty." He smiled. "You could not kill me if I wished to live. I am the master of healing and a master of life magic. This is my apprentice." He gestured behind them to the young girl. "Kira." She smiled warmly and reached out her hands for her weapon.

"Hi!" she said brightly. Areon thought she was rather pretty. She had blonde hair that ended in curls with bright blue eyes. She had to be a bit younger than Areon. Her attitude seemed to have changed considerably since they all first met.

"Well, I won't say I'm not curious as to why you have all shown up at my door. Kira and I have secluded ourselves to train," said Eanty.

Labert pulled out his satchel from under his robes. He reached inside and arbitrarily grabbed the gemstone of light and showed it to Eanty while watching around the forest.

"What have you done?" whispered Eanty, mesmerized by the shining orb.

"It was necessary. May we come in?" asked Scine.

"He is not welcome here," said Eanty, motioning to the Rapturer.

"Perhaps he should be the one to bring news to Reiquem and Elmyra?" suggested Scine. "He could travel there faster than I."

Labert looked at the Rapturer, who nodded in acquiescence. "I live very near the temple. If you are flying, it should easy to spot my house," Labert said.

"It is the master of shadow and the master of space?" asked the Rapturer.

"Yes, Reiquem and Elmyra," added Areon. "Please don't let us down."

"It's imperative that the shadow master come as soon as possible," said the Rapturer. "I will retrieve them." The Rapturer undid his black cloak and threw it at their feet, smiling nastily at Eanty, pushing off the planet with his mighty wings and through the roof of the forest.

"This way," said Kira brightly and pushed past them all. Labert replaced the gemstone and put the satchel inside his robes once more. The group proceeded into the house of the master of life and his apprentice.

When all had been told, Eanty took on the same attitude that Labert had when Areon and Reiquem told him. The group was seated at a wooden table except for Kira, who was standing behind Areon. The house was not that big; easily smaller than the Daridyn's.

"So you plan on asking help from the angels once again after you have fought and taken the gemstones from them?" said Eanty wisely.

"Think about it from our perspective." Labert tried to explain. "This person, or being, that stole the shadow essence, it killed the Dominion."

"True," said Eanty, already understanding.

"So if it possesses that sort of power it could probably kill the rest of the guardians," continued Labert. "We don't want this evil force to get a hold of any other gemstones. We tried to reason with most of the angels and the Power took the time to understand, but—"

"But I was rash against the Cherub and attacked first," cut in Areon.

"Yes," nodded Labert. "They might've died anyway by the hands of this evil entity, and if he did get the gemstones, he might know the proper alignment, and we would all cease to exist."

"The end of all life," murmured Eanty.

"We could not risk anything," said Labert.

"We can use the gemstones to lure whatever stole the shadow gemstone to us and destroy it," finished Areon.

"Do you know what guards the Temple of Life?" asked Eanty. "It is the one that destroyed the remaining dark wizard that wore the black wizard cloak."

"The Seraph," said Scine. "He does not hold very much love for my people."

"I daresay the Seraph will recognize you," said Eanty gravely. "I have met the Seraph that guards the temple. I haven't the slightest idea what will happen when we encounter it."

"What if we have to fight?" asked Areon.

"I don't know," said Eanty. "But we have to go soon. From what you have shown me, the quest is almost complete. My apprentice Kira is not ready for this journey. She has not had long to learn. We shall stay here a fortnight before heading northeast. The temple sits at the edge of the forest and farther north is the Kingdom. Our travels won't take that long; the Kingdom is close to this place."

"And we train for a fortnight?" asked Areon.

"Yes," replied Eanty flatly. "Now we sleep."

Areon sat in one of the small rooms in the upper area of the house that was braced by many trees and strong ropes. The house sort of intertwined with the trees for extra support, and it was the room Eanty had said would be his while they trained. He could not sleep.

Labert walked up into Areon's room and looked at his sad face. Areon turned slowly to face him.

"Areon, I know what this means for you," Labert said quietly.

"Where will they leave our child?" asked Areon bluntly.

"Elmyra foresaw this happening and said that she would leave the child with our friends, the alchemists," answered Labert.

"Are they good people?"

"Yes, very good, otherwise I would not have told Elmyra to do so."

"Thank you," said Areon, fighting to keep away the tears. "When this is all over, I will take Reiquem and our child to visit Belgraf."

Labert nodded and left quietly, leaving Areon to his thoughts.

<hr />

For the next two weeks, Scine, Areon, Labert, Eanty, and Kira trained vigorously. The only advantage Areon had on the group was his ability to fly; he was indeed pushed the hardest due to the fact that he only knew lower level magic and none of the master magic that they all knew. Areon possessed far more skill than Kira and soon was able to hold his own against Eanty and Scine, but Labert would always be too fast for him. They trained on the ash-colored ground outside the house everyday. Each would partner up and spar with magic. Areon truly forgot about his old sword and bow; his new weapon was magic and the ability to fly. By the end of the two weeks, Areon was so quick a flyer that Labert had trouble keeping up with him, even while in haste. The only time they left the area was to collect berries or to kill a deer for meat. The regimen began to become a bit monotonous to Areon, and he found himself almost glad to be continuing the journey by the time two weeks had come and gone.

When all were ready to leave and packed, it turned out to be a little over two weeks before the group left. Areon realized that his child would be born and tried to remember that he was not with the child because he was protecting its future. He looked out the window of his room and strapped on his bow and quiver, along with his old sword, and walked down the steps to a room of the people he had gotten to know. Kira smiled and waved at him. Areon smiled back. Labert nodded at him, and Scine grinned. Eanty swung the sack of extra food on his back that they would need and stopped. He looked at Areon and put down his things.

"Hold on, everyone, there's still something I need to get." He darted back up the stairs with speed Areon thought impossible for a man his age. He looked about as old as Labert but more worn. When he returned, he held a large sheathed sword. Areon tried to look at it more, but Eanty quickly slid it under his traveling cloak and said nothing more on the matter. "It is now time to leave. Where will we meet up with the master of death?"

"He said by the time we entered the Kingdom of Life they would be able to meet us there," Labert spoke up.

"How will that be possible?" asked Areon. No one returned a response.

"Then let us make our way to the Kingdom, for we are already behind a few days," said Eanty quickly.

"All right!" yelled Kira. "We haven't been out of here in ages." She led the way out the door with the group following her with less enthusiasm.

The Dark Forest blended together quite nicely even in the morning hours. The shadows never really started or began; they simply ran together, and the trees stayed dark during the whole march through the forest. Areon did not know which way to go, so he simply followed.

# CHAPTER L

## The Seraph

It soon became obvious to Areon that the growth of the forest had begun to increase significantly. Every step he took now took more effort due to the heavy grass, close trees, and abundances of animals. The group almost walked directly into a pool of water being continually replenished by the waterfall that shut out much of the noise of the animals in the area. Eanty stopped and looked around.

"We sleep here tonight," he said. He set down his pack of food and supplies. It was early in the day, and Areon wondered what they were all going to do. The group found a place near a group of trees and sat down in its snug roots.

"Areon, my lad," said Labert. "I will enter the Kingdom of Life clean." He motioned to the waterfall.

"I think we could all use a good bathing," replied Scine.

"I haven't washed since I was in Lalvageth," said Areon.

"Well, I'll go first," said Labert, and he walked away toward the waterfall.

Soon everyone had bathed in the waterfall except Areon and Kira. Night had fallen and almost everyone had gone and sat down to sleep for the night. Areon watched Kira by the river and walked away quietly to the waterfall. When he reached the side of it, he began to take off his cloak, which constricted immediately around his neck. Instead of trying to force it off this time, he let it touch his skin and tried to coax it into letting him take it off, giving it a false hope that it would not stop touching his skin. Soon the cloak was free, and he placed it carefully under a bush so that none could see it. He stripped down and walked from the darkness into the weakly shimmering light of the waterfall. The cold water felt exhilarating on his dirty, grass-stained skin. He scrubbed his arms clean and ran his hands through his hair. After he was as clean as he thought he was going to get, Areon walked back to the bush where his clothes lay. In the darkness a figure approached him just as he pulled on his pants, the rest of his clothes still on the ground. He waited cautiously, for he thought the others were all asleep. Kira's face became easier to see as she came within half a span of the surprised Areon. She held her arm across her chest to keep her clothes on.

"Are you finished yet?" she asked quietly but with the same cheerful voice.

Areon looked up awkwardly and mumbled, "Yes."

Kira let her arm fall and came even closer to Areon, her outfit slipping off her body.

"We could die tomorrow, you know?" she whispered sweetly into his ear before leaning in.

Areon quickly sidestepped her and grabbed his clothes. He stopped and looked back at her face.

"I'm sorry, but my love is for another," he said quietly and walked away, leaving Kira to her thoughts.

The next morning Areon awoke to find that everyone was packing up at the dawn of the day with grim faces. When Areon had secured his sword, bow, and quiver, he shot a stream of ice at the fire, which instantly went out. Everyone nodded to one another to begin the trek out of the forest.

Kira was the last to leave along with Areon. He stopped her quickly when everyone was out of earshot.

"Kira, I just wanted to say I'm sorry for last night," he said shyly.

She smiled warmly at him with her innocent blue eyes. "You love the master of shadow magic?"

"I do," he replied.

She sighed heavily. "I just thought … well, in these times it's hard to find someone." She looked away. "I figured this would happen, but don't be sorry."

They smiled at each other and began the journey to catch up with everyone.

The forest began to come into life even more so than the day before. It began to be difficult to walk, so Areon took out his sword and began cutting down the shrubs and low branches of trees. As Areon and Kira began to run to catch up they came into the clearing, which was undoubtedly for the temple that stood before them and had stood since the first part of existence; the Temple of Life.

Areon stopped swatting with his sword immediately and looked at the positioning of everyone. Scine stood with hands down looking at the temple; two spans to the left of him stood Labert with his hands together, looking intently at the temple; and lastly Eanty faced the entrance of the temple. Areon looked back toward Kira, who looked frightened. Silence hung heavy in the air.

Then the inevitable happened; the Seraph emerged from the entrance of the temple. Areon took in all its glorious features. The Cherub did not come close to the brightness of the Seraph, and Areon knew why it was the highest of the Order of the Nine. The Seraph had four faces pointing to each cardinal direction as the Cherub, but instead of only two sets of wings, it had three; the top it used to fly out of the temple, and the middle to cover its white robed figure, and the bottom set to cover its heavenly feet. The carved features of its handsome face contorted in disbelief as it looked at the masters prepared to fight it. The angel commanded respect, and Areon knew his second degree fire magic was no use against its divine white light and perpetual heavenly fire.

"The gemstone holding the very essence of life is no longer safe here, Seraph. We wish to move it to a safer place," boomed Eanty, the master of life.

The Seraph slowly turned its south facing head to Eanty, who could barely return its gaze.

"I have received no instructions from the Dominion or the Lord concerning the Gemstones that our Heavenly Father used to conceal the essences," replied the Seraph with a soft, sage voice.

"The Dominion is dead," said Areon.

"We do not die, for he has only entered a different realm known to your kind as the afterlife where his sentient life will be restored," replied the Seraph.

"Then you know what is happening?" asked Areon from the back.

The Seraph looked at him shrewdly. "I do. I am ever contemplating that beyond the mundane."

"Then you know what must be done," stated Scine.

"I received instruction when the temples were raised by the hand of the Alpha and Omega and once again received instructions to ever be in service of the Kingdom of Life from those that would assail it, nothing more."

"We will take the gemstone today," said Eanty sternly.

"You may have been able to overcome the lower orders, but I will not be overcome. You do not understand who you are dealing with; a member of the choir of the Lord's mightiest servants." The Seraph prepared to fight.

Labert put himself in haste and let it reach to each member. Eanty readied himself with prayer. Areon swiftly drew his bow and knocked his arrow within a half a second, for he was in haste. Kira put her hand on Areon's shoulder and cowered behind him, not ready for the situation. The most peculiar thing happened. Scine closed his eyes and formed a barrier of light around himself, but instantly the Seraph jerked his head toward him and the faces all swiveled around to gaze at Scine.

"You are the master of light?" asked the Seraph, completely taken aback.

"I am," whispered Scine, forcing his barrier to become stronger in order to repel an attack.

The Seraph sprung into the air using all three sets of wings to push off the ground. "The last order I received was to serve the Kingdom of Life, and the angels were not given free will." The angel flew out of sight in a northeasterly direction, leaving the group.

# CHAPTER LI

## The Temple of Life

"What happened?" Areon tried to ask Labert as they all made their way into the temple. It had vines growing over most of it, making it difficult to see what it was composed of.

Labert only shook his head to signal that he had no idea.

The temple was similar to the others, having the same pillars and the same eerie darkness. When they walked down a perfectly carved stone staircase, Areon saw what he had difficulty describing to people after he witnessed it. The sealer of death was horrible. It was something that did not exist but still moved. Black figures continually dying, killing. Areon could only think to call them dead beings.

Eanty walked up to the shroud over the gemstone of life and put his strong arms into the air. The life magic came fourth from his hands like the coming of spring a thousand times over. The shroud felt the life, and it was as though life made it disappear, rather than killing it.

Labert took Elmyra's magical satchel from within his robes and took the gemstone containing the essence of life. Everyone ran back outside the temple quickly and quietly. Kira looked at her master.

"That was amazing, Master!" she exclaimed loudly. He only half smiled, still concerned with the erratic behavior of the Seraph.

"It will only be one more night and day before we are upon the city of the Kingdom of Life," Eanty announced, changing the subject. "Follow me."

# CHAPTER LII

## What the Seraph Invoked

An old king sat upon his throne contemplating the happenings of the last eighteen years in and out of his kingdom. He rested his head on his balled-up hand and let the crown slip slowly down his sweaty forehead. His name was King Rehoboam, and he was a good king, though he had his faults. It was a solitary, sedentary life Rehoboam led, but it was better than war.

The king stood up and began to pace slowly around the front of his mighty throne carved of silver stone. This life he led would be no other way, for he had long ago lost his family. It was the price they paid for loving someone such as a king.

Rehoboam took his crown off of his balding, gray, yet somewhat still blonde hair. His strong forearms rippled as he gripped the emerald encrusted gold. The king was average height but well built and strong as a king should be in body as well as mind.

The doors of the corridor that led to the throne burst open, and the sound made King Rehoboam jump ever so slightly. However, kings quickly compose themselves in the presence of underlings.

"My Lord," said a castle guard, bowing low. The king noticed he did not wear a plumed helmet signalizing rank and was about to reprimand him, but the soldier spoke again insubordinately.

"I am sorry for this intrusion, but I thought it best to tell you as soon as possible."

"Go on then, warrior," stated the king.

"Thank you, sir," said the castle guard, bowing again. "Something flies in this direction from the south."

"And?" asked the king impatiently.

"It has three pairs of wings, sir," said the castle guard, keeping his head down. "I have done much research, Your Excellency. I think it is of the Seraphim."

Rehoboam squinted his eyes incredulously. "Impossible."

"I am quite sure of what I saw, sir," the castle guard whispered, hoping for little punishment.

"I was told by the bishop that if the Seraph were to ever need to talk to me, it would fly to the south battlement."

"The one with the sitting space and wraparound railing at the end of it?" asked the warrior.

"Precisely," returned the king curtly.

"I am stationed there, sir, and that is where the Seraph seems to be headed."

"I hope for your sake you're right, warrior." The king had compassion and clapped the man on the shoulder. "But I hope for the sake of the kingdom that you are wrong, for the Seraph only brings tidings of ill things to come."

The castle guard smiled very slightly, bowed again, and walked out swiftly.

"Warrior!" yelled the king down the corridor that led to the throne. The castle guard turned around swiftly. "Do not return to your post. I alone will go there."

The castle guard nodded and turned around the corner to the left.

The king waited until the castle guard was out of sight before running down the hall and heading up one of the many staircases to the right. Through many more memorized corridors and up many more memorized staircases, Rehoboam went until he broke out into the sunlight where the Seraph sat with its angelic face looking indifferent, its wings all folded down sadly. It turned its head so that two of the faces could see king Rehoboam with one eye each.

The king nodded in respect, not knowing what to do in the presence of something so far from the mundane.

"King Rehoboam, I presume?" asked the Seraph, its four voices as one.

"I am," returned the king with all the courage he could muster in the presence of the flaming angel.

"In normal circumstances the Lord would have sent a divine messenger; an Archangel, but I have been given orders to firstly serve the Kingdom of Life, as Bishop Tolok prayed for and received answer."

"I have read the scriptures," replied Rehoboam.

"I do not know if what I do is benevolent or not, but alas I have no free will and have not received word from the Dominion concerning events that have happened recently."

"What is this news you have borne to me?" asked the king.

"Ever have I protected the temple that your kingdom longs to guard for the Lord. You are good, King Rehoboam. But I was conflicted when a group of travelers came to claim the gemstone of life. By now they have it in there possession, and we must reclaim it."

"Why did you not stop them?" demanded the king. He felt out of place taking a tone with a being such as this, but he knew the significance of the gemstones.

"A member of the Kingdom of Light was with this company," continued the Seraph. "It was the master of light himself."

Rehoboam gasped. "I knew they had been up to something these last years. They were the ones responsible for the atrocity against me. I will act upon them immediately."

The Seraph stretched out its wings and beat them down, flying high above the king. It looked down and boomed, "If we recover the gemstone, I will have fulfilled both duties that the Lord has assigned me. I will be ready when the army leaves." The angel flew away.

———————◆————————

Later in the king's counseling quarters, Rehoboam and his four most trusted advisors sat around the table, looking at the map of the Mirrored Continents, speaking rashly due to the king's mood and desire.

"Your Majesty, I am sure if we use the stolen technology of the flying arks, we will be able to cross the sea and the Wizard Scar within days," said an older advisor.

"We will need mages for the fire and wind, but otherwise I agree," said another.

"The troops will all fit aboard, and the rest we can send across the sea for after the initial attack," said another.

The last one looked up. "Your Majesty, this is the second time in a mere nineteen years they have tried to supplant you. King Jeroboam wishes to control the entire Mirrored Continents. We have built the arks larger than any airship the light kingdom tried to build. Our spies have confirmed. We cannot guarantee that the first attack on your wife ..."

"Do not speak of it please," whispered Rehoboam. "I do not wish to think of them. Gather the warriors and mages necessary. We leave for war at dawn."

# CHAPTER LIII

## Dirk Eindee

The group was camping outside the forest next to a blazing fire. Areon could see the lights of the kingdom flickering in the night. The group had walked all day out of the forest and now nothing could be seen at night. Everyone else was fast asleep, but Areon was excited at being only east of his home that he had known for so long. It could not be that long before he would be able to see Reiquem again. With that thought, he put his hands behind his head and relaxed in the plush grass. He was ready to see the city tomorrow, expecting the same thing as the Kingdom of Light. Areon was not sure what to expect would happen in the city, but all the gemstones were acquired, and hopefully the group would wait in the city until whomever or whatever stole the shadow gem.

With this last though, Areon fell into a deep sleep to the warm, crackling fire.

For one of the first times on his adventure Areon awoke first and looked around at the new day. It was already far past dawn, yet the entire group was sleeping contently. He walked over to the fire that only smoked faintly and kicked at it, hoping someone would sense his presence and wake.

Finally Scine rolled over and saw Areon securing his bow, full of new arrows from the Kingdom of Light, around his back and looking at his sword.

"You ready to get to the kingdom?" asked Scine, rubbing his eyes and pushing the blonde locks of hair out his eyes.

"I am," said Areon sincerely.

Scine stretched and smiled at Areon. "You weren't worried the Seraph had come for us?"

Areon scrunched up his face. "Not really. I hadn't even thought about it until now," he said truthfully.

Soon Labert looked up and mumbled something about being up too early and put his face back into his hands where he started snoring loudly again.

Areon looked over at Eanty and saw he was up on his feet watching the group. He walked over the where Kira slept and gently shook her by the shoulder. She arose without hesitation and said nothing. Areon walked over to Labert and put his hand on his shoulder. Labert stood up quickly and looked around, knowing everyone was waiting for him.

"We cross the river by ferry and are then at the city gates," stated Eanty.

"Much like the Kingdom of Light," Scine told Areon. Everyone gathered up the sleeping supplies and walked out into the clearing that led to the river.

Upon arriving Areon saw the ferries tied to either side of river, except at these ferries two warriors from the king's army guarded and watched who passed to the gates of the city.

"Hold," said one warrior, holding up his hand. He handled a spear with a very large, sharp point.

Eanty emerged from behind the group.

"Master of Life," said the other, taken aback.

"My apologies. Of course you may cross," said the first warrior, obviously showing respect.

"I have dealings with the king now and again," explained Eanty as the group stepped onto the ferry. Kira beamed at him.

When they arrived at the other side, two more warriors took the ropes of the ferry and tied them to a dock where the group got off and made their way to the fabulous city gates.

Areon gazed up at the spikes on the walls and the watchtowers down the line. It was truly made for attacks. The gates were open, as it was nearing noon, so the group went through with no hassle and blended in with the immediate crowd of merchants and consumers. But as they entered the city Areon knew something was wrong with the way people were moving. Most were talking excitedly, some yelling and screaming. Many of the commoners looked to the west. As they followed Eanty, he looked around at all the people, none of whom were warriors or servants of the king.

"Something is wrong," shouted Eanty to his following companions. "Let us make our way as swiftly as we can through the city and up to the castle where King Rehoboam awaits."

Areon barely had time to take in the fabulous city. Everything was made of silver stone. Several large silver stone walkways went through the enormous city, and the houses were made of stone and stood against one another and on top of each other. The city's capacity looked to be near two hundred thousand with all the close-knit stone. After pushing through many shouting people, they were all at the stone walls that surrounded the castle. A guard at the top of one of the battlements shouted, "What business do you have at the castle?"

"We have business with the king," boomed Eanty.

"Begging your pardon, master of life," said the guard quickly while bowing low. "But the castle doors have been locked, and none shall enter until the king returns."

"Returns?" shouted Eanty. "From where?"

"Haven't you been told, my lord?" the castle guard asked timidly. "We have officially gone to war with the other kingdom. The Kingdom of Light."

The group slowly started to realize what had happened with the Seraph.

"It is my fault," whispered Scine.

Eanty turned to face the group slowly, leaving the castle guard watching to see what he was doing.

"Scine," he whispered. "Do not tell this man who you are. None of you must tell him who you are. Stay quiet and act nonchalant."

The group acquiesced quietly, and Areon began to look around, as if he had not a care in the world.

"Thank you, warrior," Eanty said, turning to him. "Our business can wait until a later date. Especially with this new affair at hand."

The guard nodded slowly and watched as the group turned to leave.

When they were once again outside the city walls, everyone burst into conversation as they followed Eanty farther east, yet still north of the River of Life.

"We are at war because the Seraph told King Rehoboam that the master of light is trying to steal the gemstone to gain power?" Labert asked quietly, looking back toward the ferries.

"It seems so. I, for one, wouldn't be the least surprised. You heard the Seraph. He said he serves the Kingdom of Life firstly. And I've heard stories of this Rehoboam. He is a bold king who makes rash decisions," remarked Scine.

"He is a good king!" yelled Kira indignantly.

"But rash," said Labert, agreeing with Scine.

"Where are we headed?" asked Areon out of breath. "Why are we heading toward those mountains?"

Scine and Labert stopped as well.

"Yes, why?" asked Labert.

Eanty spoke for the first time since they left. "Rehoboam is rash, yes, but there is more to this story that does not meet the eye. Some other reason I have feared for long years may be why the two continents are going to war."

"And what is that?" asked Scine.

"I will not say out of the hope that I may be wrong, but in order to receive answers to both the reasons we may be at war, we will consult the wisest of the wise and the secret holders of secrets," replied Eanty resolutely, looking eastward at the two large mountains that were nearly a day's walk away.

"The philosophers of Dirk Eindee," Labert said in response to Areon's enquiring look.

The company pushed on for the entire day even as it started to rain. Areon skulked as they began the arduous journey up the mountain, but when they arrived at an enormous level area halfway up and stopped, Areon was thankful. It was nearing night now, and he hoped they would be resting here. Just when he went to plop down on the muddy ground, Eanty went forward into a crevice in the monstrous mountain. He signaled the group inside.

"What are we ..." but Scine did not finish his sentence as they looked at a large stone door far into the crevice.

"This is it," whispered Eanty.

"Inside is a vast city carved out of the mountains," explained Labert to Areon. "In days long before us the two cities competed for families to live in their city. Times when numbers were needed to continue living in any civilized sort of way."

"I know one of the high counselors of their city. We may be well met, but please mind your manners. Kira, try to stay calm at all times." Eanty turned to her, and she pouted when he looked away.

Eanty slammed his fist against the mighty stone door three times, and it swiveled open to Areon's great surprise.

The inside walkway was dark only for half minute, giving one the impression they might fall off the edge into dark oblivion until Areon saw the walkway had wood railings leading to a cavernous room. The walkway turned into a ladder, which led to another way that sprawled into many more small walkways, leading to shelves upon shelves of books and ladders. These ladders led to other rooms and walkways. People walked around looking for certain books. A robed figure walked up to the party and scrutinized them thoroughly before asking pompously, "May I answer any questions to which you seek answers?"

Eanty looked at him taking charge of the situation. "I am the master of life magic."

The robed figured looked at him and took his hood down. "You are Eanty?"

"I am."

"It would not be favorable for you to lie about this at the current moment. Are you, indeed, the master of life magic?" asked the mysterious person.

"I am," Eanty returned with impatience.

"Then you are a Shadow for King Rehoboam?" said the man slyly.

Eanty reached his hand out and grabbed the man in between his neck and shoulder and squeezed hard. The man gasped and almost fell to the ground in pain.

"You … How do you know?" growled Eanty, but the man could not speak.

"A Shadow," murmured Labert. Areon looked at Labert in surprise.

"I-If you would f-follow me, your questions will be answered," the man barely spoke. Eanty released him and nodded for him to lead the way.

The group eagerly followed the man up a ladder and down a stone sided hall that led to another large room. The inside of the mountain was large. Areon knew how so many could live here. Each ladder must have led to a new room, and each room had seven or more ladders leading to more ladders. Within minutes he was lost and could only follow. Each room had new things inside; the first, a library, the second, full of people cooking, the third, for fires and socialization, and so on and so forth.

Up the last ladder they went and down a cave lit with torches on each side. But this hall did not lead to another room but only farther into the mountain. Areon bumped into Labert in front of him, but no one spoke. The robed figure knocked on the door in their way. Areon noted that it was a code of some sort, not simply a knock. The door opened and the group was ushered in.

Around a round table sat seven men. The furthest from them looked up, his face barely visible in the lowly lit room.

"What is the meaning of this intrusion?" he asked not unkindly.

"The master of life magic and Shadow for King Rehoboam," said the man with his head bowed down. Eanty gave him a stern look.

"It is serious that you know who and what I am," stated Eanty loudly.

"We are the head philosophers of our wonderful mountain city of Dirk Eindee." The man gestured at the other six sitting at the table. He then made some sort of gesture at the man that had led the group in. Areon looked back at him suspiciously and saw him smile slowly before bowing his head and exiting the room.

"Did you hear what I said?" Eanty asked even louder.

"Yes, I did, as a matter of fact," the man returned quietly.

"How do your people know?" he demanded.

"We have spies as well as the kingdom," the philosopher returned coolly.

Everyone looked around uneasily. Areon sense something was wrong.

"Why are at war with the Kingdom of Light?" asked Eanty.

"The last I heard they were trying to steal your precious essence of life," responded the head philosopher.

"It is precious to everyone, and you know this," Labert said, standing up beside Eanty.

"You know of other events," Eanty said accusingly.

"The death of Rehoboam's wife and the acquisition of his son at birth?" asked the philosopher calmly.

"You know of these events then?" he asked suspiciously. "Events supposedly commanded to be done by King Jeroboam to stop the line of King Rehoboam and cause his kingdom to fall?"

"It was not the Kingdom of Light's doing," cried Scine.

"That remains to be seen," Eanty stated, not looking at Scine.

"I do not believe it was the Kingdom of Light," said Labert. "Nor does my wife."

"Then you are wise," said the head philosopher. "For it was done by my command."

Labert and Scine gasped. Eanty took in a mighty breath.

"I might've suspected this city of something so atrocious. You will die for killing the queen," Eanty almost yelled, his temper rising.

All the philosophers seemed quite at ease.

"We did not kill the queen, she died in childbirth; but the son we did steal and planned on killing him," the philosopher said.

"And you did not succeed?" asked Eanty hopefully while still retaining the anger in his voice.

"No, we lost our spies that stole him to Moss Woods, where we assume the boy was killed. Now the line of kings will fail," replied the head philosopher.

Areon saw Eanty smile. "There is one thing that I am still wondering about before you attempt to kill us all," he said smoothly. "Why did you commit this crime against the kingdom?"

Areon froze for a moment, thinking about the last thing Eanty had said. They would try to kill the group. But what chance did they have?

"Someone self-righteous as yourself would never understand our reasoning. These times of peace cause the nations to go into a state of disbelief in God. During war everyone needs to believe in something, for they might die at any minute. But in times of peace they forget that sinning is wrong, and they will still die someday. War is the only time when people have faith." The philosopher stood up.

"You are insane," Labert remarked casually.

"And you have failed," announced Eanty.

"Oh?" said a different man at the table.

"Approximately how long ago did you lose the son of the king?" asked Eanty confidently.

"You know as well as I, almost nineteen years to date," replied the philosopher.

"This boy is the son of the king and rightful heir to the throne of Rehoboam," Eanty said proudly and confidently.

Areon almost looked behind himself. "Me?" he asked timidly.

"Yes, Areon. My number one priority ever since you were stolen at birth was to find you. All thought that the Kingdom of Light at Jeroboam's bidding stole you, but I thought differently. While other shadows were dispatched to the other Mirrored Continent, I stayed back and looked for clues after Reiquem's parents had been killed. I knew them well. Most of what I could come up with were facts that the prince had been lost in Moss Woods, and when I learned of a single boy living with a wizard outside of

Wellenore, I waited for the opportune moment to expose the truth. When you came to Kira and me and told me about your past during those weeks of staying at my place, I assumed it was you. Now is the right time for you to know, although perhaps not the right place," said Eanty, glancing at the seven wicked philosophers. "You are the Prince of the Kingdom of Life, Areon, son of Rehoboam."

"Are ... are you sure?" asked Areon timidly. He thought to himself that he did not wish for a life he had just been thrust into. He only wanted Reiquem and his child.

"So, as I said before," continued Eanty. "You have failed. The line of kings is not broken. We will inform the king immediately."

"The war is already begun," stated the philosopher.

"We will stop it," stated Scine.

"We cannot allow that."

Areon felt someone clap a rag around his mouth and the world turned black.

---

## EXCERPT FROM THE PHILOSOPHICAL ARCHIVES OF DIRK EINDEE

" ... Can good actually exist if no evil is present? It is a question I, for one, know will be brought up throughout the centuries to come. I imagine many will persecute me throughout my existence for my beliefs on the matter, but every man must do what he believes is right. Not only is it a matter of good actually being something that exists when evil is no longer present, but also a matter of people continuing to be benevolent during times when peace reigns. Do we simply trade one evil for another when war comes? I think not. Many die during war, but more go to heaven. In times of peace what good does it do one to pray to the Lord? In times of war one may die at any minute, making prayer a daily necessity. War must be invoked forcing the public to go back to its ways of prayer and fear of death and hell ..."

Right and wrong do not exist, only truths.

# CHAPTER LIV

## Death on the Side of a Mountain

Areon came to and was standing but where he knew not. He felt weak and almost fell, but strong hands gripped his elbows.

"They're regaining consciousness!" someone yelled beside Areon's ear, and his head rang in pain. He winced and tried to look around but was blindfolded by a black cloth.

"The one in the red cloak can stand on his own!" the man yelled again.

Areon heard footsteps crunching over small rocks and tried to break free but was held fast for he was weak. The footsteps stopped and he heard the same voice that belonged to the head philosopher.

"He does not matter as much as the others, he is not a master. Anyway he should still be weak. Throw them off the instant the rest start regaining consciousness, which should be any second."

Areon quickly tried to conjure fire magic, but he was, indeed, still weak. Even if he had been strong it would not have mattered. The guard ripped the cloth that covered Areon's eyes, the light blinding him momentarily. He wavered slightly at the sight before him. The entire group was on top of the mountain all lined up and all blindfolded. Areon turned around to fight his restrainer while the rest of the group began to stir, but instantly the hands that held him shoved him hard in the chest. Areon fell and watched as the other guards for the city of Dirk Eindee shoved his company off the very top of the mountain.

The mountainside did not run at an angle from whence they had been thrown but went straight down. Areon was at the bottom, and the fall would take some time before the entire group hit the ground. He put out his hands and feet to slow himself, his cloak flailing wildly in the rush of wind. Scine fell past him unconscious, but Areon grabbed him. Next, Labert came, and with his other hand Areon grabbed him as well. Eanty fell on his chest. Kira was too far to his right and the grab was impossible in what Areon took to be the last moments of their lives. He doubted his cloak could save them. He knew that he could fly to safety but refused to leave his company falling down without him to their imminent doom. He struggled to reach Kira, albeit they were close to the ground now. But in those last moments of wind and despair Areon saw out of the corner of his eye the azure sky emit a single flowing tendril that looked as if it were flying of its own accord. It came closer and closer so that Areon could see the Dragon King Leviathan swoop under them and push down hard with his wings, easily stopping the entire group from falling the rest of the way to their deaths.

Areon let go of Labert and Scine and pushed Eanty off him while looking over to make sure Kira had landed on top of the dragon, which she had. Rolling over he saw the knees of Reiquem land beside him, and she put his head on her lap and caressed his face until unconsciousness once again came over him.

Areon awoke to the wind rushing past him and Reiquem crying on his cheek. He reached up and pushed the tear-soaked hair out of her eyes and looked into them.

"I'm okay," he said quietly.

"I thought I was going to lose you. I knew you wouldn't let the group die. I had to watch you fall that whole time," Reiquem said hoarsely.

"It's okay now." Areon continued to stroke her hair. "We're together again." He noticed they were on top of Leviathan, and the sun was heading downward toward the west while the dragon flew towards it. Areon sat up and took Reiquem's hands. He looked longingly into her abysmal black eyes that he loved so much.

She smiled at him and leaned close to his ear. "Our child is a boy."

Areon, almost on the verge of tears of joy, took Reiquem in his arms and they kissed without caring if the rest of the company was watching.

Areon and everyone that had been to Dirk Eindee had let their heads clear long enough. The group needed to talk, although it seemed difficult on top of the enormous Leviathan. They all took seats upon his scales in a circle so all could be seen. Areon and Reiquem sat close together, holding one another. The Rapturer sat across from them with Eanty and Kira as far away as possible. Labert and Elmyra were hand in hand next to Reiquem. Scine sat by the Rapturer.

"Where to begin?" Eanty acknowledged the entire group.

"I know," Areon said quietly. "How did you know to save us?"

Reiquem only looked at Areon. "The Rapturer knew. Somehow, he knew."

The master of death looked at Eanty and smiled his wicked smile. "It was not your time."

"Who are you to know whose time it is and is not?" Eanty shot back defiantly, not accepting this explanation.

"I will not explain to you," said the Rapturer.

"Areon, while you were sleeping, the rest of us awoke and explained the situation to Elmyra and Reiquem. They know of the impending war." Labert said, wanting to avoid a roe between the two masters, one of life and one of death.

"And do they know why?" asked Areon.

"I have told them of Scine and the gemstone and Elmyra of you, but I left the part about your past for you to tell Reiquem yourself," answered Labert. "But before you do, we must all agree that we fly until we reach the battle of the two Kingdoms where we will attempt to stop it."

"Agreed," Eanty said gravely. Everyone else nodded toward him. "But I have one last thing that I must do before Areon explains all to the master of shadow." He stood up slowly and reached into his cloak. "I am glad we were not searched by the philosophers of Dirk Eindee, for when we left the Dark Forest I took with me Uriel, the Flame of God." He took out the mighty sword he had taken from his house and handed it to Areon. "It was your father's. He gave it to me in hopes that I would find you one day. Use it well."

"Please tell me, Areon, what is this all about?" Reiquem asked.

Areon looked to the rest of the group, who got up slowly and walked carefully across the back of the dragon to leave the two in peace.

Areon turned to Reiquem. "Do you remember when I told you long ago that I was found in Moss Woods?"

"Of course," she responded.

"I don't know how to say this, so I'll just say it, Reiquem; I was kidnapped shortly after I was born by the neighboring city to the kingdom, Dirk Eindee. They took me to the Moss Woods where whoever stole me was killed. I—" he hesitated. "I am the son of Rehoboam, heir to the throne. They did this to provoke King Rehoboam into thinking it was the Kingdom of Light, and they hoped to start a war."

A look of dawning compression swept over Reiquem's face. "Elmyra!" she yelled, and the old woman turned slowly before walking carefully back to where the two sat.

"Elmyra, is it true then?" asked Reiquem.

"Yes, dear. Labert, Eanty, and I all agree." Se looked at Areon and then back to Reiquem. "Your parents died in Moss Woods trying to save the prince."

Areon shook his head slowly. "I'm so sorry, Reiquem." She didn't let him finish, only grabbed him gently and they embraced once more while the sun slowly sank behind the horizon.

Areon pulled her away gently. "Reiquem, where is our child?" he asked.

"Elmyra and I decided to leave him with the alchemists," she replied, almost regrettably.

"Are you okay?" he asked her with concern. "Perhaps you shouldn't be here with us."

Her face grew stern but relaxed. "I am fine," she said.

"Promise me you won't fight with us if it comes down to it."

She turned away and nodded quickly and changed the subject.

"What will we do now, Areon?" she asked. "Can we really live with your father?"

He shook his head. "I don't know. We will do what we wish when the time comes. I haven't completely accepted this astonishing news and don't know if I ever will. As long as I can live with you and our child, I do not care for anything else. The kingdom has lived fine without me for nearly nineteen years."

Eanty turned from the head of the dragon and spoke to the group over the rushing wind and beating wings of Leviathan. "We can be to the battle by tomorrow. Elmyra has assured us a smooth trip. Let us all sleep, save one who will watch to wake the group upon arriving."

"I will stay awake first to talk with Leviathan. The rest of you need the rest more than me anyhow," she said.

Areon and Reiquem went to the centermost part of Leviathan with the rest of the group, save Elmyra, and fell into an uneasy sleep.

# CHAPTER LV

# Uriel, Flame of God

"Areon."

Areon woke to someone nudging him gently. It was Labert.

"The sun rises to the first battle."

He took up his bow and quiver along with his old sword, which he refused to throw away. He strapped Uriel to his back with its leather straps.

"Where are we?" asked Areon, guessing he had been asleep for at least ten hours and was sore from lying on scales. The rest of the company stood near the head of Leviathan.

Labert answered, "We have just gone west of the wizard scar and can see the form of warriors."

Areon turned to the west quickly and squinted to see; all the warriors of Rehoboam's army were stopped, clashing shields against spears. The faint outline of dust could be seen drifting upward as the warriors from the Kingdom of Light ran to meet the attackers.

"Fly, Leviathan!" screamed Elmyra. Leviathan acquiesced, and although he had been flying all night over a distance that would be impossible to travel over with normal means of travel, he flapped harder, and the group had to stable itself so as not to fall.

Slowly the battle came closer and closer. When Areon got to the head of Leviathan, he could see the two kings, Rehoboam and Jeroboam in the middle of their armies. They each had three counselors beside them and were heatedly discussing the impending battle. Finally Rehoboam jerked the reins on his horse and it ran away in defiance. Areon knew the discussion had gone badly, and the battle would proceed if they did not do something quickly.

The armies now marched at each other, the front of the lines holding out spears and preparing for a warrior's death. Louder the shouts became but the warriors all faltered as Leviathan landed between the armies, his body barely fitting. The group stood magnificently on his back as the Dragon King whipped his blue-scaled head and roared, sending some of the men to the ground. Everyone looked to Areon. He jumped from the back of Leviathan and marched to a point where both armies and kings could see him. He looked over at his father for the first time. Rehoboam watched him in disbelief. Jeroboam, on the other hand, looked as though he wanted to find some other way around this bloodshed, so he waited for the boy to speak.

"Eanty!" roared Rehoboam. "What is the meaning of this?"

Areon noticed murmurs sweep throughout the Army of Light at the name of Eanty, master of life.

Eanty motioned to Areon. "Let the boy speak."

So Rehoboam turned his crimson face to Areon once more.

Areon reached back his hand and drew the mighty sword. Gasps went out from the Army of Life. The king lost all color in his face.

Areon held it high and circled, looking at the two armies and at his company. "This is Uriel, Flame of God, given to the Prince of the Kingdom of Life. You cannot fight!"

The king slowly slid down from his horse with his gaze not breaking away from Areon.

"Is this true, Eanty?" whispered Rehoboam.

Jeroboam kept his hand raised and waited while watching the Kingdom of Life. All were on their knees bowing to their prince. Eanty and the rest of the group dismounted from Leviathan and walked across the dust to where the king looked at Areon.

"He is your son, stolen by the philosophers of Dirk Eindee to invoke war. It seems their plan ended up working," replied Eanty.

Rehoboam looked at his son. Although skinny and taller, they both had the same blonde hair, the same blue eyes, and the same intelligent face.

"No," said Rehoboam. "They have failed. Warriors!" he yelled, looking back at his troops. Board our ships, I trust Eanty with my life!" he turned back to Areon. "Even if they were trying to steal the essence of life," he began to cry. "My son has been returned to me by the grace of God!"

Areon sheathed his sword, and father and son embraced for the first time.

When the warriors of Rehoboam had all boarded the arks, Jeroboam came close to where Scine, Eanty, Elmyra, Labert, Reiquem, Kira, the Rapturer, and Areon all stood and reached out his hand, which Rehoboam took.

"Your Majesty," said Labert. "We all have much to discuss."

"I had no idea the stories of the Dragon King were true," said the king.

"Elmyra is the last summoner left," Areon told his father.

"May I ride to my castle on your dragon?" asked Rehoboam.

"He is not mine, but he must obey me," replied Elmyra. "But yes, we will all go back to the castle together."

"We can discuss the happenings with the king on our way back," said Eanty.

"I shall inform the leader of my warriors." Rehoboam went to a warrior wearing a plumed helmet.

He returned to King Jeroboam. "The Lord was watching over our warriors on this day. I am deeply sorry for my wrongful accusation." He bowed low. "You are invited to my kingdom, where we will discuss a new treaty."

Jeroboam nodded and looked towards his warriors and his own kingdom. "I have felt uneasiness in our alliance for some time, but we will start anew. Look for me from the west on the first day of the next week. I will utilize our arks once more."

The two kings held arms firmly and departed.

Then Areon and his company along with Rehoboam climbed on top of Leviathan and headed back east. All save the Rapturer, who said nothing, only waved at Areon and took up his mighty wings to fly east as well.

As quickly as everyone from the Kingdom of Life had come in anger, they left in peace.

# CHAPTER LVI

## The Mystery Revealed

Everyone took turns explaining what happened and telling various tales that had happened during the eventful journey. King Rehoboam seemed mostly interested in what Areon had done with his life thus far and was particularly interested in his love with Reiquem and their child. He talked of the celebration they would have and the marriage that would ensue as soon as all could be arranged. Reiquem and Areon smiled and nodded.

After the day and night it took to return, Leviathan wished to land away from the kingdom. The group had to make a short walk up to the city where the guards did not hesitate in the least to permit the king entering with whomever he wished.

The people of the Kingdom of Life quickly filled the streets. Flowers were flung before the feet of the ones that entered with King Rehoboam. The warriors all stood before the castle in ranks waiting for the return of their king and commander.

Areon could hear nothing amidst the shouting of the crowd. They all pushed their way up through the streets and through the warriors. A castle guard let down the drawbridge after seeing the crowd trying to get to the king. When the group passed the ranks of warriors, they held off the rest of the city so that the group could make its way into the large castle entrance. The king smiled warmly at them all, as he was used to this sort of welcome, but the group looked flustered. They followed him past two rooms with circling stairs leading up on either side with red carpet all around. Two guards stood in front of the doorway to the king's throne room.

"Your Majesty," said the guard to the right. "We've just heard you were back. We assumed you had come in through the back throne room entrance."

"Why did you assume this?" asked the king seriously.

The guards looked at each other uneasily and then one spoke.

"A loud noise just came from the room moments ago."

"Have you not looked at who it is?" asked the king calmly.

They both looked at each other. "We thought it was you, sir," said one guard.

The king swept past them and pushed at the two doors hard with his mighty hands.

"Belgraf!" yelled Areon, beaming down the red carpet at his master who sat on the throne.

Everyone looked down towards the throne as Belgraf took up his hand and beckoned to the group. Labert slid forward for a moment, but then the satchel of Elmyra holding the gemstones came out from under his robes and shot into Belgraf's awaiting hand.

"I knew you would get them, my boy," said a voice unlike the one Areon knew.

Areon walked forward slowly in front of everyone else. "How did you get in here, Belgraf?"

The old wizard pointed to the ceiling; a hole with crumbling stone towered above the throne.

"How dare you!" shouted Rehoboam, but the wizard did not tear his gaze away from Areon.

"I always knew you would be great, my boy," said Belgraf. "You have power. I assume you can fly now?"

"Yes," replied Areon, edging closer to his mentor. The rest of the group stayed back.

When Areon got close enough, he noticed the green eyes Belgraf once had were no longer green but black as Reiquem's were. They were wide, and the white areas were bloodshot with madness. His unfamiliar cloak was bloody and tattered, but the most frightful part of his appearance was what the king mentioned first, "The Black Wizard cloak," he whispered.

"Areon, come with me," beckoned Belgraf. "You have already collected the other gemstones for me, as I knew you would." He smiled wickedly.

"You've gone mad," said Areon sadly.

Belgraf smiled. "What would you know of madness? What would you know of living through the wars these pathetic humans brought to the wizard counsel's doorstep? I raised you to know magic. Are you with me or these men?"

"One of those men is my father," replied Areon heatedly. "And the rest are my friends."

Belgraf rose angrily. "I have been more of a father and friend to you than they ever could be!"

"What's wrong with your eyes, Belgraf?" but Areon knew the answer.

"All magic has a drawback," answered Belgraf.

"You told me never to master one of the six magics of the beginning."

"It was necessary to utterly destroy my mind," whispered Belgraf.

"You are not the Belgraf that raised me. You stole the shadow gem for some evil purpose," said Areon.

"No," said Belgraf quickly. "Not for evil, for myself. For a selfish purpose that you would never understand. If evil is a side-effect of it, then so be it."

"Give me back the gemstones, Belgraf," demanded Areon. "We can sort this out through philosophical discussion as we once used to in times of dispute."

"Can't you understand?" asked Belgraf, his black eyes pleading for sympathy. "Thousands of years of thinking for nothing. I long for death, but in the afterlife I fear this anxiety will still be a part of me. I must utterly destroy myself. Help me, Areon. You cannot understand but trust me as you once did. Let Nothingness consume this reality."

"You are mad," stated Areon.

"Then I am forced to act alone, as I have been for these thousand years," said Belgraf. Areon felt the wizard's aura pulsate and push him from the throne back through the ceiling. The group shouted in fear, but Areon, too, let the energy flow from his body and pushed off the ground with his aura. He launched through the ceiling as well with his scarlet cloak flailing and stopped directly in front of Belgraf stopping him mid-flight.

Belgraf stashed the gems inside his cloak and looked to Areon.

"Your friends cannot help you now. Kireth!" yelled the wizard, holding out his hand. Areon's cloak quickly shot in front of him, and the fire dissipated on it. Slowly it hung down lifeless again and Areon smiled.

"I will protect this world with my life for Reiquem and our child," said Areon defiantly.

"You will try," yelled Belgraf, and flew at the boy, his old hand making a fist. Areon dodged quickly and smote the old man with his own fist. Flying upward, he yelled, "Nasai!" The Black Wizard cloak proved just as useful as Areon's, and the fire only hit the hardened material and disappeared with a cloud of smoke.

In no time Areon was back upon Belgraf, holding him by the neck. The black cloak flew up and twisted itself around his neck, but the scarlet flowed through under the cloak and pulled back, leaving Belgraf and Areon holding necks and the cloaks holding each other. Areon reached back one hand and pulled out Uriel, slashing down heavily. Blood spurted from Belgraf's shoulder, and the old wizard cried out in pain. Areon whipped around again, slashing the wind. Belgraf flew back, and the cloaks released one another. It was too late as Belgraf shouted, "Saeth!" A large ball of fire leapt out of his palm, hitting Areon in the leg, burning off his pant leg and melting flesh.

Once again Belgraf let his aura flow from behind him and rushed at the wounded Areon. He kicked him hard in the ribs; the cloaks once again locked. Areon drew an arrow and whipped out his bow. Belgraf shot fire down upon him again, but the scarlet cloak released and formed its shield over Areon. As with the Cherub, Areon knocked an arrow behind the cloak's protection. When it hung lifeless, he released but only to have the black wizard cloak knock it away with a lifeless hand that fell to Belgraf's side immediately after.

Areon grew tired. He breathed heavily, looking at his foe. The one he had sparred with so many times. Could Belgraf really want this? he wondered to himself.

Instantly he thought of Reiquem and did not care anymore. Belgraf had gone mad, and Areon would do the only thing left he could for the wizard—destroy him.

He raised up his palm pointing to the sky, and the white lightning swirled within him and reached out into the sky where Areon struck down with it upon Belgraf. The Black Wizard cloak turned inside out, forming a barrier over the top of Belgraf, but Areon foresaw this and quickly threw out his other hand, screaming the word of the old days that would help bring forth the first degree fire magic from within him.

"Flarasithe!" Areon screamed when the fire left his hand, leaving a cauterized hole that almost consumed his entire palm. It hit Belgraf, and the old man screamed out as his side was almost completely taken off by the first degree magic. Areon could barely hang in the air, his energy leaving him quickly. His vision wavered as he watched Belgraf use the last of his aura to hold his body up and take the stones out one by one and place them around the shadow gem. It was the proper alignment.

"No," Areon could barely speak. He heard a horrendous cracking noise. The shadow gem was breaking.

The gems hung in the air without anything to support them. Belgraf lost all energy, fell, and died before hitting the roof of the castle.

Areon used the last of his energy to fly toward the hole in the castle. He landed heavily where the group of friends had been watching the fight.

"Areon, the gemstones are releasing shadow!" yelled Labert.

"I have sent for the Seraph, but it will not be here in time!" cried Rehoboam. "He can reseal the gemstone if the essence is still inside. But if it is not then, only God or Nothingness will take care of it."

"It is already released," Labert said sadly.

Areon looked up, his head lolling. Darkness filled the entire sky. Shadow crept all over the castle and inside.

"There is one thing left to do," Eanty yelled at the group. "Pour our power into someone so that they may become the master of Nothingness to destroy only shadow."

"A Master of Nothingness?" asked Labert.

"It will be me. I should have stopped Belgraf. Do it now!" screamed Areon.

The group had no time to argue. None could see the world any longer. Shadow moved all over the castle and sky.

"What of the Rapturer?" asked Elmyra desperately.

As God answers prayers, he was there as he always was at the right time and place. He flew in from the crack in the ceiling, although none could see him now.

Areon looked at him through the shadow, and the Rapturer said, "Only one will die."

"No! Not this time," cried Areon

Elmyra stepped fourth and put her hands on Areon's forearm. He felt a surge of infinity flow through him, as though he was at the end of the ever-expanding universe. Stars twinkled in his vision and coldness overtook him.

The Rapturer put his hand on Areon's other forearm, and Areon yelled out quietly and began to cry. So much death; the withering of trees was the touch, and the crying of mother's were all Areon could hear.

Eanty took his place behind Areon and touched the back of his neck.

Areon felt his hair stand on end and all the pain he ever felt was cured. New skin took the place of old, and his hair and nails shown with life and grew to double the size. The smell of fresh grass filled his nostrils, and he smiled even during a time such as this.

Reiquem stepped forward crying and laid her head on Areon's lap. The darkness that he saw only increased at this, and a shroud of warm blackness and love came into his being.

Labert took Areon by a shoulder. For a moment everything stopped, and Areon watched every unmoving person in the world. Then it began to move forward again at an incredible rate. It felt like water washing away the sand.

Scine stepped in front of him and put his hand down on his chest so that Areon might see. His body warmed, and he felt at peace. The shroud of darkness cleared, and he, Areon, could see the gemstones falling from the sky now. All the essences surrounded the shadow gem that owned a crack still spewing forth shadow and darkness.

Areon stood, the group still touching him, and held out his arms to the Shadow. He yelled out and focused all the essences forward at once. Nothingness came from him, while not consuming him. It went out to the essence of shadow and destroyed the essence from the gem in the middle along with all the blackness.

All of the group fell and the gemstones beside them. Labert quickly kicked them apart except the shadow, which was now empty.

"We die anyway," Areon said dejectedly.

"Indeed, we may," a strong, low voice said gravely.

All of the party looked around, and there stood the Seraph. "Unless the sacrifice is made."

"What sacrif—" but before Areon could finish Reiquem stood up.

"I must sacrifice my very essence so there will be no unbalance," Reiquem said quietly.

"No, there must be some other way," yelled Areon. "I won't allow it."

Reiquem grabbed him as the ground began to shake under the remaining gemstones.

"We must for our child!" she yelled. "You were going to die for us, now it is my turn," she said.

"No!" yelled Areon. He looked around for support, but the group gave him none. It was the only way, and they all knew it.

The ground quaked. Everyone felt the gemstones lift off the ground and hit again.

"The universe is unraveling. You have free will. Choose quickly, mortal," the Seraph said.

Areon and Reiquem embraced for the last time. They kissed amongst the tears and Reiquem whispered, "Take care of our child. I will see you in the afterlife. Believe, and you shall be saved."

She bent all shadow she could to her will, the entire room being drained of it. All that was let free came back once again to the gemstone and inside it stayed by the willpower of Reiquem. She let the shadow flow from the outside through her and back into the gemstone until her eyes went white.

The Seraph stepped forward, putting his hands over the gemstone, letting quintessence come fourth from his being and sealed the gemstone once again. The universe was rebalanced, and Reiquem lay lifeless in the arms of the Master of Nothingness.

And Areon wept.

# CHAPTER LVII

## The Last Chapter

Kings surrounded Areon; scepters were laid before his feet. He did not know if he deserved this or not, nor did he care. The angels sat at the front of the capacious room in the kingdom in which Areon sat. The angels flew, the things of unsurpassed beauty that all, save the wicked, loved to look at and be in the presence of. They had a way of making anyone around them feel happy and warm inside, as if a light were in you, keeping you safe. They were called the Nine Orders of Angels, but Areon felt not this happiness or warmth.

Friends he had met along the way, Myriad and Infinitia, sitting together and laughing at their witty senses of humor; Scine brushing the locks of hair out of his eyes; Eanty, the wise old man could not stop staring at the angels. Even the one that people called the Rapturer sat with a half smile on his face; it was a bit crooked and demonic, but Areon knew he was not evil. They all looked happy, benign, but Areon felt none of these feelings of goodness.

More wine was brought from the back of the room, a place Areon was not used to. He longed for Belgraf's house, his wood porch, and a day in the woods. He tried to clear his mind but could not. Lords and ladies were approaching him jovially and bowing low. He knew they would have never cared for him in the least had he not …

"Areon, my lad," said Myriad. "You could do with—" but he was cut short as Areon slowly lifted his head from his hands and gave him a cold look; one that said, "You do not understand." After this, Myriad looked away and no longer laughed with his wife. Eanty was still gazing at the angels, as if longing to float up and join them. It seemed funny, a man so serious, so obsessed with something; but then again the angels were not exactly ordinary or earthly. The Rapturer seemed to be the only one knowing what was occurring. He slid his chair back slowly and looked at all the fools who were dancing and laughing and talking in the room. Then he looked out the doors and across the bridge that provided a way across the moat and into the city. The Rapturer saw all the people that were longing to join the celebration, all the people, all the world outside. He looked at the angels; the light that was streaming in from the high windows. He looked at the shadows some cast on the ground, and all the life that filled the world. He, for the first time Areon had ever seen him, pushed the brim of his round, large hat farther back so that one could see his eyes more clearly. He watched time go by and tried to gaze up into space through the large doors, the space over the city that held things that many knew not. The Rapturer looked around at all the reasons the essences were present. He saw the people, the life.

After his drawn out survey, the Rapturer slowly stood up, looked down to the end of his nose where his magical glasses now sat, which saw a week into the past and a week or so into the future. He turned to Areon; his crooked half smile flickered across his face, not for a reason of some jest, but for friendship toward Areon. It disappeared instantly afterward as he turned, knowing that he would never look at Areon again. Areon had not a clue if the Rapturer knew what was going to be, but he saw him do all this, and lastly, he saw him take off his hat and bow slightly. Areon watched with the rest of his friends as the Rapturer walked down the middle of the hall and out the doors into the never to be again sunlight.

Areon stood up slowly. The rest had no idea. No one had any idea. Nobody knew how Areon felt. Nobody knew what was always going on inside his head. Now especially that the time had come; Areon wanted nothing, not wind or sunshine, darkness or old age. Not the feeling of walking along or traveling farther than one should ever have to. Areon wanted not the feeling of laughter; he had no more laughter in him. Areon ran his hand along the table once more, as to feel the feeling that matter possessed. He watched things around him as the Rapturer had done. He almost smiled; the fairy had undoubtedly been right, although Areon thought it would be the other she had said. The dance and celebration seemed to have quit as Areon walked to the middle of the large room. It was over for him. It was the only way. He would have these feelings in this life and the next. The afterlife held no comfort. He realized this after something he had done that he did not want to think about again. These thoughts that would be ever present in his mind for eternity were it not for one thing: Nothingness. He outstretched his arms and looked towards the heavens; he raised his outstretched arms, almost as if asking for forgiveness for what he was doing. The angels jerked their bodies toward him in fear; they felt the ominous uneasiness of life ending. They flew toward him with beating wings faster than a normal human eye could catch, but it was a feeling had to late for the life bringers. Even the Seraphim, with their four ever-watchful faces, were not fast enough. The last tear in Areon's body ran down the side of his face before he was consumed by nothingness. Next came the angels that had so desperately tried to stop him. Nobody could explain what they saw, but it mattered not, for they were consumed only seconds after the things that they saw, or didn't see; they saw nothing. No more did life exist, nor death, the afterlife with it, nor light and shadow. Time ceased, and the essence of nothing consumed the universe and every dimension and form of life that it contained.

Areon raised his head from his daydream. He wanted this for the same reason Belgraf had wanted it. The wizard felt these feelings and thoughts of hatred, bitterness, and above all loneliness, but Areon did not understand then. Areon would not make the same mistake Belgraf had when he lost his mind and tried to destroy everything. His reverie of selfish destruction would remain just that, and his longing for Reiquem would be for all eternity, for Areon wanted his son to exist.

"Areon," said the Rapturer, jerking him from his thoughts. "Walk with me."

Areon stood up and left towards the back, thankful for a reason to leave, leaving Rehoboam and the rest of the party wondering why he left with the man they called the master of death.

They walked through a hidden passage behind the throne room and up a flight of stairs out into one of the wings of the castle that led to a ledge outside.

The Rapturer turned behind them to see if any were watching.

He spoke sincerely, "Areon, do you wish to know what I am?"

Areon's mind was only on Reiquem and how he would raise a child alone. He could not choke out an answer, so he simply nodded.

"When Reiquem sacrificed her very essence, I severed her soul from body."

Areon snapped his head toward the Rapturer.

"I am an anomaly, Areon, an angel made with free will. I am the angel of death. I see all who pass into the afterlife." The angel took off his cloak and threw it aside. He lifted his mighty wings to the sky.

"And?" Areon cried beseechingly, tears running down his face.

The Rapture took flight but not before answering, "You and Reiquem will be together for all eternity in the afterlife, so says the Lord."

Areon would never again see the Rapturer, but he looked to the heavens where he had disappeared and thanked God.

# EPILOGUE

On an island south of the Mirrored Continents, a boy played with an old man. The old man put out his hands to the boy, putting him in haste. The boy threw a rock as far as his little muscles could and easily ran and caught it. He laughed and ran back to the old man.

From the north a scarlet-cloaked figure raced through the sky at an incredible speed. It slowed before the brick house, and a man landed down heavily.

"Father!" yelled the child.

"You're back at last," said the old man.

The scarlet-cloaked figure picked up the boy and threw him in the air, catching him easily. He held him up and looked into the child's beautiful black eyes.

An old woman came from the house smiling at the three.

"Areon, you're back. Labert, Alexander come along, everyone inside, I'm sure Areon is tired from his dealings with the king."

The three walked to the house, Areon holding Alexander.

"Father, will you tell me more about your adventures with my mother before I go to sleep?"

"Of course," said Areon quietly.

TATE PUBLISHING *& Enterprises*

Tate Publishing is committed to excellence in the publishing industry. Our staff of highly trained professionals, including editors, graphic designers, and marketing personnel, work together to produce the very finest books available. The company reflects the philosophy established by the founders, based on Psalms 68:11,

"THE LORD GAVE THE WORD AND GREAT WAS THE COMPANY OF THOSE WHO PUBLISHED IT."

If you would like further information, please call
1.888.361.9473
or visit our website
www.tatepublishing.com

TATE PUBLISHING *& Enterprises*, LLC
127 E. Trade Center Terrace
Mustang, Oklahoma 73064 USA